Ocean Roads

Ocean Roads

James George

HUIA

First published in 2006 by Huia Publishers,
39 Pipitea Street, PO Box 17-335,
Wellington, Aotearoa New Zealand.
www.huia.co.nz

ISBN 1-86969-237-3

Literary agency services provided by Dr Susan Sayer

National Library of New Zealand Cataloguing-in-Publication Data
George, James, 1962-
Ocean roads / James George.
ISBN 1-869692-37-3
1. Title.
NZ823.3—dc 22

Published with the assistance of

Te Waka Toi

creative
nz

ARTS COUNCIL OF NEW ZEALAND TOI AOTEAROA

To AJM,
And to all those who have never returned

Contents

Kimi ga tame	For you
Haru no no ni idete	Have I gone to the awakening meadows
Wakana tsumi	To gather herbs of spring.
Waga koromode ni	Yet upon my sleeves
Yuki wa furitsutsu	Still falls the snow

Emperor Kōkō,
Hyakunin isshu anthology

I

Sand

New Mexico, USA
April, 1989

Etta looks up over her light meter to where the clouds drift like icebergs, as if the sand and burnt grass of the plain and even the distant mountain tops lie beneath water. But she can feel only dust against her skin. She blinks hard, wipes her eyes and raises her camera. She adjusts the focal length and shoots a couple of images, then turns back towards the farmhouse and its tattered retinue of outbuildings.

Sand blows against her boots, filling her footprints one by one. Beside her the posts in the ragged fenceline lean away from the wind. Her steps echo their shadows as she walks, shooting every few paces.

A WATER TANK FILLED WITH DUST AND COBWEBS.
A BARN WITH ITS STONE WALLS INTACT BUT NO ROOF.
THE ARROW OF A HAWK'S SHADOW AS IT CROSSES THE DESERT FLOOR.

She finishes a roll of film, crouches to hold the camera in the dark of her gear bag and replace the roll with another. Then she stands and walks on.

Only the main house has been preserved.

McDonald ranch.

She begins to sing to herself.

Old McDonald had a farm ...

It's open to the public for one day, twice a year. This is one of them.

Etta crouches, photographs the shadows cast by the derelict buildings, their dark sketches shortening as the sun rises overhead. She looks beyond the compound to the mountains. Inside the ranch house, forty-five years ago, a family sat down to dinner, went to sleep with the wailing of the desert wind in the eaves. Then they were moved out so men in military khaki could use their living room to assemble a plutonium core.

She looks back through the camera's viewfinder, then reaches to wipe some dust from the glass of the lens.

You were one of those men, Isaac, but I didn't know you then.

Earlier in the day a convoy of cars and four-wheel drives and camper vans had gathered at the Otero County Fairgrounds in Alamogordo. Etta had got out of her rented Chevrolet wagon, headed for the nearest soldier. She said just one word.

Trinity.

The journey from the McDonald ranch to ground zero doesn't take long. Etta holds her camera in one hand as she drives. Soldiers at gates nod them through. At the last gate there is a shimmer of movement and a herd of antelope looms out of a dust cloud. A couple of them split from the group and skitter across the snaketrails of tyre tracks. Etta touches the switch to lower the window, listening to their hooves scuffing on the sand. She raises her camera.

TWO ANTELOPE, EYES RINGED WITH DUST, THEIR BREATH STEAMING IN THE COLD DESERT AIR.
A LINE OF CARS SITTING SILENT, THEIR EXHAUSTS ALSO STEAMING.
A HEAVY MESH FENCE WITH A SIGN THAT SAYS ROAD CLOSED.

But today it isn't.

At the road's end Etta pulls on the leather mittens she uses in the cold now that arthritis seeps through her bones. She walks at the edge of the group of visitors, glancing down at the snow-pale grains dusting her boots. Clumps of creosote scrub and sagebrush struggle for a hold in the cracked ground. The sky is stained with shivering grey cloud. A ten-minute walk, then a pause at a metal fence. She checks the dial to note her remaining exposures, then takes a long breath when she sees the dark stone obelisk.

They find a gate.

Walking across the dry grass it strikes her. This was once the most dangerous place on earth.

I've been to dangerous places.

The inscription on the obelisk ends with a date.

July 16, 1945

For a few minutes no one speaks, no one seems even to be with anyone, as if they're all strangers, though in fact Etta was the only person who came alone. She checks her light meter again. Deteriorating. She raises the camera anyway.

Click.

AN OLD MAN SQUINTING AGAINST THE WIND.

Click.

A SMALL BOY CROUCHING TO WATCH A LIZARD CRAWL ACROSS THE FAINT WAKE OF A TUMBLEWEED.

She crouches next to two twisted metal spikes sticking out of the ground, remnants of the tower that the atomic bomb sat on. The first atomic bomb. The Trinity test.

You were here, Isaac, up in those hills. Watching.

I didn't know you then.

Click.

She takes three rolls of film then packs up her gear. On the walk back to the car she reaches into her bag, unscrews the cup from her small thermos and pours the water out onto the desert floor. It is illegal to take any of the small, green, glassy granules – trinitite – formed when heat fused the sand at the instant of the explosion, so she scoops up half a cupful of ordinary sand, holds the thermos upside down and screws it into the cup.

An hour later she is on US 380, slowing at the intersection with the I 25. It has begun to rain. She crosses the state border into Arizona, heading back to California.

After a couple of hundred miles of scrubby flatlands, a roadside motel sign beckons through the evening gloom.

She lies back in the bath, a flannel over her face.

In the morning she opens the curtains and looks out. A grey dawn rises beyond the saguaro and yucca. The motel sign clangs in the wind.

She takes the cup off the thermos, figuring in all the years she has been a photo-journalist she wouldn't have taken any more photos than there are grains of sand in the little cup.

Thinking also of the last shots she took before she left Trinity.

The moment when those who had seemed strangers stood together. Two lovers embraced and kissed, two old men shook hands, a mother hugged a child.

You weren't there for that, Isaac.

Maybe you should've been.

II

Rangimoana – The Sea Wind

Hills north-west of Auckland
April, 1989

The railway carriage sits on an abandoned siding, its heavy iron wheels vanishing among the toetoe. A track-switching lever stands rusting in the long grass and a seagull sits on the lever's tip, feathers ruffling with the wind. The marshes here are liquid in all but the driest summers. Small islands of grass sit like landlocked clouds. A rabbit stirs, there's a sudden stitching of a cormorant's path against the aquamarine sky.

The carriage's exterior paint peels a fraction more with each westerly; its slip into old age is almost glacial. But the interior has changed beyond recognition in the last couple of years, ever since Isaac brought out his furniture, piece by piece, from his house.

First it was a torch to help him find his cigarettes when twilight turned to dusk as he sat at the carriage's side window. Then some of his books — not his diaries with his years of scrawled notes, but the silent cinema books he'd collected over the years. Buster Keaton, Harold Lloyd, Charlie Chaplin. His projector was next, then his films, their silver cans like giant coins. He bought a generator to run it all and heat his kettle as he sat at one end of the train watching the images projected on the sheet he'd hung from a couple of hooks at the other. By and by a tin of biscuits, a loaf of bread. His pyjamas, a sleeping bag, an eiderdown and blankets.

Early spring was spent outfitting a sink and bench unit against one wall. Then a shower box, digging a trench and laying pipes so he could rig a shower head. The hardware store in Hellensville became as familiar to him as his house had once been. The salesmen looked over the counter at him, this old man in a sharp-creased grey suit and a snap-brim hat who seldom spoke, would just give a non-committal smile as

9

he lifted his money from his wallet.

He even hammered together a letter box and set it on a stake rammed into the sandy soil, though he already had a rusting tin letter box at the road end of the metal driveway. But this second box would receive no mail, just a rattling from the westerly, an occasional spiking from rain squalls. And its own curious number, written in carpenters' pencil.

1663.

One day he forgot where he put his front-door keys and had to break into his own house, as there were two things he hadn't yet brought out.

His blackboards.

He set them up on a wall, rigged a lamp to illuminate them. One of his final purchases from the hardware store was a couple of boxes of chalks. He set a wrap of soft felt around a wooden sanding block to use as a duster, nailed a scalloped framing board beneath the blackboards' lower rim, ready to catch any stray dust. He flicked the lamp on and stood at the boards, his hands against their smooth skin.

Did everything but write on them.

Until today.

He'd walked through the supermarket picking up groceries. The newspaper was the last item to go into his trolley. At the checkout counter he stood leafing through it. A small headline caught his eye.

Cold Fusion Warms Up
A University of Utah research team announced today that they have produced a nuclear fusion reaction in heavy water, at room temperature.

'Sir?'

He read on.

'Sir?'

A tap from a woman behind him made him look up to where the checkout operator stood gesturing for Isaac to put his groceries on the empty conveyer belt.

He stands now with his chalk a quarter inch from the blackboard. He stares not at its blank surface but at the hills to the west, beyond which the ocean lies.

Hello, old friends…

He draws a dot, surrounds it with a large circle. Next to the circle he draws the letter e, with a small minus symbol adjacent to it. Beside the dot he chalks in a letter p and a plus sign. To the right he draws a second figure, beginning again with a dot. But the circle he draws around this dot is segmented, like highway centreline markings. He puts the e and p in the same places. Then he draws a smaller ring around the dot. Next to this he draws the symbol μ and a minus sign.

Moving right again he draws a third figure. A dot, labelled p with a plus sign, then a small ring around it, which he labels μ and a minus sign. On this figure there is no large outer circle.

He stands back, studies the figures from left to right, watching the large circle fade in the second figure then vanish in the third.

He looks past the blackboards and out over the grass. He reaches to slide open the window, smiles when the wind hits him.

Auckland's western suburbs sprawl in the rain. Industrial parks with rows of huge roller doors set within grey walls, garish hoardings of car sales yards and appliance stores, supermarkets with asphalt car parks filled with shoppers dodging the showers, amid the rattle of wire trolleys. In a small office block Rai sits at a medical clinic's cluttered reception desk. She looks out the window to where the rainswept trees glisten beyond the strata of the venetian blinds. Imagining she can hear the whisper of the leaves, even over the rasp of coughs from the waiting room.

In the afternoon the doctor checks the wound of a small boy who had a rusty fence-nail puncture his hand. The hospital sutures ran like a tiny jagged railway across his palm where he had further torn the skin, trying in his agony to get away from the nail.

The boy wanders into the office and stands looking up at the shelves of files while Rai prepares the bill, his bandage like a white mitten. He turns and says something to his mother, and Rai raises her eyebrows.

'He said you have two lots of eyes,' says the mother.

'Eh?'

The woman points at the lens of Rai's glasses.

'Oh,' says Rai, smiling then.

The desk fan blows a sheet of paper onto the floor. The boy stands and hands it to Rai.

'Thank you,' she says.

He walks to the window. The lights in the ceiling give him dual reflections in the windowpane. Rai looks through them to the trees beyond. The wind sets the leaves shimmering like party decorations.

She goes to her pre-med studies at university in the mornings, then works three days a week in the clinic. The practice had been looking for a part-time receptionist to allow them to open for longer hours during the influenza season and they kept her on through summer. She is grateful for the money and also the exposure to patients, to a medical environment, asking questions when she can of the doctors.

She looks up again and the boy is still at the window. His mother finishes signing her cheque and calls to him, but he doesn't turn. Rai sits looking at his face in the glass, seeing both his front and back at the same time.

A trick of the light.

The children at the birthday party sit in a rough semicircle, the closest of their tiny feet no more than a skip from the clown's. Most of the feet are bare, including his. But his feet are the lone parts of him that aren't garbed with some mismatching sin against good taste. Atop his grey hair is an old straw hat, fibres frayed and dissolving, ragged around the brim and worn away in the crown like a billy goat's hat from an old movie. A shirt cut from a patchwork quilt, a holed tweed jacket falling further apart with each movement. Baggy striped pants, too short at the calf.

He moves among the children with a deftness that belies his seventy-one years, this old man who lives on a train. He rolls a cigarette with one hand, the cigarette exploding between his lips when he sets a match to it. The children screech with laughter. Balloon animals come alive from a few twists and turns. At one point he looks up beyond the faces of the children and into the eyes of their parents, shares for a second their laughter at their children's laughter.

He's still wearing his clown's suit when the woman signs the cheque and hands it to him. He puts it in his leather carry bag and heads down the driveway to where his motorbike is parked. A 1947 Indian Chief Custom, teal blue tank, forks and fairings, black leather saddle and saddlebags. He rides along the open West Auckland streets. A couple of kids point. Two youths in an old car daubed in grey rust-paint snigger at him as they sit at the traffic lights at the end of the northwestern motorway. Behind the visor of his full-face helmet he smiles. He heads north, past the vineyards and orchards. On a long straight he eases back on the throttle, watches the flatness of the horizon beyond the cabbage palms. He turns off onto a side road, changes down a couple of gears, accelerates, the pitch of the motorbike's engine rising. He slows again, stands up for a moment on the foot pedals, seeing in the cast of his long shadow another rider silhouetted against a hundred sunsets.

Hello, Caleb, he says.

When he gets back to his carriage he pours himself a vintage port and looks up at the blackboards. He takes a deep breath, takes a chalk and writes.

Happy birthday.

He sips from his glass, loads an old reel of 8mm film from a rusting can and draws the screen down.
 A flicker of images, then a much younger Isaac appears at a wooden picnic table, wearing the same straw hat he is wearing now. Next, a four-year-old Caleb and his nine-year-old half-brother, Troy, edge in from the shadows. The camera jerks and the Isaac on the screen mouths something, but there's nothing but the clacking of the projector. He speaks to the camera and the viewpoint swivels around to take in Etta's face above her outstretched arm. She raises her eyebrows in greeting then goes back to filming the others.
 The screen Isaac takes a glass from the table and raises it,

and the Isaac on the train raises his glass also. The screen Isaac then waggles a finger at the camera, picks up a pencil and waves it like a wand. The camera jerks and Troy and Caleb vanish. Isaac shrugs his shoulders, raises his hands out from his body in a gesture of bewilderment. The camera pans to either side of the table, but the boys aren't there. The images begin to vibrate. Perhaps Etta is laughing, perhaps crying. It is impossible to tell from the silence. The screen Isaac climbs atop the table and sits with an air of indifference.

The table begins to recede on the screen as Etta steps away. When she has pulled back a few yards the boys appear, hiding beneath the picnic table. Caleb waves, Troy makes a rude face.

The Isaac on the train sets down his glass, sits watching the vibrations in the dark red liquid fade. He taps the glass with a fingernail and they begin again.

He switches off the projector, stares at the white screen. He takes his glass of port and walks out onto the deck, listening to the evening sounds. A morepork, the rustle of the wind in the leaves. An hour later he's still there, still in his clown's outfit, when car headlight circles bounce across the rails and he looks up, recognising the engine pitch of Rai's Volkswagen. She stops and steps out. He reaches up and nudges the lamp forward, bringing her eyes into the light. She raises a hand to shield her face and he draws the lamp back. She reaches into the car and puts a grey sweatshirt on over her black T-shirt then walks across the stones, her flax kete in her hand.

They sit on the deck sipping coffee. She opens her kete and lifts out a small box, prises open its lid with a fingernail.

A cupcake. A single candle.

'You remembered,' says Isaac.

He lifts the cupcake out into the light. Rai glances away

into the darkness beyond the tracks.

'Happy birthday, Caleb,' she says to the night.

'Yes,' says Isaac. 'Happy birthday, son.'

Rai leans back against the metal rails, watches Isaac lift the candle from the cupcake. She chuckles at his smudged white make-up and ruby smile, his raggedy straw hat. A loose strand hangs above his eyes. She leans and flicks at it and it falls off, slips down onto his cheek, then down through the deck floor's metal mesh to the dirt between the tracks.

He fishes in a pocket, lifts out a packet of cigarettes. The lighter flash is jagged against the dark.

'Can I bum one of those off you?' she says.

'I thought you were giving up.'

'I thought *you* were.'

He sits looking at her, puts the packet back in his pocket.

Rai stands, walks to the edge of the deck, leans against the top guard rail. When she turns back there is a fine sprinkle of rust on her wrist. She brushes it off with a sleeve.

'Tell me about him,' she says.

'I wish I could.'

He turns to her.

'I wish I could tell you all about him,' he says. 'The things a father should know.'

She sits on a chair. Isaac blows a thin trail of smoke, and they watch it drift and vanish. He stands with a hiss, goes and gets two forks.

'Go ahead,' he says when he sits again. Rai takes the first piece of cupcake.

She stays for a couple of hours watching a few of his silent movies. Two shorts of Fatty Arbuckle and Buster Keaton pummelling each other, neither altering their painted-on expression. Then Isaac puts on a Charlie Chaplin film where his little tramp character picks up a red flag that falls from the back of a truck and gives chase to the truck, waving the flag. When he turns a corner he is unaware a throng of people are marching up the street behind him. When they see his flag they call out, shout slogans, get in behind him. He looks back in bewilderment, then the police appear, attack both him and the crowd.

Isaac goes back into the kitchen to put the kettle on. Rai stands and grabs the little loop at the foot of the screen and pulls it to release the spring grip to allow the screen to retract up onto its roll. Behind it, the blackboards sit with a couple of lines written in a rough scrawl.

Happy birthday

And beneath that;

A twins paradox

She stares at the word *twins* for a moment, then sits back down.

The next morning Rai sits at her clinic desk, the glass top a jumble of receipts and manila files. The phone rings and a woman sets an appointment to have her daughter's cough checked out. Rai then follows up on blood-test results, sets more appointments. The phone rings again. A pharmaceutical company rep. It rings again.

'Hey, kid.'

Etta's voice sounds close enough to be next door.

'Hey,' says Rai.

They swap news for a while, then Etta pauses, her voice fainter.

'There's going to be an exhibition of my work at the Auckland Museum,' she says.

'Wow, cool. When?'

'Next month.'

Rai leans back in her chair, looks up to where a child's drawing hangs pinned to the wall beneath the clock. A house, two big and two small figures.

'I've decided to come back and help with the selections,' says Etta. 'And do a few other things, too.'

The drawings begin to dissolve in Rai's eyes.

'You're coming home?' she says.

'I'm coming back.'

'When?'

'Next week. Is the old place still standing?'

'With any luck.'

'I'd like to spend some time there. And some time with you.'

'I reckon I've changed a bit. Since you last saw me.'

Rai sits wrapping the phone cord around her fingers. She can hear Etta shuffling papers.

'I've changed too,' says Etta.

Rai waits for her to say more, but she doesn't. When she puts the phone down Rai waits, hearing the click echo not just in the phone receiver's chamber, but somehow off the leaves of the kōwhai, off the walls of the building and the rainswept tarmac of the roads.

The phone rings in the train carriage. Isaac turns from where he stands at the sink, to his desk. To the scattering of books and newspapers and jotted notes on crumpled pad sheets, trying to pinpoint the phone. He lifts away an ashtray, cursing when he spills some ash on the floor. Then a wad of open books, dislodging the phone onto the floor. With a clang it stops ringing.

Rai sits for a moment, listening to the harsh beeping of the disconnected signal in the receiver, then she puts the phone back on the hook.

She gets off work at three pm and nudges her VW's nose to the end of the clinic's driveway. Glancing both ways, the city in one direction, the west coast in the other. She takes a deep breath, turns left to negotiate the traffic islands to head west. It rains intermittently on the winding road out to the coast. When she sees the grey stretch of ocean she eases her car down the steep incline, glancing up at the new houses speckled amongst the trees. To the west, bars of light rise like jagged branches from a sun still half-hidden in the clouds. In the small township there is a dairy, a Swim and Dive shop (that's new), a second campground now. The petrol pumps on the old station forecourt still sit like they always did, though they're rusting now and the station's windows are barred up. A For Sale sign stands among the weeds. She turns seaward, to where the wind-whipped waves fire glistening spearpoints through the gaps in the dunes. She skirts the estuary, rounds the promontory and parks in the gravel turnaround at the road's end. Beyond the spinning wheels of surf a rainbow rises.

She steps out. The puddles in the broken asphalt of the road sit steaming. A white butterfly battles the last, faint raindrops. She walks beside the fence at the edge of the beach rescue station, down past the lifeguard's tower. The low sun, free of clouds for a moment, casts the tower's bony shadow against the pockmarked sand.

A voice.

'Hi.'

Rai turns, looks up. A guy stands leaning against the tower's rail.

'If you're thinking of heading into the water,' he says, 'can you keep between the flags.'

'It's cool. I know where the rips are here.'

'Yeah, thought I recognised you.'

'Yeah, you too.'

'How've you been?'

She stops, takes a deep draw on the sea wind.

'Gone,' she says.

Five years must change most stretches of road, but not this one. Still an asphalt afterthought, it imposes itself between the sand and bush, ragged as an untidy kid's shirt-tail. She takes her patchwork leather bag from the passenger seat and negotiates the pitted surface, stops at the foot of the steep driveway, her keys jangling in her hand. She steps off the drive, crosses the creaking swingbridge over the creek and goes on up. The pale fawn honeycomb of the trellised rails sit wrapped around the edge of the deck. Support poles sprout up through the flax and nīkau. On the doorstep sits a real estate agent's flyer.

We can sell your house today!

She goes to the old shed next to the house, opens the door and feels behind the third upright beam, smiling when she finds the metal cup. She lifts it out, closes her palm around the key.

In the dusk she falls asleep on the couch. She doesn't bother to draw the curtains on the big bay windows looking out over the ocean, wakes a couple of times and looks out at the stars through the black veil of trees. She'd dropped the real estate flyer next to the couch's leg. The next morning she steps over it on the way to the kitchen. By the time she sits back down on the couch with her morning cuppa, the flyer lies crumpled in the rubbish bag.

No. No sale here. Not today.

In the morning she goes down to the beach and walks in the surf, looks along the sand to where the old man, Koroheke Rock, crouches staring out to sea. She moves up the beach, up above the high tide line, sits among the shells and driftwood and burrows her feet into the soft sand. She pushes her hands beneath the surface, the sand cool away from the day's touch. She sits for a long time, watching the dark clouds cast shadows on the water like huge schools of fish. She takes a deep breath, glances down at the first raindrops freckling the beach's face. She burrows her hands and feet further in.

Rai walks through the Saturday morning flea market, between rows of stalls hawking mock Persian rugs, silk scarves and blouses, knock-off Longines and Rolex watches. She buys an ice cream from a vendor's van, strolls past the smell of fried rice and curry, tables set out with coffee mugs, mirrors with makes of motorcycles stencilled on the glass. She looks past the smoke of a sausage sizzle to where Akiko stands looking at shoes.

'Mum,' says Rai.

Akiko turns, smiles.

'Wouldn't have thought you'd need any more shoes,' says Rai.

'Hey,' says Akiko, 'where's *my* ice cream?'

They browse for a while then sit at a table drinking coffee. A couple of guys in gang outfits stroll by with kids in prams.

'I'm gonna hang out at the old place for a while,' says Rai.

'Okay. What's brought this on?'

'Just feel I need to.'

Akiko nods.

'I'm gonna swing by home and get some of my stuff and take it out,' says Rai.

'Okay.'

'Clothes and things. Some of my music tapes.'

'Your tapes? You'll need to hire a truck then.'

Rai pokes out her tongue. They sip at their coffees, watch the hubbub of people checking the tables of wares.

'Hey,' says Rai. 'Remember Rebecca, the girl you used to teach dance to at home?'

'She gave it up when she became pregnant.'

'Yeah. Well, she came in the other day. Her little boy had grabbed hold of a fence with a nail sticking out.'

'Ouch!'

'Yeah. Looked terrible last week but it's healing.'

'She had talent. Real talent.'

'I didn't recognise her at first. She was only a year ahead of me at high school. Now she has a three year old. A mother.'

Akiko reaches with a hand, lays it over her daughter's.

They finish their coffees then Rai says goodbye through Akiko's car window.

At the old house Rai spends a couple of hours sweeping and dusting. She knows the dings on the tables' edges, the scuffs on the walls. She'd made a few of them. And some were made by Etta's two boys, Troy and Caleb. No, not *by* them, but *for* them. Little marks on the door jambs, done in pencil, just hard enough to leave a permanent mark in the wood. Height on fifth birthday, on tenth …

Some of those marks, and one of those boys was her father.

She takes a break and sits on the hallway floor with a glass of apple juice in her hand. Looking up at the walls. Most houses have wallpaper, or paintings, but this one never did, just Etta's photographs. Everywhere. Women in coolie hats bending over a rice paddy, their figures floating like water lilies against the sunlit surface. Bowler-hatted city gents smoking cigarettes on a London train platform while other spires of smoke rise from distant factories. A truck full of young faces sprouting out of camouflage uniforms, their profiles split by the shadows of their rifles. Kids lighting candles at birthday parties while blackout curtains hang behind them. Or standing in front of naked earth where their bedrooms had once been. A bare-footed boy trudging along a mountain road in a grey dawn, carrying who-knows-what in a plastic bag emblazoned with a happy face.

Once, when she was a kid, she had called Etta 'Nana'. Etta turned and stared, Rai's face tiny in the irises of Etta's eyes.

'Bloody hell,' said Etta. 'Nana?' Then, 'Just Etta will be fine, hon.'

That was the end of that.

Rai sweeps the decks free of sand. Even though she could throw a stone and still not get halfway from here to the dunes, the sand still arrives on their doorstep. She takes a bucket and mop and begins to wash the errant sand off the walls above the deck outside Etta and Isaac's big bedroom, pausing when she comes upon some screw holes.

She stands puzzled, trying to remember what had been fixed there. Then she remembers.

Isaac's blackboards.

Now she tends to what had been the garden, taking some time to oil the rusted padlock on the implement shed until she can open it and replace it with a new one. She carries a mattock, spade and small gardening fork up the slope behind the house, building in her mind the outline of what had been the lettuce and cabbage garden.

She spends an hour struggling to upright and clean the metal frame of the bean trellis, resting one end on a saw horse while she cuts away years of weeds helixed within the wires. Sitting on an upturned apple crate, she examines the dirt in the pores of her skin. Not commonplace in her life of biology books and anatomy charts.

In the superette she strikes a conversation with a sun-hatted local, seeing, in the passing seasons of his frayed woollen sweater, answers to green-fingered questions that are a mystery to her.

'What time of year do you plant tomatoes?' asks Rai.

He ruffles his brow, rolls back on the balls of his feet.

'You're at the old place above the creek, aren't you,' he says. 'The one the egghead and his photographer wife had.'

She stares.

'What ever happened to them?' he says.

She reaches into the freezer, lifts out a bag of frozen peas.

Isaac sits with the projector disassembled. He lifts a small artist's paint brush from a jar, begins to clean the dust from the lugs on the projector's carriage wheel. So intense is his concentration that it takes him a full minute to register the sound of the Volkswagen's engine.

When he hears footsteps on the carriage's rear deck he calls out.

'It's open.'

Isaac brings in a tray with crackers and tomatoes and cheese. They sit munching.

'Are you all right?' he says.

She puts down her plate, wipes her mouth on a paper napkin.

'I've opened up the house at Rangimoana again,' she says.

He looks up through the wisps of smoke.

'Been sleeping there a few nights,' she says. 'S'pose I'm kinda moving in.'

'Kind of?'

She nods.

'Yeah. Haven't made up my mind.'

'Be a bit of a hike to university and back wouldn't it?'

'Yeah. But ...' Her voice trails off.

'But what?' says Isaac.

Rai shakes her head.

'I've been doing some stuff around the place,' she says. 'Doing it up.'

'Didn't know you had a do-it-yourself bent.'

'I'm doing it for Nan.'

Isaac leans back in his chair. He flicks a leaf of ash down through the mesh to the dirt.

'She's coming home,' says Rai. 'Etta's coming home.'

Isaac closes his eyes. Etta. He has seen her three times in the last twenty years. The first was on a day he would give anything to forget. The others were attempts out at Rangimoana to cut away the weeds of pain between them. On each occasion the first slash saw them walk away from each other. She, then he.

Home.

'When?' he says.

'Next week,' says Rai.

Akiko walks to the auditorium. A couple of props men and one of the lighting guys are there when she arrives, and she sits on a stage chair sharing a cup of tea from a thermos with them. She lays her notes out on the wooden stage and crouches, looking down at her marks for blocking, at various choreographic sketches. She needs to feel a connection between them and the stage. One by one the dancers arrive, nod to her and go to change.

She works them through three routines, adjusting her notes as she goes. A change of step, a new mix of solo and group. Three pairs of men and women dancers are easier to manage than a whole troupe, but each dancer has that much more to do. She has three more weeks until opening night, and the takings in Auckland will determine whether she tours the show further.

She signals to the rehearsal pianist and his hands spread and close, fingertips searching the black and white keys as the dancers' feet search the boards of the stage. The pairs move from one partner to the other in an ebb and flow, splitting and reforming elsewhere. As sea foam breaks and reforms. Elsewhere.

At university Rai sequesters a table end in the library, medical books and anatomy charts fanned out around her. Mid-morning she takes a break, goes to the water cooler, then stands in the foyer sipping.

A twins paradox.

She finishes her drink and drops the polystyrene cup into a bin. When she goes back in she stops and asks the guy at the desk if they have books with any reference to 'a twins paradox.'

The guy sits at his computer, taps in a series of commands. He sits, with a reflection of a light blinking in his glasses. He looks up.

He writes some Dewey decimal numbers on a yellow sticky pad.

She walks searching for the numbers. Two books list

it among their indexes. She sits, opens them out and flips through their pages.

> *A pair of twins. One gets into a spaceship and travels away from the earth at 0.80/c (eighty percent of the speed of light). The other stays home. The travelling twin turns around after four years and heads home. His journey has taken eight years. When he arrives back on earth he finds he is two years younger now than his brother, as ten years have passed on earth while he has been away. The effect is due to time dilation at great speed, predicted in Einstein's theory of special relativity. Time on the spacecraft passes twenty percent slower than on earth. Time is not constant for everyone.*

She leans back, looks past the shelves to the windows. She takes her cardigan from around her waist and slips it on.

After working a full morning in the garden's dirt Rai walks through the dunes and down onto the beach where strings of tyre tracks run between her and the booming surf. She wades into the breakers and crouches, letting the water wash her soil-stained legs.

The nights here are too rough for her to just drift into sleep. She rolls in her sheets, tangled in their surf, opens her eyes to the play of the moonshadows throwing the shapes of trees onto the walls. She turns on the bedside light, sits up in the bed. She goes into the kitchen and comes back with an armful of black rubbish sacks. In the corners of the wardrobe piles of boxes and papers sit. Bills, receipts from thirty years ago. Sewing patterns, a wooden figure of a woman's torso with dimensional marks all over it. Pieces of cloth, reels of cotton. She fills two bags in no time, sits back on her haunches looking up at the shelves. She gets the stepladder from the laundry, peers onto the top shelf. A scrapbook lies among the cobwebs. She brushes some dust from the cover and steps down, sits on the edge of the bed.

Pages are torn and cut from books and pasted in. Clippings from newspapers. Jotter pad pages with mathematical notation – calculus, by the look of it. Curves to measure velocities and acceleration. Some scrawled notes about 'maximum radius'. She turns another page. A faded newspaper clipping stills her.

English-born nuclear physicist turned anti-nuclear weapons campaigner, Isaac Simeon, was committed today to a mental institution for an indeterminate time. Simeon, 40, was hospitalised for psychiatric treatment after returning from a scientific trip to Antarctica. His distinguished career included work on the Manhattan Project and the development of the plutonium bomb which destroyed the Japanese city of Nagasaki...

She runs a fingertip over the newsprint, the ink long set, beyond smudging. She turns over the top of the page as a mark, moves on.

There are bits and pieces about protest marches, pages from what looks like a medical journal. The paste has worn away from the edges of some clippings and they slip across the sheet when she turns the page. A photo comes away, slips into her lap. The Tin Man from the *Wizard of Oz*, holding a burning match in one hand. Within the exposed rectangle of fading paste where the photo had sat there is some writing.

When a man's an empty kettle
He should be on his mettle
And yet I'm torn apart
Just because I'm presumin'

I could be kind of human
If I only had a heart

She raises the photo, looks not at the Tin Man's silver face but at the match in his fingertips. She reaches into her memory of the movie, but can't place the scene.

The tiny flame flashes. Pulses.

III

A Twins Paradox

Rangimoana, west of Auckland
November, 1969

Caleb wheels the motorbike out beneath the fading paint of the shed's overhang and across the stones of the track. The 1947 Indian Chief custom Isaac had brought over from the USA after World War Two. He puts it on its stand then goes back for the petrol can. The wind sends a shiver through the leaves, twisting the ribbon of petrol falling from can to tank. Fumes rise, pungent. Above the treeline the first sunlight crackles through a keyhole in the clouds.

He swings his leg over the seat, pausing when a shimmer of colour turns his head to where Akiko stands in the doorway. The breeze ruffles the edges of her red, gold and black yukata. A slight curl of a smile glistens beneath her dark, almond-shaped eyes.

'Going anywhere in particular?' she says.

He shakes his head.

She steps out of the doorway, grimacing as her bare feet meet the scrubby grass littered with stones, puts her arms around his shoulders and kisses him on the cheek, then steps back. He kick-starts the motorbike and eases over the rutted dirt and metal, down towards the dunes and out into the wind. He rides up the broken asphalt of the road to where it snakes around the shore. A pair of takahē stride, stilt legged in the sand; two children steer tiny pushbikes with training wheels. He waves to the kids, points the motorbike on up the slope towards the hilltop, glancing in the mirror at their small figures fading behind him.

In September 1962, his mother, Etta, had taken Caleb up to her parents' house in Opononi on the south side of the Hokianga Harbour. A week before that he'd stood in the doorway as Troy packed a duffel bag with clothes and stood looking in the mirror. The army application sat on the table, the edges curled where Troy had read and reread it, then signed it.

Report for duty. Induction.

'Why would they want you?' said Caleb.

'Beat it, brat.'

'Are you taking your Davy Crockett hat?'

Troy turned and glared. Caleb smiled. After a while Troy smiled too.

'Try not to shoot yourself,' said Caleb.

Troy looked up at the photograph taped by its edge to the mirror. An old, sepia photo of a young man dressed in army trousers and a white T-shirt, sitting on a slope above Rangimoana Bay, looking out to sea.

Caleb stepped in, sat on the bed. He folded his arms across his chest.

'I just don't see why you want to go and join the army,' he said.

Troy turned, leaned against the dresser. 'You wouldn't understand.' He took the wooden chair from beside the wall, turned it around and sat on it, leaning his elbows on the back frame. 'You're the lucky one.'

'How?' said Caleb.

'You get to have one long bloody holiday up north.'

'They still have schools up there.'

'Yeah, but they're up there. You get to ride a horse to school, head down to the beach every night.'

'We can go to the beach whenever we want to here.'

'Yeah, but without Mum to whistle you back in you can stay there all day too if you want.'

Caleb looked up at the empty doorway.

'Think of it that way,' said Troy. 'No Mum or Dad on your case. No me to kick your backside. Man, you've got it made in the shade. Out in Grandpa's dinghy, catching kahawai and kingy from the rocks. They don't even make them wear shoes to school up there. You can live like Tarzan. And think, nobody up there knows yet what a bloody pain in the bum you are.'

'I'm gonna miss you. You must remember to write, if you learn how.'

Troy laughed. He reached across the gap between them and they clasped hands. Then Troy picked away the tape holding the photograph to the mirror. He put the photo in his duffel bag. The next day, when Etta eased her car to a stop in front of the gates of the army camp in Papakura, Troy insisted they let him walk in alone.

Etta sat looking out the window at the grey sky. 'You remembered to pack your raincoat?' she said to Troy.

He raised his eyebrows, then stepped out of the car. He glanced at Caleb and they both made six-gun gestures with their hands. When Troy walked in through the gates Caleb pushed the seat-back forward, slipped out, then into the passenger seat. Etta was still staring out the window. Caleb put his hand on her wrist.

On the drive up to Opononi they stopped in the Waipoua Forest. Etta eased off the dirt and gravel road and they sat for a long time with the windows wound down, listening to the bird calls from the branches. There was a loud crack and a thump and they both looked into the bush, but there was nothing to see.

'I'll write every week,' said Etta.

Caleb stared into the trees.

When they pulled onto the gravel driveway of the house, Caleb sat flexing his hands. Squeeze and release, squeeze and release. Then he looked up over the dashboard to where his grandmother and grandfather stood from their front verandah.

Since then he has seen his mother twice, the last time three years ago. Between visits all he has seen of her is her name written in small italics at the foot of photographs. *Life* magazine, *Time* magazine. The last time, he had sat on a bench at the airport, helping her run through a list of essentials. He called the items on the list out to her. Film stock, malaria pills, plastic bags that squeezed shut, hat, first-aid kit. Somewhere between hooded jacket and compass she kissed him. Somewhere between balaclava and torch she said goodbye, again.

He hasn't seen Troy since the day they watched him walk up to the guardhouse at the gate of the base.

Akiko stands listening to the sound of the motorbike fading, then goes back inside. She stands at the window facing the drive-way, looks down at the tree's shadows cast onto her hands.

She had first met Caleb at a kite-flying day, the kites' strings rising into the grey sky behind the concrete hulk of the museum. She had gone with a couple of friends, all three of them struggling to reel in a fractious kite that was bursting to investigate the stratosphere. Her friends fell over in a raucous tangle. Akiko tripped over their legs, stumbled, almost fell flat, but a hand reached to steady her. She dug the heels of her boots into the dirt and looked up.

He stood balanced, his other hand working to keep his own kite in line. She glanced up to where his kite must have been lost somewhere among the dozen or so that darted above, then stood, regaining her breath, reaching to clear the windblown strands of her hair from her cheeks.

She found herself staring not at his grey eyes or his curious half-smile, but at his hands as he wound his kite back in, fingers flexing. Delicate. Drawing the string back onto the reel, the kite back to the ground. But there was no reel, or string, or kite. It was all a mime.

She smiled.

'You're the maths genius guy,' she said. 'I've seen you around.'

'Caleb.'

'My name is Akiko.'

'I know.'

'Do you now?'

There was a sudden jag of movement and a yellow kite fell at their feet. A real one. The wind riffled its fabric. He crouched, plucked at the taut kite string, and stood with it, both of them looking along the length of string to a young man in glasses, his hands grasping the wooden reel.

'I'm not sure it will fly with you holding it,' said Akiko.

'More's the pity,' said Caleb.

He raised the kite with both hands, letting it go at the end of his reach, and turned back to Akiko. 'I've seen you too,' he said. 'You're the dancer.'

On week nights he inhabits the house at Rangimoana alone, but on Friday nights Akiko parks her red and white Morris Mini on the other side of the swingbridge and walks up the stony path. She stays until Sunday evening or sometimes Monday morning, then heads back to her small flat overlooking Grafton Gully where she closes her curtains to the snowfall of car lights from the motorway.

At Rangimoana he sleeps either in his parents' old bed or on the couch or, in the summer, out on a hammock on the deck in the sea wind. On summer mornings he sometimes stays in the hammock until well after sunrise, watching Akiko move from room to room through the glass of the French doors, the landscape shifting around her with each touch of wind on the doorframes.

She is always leaving pieces of herself everywhere, he thinks. Not in the house itself, but out on tree branches, on the old river stones that fringe the driveway. Even down in the dunes. Scarves, earrings, once a bangle so thin he had to lift it to the light to see the whole of its circle. At first he had picked the pieces up, returned them to the bedside table in her room, but something else would appear. Her carelessness had puzzled him, she the most careful of people, until one day he found one of her scarves tied to a tree branch at the edge of the dunes. The knot showed deliberation and effort. *Intention.* He ran his fingers through it, the wool soft. After that he'd stop now and then on his way past. In September's chill westerlies the scarf's strands separated one by one. The rain strafed it, a hailstorm dissolved it, until October found it gone, each fibre a single migrating bird.

He thought a couple of times of mentioning it to her, but he never did.

In downtown Auckland the smell from the morning's breakfast fry-up drifts from the Pitt Street Fire Station's kitchen, down the corridors and into all the open rooms. Troy looks up from the bathroom's basin and into the broken mirror they keep meaning to have fixed. He follows the line of the crack in the glass that cuts across his reflection from just above his navel and goes up and over his chest to where the pieces of sticking plaster hold the separating panes in place. He washes the last of the ash and grime from his face and neck, sets the towel over his shoulder and walks on down the hall to the kitchen where the other members of Day Watch sit chewing.

Monty glances up from his horse-racing gazette.

'Man takes a beauty wash every five minutes,' he says, 'God's honest truth, fellas.'

Troy hurls the towel at him. Monty ducks. He lifts up his tea mug and takes another sip.

'It's just not natural,' says Monty.

'Washing's not natural for you,' says Troy.

The others laugh. Jimbo rinses out his tea mug. Tank reaches and snatches the gazette from Monty's hands.

'Hey!'

Troy goes on to his locker and opens the door. He takes a long breath. Two photographs hang taped to the inside of the door, both crumpled and flattened out. The first, the edges more yellowed and crinkled now, the ink faded with age, is of a young man, Troy's father, Joaquin, dressed in a white T-shirt and khaki army pants, smoking a cigarette. The smoke mists a few inches beyond his face. He isn't looking at the photographer, but rather side on. Layers of distant surf fan behind him. Low sunlight – perhaps sunset – sets his face almost ablaze and casts a flattened shadow on the grass. Troy lifts one edge of the photograph, the corner dog-eared and cracked, and reads the rough pencil scrawl on its fading skin.

J.

Rangimoana. 1945.

The other photograph, ripped from a magazine, is turned to face the wall.

He sits looking at the back of the second photo, part of an advertisement for a telephone company. He is about to close the locker when a sound he knows well jolts him.

The fire bell.

The fire engine's motor guns as Troy sits in the cab, pulling his gloves hard onto his hands. He puts on his helmet as they hammer down Nelson Street, siren wailing. He looks over the buildings to where a pall of smoke rises, then glances at Monty and Tank. Time to go to work.

A few minutes earlier the woman had stopped at the kerb, holding tight onto the dog's leash. She crossed the road, stepped onto the grass of Victoria Park and let the dog off the leash. It ran barking across the grass.

She walked past the old kindergarten building, called to the dog again but it continued to run, sniffing at a set of scuff marks in the grass. Another bark, then the dog stilled, tail wagging, still sniffing at the ground. The woman strode towards it, looking to where a forty-four gallon drum sat in the centre of the playing field. The dog circled the drum a couple of times, sniffed at the hand cart leaning up against it. He looked back across the cricket pitch towards the advancing woman, then raised a leg against the drum's rusting metal.

The woman stopped and lifted a shining object from the ground. An alarm clock, two bells on either side of a circular handle. She turned it over, the movement setting a tiny ping from hammer against bell. The minute hand flicked to 8.15.

The alarm rang.

She jumped back, dropping the clock in the grass. She turned to carry on towards the drum until a sudden rip cut through everything and the flash of light burned her eyes. She stumbled backwards, fell in the grass, one hand dabbing at something on her forehead, something sticky and burning. She flailed with her hands to peel it away, and her skin came away with it. A ragged circle of fire blazed where the drum had sat. The woman called for the dog, then drifted, her closing eyelids leaving one last imprint on her scalded irises.

An alarm clock.

The twin bells oscillating almost too fast to see.

The blaze is still burning when the first fire engine gets there, a black oval like a giant footprint in the grass around its edges. Small islets of burning grass sit glistening. Jimbo steers the engine up over the kerb and onto the playing fields, the tyres tearing up the manicured grass. Two passers-by crouch beside the woman lying on the ground. Monty leaps off the engine's running board and sprints to them. Troy and Tank unravel the fire-hoses.

The first jets of water just push the flames around. The next spreads it further, the firemen doing no more than herding the flames. Nightmare musterers. Monty turns and shouts.

'Water's having no effect.'

He lifts the radio transmitter from his jacket pocket, calls for the foam tender.

It takes twenty minutes to extinguish the last of the flames, the firemen having to walk more than a hundred yards in all directions from the explosion point to douse small pockets and patches of burning film. Only the drum's base is left intact, sitting lopsided and ragged in the charred midst of the cricket pitch. An ambulance takes the woman away.

Troy crouches among the ashes. He raises his eyebrows to Monty, approaching, holding an alarm clock.

'Where'd you get that?' says Troy.

'It was just lying in the grass, next to the woman. You look like Al Jolson, by the way.'

'Eh?'

Monty points to Troy's face and Troy reaches up and brushes some ash from his forehead. He rubs it between forefinger and thumb.

'Any unlucky buggers in there?' says Monty.

'There's some bones over there,' says Troy. 'Not human.'

Monty crouches.

'The lady was mumbling something about a dog,' he says.

'Okay. Well, I know where it is.'

'Catch.'

Monty tosses the clock up in the air and Troy snatches it from amongst the last of the thinning smoke. He turns it over in his hands. The face is cracked, the hands stopped at 8.15.

'Be interesting to hear what the woman has to say when she calms down,' says Troy.

'Might be a while. State of her.'

Troy stands.

'But that's not our lookout, brother,' says Monty. 'You coming?'

Troy pokes at some of the liquid staining the grass. He leans and spits into the dirt.

'Yeah,' says Monty, 'I can taste it too.'

'Some kind of polymer in with kerosene,' says Troy. 'Polystyrene maybe.'

Monty takes a deep breath. 'Shit.'

'That's just what I was thinking,' says Troy.

'Could be just a drum full of plastic rubbish or some such.'

'Nah.'

'Yeah.'

'No, it was *mixed* together.'

Monty stares at the scalded grass. 'As in napalm?' he says.

Troy looks out over the burnt grass. He nods his head.

Caleb sits on the motorbike, halfway down the steep incline of College Hill, watching the fire engines leave. Other people from the houses on the slope have begun to move away, sensing the drama is over. In Victoria Park the wind sends the last of the foam drifting away in the fire engines' wake.

A police car sits on the grass, figures move among the foam-sodden debris. Caleb glances up once at the grey sky, then puts on his glasses, kick-starts the motorbike and rides away up the hill.

Caleb drags the old air mattress out from under the house and he and Akiko fight over it in the shallows, Caleb in his beach baggies, Akiko in a high-necked tank top with a one-piece bathing suit beneath. Once or twice the withdrawing waves begin to take her away and he has to swim out to help drag her, laughing, back in. He stands waist deep in the water, her hands in his, sea water dripping from her long dark hair. Another wave lifts her and she and her inflatable roll right over him. When he shakes his face free of the water, she is lying – beached – on the inflatable, her face concerned for a moment, then smiling.

'Oops,' she says.

He smiles.

'Thanks a lot,' he says.

They drag the air mattresses up the sand and lie back on the face of a dune, looking skyward.

'When are you going down to the hospital?' she says.

'Maybe tomorrow.'

He grabs a handful of sand.

'It pisses me off,' says Caleb. 'Dad having to spend another birthday in that place.

He closes his eyes, listens to the surf, the screeching of the gulls.

'When he was first put away,' says Caleb, his eyes still closed, 'he seemed to have no real face. His expression was like glass, easy to look through but so much harder to look *at*.

But then he was also easy to rage against, because he wasn't a someone, he was just this name and a reason. A reason to be angry or sad or hurt or whatever. Then he started to step back into his face and ...'

'And?' says Akiko.

'And he became human again. The one thing he hadn't been, since I was a little kid. He had to begin again.'

'So did you.'

He feels her hand lie soft against his chest. He looks south to where Koroheke stands sentinel against the Tasman waves. He thinks to reach out to her hand, perhaps take it in his, or hold it against his bare skin, but he doesn't. He just lies there, listening to the engine of a jet as it climbs high overhead, heads out over the ocean.

'You never talk about home,' he says.

Akiko looks up. They both follow the jet trail until it dissipates in the blue.

'Do you write much to your family?' he says.

She doesn't answer.

The glasshouse is well ablaze by the time the fire engine arrives. Jimbo swings the big red rig in a wild circle on the dirt turnaround, sending stones scattering across the dusty lot. He shifts into reverse and backs as close as he can to the old corrugated iron shed, beyond which the glasshouse crackles with fire. The owner stands waving his arms.

'Out of the way if you would, mate,' says Monty.

Stacks of cardboard and wooden boxes burn with malevolence, the flames reaching up the glasshouse's wooden framework, their heat popping the windows. The fire crew streams out, Tank working the hydrant in place. Troy and

Geronimo unwind the hose and pick their way through the rubbish pile to the thin alley between the sheds. The first jet of water smashes a couple of the glass panes, the water cutting the plants off at the necks. Leaves and twigs fly everywhere.

There is a crunch, then another. The remaining glass panes explode one by one. The owner closes his eyes. The air inside the glasshouse ignites, the shattering glass making the air itself look fractured. Troy drops the nozzle's angle for a moment, looking into the fire. Then he raises it again, shooting water into the shadows. The last of the plants disintegrate.

And in that moment he sees other figures. He blinks and they come to him just as they had that morning, one at a time, each stepping free from the canopy of leaves, each seeming to be secure in the knowledge that no alien eyes intruded. Just the new sun rising over the ridge above them. Their number ceased at three. He waited a full minute for a fourth but there was none. Not even a rustle in the pandanus, a ripple of movement in the swamp water that would signal the vibration's origin. He raised the rifle, waiting for a moment when the line of their heads would synchronise, so he could take them all with a minimal adjustment of position.

The moment came.

Three shots, the figures falling one by one like cut saplings.

The ripples in the swamp circled outwards from where the men had fallen, then calmed. After a minute or so the swamp surface was moved only by the occasional fall of a leaf. The flutter of a dragonfly's wings. A moment later it was raining again and Troy stood, the water steaming off the barrel of his sniper rifle. Rain glistened on the leaves.

When the last of the pockets of embers are out, Troy sits apart, one foot up on an old cable reel. Jimbo and Tank sift among the debris, the mechanical rote of their movements speaking of men who have done this a thousand times before. Troy stands, his overalls rolled down to his waist, tiny crystals of water dripping down onto his bare skin as he drinks water from a child's drink bottle.

He glances at Monty, the older man packing his gear into a neat pile at his feet. As if his patrol is about to roll out. Troy smiles. Habit, always be ready to move. He had met Monty in a bar in Vung Tau in the far south of Phuoc Tuy Province in South Vietnam. Monty had turned from the bar, juggling bottles and glasses, and spilt Troy's drink. They nodded to each other and Monty put Troy's next beer on his own tab. They nodded to each other again, later, when Troy was drafted into Monty's patrol. After a month of rotting webbing, cold rations, mornings watching the light around them sharpen with the dawn, though the sun was invisible above the jungle canopy, they nodded to each other again when they assembled for a meal in the mess back at base in Nui Dat and sat whispering, punctuating their whispers with hand signals. Then Monty had looked up at the overhead lights, the rows of empty tables, plates and cutlery.

'What the hell are we whispering for?' he said.

'I was whispering cause you were,' said Troy.

They nodded again, then laughed.

Habit.

Jimbo and Tank walk back to the engine and climb up onto the running board. Monty turns to Troy.

'You okay?' he says.

'Yeah,' says Troy. 'Why?'

'Went a bit vague on us for a moment there.'

Troy raises his eyebrows.

'You've done it a couple of times,' says Monty.

'What are you on about?' says Troy.

'You're not seeing stuff are you?'

46

Troy stares.

'Stuff that isn't there,' says Monty.

'No,' says Troy. 'You?'

'No.'

'You sure?'

'I'm sure.'

Troy screws the lid back on his water bottle.

'No nightmares?' says Monty.

'No. You?'

'Nah.'

'Then why did you ask?'

'Just making conversation. Just don't start ducking from imaginary helicopters or something.'

Troy points skyward.

'Like those?' he says.

Monty looks up into the empty sky. Troy smiles.

'Bastard,' says Monty.

In the evening Caleb stacks some twigs and kindling and makes a fire out on the lawn behind the house. He and Akiko sit toasting marshmallows, their voices soft amid the crackling flames. Akiko goes into the house and comes out with one of her handmade books and a woollen cardigan which she drapes over Caleb's shoulders. He drops a marshmallow onto the plate where the others sit steaming. Akiko sits and picks up Caleb's ukulele from the grass, begins to pick at the strings. She retunes it to an open string chord, plays a quiet arpeggio. She looks down at the book next to her boots.

'I write to my mother,' she says.

Caleb drops a marshmallow into his own plate, hissing at the sting of it.

'You asked,' she says.

He puts the plate on the ground.

'I've written to her ever since I was a child,' says Akiko. 'Letters, poems, thoughts.'

'You two get on well?'

'I don't remember.'

Caleb looks through the thin drifts of smoke at her.

'I don't remember her at all,' she says. 'I know her face only from photographs.'

She chews the last of the marshmallow, puts the fork down in the plate and picks up the book. Its cover is made from wood, the surface a collage of dry leaves and dried flowers. She opens the covers and the pages fan out in bunches. Their edges are uneven, the rough sets of paper dyed different colours, aqua, mauve, fawn.

'You talked about birthdays,' she says. 'The day I was born my mother and father carried me through streets of people shambling, slipping, falling. The sky was red, purple, yellow, black. Ash fell like dying butterflies.'

She flips through another few pages of the book. Caleb puts down the plate. He slips his arms into the cardigan's sleeves. Sparks from the fire spit into the dirt at their feet.

'Where were you born?' says Caleb.

'Nagasaki.'

He closes his eyes.

'You know about Dad,' he says.

'Yes. I know who he is.'

'Was.'

Smoke swirls. He holds his breath for a moment, then lets it out.

'I don't know what to say,' he says.

'You don't need to say anything, Caleb.'

The evening turns cold and they go inside. Caleb lies on

the inflatable mattress on the floor, a couple of beach towels spread across the fabric. Sand grains roughen the wood of the floorboards. There is still a tincture of smoke in the air. Akiko sits leaning back against the couch, one of her books beside her. She has another almost completed, just waiting to be bound. She lifts one of the hard, quill-shaped spines she uses to secure the pages, loops the ends of the paper through it. She takes another spine and does the same.

In the night Caleb lies on his back on the bed, his arms splayed. The air is hot for spring, moist. The wind kicks up during the night. He sits up several times and stares at the glass of the French doors as the panes rattle in their frames, the doors clatter on their hinges.

He goes to the kitchen and gets a glass of water. On the way back he pauses at Akiko's open doorway. Her bedside light is on and she lies on top of the blankets in her yukata, facing away from the light and towards the door. He stands there for several minutes before he realises her eyes are open and looking at him.

'Sorry,' he says.

'For what?'

'For waking you.'

'I was waiting for whatever it was you were going to say.'

He steps in. She reaches out her hand and he passes her the glass of water. He looks across the glowing tips of her hair at the light bulb behind her.

'Did people treat you different? When you were a kid.'

'Yes, I suppose so. But there were many hibakusha. Survivors of the bomb.'

'I got singled out.'

'Because of what your father had worked on?'

'No, because everyone said that Dad had gone mad.'

She moves onto her back. She has two silk scarves around

her throat, a pale orange and a light green.

'Once, when I was a kid,' he says, 'a bunch of boys ganged up on me out on the footie field. *Your old man's a loony, your old man's a loony*, they shouted. I got bashed a bit. One kid walked halfway across the field to lean over and spit in my face. When the kids walked away I lay there, his spit on my throat like a scar. I rolled over and leant my face against the grass. It was soft, empty of anger. Why do you always wear scarves?'

Her profile is lit by the lamp behind her, like a quarter moon. Caleb waits for her to answer but she doesn't. He goes back to bed and lies crossways on the blankets. He doesn't sleep.

Akiko wakes with the dawn and walks down the hall. Music comes from the gramophone in the lounge.

'Caleb?'

She knocks on the bathroom door, then his bedroom and she wanders out onto the deck. She goes out to the shed but the motorbike isn't there. She goes back inside to where the stacker arm on the gramophone whirrs and sets another 45 down onto the turntable.

She stands watching the disc revolve for a moment, then sets the shower running

Mid-afternoon Caleb sits with his legs up, cross legged on the couch.

'Are you heading back to town tonight?' he says.

'Yes, later.'

Akiko cooks a pot of rice, sautés vegetables in a pan. She tastes a sprig of broccoli from the wooden spoon, then adds a touch of cayenne pepper. After dinner they sit with a bottle of wine opened, but neither of them touches it. Caleb goes to his room and comes back with a shoe box. He takes out a half-dozen small plastic bags, each filled with coloured powder. He raises them against the light, checks how much is in each, jots a reminder in the small blank page notebook he always carries. She sits writing in her handmade book, a sentence in Japanese, one in English. He holds his notebook in one hand, both pages open, his hand stretched as if he's about to snap it shut. But he doesn't.

Akiko looks down at the shoebox.

'What are those?' she says.

'Chalk dust.'

'For?'

'For the kids to blow at parties.'

He takes the rubber band from the neck of one of the bags, sprinkles orange dust on his hands. He raises the open bag beneath him and blows a short breath and a tiny cloud blooms, then falls into the bag. She reaches to dust a few stray grains from his chin.

'How do you shave the chalk down?' says Akiko.

'Cheese grater.'

She laughs then notices he isn't laughing and that makes her laugh again. He ties the bag, raises his orange stained hand and goes into a B-movie monster pose, eyes wild. He threatens to daub her face with it. She screeches, jumps back. They both sit laughing, then he stops, looks down at the bags.

'I'm just curious,' he says, 'that's all. About the scarves.'

She glances at his stained hand, which he holds outstretched, palm up. Away from his body.

Her gaze locks onto his. She raises her fingers to loosen the scarf's knot around her throat, draw it apart. He doesn't let go of her stare either, until her hand falls away to her waist, the scarf's fabric dancing in the breeze through the open doors. He takes it from her, sits holding it.

The scar is faint, but it's there. It runs from the centre of her throat down to her chest beneath the tank top. She looks down at the scarf in his hand, takes it from him and reties it around her neck, then turns to get up from the couch. He reaches with a hand on her wrist, to stop her, realising then he has touched her with the hand stained with chalk dust. She blinks, holds her eyelids closed for a long time.

'Everyone called it the pika,' she says. 'The flash. I can't remember anyone I knew calling it the bomb.'

'Kiki ...'

She doesn't open her eyes.

'Every two years,' she says, 'the week of my birthday, I had to go for medical tests. I had to take all my clothes off and get into a white robe. They took my blood, did X-rays, an electrocardiogram. Everyone had to. They tested my heart rate, the oxygenation of my blood, made me exercise in a room with white walls to match my white robe. The white of my bones in the X-rays. They did everything but treat me. Treat us.'

He crouches in front of her, leans forward until their foreheads touch. He lifts his head, looking into the dark windows beyond her. He sets his chin against her hair, closes his eyes against her.

IV

Laila, Laila

April, 1989

In the dusk Isaac crouches at the edge of the marsh's rippling water, watching a white swan and a pair of chicks bob in the current. An island of reeds sits beyond them. He lifts a stick, reaches and touches the tip amongst the ripples.

The station-master's house was built next to a workshop on a siding off the western line. In the 1950s a band of steam locomotive enthusiasts bought the land, hoping to establish a museum dedicated to the age of steam. But it never happened. The sole piece of rolling stock that they acquired was the old carriage.

When Isaac bought the two acres of land and water the real estate agent looked at the rusting railway carriage and quoted him a price for 'taking that pile of junk away', but Isaac just smiled. The agent gave him a long look, then shrugged, fastened the clasp on his satchel and held out his hand. There was a pause in his eyes.

'You're Isaac Simeon, aren't you,' he said. 'The atom bomb guy.'

'I was hoping people had forgotten,' said Isaac.

'I remember it all being in the papers,' said the agent. 'My old man used to call you a commie.'

Isaac looked up the parallel lines of tracks to where they disappeared amongst the scrub.

'I could never tell Karl Marx from Groucho Marx,' he said.

'You sure you want to live out here in the middle of nowhere?'

'Yes.'

'All right then.'

The agent turned and walked off across the scrubby grass. As he was about to step into his car he turned.

'Just out of interest,' he called, 'what do you intend to do with the carriage?'

But Isaac didn't answer. He was already halfway up the steps, drawing open the door. He paused by the first of the inner windows, watched the agent's car move off over the grass towards the road.

He sat on one of the benches, raised his legs onto the cracked cushion of the seat opposite, set one leg over the other and leaned back. The squares of light through the carriage windows illuminated the hanging dust like a sun-dappled sea. He closed his eyes to the sun's touch.

The clown's image in the glass double doors skews with the wind, then again as the automatic eye reads his presence and opens. Isaac is already dressed in his full Quark the Clown costume as he crosses the mall's central courtyard.

He performs after a man in a black leather waistcoat playing an accordion. A small boy with jandals that squeak as he walks wanders up onto the low stage into the midst of Isaac's act and sits a couple of paces away, rests his hands on his thighs and stares at Isaac's hands. He doesn't even blink when Isaac's cigarette explodes, nor does he laugh when Isaac squirts jets of tears from a pair of sunglasses, manipulated by his hand on a rubber squeeze pad. At one point Isaac writes with chalk on a small blackboard, using both hands at once, firing out a wild scrawl of numbers that only he knows are real equations from his past. At the end of his act he tries, without success, to stuff his aged frame into a pedal car the size of a large suitcase, his creaking bones and hisses drawing more cheers from the children than if he'd managed the task. Then he hands the boy a balloon half as big as he is. He tells him if he takes it he will rise above them, above the building, even above the clouds. Isaac winks at the boy's mother's concerned glance.

The boy stares at Isaac's hands for a moment, then at last away from them, at the balloon. He narrows his eyes and begins to take the balloon's string from Isaac's fingers.

Isaac lets go.

The boy stands holding the string, waiting.

Nothing happens.

His mother grins. He lets go of the balloon and it begins to rise, away from him. He snatches at it, misses, then jumps in vain. They all stand, watching the balloon climb, up above the canvas roof of the coffee kiosk, up beyond the second floor balcony and into the mall's ceiling where it touches against the fluorescent light. Isaac closes his eyes, braces himself. The balloon explodes. The boy turns and runs, past his mother and on across the courtyard, his jandals squeaking across the squares of the tiled floor. Isaac stands watching the flakes of the balloon's skin float back to earth. He reaches, catches a flake with his hand.

Armistice Day.

Armistice Day, the voice had said.

Isaac stood in the hospital corridor with his broom, trying to coax a wing of dust from the top of the skirting and onto the bristles. He looked up the passage at the row of doors on one side and windows on the other. Armistice Day, said the voice on the radio again. He walked towards it, feeling the words spinning around inside him, coins tossed into the water of a fountain, falling, falling, and he caught them, closed his hand around them. He lifted the dust one last time, held it up to the light, then picked it off and dropped it between the bars and out the window.

'Armistice Day', he said, 'I remember.'

The nurse stood looking at him for a moment, then went and spoke to the doctor standing half in and half out of a doorway. There were angled ribs of sunlight from the window bars across his white coat.

'What do you remember?' said the doctor.

'Sorry?'

'Professor Simeon,' he said, '*what* do you remember?'

'It's my birthday,' said Isaac. 'I remember that Armistice Day is my birthday.'

It isn't quite true about Armistice Day, but almost. He was born November 10, nine minutes to midnight. The day *before* they declared peace.

1918.

All across the Western Front, starlit perhaps for the first time in years, not befouled with artillery smoke, the guns were silent. In his house that silence was broken by his infant cries.

Isaac was still bellowing away the next day when people left their homes and flowed out into the streets, houses and lamp-posts hung with impromptu streamers cut from newsprint or old rags. Old nightgowns or bloomers that had sat in wardrobes were liberated, reborn as banners. His cries could still be heard a week later amid the clatter of empty bottles. The hangovers were wearing off, the eardrums and lungs wearing thin, and the streets cleared again while people sat in front rooms and waited for those who would come back.

'It's my birthday,' said Isaac.

The doctor nodded.

'It's good to have you back, Professor Simeon,' he said.

'How long have I been away?' said Isaac.

But the doctor just smiled, touched his hand against Isaac's shoulder.

The hospital staff treated him not so much as a patient but as a survivor. As if he'd rolled free from a train or air crash, been washed ashore along with the luggage of those who hadn't made it. After that day, when a voice emerged from the radio and spoke words that dragged him from that wreck, he had to learn to communicate once more, like a child. That was the strangest thing. Through it all, he never lost touch with the most complex machinery of his mind as he climbed inside a latticework of mathematics and physics. All that remained, crystalline, but he'd forgotten how to say hello. Someone would extend a hand for him to shake and he couldn't think what to do with it. A mouth would form welcoming words or just a smile, and he'd sit, going through a random sampling of possible reactions, in growing desperation, like a traveller searching a wardrobe at the last minute for a misplaced passport.

When he had parachuted free of the world he'd packed his periodic table and logarithm chart, but forgotten to save all the tiny things that made him human.

Brick Lane.
London.
Isaac's people had dispersed from North Africa, among the numberless wandering Hebrews criss-crossing the desert. Traversing centuries like the longitude lines that marked their stopping places. A sand people, a wind people. Sometime late in the sixteenth century they boarded boats from Algiers to Cadiz, then fanned out through Spain, up into central Europe. Some headed east, blending with the Ashkenazim. A small cohort wandered west, sighting the River Thames through the rain.

Most of the Simeons of Brick Lane had passed cloth through their fingers. Tailors, seamstresses. But Isaac's mother and father shunned needle and cotton and instead stepped onto the stage. Not theatres in the grand manner, but small inns and drinking clubs. Venues so tiny an offstage prompt could be heard in the middle rows of the gallery. His mother was a singer and his father a dancer and comedian, the both of them shrugging against the shaken heads and tut-tuts of their parents and uncles and aunts at the wastefulness of their chosen life.

'A pauper you should turn into,' people would say to them. In 1920s London the terms actor and drunkard, actress and prostitute were often interchangeable. They were terms to be whispered, accompanying a pointed finger or a raised nose.

Isaac grew up in a house of recitation and music, where conversations often included sentences repeated over and over to practise their inflection, explore their nuances of delivery. It was rare for the gramophone to be silent. Its circling discs were the sole constant in a childhood where costumes came and went, strange accents were born then vanished. Isaac used to sit in front of the gramophone's horn, watching his mother and father step across the single room of their tiny third floor flat that looked out over an alley where discarded fishbones lay waiting for the day cart and donkeys pissed on the cobbles. But inside there was Schumann and Brahms and Pachelbel and the sound of soft shoes on musty boards. He slept cradling a viola. Instead of toys his cot was ringed with ballet shoes, pungent jars of stage make-up and the glues for crepe moustaches. The cot itself had been lengthened three times by the simple expedient of his father sawing away the frame and inserting other boards as bridging, then nailing it all back together. Timber offcuts and nails from the builders' merchant were exchanged for an after-dinner rendition of 'God Save the King.'

But Isaac chose neither tailor's tape nor stage door. Instead he was fascinated by the one thing he almost never got to see among the costumes and alleyways and backstage cigarette smoke.

The sun.

He became a disciple of physics.

Of light.

Rai spends the morning at university, then the afternoon in the clinic. Children with ear infections, one with bronchitis, another with roseola. One boy sits conducting a conversation between two little rubber dinosaurs. Another boy pulls the arm off the plastic skeleton in the waiting room and the vibration sets the rest of the skeleton and its skull jabbering. The boy stares for a moment then begins to howl.

An hour later Rai turns in to the overgrown entrance to Isaac's property. A few cabbage palms rise against the grey sky. Harakeke grows wild beyond the dirt road's edge. Her tyres slosh in the muddy ruts. When she pulls out of the little glade and into the clearing Quark the Clown stands up from the carriage's rear steps.

'Do you sleep in that outfit or what?' she says, looking at Isaac's garb.

'Kids' outing.'

'When?'

'I'm just about to go.'

'Oh, okay.'

'Join me. My assistant.'

She reaches up and lowers her glasses on her nose.

'Yeah,' she says. 'I can just see that.'

He smiles. 'I'm serious,' he says.

'Would it involve my arse having to squeeze into anything tight and spangly?'

A dozen cars are already there when they arrive. A miniature railway runs away though the trees. The engineer sits working a scaled down version of a steam locomotive, though no steam comes from the smokestack. While the children pile aboard the open wagons their parents set up the picnic blankets and plates and cups. Isaac gestures for Rai to park to one side of the clearing. They watch the engineer wave his black cap as the wagons roll beneath the trees.

When the train reappears there is a wild splay of hand-waving from the children. Rai takes her seatbelt off, leans back in her seat.

'I found a scrapbook,' she says. 'It had a bunch of mathematical calculations in it. Other bits and pieces.'

He turns to her.

'At first I thought it was yours,' says Rai. 'With the maths and stuff. Then I realised, when I found the newspaper clipping, that it wasn't.'

'What was the newspaper clipping?'

'Just a small article, with a reference to you coming back from Antarctica.'

He looks away.

'I've never come back from Antarctica,' he says.

'I don't understand.'

'What else did it have?'

'There were some photos of the Tin Man, you know, from the *Wizard of Oz*.'

Isaac runs a finger across his bottom lip.

'Isaac?' says Rai.

The little train appears again and stops.

'That's my cue,' says Isaac.

He gets out and moves beside the car, takes his big black doctor's bag from the rear seat. He struggles to lift out the two other cases.

'Will you help me?' he says.

Rai sits for a moment, looking out to where the children gather on the grass. She reaches for the door.

Isaac coaxes the children into a half-circle. Rai holds the doctor's bag open as Isaac slips out a paper bag of balloons and turns them, one by one, into recognisable shapes. A giraffe, a dog with a wiggling tail. He blows one up and twists it into a long handled hammer and a small blond boy with a broken sandal buckle grabs it from him, begins to assail the boy next to him with it. Isaac shakes his head, takes it back. The blond boy wails.

Isaac hands Rai a small bag with various tubs of face paint and she moves among the children, dabbing on whiskers, stars, puppy dogs' noses. Then she sits among them, begins to apply paint to her own face. A couple of kids reach for the paint, take turns daubing her cheeks. One red, one purple. One eye surrounded with a green glow, the other with smudges of blue. She goes into a mime, feigning an invisible hat on her head, a big belly-laugh. A psychedelic Oliver Hardy. Isaac goes to the case with the insulation tape and lifts out a violin. Rai covers her ears in mock horror. The children laugh.

Instead of some joke song though Isaac plucks a delicate melody, then begins to sing in a soft voice. Rai takes her hands down from her ears. She doesn't recognise the song, nor in fact the language. He moves through a verse, then echoes his voice's melody on the violin, standing dead still. The crinkled skin beneath his eyes is like the worn edges of the pages of an antique book. Then his eyes close. His thin wrists at odds with the bulbous arms of his costume, the tendons on the back of his bony hands taut as wire.

The children grow restless. Then his straw hat begins to rise, his clown's raggedy hair rising also. Some of the children point. The face of a rubber chicken appears, its body expanding inch by inch. Even the child bewailing his balloon hammer starts laughing. Isaac continues with his song, its graceful beauty bizarre against the rising chicken. Rai half expects his voice to take on a warble, some form of ridiculousness, but he sings with an innocence that sends a chill through her, as if the chicken, bulbous, ugly, is beyond his control or even his awareness. He goes through another verse; plucking and singing, then bowing the violin and Rai guesses now he is singing in Hebrew. The children laugh as the chicken grows, the rubber making hideous farting noises as it expands. The blond boy stands, takes his balloon hammer again and begins to flail at Isaac but Isaac doesn't flinch, just keeps on singing. Rai stands, steps beyond the children's feet onto empty grass. She slips off her sandals, begins to move to the melody.

Laila, Laila, itsmi et enayich
Laila, Laila, bederech elayich
Laila, Laila, rachvu chamushim
Numi, Numi, sh'losha parashim

Isaac looks up as Rai moves away from him, her eyes closed. His eyes are not looking at the children now, just watching this young woman who might or might not be his grand-daughter. The trees beyond her are a flickering chorus of leaves. He cannot move or the chicken will fall, so he stays still. All the while a boy assails him with a club made from a balloon.

A shimmer passes through her, like tender electricity. Her painted face downcast, her iridescent eyelids shading any glimpse into her eyes. She makes no sound on the grass, no dent in the leaves behind her. On and on she moves, losing all hint of deliberation, of thought, of clear-cut horizons. The borders of her movements against the leaves as transitory as the skin of a raindrop.

The chicken falls. The children shriek.

The parents call out that lunch is ready.

Running feet, laughter. Amid it all the fragile sweetness of a creaking violin. The last thing he sees before he turns away is Rai's face of many colours – still – as her body moves beneath it, her arms crossed above her.

He goes on playing, aware now of the stiffening breath of age in his fingers. The children are gone now. The two of them alone on a small circle of grass beside a miniature railroad track. He closes his eyes to the pulse of the bowed strings beneath the gnarled tips of his fingers.

Laila, Laila,
Numi, Numi, sh'losha parashim

Isaac walks up the slope of the hill behind the house, glancing back now and then to where his house and the carriage shrink with each look. Halfway up he stops, turns west towards the distant sea, waiting for his breath to stop bouncing in his chest.

A blink and the sky blurs and the years blur with them. When they clear, the marshes at the foot of the slope below have hardened to gleaming ice. The glow of the Antarctic sun is bright enough to sting even downcast eyes. He rides in a half-track vehicle with two engineers and three American geologists who are measuring the chemical composition of a lake in the Taylor Valley, drawn by the rumour that a form of algae lies beneath the surface. Something living. A profound find in a continent where the only green for a couple of thousand miles is that of military fatigues.

When the geologists take a break he sits with them, drinking coffee from a flask, the precious warmth being passed from hand to hand. They sit in silence looking up into a sky where the possibility of even a high altitude cirrus cloud is no more tangible than the rumour of algae. One of them looks back down at Isaac, grins.

'It hasn't rained here in a million years,' he says.

'What do you mean, a million years?' says Isaac.

'I mean a *million* years.'

He stands and walks along the lake's edge, the water cobalt blue, as if a second sky is captured in the valley floor. He lies on his belly on a rock, looking across the water, looking for the right angle to catch the face of the glacier both above and within the liquid. Shadows loom on the dry stone. He rolls over and looks up to see the geologists standing over him. All of them smiling. One produces an American football from somewhere within his pack. In the long Antarctic twilight the four of them play an impromptu game of touch football, booted feet shifting on the ice. The dry air tires them in minutes and they lean wheezing or spitting into the snow.

In the broad daylight of the evening they set up two tents, pair off after a game of paper wraps stone, and stretch out in their tents, passing chocolate bars and mugs of stale coffee between them. Isaac lies awake most of the sunlit night, listening to the wind. In the morning he trudges out of the tent, heading for the latrine drum. Halfway there he stops. Where they had played football the day before, their boots had compressed the snow beneath their feet. The wind had then blown away the loose snow around their prints, leaving them raised, as if the men had been whisked away out of their footwear. He walks amid the field of phantom shoes, raises his arms as if willing them to rise and walk. A sorcerer's apprentice.

At the next children's party, most of the children are five and six year olds who clap and scream or sit wide-eyed on command. They seem to accept Rai's smiling incompetence as a deliberate part of the act, and she is an instant star. Isaac tells some corny jokes to warm things up, then fumbles through a dance routine, each mistake (intentional, she suspects) bringing laughter from the audience.

He does some comical mime, and Rai is amazed at what she thinks she sees but doesn't. He plucks objects out of the air, then returns them to nothing again. He finishes his act with some magic, pulling a top hat out of his bag and snapping it into shape. He spins it on his fingertips then flips it over and asks the birthday boy to blow on it and repeat some mumbo-jumbo words. Isaac raises his arms skywards then flips the hat back over and lifts out a little wooden toy train and hands it to the boy with great ceremony. The boy takes the train, shrugs. He sits, puts it aside and goes back to scoffing his cake. In the car on the way back to the train Isaac stares at the glass of the passenger window. When Rai stops at a traffic light, his eyes are closed, fingers fidgeting with the wig in his lap.

'I'm not sure that boy was impressed with the toy train,' says Rai.

Isaac nods.

'Probably wanted some whirring thing that morphs into giant robots and then into rocket ships,' says Rai.

Isaac smiles.

'But every toy train should have a boy,' he says.

In the morning the phone rings. Rai turns from the sink, wipes some soapsuds from her hands.

'Hey, kid.'

'Hi, Etta,' says Rai. 'Where are you?'

'Honolulu. Been catching a couple of days of sun. I'm flying out tomorrow morning. Have you got a pen?'

Rai writes Etta's flight number and arrival time on her hand. When Etta says goodbye Rai waits to hear the other line click, but it doesn't so she hangs up herself.

Etta looks out her hotel window to where the new sun rises in the Hawai'ian morning sky. Glistening off the windows of the high-rise hotels. She hires a car for the day, heads out of Waikiki and up into the gap through the hills on the Pali Highway. The Koolau Mountains beckon from beyond the palm leaves. An army truck goes by, cutting through the gorge. She glances into the rear-view mirror, into the dark of the truck's tray beneath its khaki awning, but there's nothing to see. She takes the meandering road around the windward coast. A wrong turn takes her into the entrance of a naval base. A white uniformed sailor looks out through the Perspex lens of a guard-house's window. She does a three-point turn and heads on up the highway.

As long as the ocean is on her right she is heading in the correct direction, knowing that as she is on an island she must either run out of road or do a complete circle and arrive back where she started. When the most ardent of the waves hit, sea spray drifts right onto the road and mists the car's windscreen. She looks through the wet windscreen at the dark shapes beyond.

When the last helicopters of the American withdrawal from Vietnam flew away from the smoke-stained Saigon sky on 29 April, 1975, she sat leaning towards the window with her camera held high, shooting film with her motor drive. Above the shouting faces, the tear-and tiredness-stained eyes. When the photos were later developed, all that came out was a skitter of shapes, chunks of helicopter and sky. It was a fair summation.

That last Saigon morning she had woken to the footsteps of people going from room to room raiding the hotel's minibars of what few bottles they had left. She filled the pockets of her flak jacket with film, put her passport and money in the belt around her waist, strapped her film bag to her back and walked the corridors, shooting the chaos. Bing Crosby trying to croon 'White Christmas' over Led Zeppelin's 'Stairway to Heaven' on warring transistor radios. A voice arguing in French with another arguing in English and another in German. A woman sobbing until the sound of a slap stopped her. Then there was a loud crack and a western man in a grey suit and briefcase stood holding a pistol over the body of a small Vietnamese man whose sandals were made from rubber tyres, cracked and petrol stained. His head was haloed with a growing ring of blood. A handful of people stood gawking at the sputtering body, wondering what to do. Who, if anyone, to call. The sound of another gunshot from down the corridor drove them to the floor.

The lobby was filled with smoke. Etta kicked a glass door open, stepped out over the fragments. The street was bedlam, people calling out for help or clinging to each other and praying, as if they were in a free-falling elevator. Etta walked the streets shooting photos, her mind in the same motordrive mode as her camera. Past the bar girls of Tu Do Street; past legless men begging in doorways. Past streams of paper blowing in the wind. Past the shouting figure of a Saigon policemen. He was standing in the centre of the street like a traffic signalman, but instead of directing traffic he was shooting at it. Cars and rickshaws and cyclists dodged him and moved on.

Crowds had been beseeching and besieging the American Embassy and the departure point at Tan Son Nhut airport for weeks – the local rich, clerks who had worked for the Americans or ARVN, women with Amerasian babies strapped to their backs, prostitutes dressed like Miss America contestants, assorted businessmen, hustlers, drug dealers, taxi drivers and tailors to the American officials whose number was fast evaporating. Private militiamen, Vietnamese mercenaries, kids with photos of US GIs with their mother or sister.

She had been in and out of South Vietnam and Cambodia since she first stood photographing American troops on China Beach in 1966. Nine years, nine hundred years, nine thousand years. Shooting and shitting in open fields of tall grass, jungle so thick it was permanent night on the forest floor. The ringing echo of military acronyms poisoning her speech. ARVN, NVA, MACV, PAO, JUSTPAO, MIA, KIA.

She drives on, her half-circle of the island almost complete when she approaches a sign pointing to Pearl Harbour. She pulls into the car park of the visitors centre and walks through the exhibits. Photographs of ships and more ships. Fading images of young men, some with name tags tacked to the wall beneath them. A few grey-haired veterans walk among the sightseers, offering directions to the ferry out to the monument, or personal memories of the day the Japanese bombed Pearl Harbour. She stands looking at the photos, rows of young men in American uniforms. She plays with the clasp of her camera bag a couple of times, but doesn't take it out.

They show a short film on the bombing, then a small boat

takes the visitors out towards the island where the battleships were moored on 7 December, 1941. The concrete plinth of the USS *Arizona* monument looms. Etta holds her hand above the warm water. The visitors climb from the rocking boat, up onto the still steps of the monument. Hundreds of names are etched into the walls, mirroring those whose bones lie beneath the visitors' feet, beneath the water's gentle waves. Children run, play tag with each other, shouting, 'You're it!' Then a marine claps his hands, calls out.

'Please. Remember, this is a cemetery.'

A Japanese woman with a camera stands focusing on another woman as she drops a floral lei into the water. Small bubbles break the surface beneath the lei, oil still leaking from the sunken *Arizona* spreads around the petals. Two other women recite something. Etta takes her camera out, but again, takes no photos. On the trip back to shore she holds her arm out over the water, feeling the warm air rise.

After Vietnam she had gone back to London. An assignment from the German magazine, *Heuer*, took her back to Vietnam in 1979. A 'then' and 'now' article. In Hanoi she stood watching streets filled with people carrying pink plum-blossom sprigs home for the Tet holidays. Municipal works trucks filled up craters in roads that had been bombed a decade earlier. There were a lot of craters to fill. As she walked among the craters, her boots scuffing on the wounds' jagged edges, she had a feeling they would be the last bomb and artillery craters she would photograph, and they were. She flew on to New Zealand, arriving in time to see an eight-year-old Rai and three other children from her class do a rendition of Abba's 'Dancing Queen' at their school's end-of-year concert. Rai wore hot pants, and knee-length boots that Akiko had painted gold. A headband with a feather, a boa the colour of candy-floss. Etta hadn't seen her since she was an infant. She stayed for five years, shooting occasional photosets for magazines and newspapers. She lectured in photojournalism at Auckland University. Then she went back to London.

Above Pearl Harbour, thunderheads rise behind the hills, pregnant with threat. She gauges she will not get back to Waikiki before they spill and she is right, the last few miles awash with driving rain. She puts the wipers onto full, the clattering on her windscreen easing when the rain loses its power in the caverns between the high-rises. She puts her camera back in her bag, pulls the zip tight.

The next photos she takes will be of home.

Home.

Isaac phones the newspaper about the story they'd had on the cold fusion claim. The deputy editor tells him they took it off the wire service. He writes to the University of Utah, asking for a transcript of the press conference and some data on the experiments.

In the afternoon he rides out to the coast, north of Rangimoana. He parks the motorbike and walks through a clump of trees, their branches all streaming away from the direction of the wind. The surf crashes against saw-toothed rocks. He picks his way down through steep dunes, struggling to keep his balance. He walks the hard packed sand for a couple of hundred yards, to where the sand begins to be crusted with stones, the onshore breeze filling the hollows in the rocks with water. At the bay's end he climbs over a small natural stone plinth, tufts of grass fighting their way out from crevices. He looks down to a rock pool the size of a bread-basket.

He crouches, looking at the sun reflected in the water. His

dark outline beneath it.

When he was a boy he asked his father what made the sun shine. He told his father he'd tried to look at it to perhaps find out, but it had hurt his eyes. His father scolded him.

'Yitzak,' he said. 'Promise me now. Do not look into the sun. Promise me. '

Isaac stares down into the pool, reaches with his middle finger and touches the circle of water. The sun's image ripples, almost breaks.

'But you did, Yitzak,' he says to the sea wind. 'You did.'

November, 1969

The twilight traffic is sparse. A few people sit in cars parked in the shadow of the palm trees on the promenade, eating ice creams from cones. Troy drives along the waterfront, parks close to the fountain. He puts on his long overcoat and takes an evening walk from Mission Bay around to St Heliers and back. The hem of the overcoat taps against his cowboy boots, the heels crunching the loose stones. When he gets back to his car his hair is wet at the tips. He leans back against the passenger door. A 1955 Chevrolet Bel Air two door hardtop. Its yellow body lowered two inches at the front end, the rear raised to accommodate the wide racing rims and tyres on the back. He looks to where the city lights freckle the shivering water of the harbour. Behind him, the occasional swish of cars passing by on the wet asphalt. The rumble of a truck motor turns his head, and he watches its headlights grow, the whites of its eyes turning to red as it goes by, cutting twin trails through the water on the road's surface.

He smiles.

When he and Caleb were boys, they'd gone for a walk

along the West Auckland railway tracks. Caleb picked up a stone and threw it spinning across the lines. It vanished in the long grass. 'You think it's true,' he said, 'that you can hear trains coming from miles away?'

Troy was standing with one foot on each rail. He looked up.

'You know,' said Caleb, 'by putting your ear to the tracks. You can hear them miles and miles away. You reckon that's true?'

Troy shrugged. He crouched down, then knelt. Caleb did the same. Each put his ear to a different rail. Nothing.

'That might just mean there are no trains coming,' said Caleb.

'Or it might mean the story is rubbish.'

Caleb shrugged this time. They leaned back down, swapping rails. Troy sat up, looked up and down the tracks at the empty lengths of steel, then leaned forward again. He closed his eyes, the metal warm against his cheek. He knelt there for a long time. When he sat up again Caleb had gone. He looked over to the roadside grass where Caleb stood peeing.

'I read somewhere,' said Troy, 'that when you pee in the grass next to the railway tracks the sound can be heard from miles away.'

'Shut up.'

'People at stations are standing there now, looking at each other, turning up their noses.'

Caleb turned, smiling. Still peeing.

Troy picked up a stone, shaped to throw it. Caleb shook himself dry then pulled his shorts back up and walked back over to the tracks. The two of them raised up on the tracks' mound of stones. The grass and road and even the few passing cars were below their eye level. Only the hills above them. They turned to look west, to where the lines vanished in the bush.

'Where do we go when we die?' said Caleb.

'How did we get from the sound of trains to pissing to death?'

'Just worked out that way.'

'I don't know. For all I know we go nowhere.'

'Where's nowhere?'

'How the hell should I know?'

'I can't even imagine *nowhere*.'

'You might be able to. Shut your eyes, think real hard.'

Caleb closed his eyes.

'Harder,' said Troy.

'My head's starting to hurt.'

'Did you see it?'

'What?'

'Nowhere.'

'No. Saw a bunch of things. But not that.'

'That settles it, then.'

'What?'

'We must go somewhere.'

In the night Troy sits up. He looks around. Walls, a door, a window. The sound of a clock, the over-loud buzzing of the refrigerator he needs to take a look at. He sits building every facet of the room and the flat that he can remember, placing it hard down on the ground in Auckland. Driving foundations in with his mind. Grounded.

'I am home in Auckland,' he says to the dark.

But.

There are shadows on the wall.

In Vietnam he had watched the children carrying bucket boats on their backs. He had entered a village in a rainstorm, the rain cutting bullet holes in the mud, keeping people sheltering in their bamboo and reed houses. But two round bucket boats sat upside down in the courtyard and he was halfway past them when they lifted and children's legs appeared beneath them. He stopped, stood still, not wishing for them to see him, hoping he could perhaps be mistaken for a tree or the upright of a pole house. The boats with legs moved on across the mud to the riverbank and slipped in, turning their shells over to reveal children's faces. Staring eyes. He squatted down in the mud, his fatigues rendering him almost invisible. In sixty seconds a Kiwi or American company could appear in the village, there could be shooting. Death. But for now the boats with legs slipped away, hands using flat cut slices of sandalwood as paddles, the faces looking once back towards him. He smiled.

The next time he saw bucket boats it was also raining. Then he heard the engines from the Phantom jets.

He lies awake in bed, looking at the edges of the curtains, slipping back into sleep only when the thin slivers of light between the fabric and the wood brighten, begin to cast pale lines across the walls.

Caleb looks up into the afternoon sun, checks the Indian's rear-view mirrors and pulls out to pass a grey-haired man in an old Austin. The traffic is light heading south, though he still manages to find himself almost wedged between the rear of a delivery truck and a car, crinkling his nose at the exhaust fumes. He checks over his shoulder and pulls out.

At the red pebbles of the turnaround outside the complex's main gate he slows, looks up at the sign. Mount Iris Psychiatric Hospital. He parks the motorbike and goes inside, a cardboard box in his hand. The echoes here always unnerve him, as if the hospital buildings are underwater. He stands listening to the keys clanging on the orderly's key ring. A square of reflected window-light hangs on the wall opposite, streaked with the shadow of steel mesh. Dark scars on its pale skin.

The orderly glances across at him. 'You wouldn't have a file hidden in that box would you?' he says with a sneer.

'No room,' says Caleb, 'what, with the revolver and the dynamite, and the breakfast your wife cooked for me.'

The orderly's sneer tightens. He opens the door and holds it ajar, standing with his feet together, calling to the next orderly. Caleb walks through, crossing each square of fractured light, casting his own transient shadows over them.

'Did they search it for atom bombs then?' says the orderly.

Caleb looks back and the orderly begins to laugh. When he closes the gate behind him he is still laughing. Caleb stops at the end of the little hall where another orderly opens the door to the visiting room and Caleb steps in, looks across to the desk and chair by the window where Isaac, dressed in hospital pyjamas, stands to greet him.

Every couple of weeks Caleb rides down from Auckland to visit his father and every month there's a different joke from a different orderly. He looks around at the clinical drabness of the visiting room. Caleb's bootsteps echo on the polished wood, as if another walker follows him across the room to where Isaac leans on the back of his plastic chair next to the small table.

A woman and a child enter, an orderly behind them carrying two chairs. When a patient has a visitor, staff bring the furniture in a few moments before, then take everything away after the visitors have left. Nothing is left to be a weapon or a missile. A young man appears in the doorway, face expressionless, eyes downcast. He sits on one of the chairs and stares into the smoke-glass window beyond the steel mesh. The woman takes the child into her lap.

Caleb nudges the package across the table. Isaac tears the seal off the package, unhooks the lip, looking up when he senses the cellophane with his fingertips. He fumbles with the paper trimmings, drawing the small cupcake out into the light. Caleb reaches into his pocket and lifts out a single candle and a small matchbook. The orderly moves into the room, stands leaning against the wall. He looks down at the matchbook.

'Go ahead and light it,' says the orderly to Caleb. 'Then give me the matches.'

'One year old, again,' says Isaac.

Isaac watches the candle burn for a moment then leans forward to blow it out, but he doesn't. He looks up at Caleb.

'You do the honours,' says Isaac.

Caleb leans in, takes a deep breath and blows the candle out. He breaks the cake in two and they sit chewing.

'You thought you'd eat the cherry on the way down,' says Isaac.

'Every man has his weakness.'

The two have met here in this room for the last six years. The first few times Caleb came he changed out of his school uniform and into street clothes in the rest room at the railway station. On the first visit Isaac just sat, looking over at the square of sunlight in the window frame. The boy looked for openings, showed Isaac some drawings he'd done at school, opened some of his mathematics schoolbooks to see if his precocious workings in differential calculus would prompt a response, but Isaac just stared, now and then winding the belt of his dressing gown around his waist, his head angling this way and that, eyes alighting now and then on his son's face, no more flicker of recognition than he showed to the table or chairs.

Isaac stands and goes to the window. He reaches a hand to the mesh, runs his fingertips over the metal. He glances sideways, and Caleb sits watching a hundred pale silhouettes of his father's face in the petals of the smoke-glass.

Isaac leans back against the wall. The visitor's child sits staring at him. Isaac glances at the child, then winks at Caleb. Isaac starts to move then freezes, begins to lean sideways, as if into a strong wind. He trudges forward on the spot, his feet sliding beneath him in silence. He grimaces against the invisible wind, clasping the hat hard against his head, squinting in the distance. The child stares, wide eyed. Isaac gestures to open an imaginary door and pulls it shut behind him, his body no longer fighting the wind. He breathes hard, reaches to wipe his brow.

'Cigarette?' says Caleb.

'Don't mind if I do.'

Caleb reaches into a pocket, mimes lifting out a packet of cigarettes. He opens the imaginary lid and tosses one into the air. Isaac catches it, rolls it from finger to finger, from one hand to the other, then flicks it up into his mouth. The child stands and claps her hands together. The woman takes her back into her lap, whispering something into her ear.

Isaac reaches into his own pocket, mimes lighting a match. He leans back, smoking the invisible cigarette.

'How sane do you have to be before they let you out of here?' says Caleb.

'Perhaps you're approaching it from the wrong direction,' says Isaac.

'I'd like to approach it from the direction that would see you home.'

A bell rings and Isaac looks up and smiles. Caleb raises his eyebrows. Isaac walks towards the door. The orderly reaches for his keys.

'Come on,' says Isaac. 'You've timed it just right.'

Patients line up along the inside edge of the corridor. No one speaks. Some of the patients wear dressing gowns covering either their pyjamas or their modesty. One wears a red cravat over the collar of his robe, giving him an air of dignity ruined by the fact that when the wind blows his robe open he is not wearing pyjama bottoms. Isaac seems not to notice any of them. He stands alone on the window side of the corridor, the dappled spring sunshine through the tapestry of trees softening the greyed edges of his hair.

The patients amble or trudge out into the gardens. Isaac reaches to brush away a few blades of new cut grass from a bench's wooden slats. He sits, stretches his legs on the gravel path. He makes no move to speak and they sit in silence for several minutes.

Caleb lifts a twig from the path, leans back and begins picking at it with his fingertips. 'When you were railing against the bomb,' he says, 'against war, did you ever think of taking it a step further?'

'What kind of a step?'

'Make your point at all costs.'

'I'm not sure anything should be done at all costs.'

'You believe that?'

'I believe I need to.'

Isaac leans towards the splay of shrubs beside him and breaks off a twig. He sits forward and begins to trace a jagged line in the stones of the path, smoothing it with delicate strokes, the twig a makeshift pencil. The rough shape of a tree begins to emerge.

'What would happen if any of the patients just wandered off,' says Caleb.

'I don't know. Shall I put it to the test?'

'Do you have your pole vault with you?'

'Actually, the fences aren't that high.'

'They'd sure seem like it if you got stuck in the wire with a searchlight beam up your arse.'

'This isn't Colditz.'

'Might as well be.'

A cormorant drifts overhead, a wayfarer from the tidal marshes to the west.

'Shit,' says Caleb, 'there are crazier people than you running the country.'

'It's comforting to know some things never change.'

'Why Antarctica?'

'What?'

'Why did you, you know, in Antarctica?'

Isaac leans back. 'It was as good a place as any, I suppose,' he says.

'That's a copout.'

'It's an unanswerable question. Does one get to choose where and when to break down?'

'I'm trying to understand.'

'I know you are, but you're asking me something I can't answer. Why didn't I go loony at Los Alamos, or at Nagasaki, or…'

His voice trails off. Caleb wipes his hands together, setting the last of the dust from the twig free.

Isaac turns back towards the pale bulk of the hospital building, with its ornate verandahs and lacework railings, its snakes–and–ladder–board network of support poles and eaves. Sitting high on its contoured mound like the superstructure of a ship.

'Only my body is here, Caleb.'

'And your mind?'

Caleb changes down through the gears and brings the motorbike to a stop. The pointsmen raise their white gloved hands fifty yards from the intersection, steering the line of cars away from Queen Street.

He puts the bike on its stand. The onlookers on the footpath form a ragged line from streetlamp to streetlamp. He turns to peer up the hill to where the ranks of protesters come chanting down the slope to the Town Hall. Placards bobbing. Slogans scrawled. Two teenagers bookmark the end of a huge white banner strung from poles held aloft, covering half the width of the street. The painted lettering has the jagged edges of knife wounds. He reads the signs.

Yanks, get out of Vietnam
Join the army, learn to kill
Stop this bloody war

He watches them pass, many of them wearing faded jeans and T-shirts. Around his age. Some – in contrast – garbed like accountants. A woman pushing a pram sweeps back her long hair from her eyes and shouts. On the kerb a couple of middle-aged men with short-back-and-sides haircuts stand with beer glasses in their hands, shouting abuse. An elderly man in the crowd swears at the woman with the pram, but she doesn't seem to notice.

Caleb walks up Wakefield Street to Max's Coffee Shop where he sits his satchel against the leg of the piano. He draws the stool closer and raises the keyboard cover, his fingers searching the coffee-stained keys for some hint of a melody. The place is almost empty. He guesses many of its regulars are in the protest march. Three young men come through the door and Caleb raises his eyebrows. One of them, Weston, holds Caleb's glance. Caleb dallies in an improvised prelude, segueing into a syncopated opening to Rachmaninov's Rhapsody on the Theme from Paganini.

He plays through four tunes, nodding to the couple of people who drop coins into the beer stein on the piano's top. He does a couple of Beatles tunes, then a jazzy rendition of 'Amazing Grace', the room beginning to fill up with people. He stands and bows and walks to the table where the three young men sit.

Michael pushes his cigarettes across the wooden table top. Caleb takes one. The waitress brings four coffees. When she goes, Dominic lifts a shiny flask from the pocket of his leather jacket, unscrews the cap and pours a thin trail into each of their cups. Weston raises his cup, nods at Caleb.

'Our esteemed mathematician,' says Weston. 'What was the subject for today?'

'Some riffing on the basic properties of n-dimensional Euclidean spaces,' says Caleb.

'I love it when you talk dirty,' says Dominic.

'How's your old man doing?' says Weston.

'Still there,' says Caleb. 'Why?'

'He could be useful,' says Michael.

'As what?'

'For the cause, man,' says Michael. 'For the cause.'

'Cause?' says Caleb. 'You're posing as a radical to pull the chicks. They think you must be dangerous. Do you tell them you're living with your granny?' Caleb lights the cigarette, leans back. 'So, did you join the protest march?' he says.

Weston reaches into his pocket and lifts out a marble, a cat's eye. He twists his fingers, sets it whirling on the tabletop. The spinning core radiates an echo of the overhead light, like a candle flame. Caleb stares at it, intrigued by its sudden presence among them.

'Not my scene,' says Weston, smiling.

Caleb picks up Akiko from the university. A light drizzle hovers. He eases the motorbike into the Symonds Street traffic then up the hill. The gully opens up to their left, the bridge and the hospital sit on the horizon. The bike's engine rises in pitch as he changes gears. A traffic light flickers against the background of trolley bus cables. Orange to red. Caleb stops, looks into the interior of the car in front where the driver looks up into her rear-view mirror. The lights change and he moves on. A fire engine comes around the corner, slowing at the free turn, watching the traffic pass. The fire crews' faces are half hidden beyond the rainswept windscreen, the wiper trails like hooded eyes. He rides on, glancing back once when the fire engine pulls up beside him at the next set of lights.

Troy sits drumming his fingers on the steering wheel, looking out the window at the motorcycle. He would know it anywhere, even after all these years. The woman he doesn't know, but somewhere in the rider's face is a face he knows. Even with the passing years. A faint smile stirs. The light changes to green but Troy doesn't move, just sits watching Caleb accelerate away through the traffic. Looking long up the street after they've vanished.

The wiper blades cross, sending skitters of water down across the glass. The rain begins to sting his skin, even though the window is wound down only an inch.

He swallows hard

The wiper blades cross.

He takes a grip on the steering wheel. Hard.

The wiper blades cross.

It was the shape of the bucket boats at the edge of the Vietnamese village that drew his eyes. About the size of a Kiwi kid's backyard paddling pool. He moved through the pandanus leaves and wild orchids, keeping the boats' circular forms dead-centred in his pupils. He remembers now hearing engines – not helicopters but jets. Phantoms. He couldn't see the sky through the jungle canopy, let alone sight a jet, so he moved on. The village was empty, only a scurrying rat moved in the dirt. He skirted the huts, keeping low, peering in windows, leading with the muzzle of his rifle. He avoided standing or stepping over any kind of indentation or elevated shape on the ground, zig-zagging towards where he could hear a small stream. He crouched, still, allowing his ears to hone in to the sound of the water. He moved again, hearing the jets' engines rise in pitch as they banked. The water glistened. He swept the rifle's barrel across in front of him in a wide arc, his finger touching the metal of the trigger. He inched towards the water, not even hearing his own footsteps in the mud above the shrill whine of the Phantom's swoop. Only then he realised the nearness of it. Low. Dive height. Napalm height. He began to sprint towards the river, all thoughts of stealth now gone. He saw a swingbridge across the river and made for it, then, knowing he was not going to make it, he dived instead headfirst into the water. Seeing at the last second, just before he broke the surface, the upturned faces of the boy and girl sheltering against the riverbank.

When he hit the water he let go of his rifle and grabbed the two children and dragged them beneath the water with him. The fire stamped through the trees, the water's surface, the whole world turning blood red. Even underwater the heat scalded his face. He closed his eyes, hugged the children's flailing bodies to him. After thirty seconds he pressed his lips to first one of their mouths, then the other, giving them a few more vital seconds of oxygen. Thirty seconds later his eyes began to cloud, red streaks and white sparkles exploding within his irises. He had to rise. Now.

He did.

Still hugging their bodies to him.

He lifted only his mouth from the water, taking the tiniest pockets of air from just above the river's surface. The stink of kerosene overwhelming. Any more than tiny gulps and the heat of the air would collapse his throat. A lifetime later the fires began to fade and he looked up to where uniformed figures started to appear dotted amongst the blackened stalks and ashes.

Voices.

American.

Click.

A woman's face.

Click.

'We gonna sit here all day?' says a voice. Monty.

'Enterprise to away team,' says Tank.

The children and the photographer and the burning jungle vanish.

Monty puts a hand on Troy's arm.

'You okay, cuz?' he says.

Troy takes the gearshift out of neutral.

'Yeah,' he says, 'yeah. Just went to sleep for a moment.'

'You know that bloke on the bike?' says Monty.

Troy nods.

'My brother,' he says. 'Well, half-brother.'

Monty raises his eyebrows.

'Full of secrets, ain't ya, Henare,' he says. 'Long suspected you had half a brain, now we find out you got half a brother too.'

Da Nang, Vietnam
November, 1969

Etta stands on the beach, listening to the distant buzz of helicopters, as inevitable here as the monsoon. The UHB1 (Huey) gunships; the double-rotored Chinooks that carry artillery pieces or sometimes whole companies of US Marines. CASEVAC crews ferrying wounded. From somewhere there is a taste of acrid smoke amid the sea breeze, but she can see no smoke. She walks a few yards closer to the sea, then sits and takes off her boots and socks and walks into the sea, the salt water soothing the hard, scuffed soles of her bare feet. She ties her boots together by their laces and fastens them through a loop of her jeans and walks in the shallows along on up the beach. A pair of boots swinging against her legs, two cameras swinging against her chest. A backpack with a spare lens, a water bottle, bandages, malaria pills, clean underwear, batteries for her light metre. She smiles, thinking she must look like a crumpled, khaki Santa Claus.

A hundred yards away, a trail of small figures climbs a steep dune. Children, spreading something between them. She gets closer. They carry an enormous sheet of cardboard. Near the crest of the dune they pause, hoist the huge square over their heads, the US army lettering faded. Little more than the kids' legs are visible now. A parasoled centipede taking the afternoon sun. They stop at the peak, lower it to the sand. She guesses what's coming, stops to watch.

Four or five of them climb onto the cardboard, a couple more struggle to, the last with a flying leap which misses, sending him face first into the sand. The others hang on as they gather speed, veer left and right. One by one the children lose their handholds and fall off, cartwheeling in the sand. All but one, who rides it all the way down to the bottom, his arms extended, his body a cross on the sheet and the flame-yellow of the sand.

She gets airlifted out of the jungle between Da Nang and Phuoc Son in a Chinook helicopter. She checks back into her usual room at the Caravelle Hotel in Saigon, stands next to the window and raises a page of negatives against the glass. She picks up her viewer, holds it against the page.

THE RIGHT SIDE OF THE TERRIFIED FACE OF A SMALL GIRL PEERING AROUND THE EDGE OF A WALL, AT ANOTHER SMALL GIRL LYING WITH THE LEFT SIDE OF HER FACE BLOODIED BEYOND RECOGNITION.
AN M-21 TANK, ALMOST OUT OF FOCUS IN THE DISTANCE, PASSING ACROSS A STREET WHERE, IN THE FOREGROUND, A LARGE, BLACK DUNG BEETLE CRAWLS.
AN AMERICAN SOLDIER LYING IN A BED AT BONG SON IMPACT HOSPITAL, READING. ON THE WALL BEHIND HIM, JUST BEYOND THE STAND AND BOTTLE WITH HIS INTRAVENOUS DRIP, A PAGE FROM A NEWSPAPER HANGS PINNED. A FADING PHOTOGRAPH OF THE APOLLO 11 MOON ROCKET TAKING OFF FROM CAPE CANAVERAL.

She stretches out on her bed for a while and tries to sleep, but can't. She lies there looking up at a fly on the ceiling, its body and wings still. She had last lain in this room a few months ago and thinks now the same fly was there then. She blinks and it vanishes. She blinks again and it's still there. She turns over and stares into the cheap wallpaper.

A few months ago she lay with the small television on, listening to people talking without wanting to know the conversation, just needing to hear voices. She meandered in and out of sleep. When she awoke again it was dark, but the television cast jerky shadows on the wall. She turned over to look at it. The picture was blurred, crackled, the figures fuzzy like snowflakes. She went to the TV, slapped its lid a couple of times. The screen shook for a moment, then settled. Nothing had changed. Then she realised there was nothing wrong with the reception, it was just how far those pictures had to come home.

All the way from the moon.

A few days later she was walking in Saigon when a sudden glimpse of a parachute caught her eye. A television in the window of a department store. A few other passers-by stopped. She had seen so many parachutes, from airborne soldiers landing to jet pilots bailing out, but this parachute carried a metal craft, almost a cocoon, in the shape of a Vietnamese peasant's hat. She stepped closer. Helicopters circled the object, though none of them shot at it. The craft landed and she realised what it was. Three tired faces emerged from the craft, sank into the softness of a life raft.

Safe.

She turned away, glanced at a row of blank screens. Her memory pushing images into their frames.

A SOLDIER REACHING WITH A CIGARETTE LIGHTER TO SET FIRE TO THE THATCHED ROOF OF A HUT, WHILE AN OLD WOMAN STANDS CRYING BEHIND HIM.

A STRIP OF BOMBS FROM HIGH LEVEL B-52S, SEEDED TOGETHER LIKE A GIANT STRING OF FIRECRACKERS.

A ROAD SO FULL OF CRATERS THAT PEOPLE WALK NOT ON THE ROAD BUT ACROSS THE TOPS OF THE MOUNDS OF DIRT BLOWN OUT BY THE BOMBS.

The moon landing celebrations were all over the news for days. Etta lay on her hotel bed reading a newspaper. Of the three astronauts, only two landed on the moon's surface. The other never got to set foot there, have his tourist photos taken among the craters and deserts like the others. She was tempted to think they'd drawn straws or played poker while airborne and he'd lost, but of course he'd known all along that he'd have to stay in orbit, further from another human being than anyone had ever been. The world's loneliest spectator. From his newspaper photo he looked like a sweet guy, too nice to be stood up on the greatest date of the century. But there he was, orbiting, waiting for when the two astronauts who *had* landed needed him. Content to forever be the man who didn't walk on the moon, just so others could.

Of the three of them, he'd be *her* guy.

A week earlier she'd been helicoptered in to the landing zone south of the Long Hai Hills, sitting between two US Marines having a conversation about whether the Jefferson Airplane or the Grateful Dead were more tuned in. Every now and then when the chopper turned side on to the wind a breeze came in the open door, past the heavy machine-gun's barrel, carrying an acrid, spicy smoke that tasted like burnt cinnamon.

The marines saw the crashed Phantom jet from the air, hovered over it. No one spoke. They circled like a shopper in a crowded car park. The jet had hit tail first, engine first, so its rear end was stuck in the jungle mud but its nose still stretched skyward like a metal finger, pointing. A couple of half-crushed trees held it up.

'Call it in,' said the sergeant.

A crackle on the pilot's radio. Outward, inward.

'Bodies?' said the pilot.

'Unknown,' said the soldier nearest the door, clicking a bandana of bullets into the machine gun.

'Let's find out,' said the sergeant.

Etta didn't see the bodies in the trees until her own boots were ankle deep in the mud. Next to her a snake moved between branches. Macaws called from the treetops. The first body they found, strung upside down in the trees by ropes made of vine strands, had nothing left above his waist but a thin helix of bone, the spine that once held him upright. There were traces of human tissue on the leaves, a couple of the rock pools were a dirty red.

The machine gunner spat into the moss.

'Booby trapped,' he said.

The others nodded.

'What set it off?' said the soldier who'd been talking about the Grateful Dead a few moments earlier.

They debated it for a while, how the booby-trapped body could be prompted to explode so high up. Then a couple of large birds slipped down through the highest leaves, began to pick at the flesh of one of the other bodies.

'Damn,' said the machine gunner. 'That's how.'

'Better them than us,' said Grateful Dead.

Another soldier crossed himself.

The crew from the second chopper appeared. The officer shook his head at the birds. He raised a handgun, began to shoot at the other bodies, the bullets making little tufts of smoke and fabric and flesh as they hit. One shot piercing an unfeeling leg, another a silent chest. A couple broke through to the tree trunks beyond. None of the other bodies exploded.

The officer holstered his pistol.

'Bring the boys down,' he said.

Etta kept her camera's lens cap on.

The marines followed a trail zig-zagging along a river bank, the river snaking out of the thick bush and into a plain peppered with stands of elephant grass six feet high. A couple of times shudders through the stalks brought the troop to a crouch, M-16 snouts hovering in lazy gestures like a dragonfly's path. Both turned out to be water buffalo. The second buffalo fell section by section, front legs kneeling in sudden prayer, head and neck crumpling as pieces of its hide bounced like hailstones with each tug of a bullet.

'What did you do that for?' said the officer.

Grateful Dead stood with a thin curtain of smoke dissipating from his barrel end. He shrugged. They moved on.

Lunch was taken with a towering rock wall at their backs, guards crouching in a triangle around them. No one liked the pumpkin soup, and the beef looked like putty. Thunder rumbled to the north. Etta sat making sure all her photographic equipment and the zip-locked plastic bags with her film in were watertight. In the afternoon the rain was a forest of needles, and they stepped back into the thicker bush, caped their slickers over their heads, peering out, watching for more movements in the grass. The first small fist of blue sky brought the first exchange of gunfire. Two men in black livery came upon the company sheltering in the jungle's edge. A moment when all eyes stared in surprise. Then the Americans opened up.

A corporal kicked at one of the bodies, lifting the man's skinny arm with the toe of his boot. Turning him over onto his back.

'Were they armed?' said the officer.

'One of them was. I think.'

'Okay. Write it up.'

That was the first day.

On the second day the marines walked for miles, once completing a giant circle, a couple of the newer recruits ducking with their guns ready when the scout came upon the path they'd knocked down that morning in the tall grass. The point man stood smiling, shaking his head.

On the third day they crouched again, this time when the officer called in a napalm strike.

Some of the platoon had already cased the village more than once. Six or seven houses with thatched roofs, a common hut where kids sometimes sat chanting. Two bucket boats by the river. There had been rumours that a troop of Vietcong were using the village as an ammunition store. That wasn't uncommon. Tunnels often burrowed beneath the edges of fields, beneath long-drop toilets. In the darkened hutches people lay breathing through bamboo straws. Marines were as likely to stumble over them as they were to find them with deliberation. Which wasn't often.

And most of the tunnels weren't for weapons. They were for sheltering when men with guns, one side or the other, appeared.

The marines crouched in the trees, then backtracked, following their own bootprints, when the officer received the air-force acknowledgement. A flare was fired. One soldier began to sing.

Shall we gather at the river...

'Not on my watch, corporal,' said the officer.

Etta looked at her light meter. The soft rain shower was hardening. Like a game of pick-up-sticks falling from the sky. Steam rose off the warm mud. The marines raised their collars.

Etta shook her head. The murk would make decent photos next to impossible.

The radio man moved next to the officer.

'There's a New Zealand infantry platoon in the area,' he said.

'How close?' said the officer.

'Couple of miles. Maybe less.'

'Maybe?'

'Affirmative.'

'They would've seen the flare.'

Etta lowered her camera, stared at the radio man.

She heard the jets' engines but never saw them. All but the officer and the scout and Etta lowered their heads. She raised her camera again, with one hand, the other hand raising the kerchief over her nose and mouth.

Sometimes a sound is so loud it doesn't register with the ears, just the sudden shift of earth beneath the feet. Then the metallic whine begins, and a crackling, like someone crumpling paper inside the ear canal. Thus it is with Napalm B. Then there's just silence, as the tongue catches against the roof of the mouth, the taste of kerosene seeming to seep through every pore. No one looked at the flames, they were too bright. Like the sun had fallen into the trees.

They all waited.

The flames' intensity dulled a fraction.

One man stood.

'Brauer,' said the officer, 'get your ass back down.'

A couple of minutes passed, flaming torches falling from branch to branch. Some of them leaves, some of them birds. When the marines moved at last the fires were all but out, just smouldering ash, glowing like discarded cigarette ends.

'Fan out,' the officer shouted, 'no further than twenty yards apart.'

Etta had started clicking the shutter button when the ground shifted, even while her head was turned away. The smoke went from orange to black as the kerosene burned. She moved with the platoon, the soldiers all with rifles raised, knowing burrows could open right next to their feet.

Sometimes after a napalm strike they would find bodies frozen mid-gesture. Shrunken limbs ragged, skin indistinguishable from the fabric of their clothes. Their body fat hissing. But this time there were none. The platoon stood with raised eyebrows, the officer making a slow sweep around him with his arm. Soldiers began firing into the remnants of earth mounds, into overlays of fallen pandanus leaves on the ground. Anything that looked like cover. A private lifted the rims of two blackened hulls of bucket boats, slipped grenades beneath. The platoon ducked. The bucket boats sailed up into the air, the wood dismantling in mid-air, spraying fibres afire.

Then Etta heard a soldier shouting at someone in the river. The others raised their rifles again. She moved in, shooting images as she walked, stopping only when the figure in the river turned, looked past the blackened faces of the two children he was holding, straight at her.

A triangle of blackened faces.

An unholy trinity.

She took one more photo.

It won her the Pulitzer Prize and lost her one of her sons.

V

Astronaut's Eyes

When Troy was a boy it was always easy to trace his whereabouts by the trail of mayhem. Firecrackers would appear from nowhere in the middle of May and find their way into letter boxes. A rear-view mirror from an expensive car would appear stuck with insulation tape to the handlebars of Troy's push-bike. One Guy Fawkes night her neighbour's garden gnome bore scorch marks on his back from skyrockets that had been strapped to his waist in a failed attempt to get him to fly. While everyone else scattered, Troy had stood watching him bounce around shooting sparks, cursing when he didn't take off.

But then sometimes Troy would just go quiet, walk down to the beach and stand or sit still. Stare at grains of sand in his hands, or just his hands themselves and their shadow on the ground. Etta was never worried when Troy was on his wild escapades. In mischief he always had a sense of indestructibility in his stare.

It was when he'd go still that the chill used to creep up from her fingertips.

She'd found him once, sitting on a dune.

'Troy,' she said.

He looked up, out to the open sea. He sat for a long time, running sand through his fingers.

'Troy,' she said.

She ran her fingers across his fringe, straightening it. But the sea wind just blew it loose again.

'Hey, hon,' she said, 'what's up?'

'What's a mongrel?' he said.

'It's a dog with bits of this and bits of that. Why?'

'The woman in the shop called me a mongrel.'

'What?'

'I was looking at a frame thing, for photos. She tried to grab it from my hand. It fell and the glass broke. She called me a mongrel. I made a fist.'

'You hit her?'

'No. I just left.'

'What were you looking at the frame for?'

Troy shrugged.

She reached for his hand, but he stood and walked down the slope of the dune, his footprints like stitches on the sand. She stared at his tracks, at the stalks of marram grass rustling in the wind.

Troy's father had hair the tinge of marram grass.

Joaquin.

She drew him before she knew him.

A line of young men in uniforms, as there were everywhere then. February, 1944. The summer the Americans arrived. She had just turned nineteen and was a trainee teacher at the local school. She rode her bicycle to and from school and would often stop on fine days and lift her sketchbook and pencils out of the flax kete hanging from the handlebars. Stop and sketch whatever caught her glance. A tūī in a roadside rimu, a stand of toetoe all leaning with the wind. One dry morning she crested a hill and stopped pedalling, eased over to the dirt verge. The fields bordering the scrubby grass against the marshes were filled with a scattering of white tents. Soldiers stood at small campfires. Steam rose from billies.

She put her pencil between her teeth and walked to higher ground and sat and drew the tents, then turned the page and sketched the soldiers. A hand gesture here, a facial expression there, none of which she could see for sure, they were too far away. Then a couple of faces turned for a moment from their breakfast fires. One looked away again at some rumble of laughter, but the other stayed staring across the marsh to where she sat on the small rise. She imagined, then drew his eyes, his hair. Then one hand waving to her.

When she looked up, he *was* waving.

She packed up her things and rode on.

To the small town the arrival of the marines was a thing of wonder. An official welcome was arranged, complete with brass band and speeches. The dignitaries' sashes of office flapped in the sea wind. The mayor lost his hat and it rolled in the sand. A small boy picked it up, but instead of returning it, made off through the sandhills, to the cheering of his friends. A week later there was a dance at the surf club hall. Behind the hall they lifted the dirt from the hāngi pits just as the sun was sinking, so the steam rose against a rusting sky.

With the blackout, the village hall stood in darkness. Within, a false wall had been set up a few paces inside the door. A metal bean trellis had been dragged inside and hung with black-painted sheets to shield the hall's inner light when the outside door was opened. Etta said hello to the people she passed heading up the steps and at the entranceway. She stood by one of the long trestle tables overlaid with white sheeting. Around the hall stood lanterns made from beer crates wrapped in some kind of red film, perhaps cellophane, and centred with hurricane lamps. The soldiers stood and sipped from their glasses in sunset colours.

The air was humid, muddied by cigarette smoke. A band played on a small stage made by stacking four-by-twos a half-dozen high and overlaying them with deck timbers. The school headmaster's fingers moved over his accordion's keys, the eldest Hawkins boy played his saxophone. Wade the butcher stood wrestling with his trombone. Others tapped on snare drums, an upright piano.

She danced with a couple of locals, then a couple of Americans. After a half-hour she cadged a cigarette off a friend and stood smoking at the edge of the lantern-light. She turned to see a young American soldier a few paces away, looking through the smoke. His boots were shined to a glare and he had his heavy overcoat on. Etta looked at the punch bowl, reached for a cup.

'You'd better be careful,' said the soldier, 'the army likes to keep its secrets.'

She puzzled for a moment. He raised a hand, made pencil gestures in the air.

'How on earth did you see what I was doing?' asked Etta. 'From that distance?'

He pointed to his eyes, a fingertip towards each pupil.

'I'm a sharpshooter,' he said.

He looked at her hands, at the cup. She raised an empty cup to him.

'Thank you,' he said.

'You might not thank me when you drink it.'

She expected him to smile, but he didn't.

'I'm Etta,' she said.

'Joaquin.'

They danced a couple of times, slow waltzes. The dances were stately, the dancers' movements formal. He stood on her toe once and she yelped and he winced and she laughed. Then the band stepped from the stage, heading for the drinks table. There was silence for a moment until one of the Americans set a Harry James record spinning on the gramophone. The ancient soundshell began to tremble.

Joaquin held out his hand, his right hand fingers clicking. For all his formality there was a featherlight sense in his hands, the movement of his feet. Etta stepped closer, reached up and slipped the pins from her hair. Joaquin took off his hat for the first time, fired it in the general direction of the bench. His grip was steady but not the usual local bloke's cruncher. In a second they were away, his arms sending her out to full stretch, only his fingers keeping hold of her. She spun back towards him, his body bristling, his uniform a shimmer of movement. She began to laugh, go with his steps, the two of them segueing from one Jitterbug move to another, the other dancers radiating away, leaving them in a nucleus. His eyes widened and he dragged her into a dip then set her spiralling across the boards. She stood her ground, shimmied, challenged him with her eyes and he took her in a rough grasp. She slapped his chest with her open hands and he dipped her again, both of them laughing. She separated from him, only their hands tethered, his fingers never letting go of her. She could feel her nails digging into his palms as they moved from step to step. At the song's crescendo he let her go all the way down to an inch above the floor, still with a grasp of her hand. Her forearm muscles burned. Then she was floating, weightless, as he drew her back up, took her, dipped her once again, letting her fall almost to the floor, her back arched like a bow. Her hair over her eyes, criss-crossing the glare from the hall lights in her pupils.

The music stopped and he reeled her back in, his stare moving away from her to some spot over her shoulder. She turned but there was nothing to see. When she looked back, he stood rubbing his fingers into his palms. She straightened herself up, the tips of her fringe wet against her forehead. When she raised a hand to brush it away from her face he stilled, looking at the blood on her fingertips where her nails had dug into his hands.

'Shit!' said Etta. 'Sorry.'

'I've had worse,' he said.

After the second number Joaquin picked up his coat and they went to the door, then out onto the small concrete deck at the top of the steps leading down to the sand. Two couples sat staring into the light rain. A few drops fell on Etta's bare legs. Joaquin raised his coat, lay it over her legs. They talked into the rain.

'Have you always lived here?' he said.

'No. I'm from up north. The Hokianga.'

'Hokianga. What does that mean?'

'The returning place.'

He nodded his head, ran his fingers over the moist concrete.

'Where I come from,' he said, 'about the only spray or rain we get is dust.'

'I've been around the sea all my life,' she said.

His eyes were soft in the misting rain.

'My dad was a fisherman,' she said. 'I used to go out with him in his boat sometimes. If the sea was calm he'd let me hold the tiller. Mum would go spare when I got home all covered in spray, like a bedraggled cat in the rain.'

She straightened his coat over her legs. A shout turned his head to where a sergeant stood calling.

'I'd better go,' said Joaquin.

Etta stood, straightened her skirt. 'All right' she said.

She walked with him, out to the front door. An army truck stood with its motor running.

'Will I see you again?' said Joaquin.

'You never know where I might appear with my sketchbook.'

'I'll look forward to it,' he said with a shake of her hand.

When he settled into the truck he said something else, but she couldn't hear it over in the grumble of the truck's engine, so she just waved. He did too.

One hand raised.

Still.

Etta stood at the blackboard in the one-roomed school. The smaller children worked on basic addition, using small twigs Etta had cut from a felled kauri as counting sticks. The older children tackled long division, some glancing up to snigger at the small children grappling with numbers less than ten. In the afternoon she allowed them to relax with an hour of art, and attempted to keep the youngest from covering themselves in paint.

She sat back in her chair, lifted her own sketchbook from her kete and began to doodle, glancing up now and then at the class. Not realising until she was almost done that she had sketched an army truck. A row of soldiers without faces, except for one.

'You said it rained dust,' said Etta from where she stood at the edge of the road, holding her bicycle with one hand, looking up into the army truck's cab. Joaquin looked down from the driver's seat.

She had eased her bicycle over to the ditch when she saw the truck coming down the loose gravel and dirt road. When it had pulled up beside where she stood, she saw Joaquin smiling down.

'Corporal,' said another voice from inside the truck, 'can we move on.'

She stepped closer to the truck.

'Can we meet somewhere, when I'm next off,' he said.

'Corporal,' said the voice.

'I'd like that,' said Etta.

He nodded, then she heard the truck's motor gun. She stepped back.

Etta sat on a rock above the cliffs for an hour, gauging the time by the height of the sun. She watched a cloud ease into the sun's path. When she looked back down again Joaquin stood with his cap in his hands. She reached for the picnic basket she'd packed.

'Allow me,' he said.

They eased their way down the steep track to the beach. Joaquin winced once as the sea spray arced over the rocks and hit him. When he saw her staring, he smiled.

He walked past her, crouched in the sand. He scooped his fingers into it, raised them in front of his eyes to watch the sand fall. He brushed his hand clean against his khaki trousers. Etta took off her shoes and they picked their way over the dry sand up into the dunes.

He set the picnic basket down.

'So,' she said. 'Where is this place where it rains dust?'

'Home.'

He cleared his throat.

'New Mexico,' he said. 'Animas. Just north of the Animas.'

'Animas?'

'Mountains. A range of mountains.'

'Tell me about it.'

And he did. About sand – desert sand, not sea sand. About rain squalls that boomed inky black in the sky but never reached earth, of dust storms that did, wind gusts hard enough to blow tethered horses over, coiling, choking in their ropes. Of springtime in the mountains where the morning fogs would be enough to make yellow and mauve and purple flowers cover the cracked dirt of the canyon floors.

'Was it your family's ranch?' said Etta.

'No. We worked for Señor Tucker. Ever since my grandfather came up from Mexico.'

'*May*-hee-co,' she said, pronouncing it like he had.

He told her of wolves they'd hear in the night. How Señor

Tucker would get angry with the sound and send the men out with ropes and traps and guns, but they'd never catch them, just end up at a boundary fence that sparkled like electricity in the moonlight.

'You didn't go past the boundary fence?'

'The wolves were someone else's problem then. If they even existed.'

'If?'

'We'd never seen them. Some of the vaqueros thought maybe they were ghosts of wolves.'

'Vaqueros?'

'Hombres del pais. Cabballeros, cowboys.'

So she told him about the ocean, about its moods. Sometimes friend, sometimes foe. They went down to the water and he took off his black army boots and they both walked the shallows barefoot. He was skittery at the sound of the waves. Once when they wandered out too far and the tide engulfed them up to their calves he clasped her hand tight. She could feel him shiver. He stepped back, made an extravagant theatre of protecting her, as if it was she who needed it. He didn't see her smile.

'Can you swim here?' he said.

'Nah. There's a rip. There's a much better spot to the south, past the point.'

They walked on through the shallows.

'Maybe you could show me some time,' he said.

When they walked back to the edge of town a couple of the locals stared for a moment, then turned away.

The next time he was off-duty they went down to the blowhole above South Bay. The blowhole would play when the westerlies pushed in swells that filled the cauldron with waves like rushing bulls. Between big waves she led him across the rocks. They sat eating smoked snapper sandwiches, sipping from a bottle of soft drink he'd purloined from the base.

'So when does the show start?' he said.

'Waves need to be a little higher,' she said.

He looked into the rocky aperture, shook his head. By mid-afternoon it was a howler and they had to sit on the blanket with the basket tucked between them to stop it from blowing away.

'Give it a minute,' she said.

He glanced up, just as a huge swell hit the cliff below. There was a sudden suck of air and the surf erupted through the rocks like a geyser, drenching them both. They gathered their things and moved back onto the sandy grass. She got out her sketchbook and made a few pencil lines. He stood and walked all the way to the edge of the cliff, glanced over, almost far enough to topple, but she caught him with her pencil, secured him to the page.

'Hey,' she said, 'take off your tunic.'

'Why?'

''Cause I don't want to draw you in uniform.'

He had a white T-shirt on underneath, stood with the wind billowing the sleeves. When he sat back down he looked at her sketch, looked at it for a long time, until she began to feel he was no longer there.

'You okay?' she said.

'I was just thinking, about last time I'd felt the sea. Before we came here.'

'What about it?'

He took a deep breath.

She reached out, touched his hand.

'Joaquin,' she said, 'what about it?'

'We were on an island, surrounded by a lagoon. We landed

on a beach so smooth you could think we were the first to walk on it. But it'd been raked over to hide the mines. After the first hour I couldn't tell my compadres from the seaweed. We just kept landing, boat after boat. At the evening muster half our platoon didn't answer their names.'

Etta swallowed, looked down at the waves.

'In the evening I just walked out into the lagoon,' said Joaquin. 'Went a half a mile and the water was still not above my chest. I felt like I could walk across the world, all the way home.'

Joaquin flexed his fingers above his shadow. They lay back on the warm sand, spread like starfish, just their fingertips touching.

A couple of weeks later he commandeered a motorcycle, a cantankerous contraption with a putt-putt motor as irritable as an old sly-grogger's dog. He lifted a small carton from the motorcycle's saddlebag. She slipped the string down its sides, opened the lid.

A camera.

'It's a Beau Brownie,' he said. 'I won it in a poker game.'

He handed it to her.

'For me?' she said.

'I thought of your drawing, of pictures.'

She turned it over in her hand.

'Is it true you won it in a poker game?' she said.

He grinned. 'No,' he said. 'Cost me a couple of days' pay.'

She frowned, shaped to speak, but he raised two fingers and touched them against her lips.

'Don't say it,' he said.

'All right,' she said, 'can I say thank you?'

They doubled up to Frenchman's Point Lookout, where

the corrugated-iron toilet block walls had blown over in a gale and no one had got around to putting them back up. So the toilet sat uncovered on the promontory. The locals called it the best panoramic long-drop dunny on the west coast.

They walked down to where the nīkau palms grew wild against the hillside, the leaves like green flames. The sun was setting, so she knew he'd have to head back soon. She fumbled with the Beau Brownie and he grinned, shook his head. She took one photo, her first. Joaquin in his T-shirt. On the hillside, looking out to sea.

The kiss was almost an accident, a nerve reaction. He looked away and said he'd never meant to, and she laughed and said she had. Then *he* laughed. She had only meant to kiss him, but his hands were islands of warmth in the cold air. He hesitated a couple of times, the second time at the snap of her suspender belt breaking. He looked up, and she thought for a second she could see something flickering in the distance within his eyes. He began to slip away from her, but she reeled him back with the strength of her own stare and he swam above her, her arms wrapping him like a gift. She glanced sideways to where his fingers dug into the dirt, anchoring his shuddering body.

Her breath against his cheekbones was hot.

But his tears against her eyelids were ice.

He raised himself and turned, rolled away.

'What is it?' she said.

He slid a couple of feet down the wet slope. She moved behind him, put her bare legs either side of him, her arms crossed over his chest. Each palm against a nipple. Her chin on the muscle of his shoulder.

'We're heading out,' he said. 'Soon.'

'I guess I knew that,' she said. 'The look in your eyes.'

She lay back down, drew his face against her. His wet hair

against her own wetness. He turned his face side on, closed his eyes against her.

The baby grew inside her one teardrop at a time, a drop for each mile he sailed away from her. Each heartbeat echoed the slam of the army truck's rear door as the marines decamped.

When she was carrying the child, she loved him, she loved her, she hated him, she hated her. Whoever the child was going to be, it didn't seem like much of a trade.

Those times when Troy was a child and he'd just go still, she'd think of that raised hand in that first sketch she'd made of his father. The stillness of his and her figures on the sand. She wrote to the US consulate a couple of weeks after Troy was born, asking for information about Joaquin. A form letter came back saying that the place where Private Alvarez was buried was called Tinian.

She sat in the twilit dunes at Rangimoana with Troy, wrapped in a blanket, laying across her lap. He looked up into the fading light, and she searched the moments between those sleepy infant blinks for something in his eyes she could hold on to. A sign for a traveller to navigate by. But the only thing there was, was something she couldn't quite put into words.

She lies on the bed of her Saigon hotel room, watching a fly sit still against the peeling paint. She glances at the television screen, its blank face a dull grey with the power off. But in it she can see those astronauts ghosting amid the crackling picture. She closes her eyes, sensing she knows now what she saw in her baby's stare that afternoon on Rangimoana Beach.

It was *distance*.

Joaquin's eyes and hands had a sense of closeness in them. Closeness to the earth. Hombres del pais, he had said – men of the land. But Troy's stare has always inhabited a different orbit, a distant orbit. As if he looks not across dirt or sand or even a swollen, rainswept river with napalm smoke swirling, but just blackness. Waiting for his compadres to return.

Her son has astronaut's eyes.

VI

Canon in D

Auckland
December, 1969

The dancers move in a circular stream around where Akiko stands like a river stone in their centre. She feels the beat of the music, the beats of the dancers' shoes. She closes her eyes, counts in her head when they should change movements. Then, with her eyes still closed, she calls out.

In the seaside village where she grew up, the boats put out on the dawn tide and came back early afternoon. When they returned on a good day, fish would sparkle in the baskets, like a fire that would keep the village warm. On bad days the fishermen spoke of good days. Everyone took their breath from the sea. The sea wind kept the green in the leaves of the trees rooted into the cliff faces. It took the fishing boats in an invisible hand at the workday's end and eased them back into the cove.

All the children had heard the story that if the sea wind stilled, the boats could not find their way home. But Akiko was different – she knew that the wind didn't need to go still, that her mother and father already could not find their way home. The day she was born was the day her parents began to die.

In Nagasaki there is a statue. A figure sits on a rock, naked but for a discreet fall of cloth from one bicep down across his midriff. He is in a half-lotus, one leg lying flat on the rock base, the other straight down with a foot on the ground. One arm points skyward, the other fans out over the land. His eyes are closed. Pigeons sit on his arms and legs, sometimes even on one of his stone fingers. To a pigeon, and a traveller unaware of where the statue sits, the gestures may just as well be the shape the stone has become with wind and rain. To recorders of history the raised arm points in the direction from which the aeroplane, a B–29 bomber nicknamed Bock's Car passed almost beyond sight of the ground and dropped an atomic bomb.

The hibakusha were sent anywhere they could be sent. To relatives far away, to hospitals, to cemeteries. In Nagasaki, Akiko had known many other children with scars on their skin. She had said goodbye to some. One November day when she was six years old she went with the other children of her class to the forest to see the last of the autumn colours. She walked across the crackling forest floor, looking up at the leaves twisting, falling from branches. She held out her hands but none of the leaves fell into her fingers. She snatched at some, tried to grab them, but couldn't. She stood watching one fall all the way from a top branch down to the frost-hardened ground. She crouched, lifted its brittle skin into her hand. She held it for a moment then put it in the pocket of her coat.

When summer came again she would stop on the way to school at a municipal garden that was tended by a hibakusha man who had no ears. His skin was burned smooth, like a flat stone, with small flakes hidden within it; like a mosaic. He tended row after row of chrysanthemum bushes, most of them white or yellow. It was rare that he spoke or even looked at people's faces, though many out walking would stop to compliment his skill as a gardener. One day he saw Akiko walking among his rows of bushes. He was crouched in the gravel, reaching among the leaves with a pair of secateurs. She stopped, looking at the secateurs' blades. He dropped them in the gravel beside him, wiped a hand across his brow. When he pushed his hat back on his head she saw his mosaic skin. She nodded in respect to him and walked on. The next day she returned. On the third day he gave her a chrysanthemum, cut by his own hand. This time he nodded in respect.

The next day Akiko took two sheets of rice paper and sat the chrysanthemum between them and pressed it flat. Each month the man without ears gave her another flower and she pressed them all between sheets of paper. Within a year she had made a book of them, using thin slices of wood for a cover, leaves and bark and twigs fastened to them with glue. Thin sharp needles of beach grass formed their spines. One day the gardener was gone. The next day there was a new gardener.

Hibakusha.

When she first arrived at Auckland Airport, it didn't look like the pictures of New Zealand in the brochures she'd read through about the exchange student program, but it did smell of the sea. That was the first thing she noticed. She walked across the tarmac with the other passengers, looking past the concrete runways to the water. She nodded to herself.

They are island people here.

Ocean people.

That much she knew straight away.

Back home she had attended the interview in her best school skirt and blouse. Queued with the other applicants from high schools in the Nagasaki prefecture. She had sat toying with the edge of the application form. The interviewers never took off their coats, never moved their polished shoes beneath the table. One was from New Zealand, the other from Hokkaido. When her aunt and uncle and cousins lined up that evening to ask her how the interview had progressed she looked at all of them then lay on her bed, looking up at the ceiling.

In the night she woke, felt beside the bed for one of her hand-made books, sat up and reached for her quill and ink dish.

Today an old man stopped me in the street to ask for directions. I didn't know the place he spoke of and told him so, but he kept holding his hand next to his ear. After a while he shook his head and shuffled away.

Today I had a pain inside. I felt around down past my navel and then across. Nothing I did made it worse or better. Every week I have a pain somewhere different. I can't make them stop so have made them my friends.

Today my uncle died. He was hibakusha, but few people knew, because he had no scars on the outside.

Today I saw a rainbow over the Urakami River. After a while it drifted out into the bay and I couldn't see it anymore.

Today I found out that New Zealand is also a scattering of islands. One of them was named after a fish.

Today I stood watching a chrysanthemum in the rain. Some of the drops that fell onto the petals never touched the earth.

Today I miss you a little less.

She stood with her suitcases by the luggage carousel at Auckland Airport, waiting for the liaison person from the student exchange programme to come and collect her. The other passengers stood with their arms around their husbands or wives or children. After they'd gone there was one bag still on the carousel, going round and round, uncollected. Akiko sat on her suitcase, watching the last bag. It was black with a white label flapping as it moved. A man dressed in a uniform came and looked at it, stood next to her, watching it. The label flapped as it came out again, shuddered with the carousel's movement. They both watched it go back through the dark curtain, then the uniformed man left.

The woman arrived apologising. She took her glasses off and rubbed her eyes, and said something about traffic, then put her glasses back on. She took a couple of deep breaths. She handed Akiko a small furry toy, a kiwi, then shook Akiko's hand. One of the kiwi's shiny plastic eyes was loose, dangling by a thin thread. Akiko watched the eye wobble. When they walked away the eye wobbled again and fell off and rolled under the carousel. As one eye rolled away over the floor tiles she covered the kiwi's other one up with her hand.

Troy stands in the fire station's shower, arms outstretched, eyes closed. His hands press against the cubicle's wall. He takes a couple of deep breaths, conscious of his chest's every expansion and release. He opens his eyes, blinks within the stream, seeing in the sparkling water glimpses of flames curling around him like a toxic lover. He blinks again and they've gone. When he steps out of the water, he feels a sudden chill bringing out bumps on his nakedness. He looks around the room for a moment, then begins to dress.

He nods to the guys coming in to start the new shift and walks out to the Chev where the turning of the key dismisses the silence. He sits listening, sensing in every piston cycle the work of his own hands. All those days and nights lying on a wheeled board under the engine, looking up into its heart. He loves that view, the engine's inner workings open above his eyes. Open to him. For him a car junkyard is at once a source of riches for the mechanic but also the loneliest place on earth.

After getting out of the army he had gone to the USA, intending to bum around California for a while before heading home. But instead he headed inland, drifting towards the rising sun. He worked on the sly as a truck driver for a while, then as a mechanic in an oilfield. With his gift with engines no one asked him about work permits.

He bought the battered '55 Chev in West Texas from a dishevelled woman with scar tracks on her bony arms, her dirty hair hanging limp like corroded wiring.

'Another twenty bucks and you can hump me,' she said, leaning against the doorframe, yellowed fingers grasping a crumpled cigarette.

'Actually I just came for the Chev,' said Troy.

'Fifteen?'

'The keys?'

He glances into the rear-view mirror, pulls out into a gap in the traffic. In an hour he is out of the city, searching for a road with no lights at the edges, just open fields, or bush. Branches instead of buildings. He accelerates on the empty highway. The flashing dots of the road's centre line flicker like flakes of metal swarf in the Chev's headlights.

In Abilene, Texas, he'd had the Chev repainted cadmium yellow. In Levelland he dropped in the 327 cubic inch engine, bought from a guy with his leg in a cast, who'd totalled his Corvette Stingray. He fitted the Holley carburettors in El Paso, the fuelie heads in New Orleans.

He sat sometimes in desert twilights, out on the sand, among the saguaro and chaparral. Looking at the Chev's yellow body slip into synch with the sand. Troy saw his own sweat in each turn of the torque wrench. When he tired of drifting he worked his way home on a cargo ship, checking every day on the air- and water-tightness of the container on the ship's deck. He peered into the darkness of the container on the Auckland wharf, took a cloth from his back pocket to wipe the travelling dust off the car's windows.

On his last road trip before leaving the States he'd driven up through the Panhandle, then into New Mexico, heading on a whim up to Santa Fe, then Alamogordo, the Chev's shadow lengthening like a comet's tail in the desert twilights. He drove on until the military turned him back. Two uniformed guys in a jeep, emerging from behind a dune. Both wore holstered pistols. There was no sign that said he was entering a military site. But for all that, he knew where he was.

Jornada del Muerto.

The Trinity site. The atomic bomb site.

The only things he knows about his father is that he was born in the deserts of New Mexico and died on a Pacific atoll. An atoll where they built the airfield that launched the B-29s that dropped the atomic bombs on Japan to end World War Two. His father's blood was in that coral runway. And that bomb was in his stepfather's blood.

He meets Monty in the public bar of the Wayfarer where they sit amid the dim lights, the drinkers mostly elderly men, some in overalls, a couple with cloth caps and black-rimmed glasses held together with sticking plaster.

'Let's check out the Bangkok Bar,' says Monty.

'The what?'

'Next door.'

They walk out onto the street. A car pulls up, double-parks. American. Long lean lines, sharp-pointed fins on the fenders. A young woman steps out of the passenger's side. Tight T-shirt beneath a loose-hanging leather waistcoat. Hip-hugging jeans with flared bottoms. She fires a cursory glance in their direction then walks on.

'Nice,' says Monty.

'Yeah,' says Troy, ''59 Plymouth Fury. Those mag wheels look a bit ostentatious though. They should've kept it stock —'

'Not the bloody car, Henare, the bird!'

They sit looking at the imitation Asian décor, fading prints on the walls, umbrellas over the tables, even though the bar is inside. Monty looks up at the ceiling.

'Place must spring a serious leak when she pisses down,' he says.

The background music on the scratchy record pings away through tinny speakers.

'Is that a sitar?' says Monty.

Troy nods.

'Sitars are Indian ain't they?' says Monty.

'Far as I know.'

'Yet this is the Bangkok Bar.'

'That's what the sign said.'

'Geography not their strong point then.'

Monty lifts a packet of tobacco from his pocket, a small clutch of papers. 'You gonna play inscrutable all day or actually say something,' he says.

'Just thinking,' says Troy.

'Ah okay, I'm with ya now. Energy drain, puts all the other lights out.'

Troy stands and goes and gets another couple of jugs of draught.

'How come you bailed out in the end?' says Monty. 'Figured you for a twenty-year man.'

'Could say the same about you,' says Troy.

Monty smiles.

'Thought I'd put out fires,' he says.

'Rather than start them.'

'Something like that.'

'Thanks for the heads-up on the job, by the way.'

'What else would you have done.'

'Dunno.'

'We did our time,' says Monty. Then he smirks. 'And

you, *you* got your pretty face in the newspapers all around the world.'

Troy stops with his beer glass half-raised, watching Monty's face dissolve in the liquid in the bottom of the glass.

The rising moon fades into the clouds. The girl in the batik blouse and black leather pants stands between the noses of the two cars, her arms raised as the pitch of the engines rises. She drops her arms, closes her eyes as the gravel dust engulfs her and the noise sweeps away beyond her.

Troy's Chev inches ahead, then suddenly races alone as the Valiant vanishes in a coil of black smoke. Blown engine. The Chev carries on to the last lamp-post before the crossroads then slows and does a U-turn and heads back. As it passes the smoking hulk of the Valiant, Troy extends his arm out the window and money changes hands. The girl walks down the faded centre line, her calf-length boots crackling on the loose stones. She stops at the Chev's open window.

'Which way are you headed?' she says. He looks at her long, straight hair, the butterflies painted onto her cheeks. Her eye shadow smudged like a bruise.

Troy points to the Valiant.

'What about your mate?' he says.

The girl shrugs. She opens the passenger side door and leans back in the seat. She runs a finger along the rim of the door, tapping her nails against the windowglass. She raises a hand to the black band she wears around her neck, a finger against a small metal locket attached to the band. He drives on up the street, the hum of the motor rumbling through the floorboards.

'Anytime you like,' he says.

'What?'

'The routine.'

'Screw you.'

He smiles.

They reach the city and he pulls off at an exit, turns to her. Her eyes shadowed off and on as they pass through a glade of trees. He takes one hand off the wheel, reaches across the gap between them, fingers extended towards her cheek. But he doesn't touch her, instead reaches down and pushes the button to flick the radio on.

For those who come to San Francisco, be sure to wear some flowers in your hair...

She turns to stare out the window.

They cruise Karangahape Road, the gaudy lights from the burger bars bleeding against the rain-streaked windscreen. They stop at a rundown takeaway, buy a burger and some cigarettes and drinks, then drive on. The girl sits sipping a soft drink through a straw. A crumpled wad of paper lies on the seat between them, the smell of mayonnaise and steak sauce vying with the scent of engine oil from Troy's jeans.

Midnight he races a Ford with a small-block V8, sheets of rainwater rising from puddles, kicked up by spinning tyres. He pulls away on a long right-hander heading towards the harbour. A few crumpled dollar notes pass between loser and winner and he heads on into the dark, slowing to stop in Okahu Bay.

In the night he leans over the girl on the back seat, her sleeping figure pushing back into him, his arms looped around her waist as he curls into the frame of the back seat. He blinks against her hair, a finger tracking across the bare skin of her hip bones where her blouse has ridden up in her sleep.

'Is any of it what you thought it would be?' he whispers over the rise and fall of her sleeping breaths. Soon, he is asleep too.

In the last dark before dawn Troy slips away from the girl

and steps out. He walks down to the water's edge. The tide has withdrawn a hundred yards out into the marina, leaving some of the shallow-draught boats high and dry on the sand, a tired lean to their masts. When he turns back towards shore he sees the girl's figure in the streetlights, her thumb raised to the early risers passing by. By the time he gets back to the Chev she and her thumb are long gone. The footpath as empty as the pocket of his leather jacket where his win money had lain curled into a tube.

He shakes his head, gets back behind the wheel.

Akiko sits out on the back lawn of her flat, looking at the sunset, watching clouds lose their clear borders and fade into the pink sky around them. Beyond the clouds lightning flashes away to the east. She listens for thunder, but there is just city noise. The storm must be far away. She sits on the grass, watching the day slip away beyond the lightning's edge. A last fanfare of light. She is still sitting there when the sound of the motorbike turns her head towards the driveway.

Caleb steps from the Indian. He walks across the grass, sits next to her. At the first flash of distant lightning he looks up.

'You're counting, aren't you,' says Akiko.

'How'd you know?'

She smiles.

'Because I did, for a while,' she says.

He frowns.

'Stopped the count at thirty,' he says. 'Maybe it's phantom lightning.'

'What's that?'

'I just made it up.'

Another flash turns the outlines of faraway trees into jagged green candle-flames.

'If you did something,' says Caleb, 'for the right reasons, but it's the wrong thing. Would a person get forgiveness or damnation?'

'I suppose that would depend on the thing and the reason. And whether you believed in damnation.'

'And forgiveness?'

'I think everyone believes in forgiveness.'

A fork of lightning skewers the clouds.

'Are you still counting?' says Akiko.

'No,' says Caleb.

Troy walks through the dawn quiet to the fire station's front door. He glances at the streaks of rain beginning to gather on the glass. He reaches for the handle, pausing for a second when his own shadow darkens the trails of water. He is halfway through the door when the sound jolts him.

The fire bell.

The building is well ablaze, shedding its skin like a figure in an anatomy chart. Girders glow red, some entering the realm of white heat. One engine from uptown is already at the scene when Troy's crew arrives, four fire-fighters wrestling with hoses whose jets just whip the burning solution back onto their protective fire suits. Amid the chaos something catches Troy's eye. The cylindrical skeleton of a metal drum. Beyond it, past the glowing girders, burning veins of kerosene and polystyrene hang from the surrounding trees.

They have to stop the fire migrating. That's all that's important; this building is already history. The fireman move further in, the stench of kerosene barbecues their throats.

They put on their smoke masks, though in fact there isn't much smoke. Just kerosene fire, burning at a thousand odd degrees, in a ramshackle downtown warehouse street, on a Friday morning in the rain.

The foam tender saves them, saves the buildings next door, though it takes an hour. The firemen's eyes sting, secrete acid tears onto their heat-swollen cheeks. Troy sits on the engine's running board. There is a respite of silence, punctuated only by the coughs of the exhausted men.

Geronimo hands around metal mugs with lukewarm water from the hydrant.

Monty stands, looks at Troy.

'Yep,' says Troy. 'Same stuff as last time.'

Monty lifts his helmet off, whacks it down on the blackened footpath.

'I will personally kill whoever's setting this shit off!' he says.

Troy reaches up, draws him back down.

'Save it, brother,' he says. 'They're long gone. Probably sitting back in their tree-house laughing at the news on the radio.'

Tank looks up from where he sits against one of the fire engine's tyres.

'What are you two on about?' he says.

Troy stands and walks to the grimy front door of what had been the loading dock's office and kicks in the glass with his right boot. He lifts a sheet of glass, smeared with a thick filmy resin. He lays it on the asphalt – wet from the fire hoses – walks a few paces to where a piece of wood sits smouldering. He holds the wood over the glass, then drops it and steps away just as the resin on the glass ignites. A full minute later it is still burning. Troy kicks it a few paces away and turns a fire hose on it, drenching it. But still it burns.

'Napalm,' says Monty.

Tank looks up. 'I think you blokes spent a bit too long in the jungle,' he says.

The others look away, each to his own thoughts. All sipping from their mugs, swallowing the taste of kerosene along with the hydrant water.

When his shift is over he goes home, sits on his front steps, a metallic tincture sour on his tongue.

Napalm.

Someone has concocted a recipe for napalm.

He has crossed an entire ocean, a hemisphere, left behind the clatter of M-60 machine guns and helicopter blades, and he can still taste it. Not from some obscene trick of memory, but in the here and now. He goes inside, runs the tap and drains three glasses of cold water, then a fourth, and leans – bloated – against the bench. He walks into his sitting room, sits on an old wooden chair, staring at his hands. At the rivulets of water on his skin, in the lifelines of his palm.

In the afternoon he goes for a drive. The Grey Lynn streets are alive with children. Tiny tots play on jungle-gyms in a park. Their mothers in their wide-brimmed Polynesian hats sit in leaf shadows. Elderly ladies sit on benches, the sun lighting their blue-rinse hair. He heads downtown where a troupe of Hari-Krishnas' drums echo in the concrete canyons of Queen Street. Suited men with briefcases walk past a newspaper boy calling out, advertising his wares. A young bearded man stands busking with his guitar on the corner of K Road and Symonds Street. Troy takes it all in as he drives, reminders of life back in the world.

The World.

The catchphrase American draftees used for anywhere but Vietnam.

He smiles, drives on.

There are road works on Anzac Ave. A car horn blares and a workman shakes his head. Troy turns past the courthouse and the Big I hotel and into Princes Street, slowing to glance at a group of teenagers kicking a rugby ball just inside the gates of Albert Park. A couple of figures step out onto the pedestrian crossing, one the young oriental woman he had seen riding pillion on Caleb's motorcycle. He watches her pass then starts to move away, but doesn't. Instead he eases into an empty space and gets out of the car, looking to where she walks down beside one of the old villas that front the tree-lined street.

She slows to speak to a couple of people, then walks on to a squat building sitting away from the others. Troy gets out and strolls down the tree-lined lane to the building she went into, pauses where the sign says Auditorium.

The foyer is empty, enlivened only by numerous bills advertising events or what looks like the current cause of the week. He can hear voices from inside. He pushes open an entrance door and slips into a darkened aisle. Voices come from a stage that is lit by two banks of overhead lights. He sits in one of the empty seats, raises a foot against the armrest of the chair in front. Music starts, an orchestral piece, strings behind a harpsichord. He reaches back a thousand years to Isaac's chaotic record collection in the house at Rangimoana. Pachelbel's Canon in D. A group of dance students totter onto the stage and take positions, seeming precarious on the tips of their pointed ballet shoes. They wear coloured knee-length socks, some over stockings, some over bare legs. Troy squints against the bright stage lights as they drift from green to blue, then a pale pink. He focuses again when the young woman he had followed steps from the edge of the stage and claps her hands, the entire troupe stilling. He is too far away to hear any distinct words over the music. He tries to interpret her conversation, her stance. She takes a step back and the dance begins again.

She stops them twice more. The second time their faces dissolve into laughter, the moment so easy, so graceful, that he could accept it as a scripted moment in the performance. She never once steps into the circle of their feet, but remains just beyond their toes. In the shadows. He looks at the assembly of figures in stage-lights, then off to the edges, into the darkness where he sits silent, unnoticed.

He had lain prone on a rock ridge once, watching some New Zealand infantry moving down a jungle path in single file, their bodies fading in and out of the morning mist. He could hear them talking, breaking into the world of silence, cursing at each other, at the heat and flies and mosquitoes. His spotter, Manu, had winked, made silent bang bang bang sounds with his mouth. There was every possibility that somewhere, even within earshot of where they lay, NVA or Vietcong snipers could be waiting. He lifted his rifle, used his scope to scan the trees around, trying to pick leaves disturbed by wind from those set moving by human hand or foot. He looked over the top of the jungle to the jagged green horizon, a few tufts of smoke from distant burning villages fading against the sky.

A tap on his shoulder. Manu. Troy's finger touched against the trigger, all bar the circle of the world within his scope's lens drawing away.

'Right, two degrees,' said Manu.
'Range?'
'Four hundred, four-fifty maybe.'
'Okay'
'Got him?'
'Yeah,' said Troy.

Manu lowered his binoculars and squinted into the distance.

'He's making an awful lot of a ruckus for a VC,' he said.

'Kid?'

'All the way up that tree?'

'Does it matter?'

'Not if he starts shooting.'

'Or we do.'

'Or we do.'

A moment's silence, the infantrymen still picking their way through the trees beneath them. Their scout stopped, a hand raised against the leaves. He crouched, looked around the valley, but showed no recognition of spotting either the New Zealand snipers on the ridge or the shadowed figure moving against the leaves a quarter-mile away.

Troy and Manu saw Troy's muzzle flash before they heard the crack of his ammunition breaking the sound barrier. An arrow's path of leaves skittered above the patrol. The scout dropped, suddenly, and shouted 'Down!' and the line of figures dived into the stinking mud. Troy didn't move, just lay statued, drawing a line with his eyes, back from where the path of his metallic raindrop had cut the VC sniper from his sanctuary, spattering the leaves with his lifeblood.

He blinks his eyes, back in the auditorium, where the young Oriental woman stands, her eyes closed, alone now in the centre of the stage. She lifts her arms, tilts off-centre so her weight is pulled to one side, her body tensed. The music begins again, and she ignites within it.

The students draw away to the edge of the light, watching her, and Troy notices now she also wears ballet shoes beneath the tips of her jeans. She follows the pattern the others had danced, then stops for a second, staring above her. She moves on, no longer shadowing the melody's recurring motif, but leading it. Each footfall guides the notes, as if a mother to a daughter. Minutes compress, seconds stretch, then the music fades. Troy sits forward, expecting her to stop, but she doesn't. Pachelbel's harpsichordist retreats back into his pocket of history, but her body inches beyond even the music itself, when nothing but the hum of needle on empty grooves fills the auditorium. There is a click click click now as the stylus bounces, but the woman on the stage just keeps on dancing. Her point shoes call to the stereo's needle. She dances no longer to melody, but to a discordant scratch.

She stills.

Her eyes close, one arm a half circle upward, the other down, a taut curve to her spine. Her shadow's outline is that of a question mark.

People stare, no one speaks.

Troy stands, walks down the aisle from the shadowed upper seats, steps up onto the stage. His boots clatter on the wood. People admonish him, but he ignores them, reaches to touch a single finger against the dancer's quivering hand, her eyes still shuttered.

She jerks back into the world, stares up at him. Shock in her pupils.

'Where did you come from?' she says.

He straightens.

'Sorry,' he says.

'What?'

He steps back.

'Damn,' he says. 'Sorry. I just thought…'

She glances around at the assembly, all staring at him.

'What did you think?' she says.

'I just thought, I thought you weren't going to come back, from wherever you were.' He swallows. 'I'm not making sense,' he says.

Feet shuffle, there is a low hum of conversation. Troy stands a few feet away from her, staring now up into the light beams. A sheepish smile on his face. She shakes her head.

He gives her an exaggerated bow, like a musketeer.

'I'll go now,' he says.

'Perhaps you should,' she says.

He takes the steps off the stage, glances back. She is still there, in that circle she drew about herself. At the exit door he looks back once, a last glimpse before she dissolves in the glare of the lights.

We are the unwilling
Led by the unqualified,
Doing the unnecessary
For the ungrateful

(Scratched onto a wall, Phuoc Toy, 1968)

One fine morning in the Long Hai Hills on Troy's second tour in Vietnam in 1968, one of his patrol mates, Davis, dropped to the ground. Troy saw the skitter of leaves, but only *after* Davis fell. He never heard the shot. He and Monty rolled over on the jungle floor, looking around, the leaves returning to their normal positions. Troy saw in the slight upward angle of their path that the shot was from an elevated position. He signalled with his a hand easing on an upward curve.

Sniper, high in the trees.

Monty signalled to the rest of the patrol. No one returned fire, there was nothing visible to shoot at. Just branches and leaves, an occasional dew drop. There were no more sounds of shooting that morning, just the spades of the burial party an hour later when it was judged to be safe to move. Charlie was long gone. Maybe it was just a stray shot. Maybe not.

By midday it was raining and the red stain where Davis fell was cleansed. Not even a taste was left for the ants. They sat eating cold C rations, and Troy kept thinking of the rain washing away that red marking. Once in the Deep J they'd stumbled into a gully where someone a hundred or a thousand years ago had scratched figures onto the rock walls. Some kind of ancient language.

They all had a comical go at deciphering it, all the attempts beginning with *There once was a lady from Long Hai…*

As he sat spooning the rations into his mouth, he thought then how time was compressing. How some ancient tribesman's scratchings had seen centuries, but the blood signatures of modern men with their technology, weapons and civilisation had not even lasted through a single rain shower.

Back at base they sat under the trees, the killer Vietnamese sun sending rifle trails of sunlight through the leaves. A bare foot left in its path would start to itch after a few minutes. Beer would feel warm enough to have been already drunk and pissed out. Brownie Hohepa sat down with his guitar.

'A song, Brownie,' said Monty. 'If you please.'

'Not Ten-Bloody-Guitars,' said Gus.

Brownie looked up into the leaves, then began to strum, his voice following.

And they'll all come to meet me,
The girls'll swivel their hips to greet me,
Monty chimed in.
Your sister'll bare her tits to treat me,

Then the whole patrol.

And then we'll smoke, the green, green grass of home.

The troop broke into laughter.

They sang another couple of songs then Brownie headed for the latrine. Monty picked up the guitar, stabbed at a couple of chords, went into chunka-chunka rhythm. He began to croon in a bad Elvis Presley impersonation.

I got the one, two, three, four, occupation Long Hai Blues...

Troy had been sent to Vietnam as part of the 182-man rifle company   Victor 1 – in May 1967, to join the 2nd Battalion, Royal Australian Regiment, at Nui Dat. A second rifle company, Whiskey, joined them in December 1967. In March 1968, the two New Zealand companies merged with the Australian 2RAR to become the ANZAC infantry battalion.

In Troy's role as a specialist sniper, a reputation, then designation he had carried since he was with the New Zealand infantry in Malaya in 1965, he was sometimes loaned out to other allied forces, the Australians, the Americans.

He'd watched from a hill once, as an American company waded across a rice paddy the size of a half-dozen rugby fields, their boots slowed to sloth speed by the mud. Time-lapse soldiers. He couldn't help thinking as a sniper that if they'd had different coloured uniforms he would've been expected to decimate them and, given their terrible footing, would've done so without raising a sweat. He looked over their heads at the far hills, waiting for the crack of shots from an enemy position, but they never came. He wondered if in the hum of the soldiers' conversation any of them had thought, as well armed as they were, that one sniper and spotter could have planted them all amid the season's crops.

His brief was simple. Work in a two-man team with a

spotter, always be on the move. Always look for high ground, look for targets. Through bamboo glades, through smoke haze, sometimes just at his guesses at the source of tracer fire. Once even onto the deck of a cart pulled by a donkey.

The four uniformed NVA soldiers rolled about in the cart, trying to find cover, but there was none. The canyon's moss covered walls sent an army of echoes chattering, shielding Troy's position. Birds scattered like the paths of skyrockets. He deliberated each shot, blinking through the smoke wafting from his rifle. A chest shot, a throat, the couple of inches of certain death around an ear. He had been well trained. After maybe thirty seconds he stopped shooting. The rifle's barrel steamed in the humid air. Down below, a hat rolled in the road, then stopped. The donkey, freed from the choke of command on its ropes began to meander. To the edge of the road, to a few sprigs of flowers, then back across the rutted dirt to where a muddy creek ran. Birds began to drop to tree branches again; the bush sounds returned. The donkey craned its neck to get close to the water, right on the ditch's edge. Then it began to slip, wet dirt giving way, the donkey's hooves scrambling as it fell, dragging the cart of corpses into the creek. In the water it stood again, still tethered to the broken cart. Shook its face free of water again and began to drink.

Troy rolled over. He and Manu took a swig each from a water bottle, then moved on.

Six months into Troy's second tour he was lent to an American unit, operating a small fleet of patrol air cushion vehicles in the Plain of Reeds. The PACVs had been developed for amphibious work, often as safety vehicles at airports, able to cross terrain – even water – quicker than any other vehicle. In the Plain of Reeds they had a different use. Scouting unidentified boats, sometimes even just the shambling local approximation of kayaks. After a jeep with Australian logistics clerks had been shot up by what had looked like an old geezer and his missus paddling a decrepit canoe, nothing and no one was to be regarded as harmless.

The last of the ten days he spent on the PACVs his patrol was called to investigate an area of marshes where a US pilot had parachuted from a stalled Starfighter. After an hour cruising the inlets the marines sighted a small group of figures among the sodden grass and veered left to check them out. The figures bunched, still a quarter mile away, appearing no more than a tree stump. If the American scout hadn't caught a glimpse of them in his binoculars, moving before they froze, he might've mistaken them for a half-buried tree or a rock and moved on. The shooting started a couple of hundred yards out as the PACV bore down on them, the figures realising their fakery had failed. The Americans fired back. Troy stood with his sniper rifle, the grind of the craft's engine behind him drowning out the sounds of shooting. His fingers picked the figures off one by one. The Americans stopped shooting, left him to it. The last of the seven figures to fall did so straight backwards in a silent movie pratfall, his flax hat rising almost in salute as the bullet knocked on his forehead.

They discovered while they were searching the dead for any useful information, that other than the pratfall guy, all the others were little more than boys.

Troy sat back against the glass of the cabin window, closed his eyes. There were a couple of slaps on his shoulder from his patrol mates.

Then someone yelped, high pitched and frantic. Troy opened his eyes. One of the marines in the water rolled up his pants leg, stood staring at the black figure of a leech on his calf. The others who had been in the water began to scramble back on board. The air filled with cursing.

Troy opened his pack, lifted out his rations tin and a crumpled copy of a car racing comic. He sat chewing on a cracker, flipping through the pages. He stopped at a page full of advertisements for auto parts, spares for doing up streetcars into hot rods. There was a photo of a drag strip, the camera looking over a driver's shoulder to where tarmac stretched away beyond the end of the quarter mile strip, into the distance. The edges of the tarseal converged at the horizon. He closed his eyes again.

The day he saw the bucket boats burning he sat beneath the stink of the napalm smoke, beneath the river's surface, his feet dug into the mud. Trying to hold fast against the current. He held his breath as long as he could, then raised his lips above the water for a second. The burning taste of kerosene tore at the roof of his mouth, even though the worst of the flames would've passed. He raised his nose and mouth above the river, taking small gulps of air, just a mouthful until the burning came with the oxygen. Then he dipped below the water again, held the girl's mouth to his own and breathed out. He raised his lips to the air again, sank down, gave some breath to the boy. All the time the blinding flash of the napalm strike was still singed into his eyelids, like a movie playing over and over. Neither the boy nor the girl had their eyes open. The boy was bleeding from a head wound, the blood winding away like a pink streamer in the water. Troy couldn't keep them down any longer so he rose, lifting all three of them. He slapped the boy on the back and water gushed from his mouth. Troy slapped him again, then did the same to the girl.

He needed to get them all out of the reeds, across the water to the bank, get them on their stomachs so they could spit their lungs clear. The smoke was clearing, even the retching stench drifting away with it. He tried to take a step but couldn't. Then again. It wasn't the suck of the mud. In his mind he could see his legs rising out of the water, lifting the three of them up and away, away out of that stinking water, through the rancid air and away through the trees to a place to breathe. He could see all those things, but he couldn't do them. Time began to pass. The sun sinking, rising again. Sinking, rising. A couple of days passed, then months, years, while he still sat in that river. Sat in that river holding onto the two kids he'd seen as he was running for the cover of the water. Two tiny faces just below the level of the riverbank, staring up at him .

The boy's head toppled forward, his nose in the water. Troy lifted him back up, willing his legs to move, but they didn't. He closed his eyes again, sensing now a warmth around his abdomen, realising after a few seconds that he was pissing himself.

The smoke had almost gone by the time the voices of the soldiers echoed across the river. Calls to comrades. Even laughter. One doing some kind of bird call, as if they had stumbled into a cowboys and Indians movie. Three of them stood on the riverbank, their stare settling on him.

'Who are you with?' said one, American.

Troy didn't answer.

'Don't you recognise an officer?' said another soldier.

Troy spat into the water. Spit, piss, blood, kerosene and polystyrene. Then another figure appeared and he saw the glint of a camera lens. He turned the kids' faces towards him, away from the camera, the photographer's face masked by the camera and the helmet they wore, their features coming into the light only when they lowered the camera and a woman's voice echoed inside him.

'Troy?'
He looked up. The children didn't.
'Troy?' she said. 'Troy?'

VII

Woman in the Setting Sun

Honolulu
April 1989

Etta goes through customs at Aloha Airport. The officer leafs through her dog-eared passport, page after page of stamps. The officer closes her passport and gestures her through the gate.

The departure lounge is packed, piped muzak backing conversations in a dozen different languages. Etta sits against the viewing windows, so the light is behind her. She raises the camera now and then, not clicking the shutter control, just getting her eye in synch with the movement around her. Scoping how to capture the intent behind gesture. Two soldiers in lace-up boots walk by, a family of tourists with the kids smacking each other behind the parents' backs. A young couple in baseball team gear argue over something in a paper bag.

She buckles in to her window seat as her plane taxis out to its holding point. When it turns in its wide arc to get on to the runway she looks up the length of tarmac, where the runway thins to its vanishing point. She knows they asked her to do the shoot at the Trinity site not just because of her reputation as a photographer, but because of her personal history. Her stake in that ground. She looks down at the faint trails of rubber stretching as far as the eye can see. Ground, stakes in the ground.

When the jet's engines rise in pitch she leans back, feeling the acceleration and the jet's sudden freedom as its wheels let go of the ground. The woman in the next seat smiles.

'Visiting family?' she says.

Etta glances at her, then back to the small window, the details of Oahu fading beneath them.

'No,' says Etta. Then, 'Yes.'

The woman's eyes narrow, then she turns forward. Reaches to rummage in the pocket in the rear of the seat in front of her. She takes out an airline magazine.

Etta looks out the window. Keeps looking long after any landmarks then any land at all have been obscured by cloud. Until there's nothing to see *but* cloud.

A whiteout.

She raises a hand against the rim of the aperture, taps her fingernail against the glass.

Click.

Auckland
VJ Day, August 1945

Etta sets the infant Troy in his bassinette down on the bus seat then sits beside him. The fields they pass are green with the winter rain, water from some of last night's showers still sitting in the hollows. In the city there is noise everywhere, echoing off the concrete walls of the buildings, off the shop windows shaking with the riotous movement of people on the footpaths and streets. Bits of paper rain down from office windows. Men in uniforms and in civvies celebrate with office workers, stevedores in overalls, women in elegant hats or with their hair streaming. Strangers shake hands or kiss. Etta reaches down, brushes a piece of paper from Troy's cheek.

She waits for an hour in a hallway of the US consulate, glancing up at the stern faces looking out from the photos on the walls. Whenever anyone opens a street-facing door a surge of laughter and singing crashes against the wooden walls. She leans back, closes her eyes to it all.

A tall officer in a starched and pressed uniform appears in a doorway, nods in her direction. She lifts the bassinette and walks in. There's a stack of manila envelopes on the left of his desk, another on the right. The straight span of his shoulders is like a tightrope between them. The lines are broken only by the ragged weave of his cigarette's smoke.

She says her piece and he leans back, looks over her head.

'I don't see ...' he says.

A church bell chimes, fireworks clatter, a couple of klaxon horns honk. Etta turns, looks out the window. The officer doesn't move. Troy stirs in his bassinette, tries to roll over. Etta bends down, lifts him out, wrapped in a woollen jumpsuit. She stands and walks to the window and back, rocking him.

'I'll close the window,' says the officer. 'The noise.'

'No, it's all right, it's been a long time since people have been so happy.'

'Yes, it has.'

'I drew a sketch of the camp once.'

The officer stubs his cigarette into a glass ashtray.

'What camp?' he says.

'Where they – where *he* – was stationed. Out on the coast. Rangimoana.'

He stares.

'Joaquin said later that the army wouldn't approve. That they liked to keep their secrets.'

'There is a war. Was a war.'

She nuzzles Troy against her chin. His brown hair is lighter than hers.

'Miss,' says the officer, looking up at his hat sitting on its rack, 'if you and Private Alvarez had been married then it would be a different matter, but...'

'No it wouldn't.'

'Officially, I mean.'

'I know what you meant.'

She glances down at the bassinette.

'Would you mind lifting this onto the table?' she says.

The officer stands, walks around to her and sets the bassinette onto his desktop. Etta lays Troy back among the blankets; his small figure against a backdrop of official papers, scatterings of troop movement orders. A cigarette butt smouldering in an ashtray.

'Do you know where Tinian is?' she says.

'Yes,' he says. 'Why?'

More firecrackers in the street. For a moment she thinks she sees the officer wince. He lays his hands flat on the table. Outside someone has gotten hold of a bugle and it sounds as if they're strangling it to death. As Etta turns to go she hears papers ruffling. She turns back to see the officer shift a folder from the pile on his left to the pile on his right.

She walks among the crowds still celebrating. She lifts her camera from the pram's carry-all and takes a handful of photographs. A whole gallery of faces coming to her, people caught in a moment of joy. Each instant in their faces says more than all the politician's speeches and newspapers' triumphant editorials.

Troy turns two and then three. Etta loses her job as the school's trainee teacher. The board of education officers notify her by mail that she has been reclassified as unsuitable. She writes back, asking for a reason. None is given.

Without a ring she doesn't qualify for a war widow's pension from either New Zealand or the USA. She and Troy survive on the money she gets from cleaning the toilets and sweeping the classrooms of the school she once taught at. She looks up from her broom or rubbish pail at the times-tables on the blackboards she had dusted clear hundreds of times. Her meagre wage is supplemented by a money order each month from her parents. Etta takes Troy over the hill in the ramshackle local bus to collect it. She returns back to Rangimoana from the post office, her thumb out to the intermittent passing traffic. When there are no rides Troy walks the stony or muddy road beside her, avoiding the ruts of the road, half-slipping on the stones, the soles of his second-hand shoes thinning.

One night she spends an evening arranging photographic prints and negatives into folders made by gluing two sheets of paper together then folding them over. She has taken over forty photographs of Rangimoana, in all shades of light, the black sand streaked with the tones of sunset, or lightened with the dawn. She bundles some of the prints up and writes a covering letter to the newspaper, suggesting a photographic article for the Saturday magazine. The point where land meets sea, in all seasons.

A couple of weeks later the postman whistles from the letter box. The response is a typed form reprinted on a Gestetner copying machine. Only her name and the signature are in pen. She slips the letter back into its envelope and puts it into a dresser drawer. She crouches, tapes a small rectangle of paper onto the drawer and writes *rejections* on it. Through the winter and into the spring she receives four more rejections while all the time walking with her camera, stopping to catch angles of the sea's anger and joy, the changing colours of the sand, morning and evening light on the hillsides. She shoots only one in ten of the images she lines up; film being precious. On her next trip into the city she sits with the telephone directory at a table in the downtown post office, copying out the names and addresses of the handful of photographic studios and agencies and freelancers. She writes to them asking if any is willing to take her on as a part-time apprentice or cadet. She gets interviews with two, watches one face tighten as she mentions it's a two-hour ride for her into town, another's raised eyebrow as she arrives at the door with Troy's hand in hers.

Summer comes and goes, the open ground beside the estuary filling with tents over Christmas and New Year. February brings an exodus back into town. Easter sees the last of the long-term visitors. A week after Easter she leans back against a driftwood log, Troy stomping around in the black sand. His sandaled heels dig tiny indentations. He stops now and then, crouches to look at them.

'Troy,' says Etta, 'don't go too far.'

'Can we go swimming?'

'No. It's too rough today. We'll go swimming tomorrow.'

He makes a face, wanders off in a huff and sits with his back to her, looking out at the waves. The only stillness in a landscape that never sits still.

A ring of petrels orbits the clouds. Troy points up, shouting at them.

'Yes, hon,' says Etta. 'I see them.'

She watches them circle, their wings making a mechanical tap-tap-tap. They drift away, but the sound keeps echoing. She stands, looks up and down the beach. Troy turns to face her. There is a rumble, coming closer. Etta walks to him, bends and lifts him against her, just as a motorcycle comes roaring through the gap in the dunes.

The rider crosses the tide lines, a wake of black sand flying. At the waterline he turns, stands up on the pedals like a horseman on stirrups, his body silhouetted against the waves. Rolled-up sleeves, a long fringe of hair above his spectacles. The sun's glare sets their lenses afire. Then he stops, looks up the beach at the woman and child. He stills the engine, walks the motorbike up out of the shallows and over the sand.

'My apologies,' he says, 'I didn't know there was anyone here.'

'It's all right,' says Etta. 'We don't get many strangers here these days.'

'Is that a blessing or a curse?'

'An observation.'

He stands looking at the two figures, then his eyes narrow to a squint.

'Ah,' he says.

'Ah, what?'

'It's not important. Tell me, is there a watering hole around here?'

'You must be mistaking this for civilisation.'

'Actually, I'm trying to get away from civilisation.'

He wipes some road dust from his forehead with the back of his arm.

'You don't look like a beer-drinking man,' says Etta.

'I'm not sure how I should take that.'

He looks away and takes off his spectacles and wipes his eyes with his sleeve, then wipes his spectacles too and puts them back on. He takes a few gulps of sea air, leans on the handlebars. He turns back to her, his grey eyes sharper now through the clear lenses. Etta clasps Troy's hand.

'Would lemonade suit you?' she says to the rider.

'Down to the ground.'

'You sure aren't from around here, then.'

Etta takes Troy's hand and turns towards the dunes. She crosses the fallen log that bridges the creek and goes inside. She lifts the cloth from atop a glass pitcher of lemonade and pours two glasses. She picks a lemon pip out of one, wipes her hand on her shorts.

'Let's go back over the road,' she says.

Troy frowns but follows.

When they returns to the beach the rider is sitting on a driftwood log. He turns. She puts the tray down in the sand, lifts one glass and hands it to Troy, motions for the rider to take the other. They sit back, sipping.

'The name's Isaac,' says the rider.

'Etta. And this is Troy.'

Isaac raises his glass.

'Thank you,' he says.

He crosses one leg over the other. Etta notices that his boots are army regulation. He lifts a gold case from his pocket, offers her a cigarette. She nods and takes one. He fishes a cigarette lighter from another pocket. Etta looks down at the lighter.

'A Zippo,' she says. 'US Army issue.'

'Yes. How did you know?'

'I've seen one before.'

Isaac sits smoking, Etta standing a few yards away on the sand, alternating sips from her lemonade with Troy.

'Were you in the services?' says Etta.

'Not quite.'

She raises her eyebrows.

'More a case of being in league with them,' he says.

Troy gulps the last of his lemonade. He stands and runs down the beach, circling in the shells.

'He looks like a handful,' says Isaac.

'You can't imagine.'

Etta puts down her glass.

'Before,' she says, 'when you said *ah*, what did you mean?'

'Nothing.'

'Come on.'

'Look, to be honest I'd rather not say.'

'I've heard it all, don't you worry.'

'All right, if you insist. The stern-looking woman in the little wagon contraption said, when I asked, that there was no one up here but a couple of nutty old codgers who think the Boer War's still on, and that Hori floozy with the bastard child.'

Etta runs the palms of her hands hard across her knees.

'And I don't qualify as either of the old codgers,' she says.

Isaac glances once more at Troy, then back at Etta.

'You know,' he says, 'I'd rather you hadn't asked me to say that.'

Troy walks across his path, his shadow fleeting in Isaac's eyes. Isaac turns to watch him chase a gull's shadow.

'I found this place by accident,' says Isaac.

'Most people do.'

'Do they tend to stay?'

'Not for long. Some do. Some come back over and over. Some people come here to escape.'

'From what?'

'Take your pick.'

Isaac looks for somewhere to toss his cigarette. Etta holds out the tray. He baulks.

'It'll wash out,' she says.

A half-hour later he kick-starts the motorbike, twists the accelerator grip. Etta steps back towards the creek, then forward again.

'What did you mean,' she says, 'in league with the army?'

'I'm a scientist,' he says, 'not a soldier.'

She steps back again. He turns the motorcycle about and waves to her then heads off back down the beach until she loses sight of his figure among the waves.

The next day she and Troy ride up to Frenchman's Point. She leads Troy by the hand to where the slope begins to steepen, then stops. They sit in the grass, looking down over the ocean. Tangles of undergrowth fight the hillside's dirt.

The bush has thickened since she was last here. Troy wants to go exploring, but Etta holds him close. He fights her grip, then settles, sits against the hillside. Etta looks beyond him to where the waves are overlaid in the sweep of the bay.

Isaac enters the office at Auckland University that he shares with two other lecturers. He glances up at the calendar on the wall, aware he is the temporary one here, lecturing on physics for six months until he takes up a teaching appointment at the California Institute of Technology in the American fall term. His work on the Manhattan Project at Los Alamos and then on the Crossroads series of nuclear tests in the Pacific in 1946 has opened doors for him that otherwise would not be open, as they have for so many of the other atomic bomb physicists. He sits and leans back in the creaking chair, looks up at where his Oxford degrees sit dusty and fly-spotted on the walls.

Atomic bomb physicists.

The letter from the British Ministry of Defence sits unopened on the blotter in the centre of the desk. He raises it to the light, leans back again, tapping against the paper with a fingertip. He considers making a paper dart from it, setting it sailing out the window. Instead he stands, peers down at the Friday evening traffic working its tired way out of the city. He looks west at the rows of gabled roofs, beyond which hills beckon.

In an hour he is free of city clutter, into new suburbs where a bulldozer sits waiting for Monday, its caterpillar tracks caked with dirt. Children play on open ground, chasing rugby balls or just playing tag. He steers the Indian down the winding hill road into Rangimoana. His saddlebags carry a sleeping bag, two changes of clothes and two packets of cigarettes.

He could ride straight down past the campground and onto the beach, but he doesn't. He skirts the estuary and crosses the little wooden bridge and rides on along the worsening road surface to where the Fibrolite cottage sits beyond the creek.

Troy sits on the grass, pushing a solid block of timber through the stems. He looks up as Isaac turns and stops. Etta stands from her gardening, raises an arm to shield her eyes from the lowering sun. She shows no interest for a moment, and he realises he is backlit; his features may be invisible. Or perhaps he has misjudged the moment, the ride out here. Then she looks beside him to the motorcycle, lowers her raised arm and smiles.

They sip orange cordial at the lone table. Etta has brought Troy in and closed the door. He lies on the floor, grappling with a couple of stuffed toys which appear to have begun life as socks. He pushes one across the floor, making an engine noise. A manila folder sits on the floor next to Etta's chair's foot. Troy crashes his motorised sock into it. A couple of envelopes fall out.

'Careful, hon,' says Etta.

She reaches down and pushes everything back into the folder.

'Rejection letters,' says Etta, following Isaac's gaze.

'Rejection?' he says.

'Every newspaper and magazine in the country. Or it sure seems like it.'

She stands and goes to a cupboard, lifts out a cardboard shoe box and brings it back, setting it on the table. She has glued a cardboard divider in the centre of the box. Developed photographs in one compartment, negatives in the other.

Isaac leafs through the photos. The beach in different light, the sky, the waves.

'You took these?' he says.

'Yes.'

She stands again, goes to a woven flax bag and lifts out a Brownie camera. Isaac turns it over in his hands.

'I had one of these in the States,' he says. 'Where did you get this one?'

She doesn't answer, just stares at him for a moment, then puts the camera back in the bag. He looks through the photos again. Halfway down the pile the shots of the beach end and he comes across photos of people on a city street, caught in wild celebration. Two sailors raising bottles, a woman in a long skirt caught as she turns to watch a car go by with a half-dozen people clambering over the fenders and bonnet. The further Isaac delves the closer the shots are: a welter of faces caught in luxuriant smiles, an old man snoring against a shop door frame. Three young men in army clobber singing fit to burst. A young girl, eyes squeezed closed.

'The noise of the firecrackers,' says Etta.

Isaac looks up.

'The war was over,' says Etta. 'Was it like that where you were?'

'After a fashion, yes.'

She seems to be waiting for him to say more, but he doesn't. She moves to close the box, but he doesn't let go of the photos.

'These are good,' he says. 'The faces.'

'I have a part-time job, working a day a week as an assistant to a wedding photographer. It's a start, and I've managed to scrounge some bits 'n bobs.'

She stands.

'I'll show you,' she says.

She leads him behind the cottage to where a small lean-to stands. She swings a corrugated-iron sheet away from the lean-to's entrance and steps in. A tub, a couple of taps. A tea chest with an army issue footlocker across it. She opens the locker to reveal a couple of vials with cork stoppers. Three jars with coloured solution. Two shallow trays. A half-dozen photographs pegged to a length of clothesline twine.

He looks down at the tub, the small bench and the jars.

'It's a darkroom,' he says.

'You seen one before?'

'Now and then. At Oxford or on the Hill.'

'The Hill?'

'Los Alamos, a place where I worked during the war.'

He glances down at Troy clasping his mother's legs. Her skirt rises up as the boy tugs on at it, tries to drag it away.

Isaac sits against the outside wall, Etta on the step. Watching the sun fade into the dunes. Isaac takes a draw on his cigarette, then sees her looking at it, hands it to her.

'You have a talent for faces,' he says. 'People.'

She takes a long drag, leans back and blows a smoke ring.

'There's a magazine after an article on me,' says Isaac.

He lights another cigarette for himself.

'They've submitted some questions,' he says, 'background bio material et cetera. I was one of the few on the hill who didn't have a strange foreign accent.'

'You *do* have a strange foreign accent.'

'Thank you. Thing is, they've said they need a couple of recent photos. I didn't think of it until just now.'

She looks out at the sunset.

'I don't have any photos,' says Isaac. 'To be honest, I've always been a bit camera shy. I won't be back in the States until after the issue's published so they're pushing me to arrange for a local photographer.'

She stops blowing smoke rings.

'I'm beginning to like this idea,' she says. 'What's the magazine?'

'*Life.*'

'Life? Life of what.'

'Just – *Life.*'

'*Life.* You mean *Life* at the movies, *Life* at war, *Life* that sells a million copies a week. That *Life*? They want to do a story about you.'

'Yes.'

'You're joking.'

'No. So, will you take the photos?'

She begins to laugh.

Etta tells Isaac that Walter and Ruth back over the bridge into town will do him bed and breakfast or if they already have a tenant he could try banging on the door of the surf club, but he takes his bedroll across the track to the dunes, spreads it out and slips into the sleeping bag.

In the morning Etta crouches above him, wearing a pair of khaki shorts with her nightdress tucked inside them. Her long hair is wild in the morning breeze. She reaches out with a chipped enamel mug, the steam from the hot tea rising against the greying light. He takes a sip, then flicks some sand from his lips. Etta stares out to sea.

'I'm *not* a floozy, by the way,' she says.

'You know those weren't my words.'

She nods.

Isaac rides the back-country roads, where orchards sit hidden among sheep-scattered hills, or valleys of untamed bush. Some of the bush he rides through is so thick the sunlight shatters, sometimes vanishes altogether. He blinks, conscious now he has picked up speed, a corner seeming to tumble towards him. He eases back on the throttle, fingers pressing on the brake. He stops the Indian, sits breathing hard. A blank page has passed through him, and it has rendered the last half-mile of road invisible.

In Rangimoana there is no sign of Etta and Troy. He turns off the motor, sits in the silence, becomes aware within a few seconds that it is anything *but* silent. The ocean, the calls of gulls, the wind. He sits thinking that in the time he has been in Auckland his passage remains almost unmarked. Three or four changes of clothes, few possessions. No furniture that isn't owned by the university. No friends beyond the faculty.

He walks into the twilit dunes, scuffing the marram grass with his bare toes. He sits in the cooling sand, listening to the heartbeat of the waves. He raises his left arm against the horizon. A scattering of gulls haze out beyond the breaking surf. One dives, then another, falling and rising and falling in the burning pink light, and in their search he sees Etta crouching in her shorts in the sand, staring into the surf.

Etta picks up Troy from Walter and Ruth's and steers her bicycle along the road. Troy sits laughing on the carry rack, fingers gripping the metal frame, the knuckles turning pink with the intensity of his grip. His legs dangle. He leans back, looks skyward. She taps him atop his head and he laughs louder; she speeds up her pedalling, the cycle bouncing on the ruts and stones until with a skid of brakes they stop outside the bach. She brushes herself off, looks towards the dunes where the motorcycle sits on its stand, backlit by the red flames of wattle flowers.

Inside she pours some milk from the urn into an old pewter mug and she and Troy pass it back and forth. She goes to the washbasin and takes off her work clothes, bends over and reaches for the tap. A few minutes later she ties a short length of woven flax around the pony tail in her newly wetted hair.

Troy sits on the floor, cradling the mug, scooping out the last of the milk with his fingers. Etta crouches beside him.

'Motorcycle,' says Troy.

'Yes, I saw it.'

Troy starts making flicking motions, imitating Isaac's Zippo lighter.

'How about a walk on the beach?' she says.

He turns and flicks some milk into her face.

'You could've just said no thanks,' says Etta.

'Motorcycle,' says Troy.

Etta looks down at him.

He leans back and holds his fingers above and below his eyes, peering through make-believe spectacles. Etta laughs. They walk down to the dunes. She stoops to avoid the pōhutukawa branches, brushes through to where the empty beach opens up. She takes off her sandals, loops their straps through her shorts' belt and buckles them shut.

Etta sits on a driftwood log, raises a forearm above her face, stilling when her stare settles at Koroheke's feet. A gull cries and she looks up, follows its falling arc down past the rock's shadow to where a figure ripples in the fractured light reflected off the surf. He comes closer. A rumpled check shirt, open down the front, tattered trousers ripped off just below the knees. The circle of a straw-boater hat. He carries a piece of driftwood over his shoulders, his bare feet scuffing the shallows; his footprints vanishing in seconds with the bloom and fade of the tide.

He turns and walks up through the dunes, still fifty yards shy of where Etta and Troy sit among the driftwood. He doesn't appear to see them. Etta takes Troy's hand and they walk down the beach, turning where the footprints veer up into the trees. They step through the rotted remnants of an ancient fence, her sandals knocking against her hips. At the edge of the small clearing is a pūriri tree. A spray of branches, sun-specked leaves glinting. Isaac sits among the roots, the length of driftwood laid across his lap, his eyes closed to the speckled shadows on his cheeks. A dry leaf crackles beneath Etta's feet and he opens his eyes.

'Well, mister scientist,' she says, 'you're starting to look more like a beachcomber.'

Isaac gestures for them both to sit next to him. Etta sits, but Troy walks up to the nearest dune, struggles to climb it, each step forward followed by a slip back.

Etta breaks off a piece of grass.

'Do they have beaches like this in England?' she says.

'I don't know, to be honest. I never spent much time at the seaside. I can't even swim.'

'I can teach you, if you'd like.'

'Not sure about that. Last time I tried I just got a thorough dunking.'

'Where was that, at home?'

'No. When I was stationed in the North Pacific. Calmest water I'd ever seen, but to no avail.'

'North Pacific?'

'Yes.'

She looks up at Troy, perched in a precarious crouch in the sand.

'Have you ever heard of a place called Tinian?' she says.

'Yes. I've been there. Why?'

'What's there?'

'An airfield, small town. Army base.'

'A soldiers' cemetery?'

'I guess so. Why do you ask?'

Troy stands, begins to slip again, the dune crumbling around him.

'Come down, bub,' says Etta.

Troy turns to look at her and loses his footing and slides down towards them, laughing.

Isaac smiles.

'Say,' he says, 'you wouldn't be a devotee of silent movies at all, would you?'

'Every Saturday morning at the Odeon.'

'The Odeon? Sounds very grand.'

'It was a corrugated-iron shed with a projector that broke down just at the moment the films became interesting.'

'I have a collection that would make Sam Goldwyn envious. I can bring them out, next time I come.'

They look at each other for a moment, then Etta turns out towards the reddening clouds. Isaac takes a pocket knife from his shirt pocket, cuts a length a few inches long from the end of the piece of driftwood. He begins to whittle at it. Troy sits watching Isaac. In a half-hour a stick figure emerges from the wood and Isaac holds it up and Troy takes it. He turns it over and over in his hands, then stands with it, mumbles something to it and spins around, pointing the wooden figure as if it was a gun. They walk back down the beach.

Past midnight Isaac lies back in his sleeping bag, watching the moon out over Koroheke, the ocean subtle tonight, almost a whisper between conspirators. In the morning Etta crouches with two steaming mugs.

'You'd better speak to Walter and Ruth about lodgings,' she says. 'Or the constable will arrest you as a drifter.'

'I am a drifter.'

The next time he comes he borrows a sidecar and attaches it to the Indian. His projector, a bedsheet and four film tins are lashed to the seat. He carries a wooden rectangle strapped to his back, a painting sitting in its frame, covered over with a couple of squares of butcher's paper tied with string. He had picked it up in a Saturday morning jumble sale in Taos, New Mexico. A woman all in black, dress long enough to touch the dirt of the path she stands on. The trees and grass scrubby, half-shorn. The woman looks away from the viewer, towards the distant hills where the sun has fallen. The sky orange, yellow, red.

Woman in the Setting Sun, by Caspar David Friedrich.

He steps off the motorcycle, stands with the painting in its plywood frame roped to his back like some ancient woodcutter. Etta walks across the grass. She helps him remove the lashings and peel the covering of paper away.

'Gawd,' she says, 'what on earth is this?'

'I've nowhere to hang it, thought you might.'

'It's hideous.'

'Is that your considered opinion?'

'Nope. My considered option is that it's a monstrosity.'

'It'll grow on you.'

'I'm hoping it'll grow legs!'

He sits back on the motorbike, shaking his head.

'Why is she looking away from us?' says Etta.

'He never painted faces,' says Isaac.

Etta stands wide-eyed, then carries the painting into the bach, sets it down on one end against the wall. Isaac sits at the table, looks down at an old matchbox sitting beneath one of the chair legs that's shorter than the other. He can hear the generator humming outside. Etta glances down at the painting a couple of times while she's boiling the kettle.

'I hope your taste in films is better,' she says.

She makes dinner from some green beans, parsley and potatoes. Isaac rigs the projector and stands on a chair to tack the bedsheet to the low ceiling, then aims the projector's lit aperture at it. They watch Buster Keaton's *The General, The Navigator* and *Steamboat Bill,* and a couple of Chaplin shorts on the last reel.

Isaac sits at one end of the couch, Etta at the other. Troy sits between them, staring wide eyed at the screen. Then he begins to yawn.

'Bit late for you, huh,' says Etta.

She lifts him, steps towards his small bed.

'Hang on,' says Isaac, 'I'll pause the projector.'

'No, let it go.'

She leans over Troy, settling him into the blankets, his eyes blinking slower and slower. She sits for a moment beside him, her back to Isaac, her face leaning on an upraised arm, mother and child silhouetted in the staccato light from the flickering screen.

When he walks into Walter's kitchen Ruth looks up from the sink.

'You'll be staying just the one night?' she says.

'I don't know,' he says.

She makes him a cup of cocoa and they sit, the lone candle burning down to a stub. They can hear Walter snoring from the sitting room.

'She's had a hard time of it,' says Ruth.

'It must've been tough bringing up the boy on her own.'

'That's not the half of it.'

He sits swirling the last of his cocoa, then goes on to his room.

The next morning Etta answers his knock on her door and they go down to the strip of wet beach before the shallows. She guides him with her left hand raised, her right hand carrying the camera. She poses him against a backdrop of sand, the ocean just out of frame.

'You said this Los Alamos place was in the desert?' she says.

'Almost.'

Etta fingers the shutter control. Click.

'Why?' says Isaac.

'Those sand dunes could be mistaken for desert. Might be appropriate.'

'Good point.'

'Hang on, I'll crouch. Then they can't see the ocean.'

'Apart from the seaweed.'

'Move left a bit, yeah, there.'

'And the shells.'

'Will you stop it!'

He laughs and she photographs him laughing and he stops. Then he begins to laugh again. She takes a half-dozen or so photographs, each with a different aspect; backlit, sidelight, full face, three-quarter.

'Take your glasses off, will you,' says Etta.

He does so and she lowers the camera, surprised at the sudden sweeping away of years from his face.

'How old are you, Isaac?'

'Twenty-nine. Why?'

'When I first met you, I thought you were older.'

'Perhaps I was.'

She stands with the camera lowered, then raises it again, centring him in its rectangular eye.

Click.

She looks once more through the viewfinder, the land and sea shifting around him. This man not of soil or sand but books. A man who admits to having crossed the ocean without a single pair of Sunday best shoes, but made sure to pack a brand-new American motorbike and a copy of the world's ugliest painting.

She nods him further back, into the shallows. Sea spray finds the crotch of his trousers. He yelps.

Click.

'You look like you had an accident before you could get to the privy,' she says.

He laughs, and there is a hint of a child peeking out for a moment then withdrawing. She takes another then lowers the camera and he relaxes, losing the stiffness he had in her camera's eye. She points out to sea and he follows her eye line, and she raises the camera, catches him unaware.

'Isaac,' she says, and he turns back to her.

Click.

'Hey!' he says. 'No fair.'

'One more.'

They walk down to the waterline and she steps into the surf, ushering him forward. His long hair blows across his scalp and he reaches to tug it into line.

'No, leave it,' she says.

She walks them further into the waves, the water crashing against their waists. She has to lift the camera high out of the water with each oncoming wave, lower it again in the troughs. She reaches out, undoes the buttons of his shirt, the sides flapping away, leaving him almost bare above the waist. He shows no prudish modesty, just a tired smile, the formality and consideration of his city mannerisms and banter fading, a rawer man emerging. A man of waves and troughs.

Click.

Etta puts the prints in with the next batch of negatives she takes from the wedding photographer to be developed. She takes a train into the city, meets Isaac in Albert Park and they spend an hour looking at them, laid out on the grass. She sits tapping her fingernail against the prints of the last three photos she took. Isaac in the waves. The next day Isaac slips the envelope of photographs and negatives over the counter at the post office.

'Air post,' he says.

'That's expensive,' says the woman at the counter.

He nods, reaches into his billfold.

He rides out every weekend, bringing the Friday dusk from the east with him, his eyes blinking into the rising sun as he returns each Monday morning. He carves little wooden figures for Troy in his lunch hour at university, looking over his knife to the clock-tower's spire. Stick figures at first, then graduating to cars and trucks. He uses wooden dowel pins for axles, cut-down cotton reels for wheels. He puts them in his bag and kick-starts the motorcycle.

When she and he are on the sand Isaac stands close, close enough to feel her quiet breath on his chin. She straightens, her shoulders and back seeming to stiffen. Then she relaxes, a giving grace he has not felt from her before. He moves close enough to kiss her, but doesn't attempt to. He looks out at the sea.

'I'm sorry I made you say that stuff about the Hori floozy,' says Etta. 'Your lips didn't deserve to say that.'

'Thank you.'

He spends half his nights in Rangimoana in the small hard bed at Walter and Ruth's, the other half somewhere in the dunes. On the dunes nights he wakes to sea mist, the westerly skimming the surf's tips. One evening he builds the figure of a woman with sand, sits against it, sleeps against it. In the morning he sits up, yawning, a sudden whirl of scraping hands when he sees Etta walking across the beach towards him. She sits, looking puzzled at the wild scratchings on the beach's skin.

'Bad dreams?' she says.

'Something like that.'

They walk down the beach to Koroheke, the algae soft, slippery against their bare feet. She turns, looking out to the horizon. She stands for so long he feels himself begin to vanish, but then she reaches for his hand and they both look west, the sun rising over their shoulders, the silver ocean stretching away.

'Funny,' says Isaac. 'I took the turnoff to here on a sudden whim. The first time I came.'

She nods.

'I could've gone anywhere,' says Isaac. 'North, south.'

'But you didn't.'

She looks north.

'You ever think about home?' she says.

'Now and then. It's been a while.'

'Me too.'

He looks over her shoulder to where the beach stretches away.

'When I first arrived here,' he says, 'I had this idea of riding the length of the country.'

'You still might.'

'You could come with me.'

'And Troy?'

'The three of us. We could stop off, see your folks.'

'Go all the way to the cape. I've never done that.'

'Cape?'

'Te Rerenga Wairua.'

'What does that mean?'

'The leaving place of the spirits.'

He smiles.

'What's after that?' he says.

'It's just ocean roads after that.'

That night, after their latest session watching his silent movies, Isaac begins to pack the film back in the tin, look around for his sandals and straw hat, but Etta appears behind him, a blanket and a quilt in her arms. Another pillow. He watches all this with glances at her, his hands busy with tins and boxes. She appears once more, this time carrying an inflatable mattress, the rubber scent tart. She sits cross-legged on the floor, begins to blow into the nozzle.

In the night he rolls over on the mattress, trying to brush strands of his hair away from his eyes, then he stills, realising it's *her* hair against his eyelids. He reaches across, touches a hand against the warmth of her body. Then he closes his eyes, goes back to sleep. The next time he wakes, Troy is between them.

In the afternoon, when the school has emptied for the day, he takes her to work on his motorcycle. He sits with the motor running, watching her walk up the deserted byways of the school yard. She glances over her shoulder, winks at him, affects a movie-star walk; mincing steps that don't quite go with her fading headscarf, frayed blue overalls with a rag hanging out of the backside pocket. He has said he will loan her the money for her photographic materials, but she won't take it, perhaps sensing it would be a loan he has no intention of keeping her to. He buys things for Troy and gives them to her via anyone in the village who will act as middle man, Etta's eyebrows rising at her sudden popularity. On market day or walkabout Sunday he matches her steps, her best dress curling against him. There are some sideways looks, some turned-up noses, but she disdains them. He teaches her how to ride the motorcycle, Etta steering them both around the bay. Isaac smiles out from the pillion seat, nodding to the people they pass, those who look up from their gardens. She in turn teaches him how to swim, the two of them floating in the tender waves of the little sheltered cove south of town.

'Who was Troy's father?' he says one day as they sit in the marram grass.

'Don't ask me that.'

'I just want to know, Etta.'

'Yeah, I know, but…'

She closes her eyes. He touches her hair.

'If and when you want to,' he says.

'If and when.'

He doesn't go back out to Rangimoana for a week and when he does she says little to him, just talks about photography. They sit in her darkroom, Etta absorbed in the act of bringing photos out of the solution and into the light.

In the night she comes to him again, easing onto the mattress beside him.

'I can't sleep,' she says. 'Been lying staring at the ceiling.'

'Me too.'

She goes silent and he wonders if she is drifting into sleep. Then he feels her eyelashes against his cheek. Her voice comes out of the dark.

'If and when,' she says.

'Yes.'

Isaac is standing in the shallows when Etta rides past him on the Indian, the tyres kicking up a parabola of water behind her. He steps up out of the water and she circles him, kicking up sand now. She rolls to a stop, reaches behind her and lifts the camera from the saddlebag. The beach is deserted. She steps off and walks past him.

'I told Walter I'd be by in another hour or so to pick up

Troy,' she says.

He looks at her, then at the camera.

'Can I take another couple of photos?' says Etta. 'Just for me.'

They walk to the north end of the bay, the bush-covered cliffs on two sides. She raises the camera. Isaac squints into the sun, his glasses catching the light's edge. Etta shakes her head, takes the frames from his face and puts them in her pocket. She turns to walk away but stops, goes back and lifts away his shirt. He stands with the waves making him rise and fall, as if the sea is breathing for him. She shapes to take a photograph but stops and walks back to him. She unhooks his belt and slips it from the loops of his trousers, then unbuttons the trousers themselves and lets them fall away. He doesn't protest this time.

He is naked beneath the falling fabric. The hair between his legs glistens with sea water now, his penis like a fish among the droplets. He steps free from his trousers and lets them float away. She moves seaward of him, crouches in the water, Isaac's body rising against the sea cliffs, the waves from this angle looking high enough to swamp her. She takes the scarf from her head, wipes the camera's lens.

Click.

She stands again, drawing him down with a gesture, down so far only his torso is above the waves, like a marker buoy.

Isaac gestures her forward, slips his fingers into hers. He takes her other hand, then runs his fingertips up her arms, onto the cotton of her overalls. He flicks open the top button, keeps unbuttoning until they spread at her waist then he raises her out of the fabric. He takes the strap of the camera with a fingertip and plucks it skyward, high above her head, slipping it over his own. He draws the last of her garments away. Her naked skin is aflame with the thousand fleeting hues of the sunset sea. He raises the camera, centres her in the viewfinder. Centres this moment in his life, in their lives. Her nipples are tiny peaks within their dark circles. His eyes trace her own dunes and sand-tinted slopes. The thin feather of downy hair from her navel thickening as it spreads like toetoe above her cleft. He looks up, away from the viewfinder, away from everything.

'What is it?' she says.

'I don't want to go,' he says.

She looks down into the sea foam, then back up, her face in this moment unreadable. Unreadable to this physicist who can read and understand the smallest things on earth.

Then she smiles.

Click.

Isaac changes down through the gears with his foot, heads up the hill out of Rangimoana, the steep incline revealing the vastness of the ocean. A couple of times he has to ride all the way over almost into the ditch to avoid lorries or cars coming down the hill. Faces peer out. He nods and rides on. At the hill's crest he stops and eases onto the clay of the lookout point, raises a forearm above his eyes. To the north the last bay ends at the cliffs and the road dissolves into sand. He cannot see the tiny cottage. He looks long for it, but it is lost in the sea haze.

Etta wakes to the sound of Troy drawing with a pencil on the wall. Isaac already sits up in bed, watching him. She frowns.

'You could've stopped him,' she says.

'I was curious to see what he was going to come out with.'

'Well, I can stand not knowing.'

She steps out of bed and lifts Troy away from the wall,

the pencil flailing in the air. She half expects him to kick and roar, but he doesn't, just hangs suspended in space, his arms outstretched. Looking down at Isaac.

'Come on, you,' says Etta to Troy, 'time for breakfast.'

They walk past the hanging curtain that separates the sleeping section of the bach from the rest. Isaac stands and goes to the wall, crouches, studies the pencil lines. He winds its path back from the point where the drawer's hand had been lifted away, back through his journey. He sits on his haunches and smiles, realising that among the wild fountain of marks sits a pretty fair approximation of a motorbike.

'I have to go into the university today,' says Isaac. 'Why don't you two come with me. Spend the day in town.'

Isaac has bought the sidecar and Troy sits in it, the smallest pair of goggles Isaac could find still too big for him. They give him a permanent wide-eyed stare as the wind pushes back his hair. He holds on with both hands but smiles all the way. Etta doubles behind Isaac. They enter the city from the west and Isaac takes them over Karangahape Road and down the hill and then up past Albert Park. They walk down the grassy slope, past the university clock tower and up to Isaac's office in the science department. Troy sits on the desk, pushing Isaac's globe with his fingers.

'That's the world,' says Isaac.

'All of it?' says Troy.

'Yes.'

'These bits stick up,' says Troy, running his fingers over the islands of the Pacific.

'Yes,' says Isaac. 'It's called a relief.'

'Re-lief.'

'Yes,' says Etta. Things aren't flat like on a picture. They're made into shapes you can feel.'

Troy examines the globe, runs his fingers across it.

Etta looks up at the scrawl of numbers and symbols on the blackboard.

'And is that the world too?' she asks.

'Another part of it, yes,' says Isaac.

'Your other life.'

'Yes, I suppose.'

They walk through the park and down to Queen Street. Etta stops, steps outside of Troy, so he walks between them. He looks up, his eyes wide at all the movement and noise. She takes one of his hands and Isaac takes the other.

They buy ice creams at a streetside stall, stand at an inter-section. Troy licks his ice cream, watching the reflections in a shop's door. Whenever the door opens, the glass shimmers.

In the night Etta leans over Troy lying in his blankets laid across the inflatable mattress, then slips back into bed next to Isaac. The faint moon paints his face on the pillow. Just an outline, his eyes lost to her. She looks away and the slight movement on the sheets draws his hand up to her cheek.

'Can't sleep?' he says.

'No.'

She closes her eyes against his hand, knowing in these last few nights that they are the first she has ever slept with a man. *Slept*. His warmth easing into her, not rushing in a few borrowed moments with a grass bank beneath her bones. She curls against him, her face against his chest. A nipple beneath her cheek.

He rides out on the motorcycle in the mornings and she stands with Troy, watching his figure fade. Then she and Troy spend an hour making sandcastles. She reads to him from the few crumbling books she has managed to scrounge second hand. Every day he pockets a few new words. One evening she teaches him how to write his name, and he spends days trying to perfect it. Etta adds her name and Isaac's, then the name of the village. Then the motorbike.

And Isaac she teaches too, sensing in his formality another costume, like the rag-tag clown outfits he assembles about himself for birthday parties for faculty members' children. Who'd have guessed a clown lay behind those spectacles? She teaches him about how to capture the light in a lens, and he teaches her what the light is composed of, like a musical score.

One night she reaches into her dresser drawer in the candlelight and lifts out the photo. A young man, T-shirted, looking west into the setting sun. A hillside is gathered behind him, as if to push him off out to sea.

'If and when,' she says.

He nods.

So she tells him. Of a dunny in the sea wind, of marching songs, of Zippo lighters and cameras that weren't won in poker games, of Harry James's trumpet in a tiny hall by the sea, of the slamming doors of army trucks. She says it all in a monotone. The story ends with her voice wrapped within an officer's cigarette smoke as it drifts across a baby's bassinette. He doesn't say a word, but neither does he let go of her hand.

'You said you don't want to go,' she says.

'No.'

'I don't want you to go.'

She listens to him breathing in the dark.

'Can you do me one thing,' she says.

'Anything.'

'Don't talk about love.'

'Why?'

'Please.'

He lies back down, then turns his body towards her, answers with a fingertip down across her cheek.

Isaac looks up at Professor Owens, the head of department. At his hat hanging on its rack, Isaac's own hat held tight in his fingers as he sits forward in the chair.

'Of course it's an honour,' says Owens. 'An unexpected one.'

'I'd appreciate whatever you can do,' says Isaac.

The two men shake hands.

'We never expected you to want to stay on,' says Owens.

Isaac walks down the corridor and sits back in his office chair. His hat still in his hands. He flings it at the stand behind the door, misses. He smiles. Before he heads out to the coast in the evening he stops at the post office, drops the letter to the California Institute of Technology in the slot.

Etta kneels, washing Troy's hair in the tub. She has splashes of water over the top of her shirt, on the tips of her hair. She tickles Troy beneath his arms and he laughs, half pulls away. Etta takes a handful of soapsuds and anoints the top of his head, looking up when she hears the motorbike. Troy stands from the tub, and she hands him a towel. There are footsteps at the door, but it doesn't open.

'Isaac?'

She opens it, steps out to where he stands looking over at the dunes. She waves a hand in front of his face.

'I'm not going,' he says.

She stands for a moment, looking in the direction of his stare, then reaches up and runs her soapy hands through Isaac's hair. He reaches up, sets his fingers between hers.

Etta keeps her job cleaning up at the school, while still

working part-time at the photographic studio. She and Isaac erect a corrugated-iron shed in the yard, moving her rudimentary darkroom from the lean-to behind the bach. She buys some gear second-hand through her growing network of photographic contacts. A stop bath, a print-developing tray, her measuring jugs and timer. At first she carries water into the shed from the bach in a bucket, but then she and Isaac dig a pipe extension from the bach's water tank. He runs another power cable from the generator into the shed and she installs a photographic developers' safelight and screws it into the fitting. Isaac closes the door. Etta works the switch and the tiny room is bathed in purple light. She spins on her stool, looks to where he leans against the door jamb looking at the bulb. She smiles but he doesn't acknowledge it. Etta takes the negatives from the camera and begins the process. She lifts the sheets of paper one by one from the fluid and sets them into the stop bath, neutralising the developer. Then she takes the sheets out again and drops them into the last tray, the fixer. The unexposed silver-halide seeds then loosen, vanishing as she washes them away, awakening the image in its journey from dusk to dawn.

They come together in the evenings, after Troy is asleep, glad of the looseness of their bonds during the day, glad to be in each others' orbits but only attached by a smile or a raise of the eyebrows or the touch of fingertips. They have learned to explore each other in a hush, a silent movie, leaving Troy undisturbed in his dreams. When Isaac is halfway down her body, speaking soundless words to her, she has learned to voice her pleasure just with her fingers in his hair. Tensing and releasing. She doesn't lift her chin in these moments, doesn't look to see if he is looking back at her, their pact of silence now moving into a silence of gesture. What few words they do speak are just whispers, a beat beneath the music. And no curls of their tongues or lips lead to forming the word *love*, as she has wished it so. Their language is one with a single word missing.

If he is honest, that doesn't pain him. He had detoured around such things. A brilliant child, rushing on a train of numbers and algebraic symbols through the world, glancing away from his blackboard only to a book. Never to a human face, a woman's smile. 'Always with his head off in some book,' his friends and family had said, and it wasn't a lie. The female students at Oxford had been ignored, those who tried. The same at Caltech. He had crossed an ocean and a continent, but never crossed a young woman's top step or doorway. Two years in the desert learning to make more deserts, the stab of realisation like a blade through a vein somewhere inside him. But that day when a woman stood from the driftwood log with her child's hand in hers the tracks his train had run on began to warp. Began to unravel. Leaving him standing in the sand with the realisation that he had learned how to kill before he had learned how to kiss.

But they still don't speak of love, not even when he slides the ring over her finger and she looks into his eyes. Not even when she tells him she is pregnant.

One morning Isaac sits at the table on the grass outside their bach, reading a newspaper. He feels a sting on the back of his neck and reaches, smacks his hand against his skin. When he looks at his hand there is a small smear of blood, seeping into the lifelines in his skin. He curses, wipes his palm on the grass and goes back to his paper.

The first sentence stills him, the second closes his eyes. The Soviet Union has exploded its first atomic bomb. He stands, drops the paper on the table and bashes the edge of his hand against the bach's wall.

Nineteen-fifty offers an apex in the century. More armies gather, more letters and phone calls and ultimatums are sent to open dialogue and close borders.

Away from it all a man and a woman pitch a tent by a fence, then disassemble an old bach and build something larger, something they hope will be more permanent, set against the safety of the hillside. A pole house, its back to the hillside, its face to the sea wind. The three then become a four when another boy is born. They name him Caleb.

Isaac takes Etta and Caleb home from the hospital with the motorbike and sidecar. Troy doubles with Isaac this time, sitting in front of him, lashed to Isaac's waist with the arms of a woollen sweater.

They sit out on the deck, Isaac and Etta taking turns to hold Caleb. Then Etta undoes the buttons on her dressing gown, begins breastfeeding Caleb while Isaac draws Troy a diagram of how the motorbike's engine works. Etta wipes a spill of milk from Caleb's chin, ruffles his sparse hair.

'Troy sure likes the sidecar,' says Isaac.

Etta laughs.

'When they're older,' says Isaac, 'we could take them on a real trip. As a family.'

'We are a family,' says Etta, 'aren't we.'

'Where would you like to go?' says Isaac to Troy.

'Far,' says Troy.

Isaac looks up at Etta.

'Perhaps all the way to Te Rerenga Wairua,' he says.

'Where's that?' says Troy.

'You in a hurry to become a spirit?' says Etta to Isaac.

'When are we going?' says Troy.

'First things first,' says Etta.

Isaac leans back in his chair, puts his feet up on the low table. Troy tries to do the same but his legs won't reach. He stands and walks to the edge of the deck, leans against the rails.

'We could,' says Isaac.

VIII

Chrysanthemums

November, 1969

A banner hangs between two trees at the edge of one of the university's courtyards. There are rough sketches of skeletons at each end, bookending the text.

We don't want your bloody war

A young woman sells buttons with the peace symbol on them for five cents each. Onlookers watch an impromptu street theatre where a mime stands in the centre of the actor's circle, dressed in a white body suit, her figure dead still. Her oriental eyes are made up like stamped footprints – snowman's eyes – in her arctic-pale face. She stands straight, one arm raised perpendicular against her body, palms upward. She stares along its length to her hand. She looks up, searches the sky above and around her. People watching turn to search also, but see nothing. They look back at her, following the focal point of her stare closer and closer to her as Akiko raises her arm higher, calling an invisible bird to her with clicks of her tongue. Her arm bends as it lands, then settles.

For her afternoon class she has the dancers assemble on the stage then claps her hands. She guides them through a number, a casual run-through at first, getting them to shake everything that *isn't* the dance from their fingers and toes. Then another, focusing on individual movement. A third follows, this time putting the sense of individuality into a back pocket and calling out to them to move as a single 'we'. There are a few false steps, but she keeps the dancers flowing. After an hour she gives their legs a break but questions them, calling for comments, first impressions before the sharp angles and edges fade.

'*Drags in the middle section.*'

'*I was a beat too slow. Sorry.*'

'I'm closer than I was yesterday.'

'I think my bum's too big for this stuff!'

The last comment brings a smile all round. Akiko listens to them, asks what they will do next time to change it. Discussion back and forth, then she tells the students to go out into the daylight, think and talk about everything *except* dance for an hour.

When they return their eyes are sharp again.

At Mount Iris, Caleb and Isaac walk along a gravel path beneath the trees. They sit listening to the cicadas in the buffalo grass. The northerly's spring greeting dawdles in the sycamore leaves. Caleb looks over onto the lawn in front of the main building where a nurse throws a tennis ball to each of a small group of patients. Some grasp hold of it, some just watch it go. Others seem not to notice its presence. One man shapes to catch it, but lets it pass clean through his raised arms. The ball drops to the grass but he keeps his hands raised, like a signpost at a crossroads.

'You don't have to visit so often,' says Isaac.

'It's no hassle,' says Caleb.

'Your studies.'

'I said it's no hassle.'

Isaac reaches, touches Caleb on the shoulder.

'Have you settled on your PhD research topic yet?' says Isaac.

'Still tossing up ideas.'

'I've been thinking about nuclear fusion.'

Isaac stands, walks to the garden and comes back with a twig. He leans forward, uses the twig to scratch three small circles side by side into the loose stones of the path.

'Are you aware of the work the team in Bristol did on cold fusion?' he says.

'Beyond the discovery of intermediate particles, the mesotron stuff, not much.'

Isaac points at the small circles he's scratched, focuses on the first figure,

'Say these are simple hydrogen atoms,' he says. He scrapes a large circle around the small circle, then cuts the letter e next to the large circle, nicks a small minus symbol next to the p. Beside the smaller circle he cuts a letter p and a plus sign.

'Electron and proton,' says Caleb. 'I'm with you.'

'Let's say an atom of standard hydrogen is invaded,' says Isaac.

He points at the second figure, draws a ring only a couple of inches larger in diameter around the smaller circle. Next to this he draws the symbol μ and a minus sign.

'A muon,' says Caleb.

Isaac nods.

'And because the muon orbits the proton in the atom's nucleus closer than the atom's electron would –'

'Because it's a couple of hundred times heavier than an electron,' says Caleb.

'The muon would orbit the nucleus closer in.'

Caleb leans forward. 'The muon's negative charge,' he says, 'as it orbited the atom *inside* the electron's orbit, would shield the electron's negative attraction to the positive charge of the proton.'

'And the electron would be ejected,' says Isaac, 'and we would have muonic hydrogen.'

The two men sit looking at the diagram in the dust and gravel.

'Now the proton's positive charge is shielded by the heavy muon,' says Caleb.

'It would be able to get much closer to the nucleus of a nearby atom –'

'And we'd have fusion,' says Caleb. 'In theory.'

'Sure it's a theory,' says Isaac. 'It's at least possible.'

'Where did the Bristol physicists get with this?' says Caleb.

'I don't know.'

Caleb looks down at the diagrams, moving from one to the other in his mind. Reading them.

The nurse walks past the man with the raised arms, retrieves the ball. He moves a few paces away, his arms still raised. She feigns to lob the ball to him and he laughs, agitates for her to throw it so she does. He makes no attempt to catch it. The ball rolls across the grass and gravel path, stops when Caleb sets the toes of his boot down on top of it.

'Nuclear fusion at room temperature,' says Caleb.

'Power without destruction,' says Isaac.

'It's a sweet dream,' says Caleb.

Isaac shrugs.

Friday morning, Akiko walks along Princes Street towards the university. She cuts down a path she doesn't often take, slows when she comes upon a bush of yellow chrysanthemums. A dozen large flowers vie with each other for the sun filtering through the macrocarpa branches overhead. She crouches, touches the petals with her fingertip. She reaches into her satchel, takes her nail file and clips off one of the flower's stems, then she stands and walks to her office, carrying the flower. She puts her satchel on the desk, goes into the kitchen, finds a tea mug and fills it with water. She shortens the chrysanthemum's stem and fits it into the cup, then puts it on the corner of her desk. At day's end she's about to walk out the door when she stops, looks at the flower, realising it will sit unseen through the weekend. She drives out to Rangimoana with the chrysanthemum wedged in its cup of water on the passenger seat between her satchel and soft suitcase. As the road winds out to the coast she glances down, watching the chrysanthemum move from side to side with the motion of the car. She walks up the path with just the flower in its cup. When she has brought her other gear inside she sits on her bed, takes out her handmade book, and begins to write

I am told they were your favourite flower.
We used to gather the blossoms on your birthday, set them around the table where we sat and looked at your photograph.

Akiko lies back on her bed, listens to the birds in the bush behind her. For a while she sleeps. When she wakes the sun is a couple of hours further to the west. She sits up, the house silent. She takes the flower and goes to Caleb's room and sets it on his bedside table.

Later they sit on the settee. Caleb toys with a piece of the cushion's stuffing which is coming loose, running a length of frayed fabric through his fingers. He picks up a graph–paper pad and draws three small circles next to each other. He draws them twice more, but then sets the paper back down, folds his legs beneath him.

'Distracted?' says Akiko.

He doesn't answer.

'What are you working on?' she says.

'Something Dad mentioned today.'

She glances past him to where a photo sits in his jumble of notes on the table. She leans forward, takes a corner of the photo. In the centre sits a mop-haired boy. She smiles.

'Is this you?' she says.

'Hate to admit it, but yes.'

'I love the fringe.'

'My first.'

In the photo Caleb sits in dirt or sand, bending to touch a lit match to a crumple of papers and marram grass. A tiny bonfire. His eyes are bullets of concentration. Beyond him two other figures stand, a man with black-rimmed sunglasses and an older boy holding a piece of rope, the man and the older boy sharing a smirk. She looks closer. No. It's not a rope. It's a hose, aimed at the infant bonfire.

'Is this your dad?' she says.

'Yeah.'

'And who's this?'

'Troy. My brother.'

'You don't look much alike.'

'We're not.'

She looks back at Caleb.

'We had different dads,' he says.

'When was this taken?'

'The last summer we were all together.'

Beside Caleb's father is a water tap, his hand poised above it.

'So did they turn the hose on?' she says.

'Oh yeah.'

Akiko looks back at the photograph, this time at the older boy. Noticing now he isn't looking at his brother or the bonfire, but straight at the photographer.

There are a half-dozen or so people standing just out of the circle of street lights when Troy arrives. No one speaks. He can hear the lapping of the harbour on the rocks beyond the verge. The other driver leans against a door pillar.

'Mustang,' says Troy. 'Nice.'

The other driver nods towards the Chev.

'Is the owner buried in a shallow grave somewhere or did you raid your piggy bank,' he says.

'Are we racing or talking?' says Troy.

The Mustang wheelspins against the greasy tar seal and the Chev is halfway out of sight before the Mustang driver gets it under control. At the traffic light he flicks a small wad of money in through the Chev's open passenger window.

Caleb lies back on his blankets, listening to the surf.

Once when he and Troy were kids they were playing war with the local boys in the bush above the house. Old broom and rake handles as guns, bent nails as triggers. He and Troy were on opposite sides. One side went into the bush and hid while the other side counted to sixty, then came in after them. Most of the troops were gunned down in the first few seconds, leaving only Troy and Caleb. Caleb ducked into the darkest spot he could find, giving himself time to think about what to do. With Troy's hawk-like eyes Caleb figured if he moved around then Troy would see him, or at least hear him. So he lay still, knowing Troy wouldn't just sit still. Hoping Troy would come to him.

For an hour he lay motionless, hearing nothing but the sea, guessing Troy was waiting too. Then he heard a dry leaf crack. He moved further into the fern leaves. Another crack, then a crunch of leaves. To his left, coming closer. He slowed down his breaths, peering into the thin alleyway of dirt and stones between the stands of fern and nīkau. He couldn't see

Troy, not even a shadow. A crack of a twig, almost in front of him. He craned his neck to see through the leaves, but couldn't. Another crack, then a thud, past him this time. To his right. He leapt out of the bush and into the path, spun to his right and pointed his gun.

The path was empty, except for the rock coming to a slow stop, rolling away from him.

'Li'l brother,' said the voice behind him.

He turned to see Troy standing pointing his gun at him with one hand, another rock in the other.

Caleb smiled.

'Bastard,' he whispered.

Troy smiled.

Then Caleb realised. Troy hadn't shot. Caleb raised his gun, fast.

'Ratatatatata,' he said.

He can still see the look of shock on Troy's face.

Fawn-coloured fields shine in the afternoon light. Troy leans against the front guard of the Chev. A red iron barn breaks the line of the flatlands, a corrugated half-moon. In the distance sheep graze. A top-dressing plane rises then vanishes again beyond the hills. Troy looks north, up the road's centreline. A cattle truck approaches. He watches it pass, the driver pulling into the centre of the road, hitting his air-horn. Troy closes his eyes to the swirl of dust, listening to the truck's motor fade. When he opens his eyes again a 1957 Ford F-100 pickup is easing to a stop, straddling the centre line.

The driver eyes him from the cab.

'She runs quiet,' says Troy.

'Not interested in noise,' says the driver.

'That makes a change.'

'You ready?'

Troy reaches onto the Chev's dashboard for the money. He walks around the rear and stashes his money in the long grass at the foot of a farmer's letter box. When he turns around the F-100 driver is standing behind him, flicking at the edges of some ten-dollar bills with his fingertips. He too leans and pushes his money into the grass. He brushes pollen dust from his fingers. The two drivers stand, no more than an arm's length from each other. Their stances are awkward without the shells of their cars around them. Troy looks into the driver's eyes for a second, then away. Thinking, that of the couple of dozen drivers he has raced in the last few months, he has not been given a single name. Nor has he given his. He wipes his hands on his jeans.

'I'm growing old here,' he says.

'You won't get the chance, mate.'

He looks along the length of road to the slight rise where the bridge crosses the stony riverbed. A quarter mile, maybe a bit more.

'To the bridge,' he says.

'The bridge it is.'

Troy walks back to the Chev and straps himself in. The other driver steps into the pickup's cab. Troy looks to the hills where the plane rises once again, then dips behind the hills as it moves low to dust.

'When the plane appears again, we go,' says Troy.

The F-100 driver nods. They both start their engines.

A moment of silence, the hill muting the plane's low hum. Troy has the stick-shift in neutral, the sole of his right foot sending V8 waves across the sunburned asphalt. He takes a deep breath.

Wings reappear. Troy pulls the shifter into gear. First,

second, the rev counter needle shimmering. The noise is ear-crushing. He is aware of the F-100 only by feel, not taking his stare from the centre of his lane. He closes a fist over the shifter; third, then top. Sensing in that moment that he is alone on this road. The bridge rails flash into view and he feels the shudder beneath him as his wheels take in the sudden rise in the ground. He eases back on the pedal, hears the engine pitch scream for an instant as the wheels leave the ground, only sky in front of him. An empty, blue windscreen. The Chev is no longer a car, but a bullet. A crunch as he lands again, his head banging against the ceiling. A bit of braking, a change down to third. He feels the whoosh as the F-100 goes by – too late.

The F-100 slows a hundred yards beyond. Troy pulls into the roadside stones, checks the mirror and does a half u-turn, stopping halfway across the centre line. A pause, then the F-100 moves away, shrinking into the road dust and haze of summer fields. Troy completes his turn, begins to head back over the bridge for his money, but stops mid-span.

He gets out, the Chev idling on the cracking asphalt. He sits flexing his hands, waiting while his breathing eases back to normal. Then he leans against the bridge rail and retches over the side, into the stream water. He closes his eyes for a moment, his head pounding. He opens his eyes, looks down into the water to where pallid reeds move in languid unison, like an army of sleepwalkers.

He cruises a couple of backstreet mechanical workshops in the Chev. Places the midnight hotrodders pass through during the day, leaving scrawled messages stuck to the walls amongst the crumpled photographs of young women, bare-breasted, kitted out only in hot pants and knee-length boots. Some of the messages are just in chalk, a few rough marks on the concrete wall. A where, a when, a description of the car. He reads one.

Orewa straight
One
Single headlight

He pulls the Chev out of the mechanics' yard, leans back in the seat, one hand on the steering wheel. The traffic slows near the beginning of the Newmarket flyover. He eases to the road's shoulder, craning his neck to see the reason for the hold-up. When he sees the wreck he accelerates.

The Mustang he raced last night lies on its half-crushed roof, turning in a slow spin, like helicopter blades winding down. Two bloodied faces revolve with the cab, expressionless below their mangled bodies. There are skittering reflections of smashed windscreen glass fragments embedded in their skin.

He stops and gets out. A couple of people run towards the wreck.

'Find an emergency phone,' he says to one. He gets the other to help him try and open the door. It won't budge. He opens the Chev's boot and lifts out a pinch bar and begins to pry the door away from its hinges, both men straining. Neither the Mustang's driver nor passenger have a pulse. Troy leans over first one then the other, trying to resuscitate them. He's still there when the ambulance siren winds down behind him and the ambulance men take over.

When the traffic cops arrive and set up the cordon he watches, guides the tow truck in and lifts its hook off the boom. When he pulls away he glances back once to where the officers are setting out their hazard markers, their torch-beams playing like children's sparklers over the darkening road.

Caleb peers out beneath the hood of his raincoat, eases back on the throttle and steers the Indian into the driveway. He centres Weston's old rented villa in his headlights. The image flickering both with the raindrops and the pulse of the motorcycle's engine beneath him. He switches it off. The only sound is now the rain dripping from the hood's brim onto the oilskin of his coat.

Weston answers Caleb's knock on the door, leans against the frame, chewing on a piece of toast.

'Thought I heard the bike,' he says.

Michael steps out from a room off the hallway. 'You look like a drowned rat,' he says.

Caleb raises his chin to the faces in the kitchen at the end of the hall, one supping from a tea mug. He shakes out the raincoat and hangs it on the hook outside the door. One room has Michael's leatherwork offcuts strewn on the floor beneath his sewing machine; the next has a couple of beanbags, posters of Hindu gods with multiple arms or elephant's heads. The ubiquitous image of Che Guevara's bereted head. A smell of leather, the electric train-set smell of Michael's sewing machine, some kind of incense from the back room. A smell of everything but the kerosene. Weston sees him looking around.

'We shifted it,' says Weston.

'Where to?' says Caleb.

'Old warehouse. Falling down. No one ever goes there.'

'Except for us,' says Dominic, standing in the doorway.

Caleb goes into the sitting room. JK plucks at his electric guitar, takes the joint from Dominic's outstretched fingers. JK reaches down to the amp and turns the volume up. He lifts his hands off the strings and a metallic whine begins to grow, breaking into a wild howl of feedback. Dominic picks up a cushion and throws it at him.

Weston appears in the doorway.

'Ladies, please,' he says.

JK turns the volume down again. Weston's stare moves from face to face.

'Not sure the last one made any impact,' says Dominic. 'Not much in the papers.'

'Maybe they just missed the point,' says Caleb.

'So another demonstration is in order?' says JK.

Caleb walks to the window, peers out. The villa's arched windows are mirrored on the wall of the house opposite. He can just make out his shape in the reflection, captured within the frame. He turns back.

'I don't want people involved,' he says.

'Just us,' says Weston.

'You know what I mean.'

'How about the cenotaph thingy,' says JK, 'at the museum.'

'No,' says Caleb. 'Our message would get lost. And I don't want the old diggers' ghosts on my trail.'

Weston reaches into his jacket, lifts out the marble, the cat's eye. He flicks it, giving it a twist with his fingers then releasing it – spinning – onto the wooden floor. He looks up at Caleb. Caleb stands, watching the marble spin.

Akiko sits in her Mini on Karangahape Road, tapping a knuckle against the vinyl inside covering of the door. A fireman stands in the road, with a red stop sign. Hoses crisscross the wet pavement of the footpath to where smoke comes from a doorway. A fireman comes walking out, takes off his mask. Then another. Two more emerge, take off their helmets and turn to set them back into the fire engine. Akiko sits forward, one hand reaching to beep the Mini's horn. The tallest of the firemen looks over at her, his eyes widening. Akiko reaches out the window, a single finger extended towards him. He reaches also, his cohorts standing watching him in puzzlement. The last of the smoke drifts between the two fingertips.

The fireman with the sign flips its face to GO and the line of traffic begins to move away. Akiko puts the Mini into gear.

Troy stands above the telephone in the fire-station's kitchen. The others are still downstairs washing down the gear. He reaches to scratch his nose, then notices he has left a small snowflake of soapsuds on the tip. He blows it away and reaches for the telephone book.

University of Auckland.

He phones the top number on the list, clears his throat when the woman answers.

'You have a dance tutor there,' he says, 'oriental woman.'

'Dance tutor.'

'Yeah.'

'Do you want to speak to the School of Performing Arts?

'Oh, okay. Yes. Thanks.'

The woman gives him the number and he scrawls it onto the back of a cigarette packet. Another receptionist. He asks the same question as before. Silence.

'Oriental woman,' says Troy.

'Can you give me her name, sir.'

'No. I forgot. Sorry. Can you get it for me?'

The sound of a hand closing over the mouthpiece, muffled voices. Then another woman comes on the line.

'Akiko Io,' says the voice. 'Dance and choreography?'

'Yes,' says Troy. 'Probably. When's her next class?'

'Hold on.'

Footsteps on the stairs. Tank comes in and goes straight to the refrigerator.

'Nine until noon tomorrow, in the auditorium,' says the woman. 'Do you want to leave a message for her?'

'No, that's cool. Thanks.'

The kitchen is full of movement and noise now. Monty reaches for the bread. Geronimo rummages in the cutlery drawer. Troy reaches down, picks up a serrated knife, cuts off a slice of cheese and walks on – chewing – out the door.

Akiko lies back in her bed, the curtains open to the darkness. She prefers to sleep with light, though not a bulb over her head. She might leave the hall light on but shut her bedroom door, or she might forego her bed and just curl up on the couch in the small lounge, a rectangle of light coming through the servery opening from the kitchen. When she moved in here the first thing she did was to set up her bed against the wall by the bay window. Put up the wooden shoe-trees she uses to hang her scarves in the little alcove. And in this way she sleeps, the summer wind through the open windows setting the scarves flickering above her as she rolls over in her sleep.

In her first year in New Zealand she had eased into others' lives like a latecomer at a crowded theatre suddenly finding a spare seat. There were couches and kitchens; sips of weak tea at Formica tables. Photographs sitting on mantelpieces above open fireplaces. Mothers and fathers, sisters and brothers.

She turns over, fluffs the pillow and lays her head back down, the lights from buildings just visible in the murky glass above the bottom of the window frame. Beyond that, Rangitoto, beyond that only stars. She looks into them, like a school of fish an inch beneath the cast of a net.

Troy looks down at his watch. A couple of minutes past noon. He stretches his legs on the grass outside the university auditorium, listening to the thumping of footsteps on lino floors. Around the quadrangle, doors begin to open and a stream of students comes out, splitting in all directions. He sits for fifteen minutes, watching, until the whole courtyard and grass mound is awash with people: talking, peering with deep concentration at open notepads. A few glance in his direction, many of them in jeans, shirts and scarves in wild colours. He suddenly feels self-conscious in his black T-shirt and trousers, his hair shorter than anyone else's.

He walks over to the drinking fountain and bends close, taking the cool liquid onto his tongue. When he finishes drinking he wets a hand and runs both palms up over his face and up through his hair. He dries his eyelids and cheeks with a dab from his raised shirt. When he lowers his shirt again she stands a few feet away, looking him.

'We meet again,' she says. 'Coincidence?'

He shakes his head.

'I didn't think you were a student,' she says. 'Fighting fires and all.'

He glances at the cafeteria.

'Would you like to get a Coke?' he says.

The scarf around her neck catches a hint of wind, ruffles. She steadies it with a hand.

'All right,' she says.

They sit at one of the outside tables, amid the crackle of potato-chip packets, the slurp of drinkers sucking through straws.

'So,' she says.

'So I'm curious,' says Troy.

'That's all?'

'I don't know. It's a start.'

'Then what are you curious about?'

'About what you saw, the other day when you were dancing.'

She sips from her drink. The white of her cardigan is stark against her black blouse.

'I'd have to trust you first,' she says.

'Trust?'

'Yes.'

'You have to trust me just to tell me that?'

'Yes, of course. Do you think it's a small thing?'

'No. I guess not.'

She sits forward. 'And why should I trust you to tell you what I see when I dance?' she says. 'When you don't even trust me with your name.'

'Troy.'

A suggestion of a smile flickers. She sits back again.

'Are you testing me?' she says.

'Testing you? Why?'

'As the older brother.'

He takes a deep breath, steeples his hands in front of him. At the counter someone drops a tray. It clatters on the floor, spilling a teapot and cup. Steaming tea splashes. Neither Troy nor Akiko react.

'You haven't changed that much from your photo,' says Akiko.

Troy's back stiffens, he feels the breeze from the door around his legs. He sits looking at her for a moment.

'Which photo was that?' he says.

'You and Caleb and your dad. You pointing the hose at Caleb.'

'Stepdad,' says Troy.

When Troy says nothing further she takes another sip from her drink. She sets the bottle down, the liquid swirls in the glass. She touches the scarf around her neck again. Troy watches her fingers tighten then loosen then tighten the fabric.

'You know I didn't need saving,' she says. 'From the dance. I *was* coming back.'

'No. I didn't know that.'

He leans back, looks out over the quadrangle.

'Whether you believe me or not,' he says, 'I didn't know.'

She frowns for a moment, then nods her head.

Akiko stands at the head of her afternoon class, looking up into the floor-to-ceiling mirrors at the rows of students behind her. She walks down through them, calls out steps and they respond. She turns around and walks back, each of her words shifting their feet into a different pattern. The floor resounds with their weight, two dozen heartbeats. Outside it may be bright sunshine or heavy rain, but none of that matters here. They are alone, she and the dancers, and the world outside is not a party to this. Another change of step, faces smiling as the rhythm seeps back from the floorboards, back through their feet, and they realise the parts of the creature that they are. A few heads nod and Akiko acknowledges them with a blink or a widening of her eyes to get them to focus on the pulse of the music. For ten minutes they move, not knowing what step will come next. She walks to the back of the hall and stands watching them. Her bones feel their current as if she dances with them.

Caleb stands toying with one of the sprigs dangling from the plant basket hanging from the rafters of Akiko's verandah.

Akiko opens the door, chewing on a wafer.

Soon Caleb sits among her record collection, his bare feet on her Arabic rug, his boots standing up by the settee leg. He looks over the top of an album cover, at her fidgeting in the kitchen.

'You okay?' he says.

'Yes, why?'

'You look …'

He looks back at the album cover.

'You could've at least finished that sentence,' says Akiko. 'Don't keep a girl in suspense.'

'Sorry. I don't know what the next word was going to be.'

'Beautiful?'

'Yeah, that was it.'

'Liar!'

He puts a disc on the turntable, sets the stylus into the grooves. When she walks into the room with the wine glasses he turns, reaches a hand across to her. She goes to hand him a glass, then realises he is reaching for her fingers. She stands, staring down at his hand.

'Hey,' he says, 'you're drifting again.'

He shapes to put an invisible rose between his teeth, then stands. She sets the glasses down on the table, steps towards him and they move together, a crash of torsos. He stares, wide-eyed, shocked at her sudden ferocity. But it lasts for just a moment, then she clothes him like a sheet. He goes to grasp her too but she dances away and his hands fall empty. He steps forward to follow her but his legs freeze. Then his hands. He tries to flex his fingers, but they just stiffen. A sudden wave of tiredness washes through him and he blows out a breath. Akiko's eyes widen but he smiles her concern away. He stands tapping a foot to the rhythm, waggling a finger at her to come closer, but she circles instead. There is a shuddering in his bones. He totters for a second, collapses into the chair. She stands with her hands on her hips, bidding him towards her. When he doesn't move she stops dancing, reaches and turns down the stereo.

'Are you all right?' she says.

He reaches for his glass, uses strength he shouldn't need just to close his hand around it. She sits on the arm of the couch, next to him.

'Caleb?'

'Just a little tired,' he says. 'That's all.'

He finishes his glass of wine, the feeling coming back to his limbs inch by inch. He yawns a couple of times, then heads off, riding to clear his head. On the open road back to Rangimoana the headwind grips him. He rides blinking his eyes, his eyes dry behind his glasses.

He lifts one hand from the handlebars; it opens and closes without pain. He changes gears and rides on.

The house has been burning for less than ten minutes before the fire crew arrive, but that's enough to eat away half of it. Geronimo is the first on the ash-strewn lawn, then Troy and Monty and Jimbo. Tank works the water valves. A man steps from foot to foot by the hedge, nervous eyes scanning the property.

'I can't see everyone,' he shouts.

'Who's missing?' says Monty.

'There's an old bloke lives with them. I can't see him. Or the toddler either.'

Troy looks at the ragged jumble of people sitting on the footpath, the younger of the two women screaming.

'That's us, mate,' says Monty.

Troy and Monty sprint down the path, looking for a side entrance, the front verandah an open mouth of flame. Troy nods towards a path overgrown with weeds. They kick overhanging branches and bits of the hedge away, the burnt timber giving way as they reach the back. A rickety porch, soot-stained windows. Troy fixes his helmet tight to his head, pulls up the collar of his heavy jacket. Jimbo and Geronimo appear beside them, hands working the firehoses' nozzles. A nod to Monty and they smash through the glass of the rear door.

Troy peers through the smoke. A jet of spray crosses between him and Monty as Geronimo finds his target, sending them further into the house on a river of high-pressure water. Troy shakes his head clear, counting, guessing how to rebuild the crumbling architecture in his mind. One room, a bathroom, then the kitchen. Find the hall, then the doors that lead off it. An old bloke, the guy said, and a toddler. Monty takes the left side of the hall, Troy the right, feeling their way down the disintegrating walls as Geronimo's water jet crashes against their backs. The hose knocks off Troy's helmet. He reaches for it, misses, snatches again and grasps it, jams it back on his head. On the bed the figure of the old man looks tiny, like a small sack of rubbish or grass clippings. The walls are gone now, just the solid wood uprights remaining, and they're well aflame. A piece of wood cracks against his helmet, then another. He grabs the old man, drags him over the floor, then crouches, lifts him over his shoulder and walks, dodging tiles and ceiling fragments and flames, back down the corridor.

'Monty?'

No answer. He can't wait. He stumbles through the door. Geronimo steps aside and Jimbo takes the old man from Troy, carrying him over to the grass. Monty lies on the grass, pouring water over his face and hands, taking a few gulps into his mouth. Off to the side an ambulance man holds a child, the kid's eyes wide and staring, looking once over at Troy, then back at the fire.

When they get back out to the street a television crew has set up.

'Smile, cuz,' says Monty. 'The cameras are after you again.'

Troy glances at the camera, then away. Monty reaches over, fingers Troy's singed hair.

'You need to keep a tighter rein on that helmet, brother,' he says.

'That bastard Geronimo's loose with that hose!'

Monty bursts out laughing. The cameraman steps closer, almost between them, getting in Troy's way. Troy looks at him, then reaches and gestures him and his camera to one side.

The next evening Akiko stands at the bench, slicing carrots on the chopping board, when the news comes on. Politics, cricket, then a story about a fire. She takes a capsicum from the basket, glances back up at the screen, her cutting fingers falling still when she sees Troy in his fireman's outfit glance at the camera.

She picks up a tomato, then looks back once more at the screen. An item now on a Vietnam war protest at a university. The screen fades from her eyes. She looks back at the tomato, tart juice seeping down over her wrist and into her palm.

She looks up.

'Tell me,' she says, 'what do *you* see?'

Caleb flicks on the television and waits for it to warm up. When nothing happens after a few minutes he walks to it and thumps the top cover with the palm of his hand. The newsreader appears, frowning over his black-rimmed glasses. Caleb smiles; Harold Lloyd reading the news. He goes out to the kitchen, hears a reporter's voice say something about a fire. He opens the fridge door, examines the contents for something edible. He walks back into the lounge where the news has now shifted to a demonstration. He watches a few minutes, sipping on a glass of flat Coke, then lies back on the couch, turns away from the glare of the overhead light, blinks once, then tries to refocus his eyes, a little disoriented by the sudden change of light to dark. He realises when he sees the night beyond the windowglass that he must've been asleep for hours.

When he goes to stand his legs spasm. He sits back down, closes his eyes.

Akiko walks down her small hallway, picks up the phonebook and phone. *Fire Service.* She phones the first number listed. The woman's voice is stern, formal.

'The firemen that were on the television news last night,' says Akiko, 'can you tell me what station they were from?'

'Which blaze are you referring to?'

'The one on TV.'

'That's not much help.'

'Okay, it was a private house, don't know the suburb, but it was near the city. I could see the tall buildings in the background.'

Silence on the other end.

'I'd like to send them something,' says Akiko. 'You know,

a card or a gift.'

An exchange of voices, then another person comes on.

'There were engines from at least three stations at that fire,' says the woman.

'Then let me have them all.'

After the woman tells her, Akiko finds the number for each station and phones around, asking for a fireman named Troy. At the third station a fireman tells her that he's out the back on washing detail and tells her to hold on while he sings out, but she says not to worry, she'll call back later. But she doesn't. She gets in her car and drives up Ponsonby Road then takes Hopetown Street across to Pitt Street, stopping outside the fire station, looking at the engines behind the big doors. Then she carries on up to K Road, cruising the inside lane until she sees a fish and chips shop.

She drives back down to the station with a dozen pieces of fish and all the chips she can carry. She loops the strap of her bag over her shoulder and knocks on the station door, holding a cardboard tray and a steaming wad of newspaper.

A large man answers, unshaven. He follows his nose towards the wrapping of newspaper, then looks up at her face.

'I do hope you're looking for me,' he says.

'They're for everyone. I saw you guys on the news last night.'

'Flaming heck! Good timing.'

She hands him the package.

'Is Troy in?' she says.

'Hang on.'

Another fireman passes the doorway, stops when he smells the food.

'A Samaritan,' says the large man. 'Give Henare a whistle will you.'

The other fireman glances through the door at Akiko and

smiles, then heads up the stairs.

'Montgomery, at your service,' says the large man. 'Call me Monty. I'm rumoured to be the watch commander here.'

She glances to her left to where the fire engines loom, dwarfing her. When she looks back Troy stands at the foot of the stairs, wearing fireman's trousers but only a singlet on top. She takes a couple of steps towards him, wincing when she sees the reddened skin on his throat. The paperthin peels on his forehead.

'Ouch,' she says.

'About sums it up,' he says.

'Perhaps you should learn to duck.'

'I've often thought about it.'

She laughs.

'Sorry,' she says.

Monty walks past Troy. He turns and raises his eyebrows, then heads upstairs.

'So now I've seen where you work too,' says Akiko.

She undoes the clasp of her bag, then does it up again.

'I have to go,' she says.

'Do you?'

She raises her arm as if she's going to touch it against his, but she doesn't.

Troy nods.

'Thanks for the fish and chips,' he says. 'It's good to see you.'

'Is it?'

'Yes. Yes, it is.'

Akiko opens the door, nods once to Troy and steps out into the traffic noise. She stands on the empty pavement, fishing into her bag for her car keys. She finds them, stands with them jangling from her fingers.

'Well,' she says, 'we know where each other is.'

Caleb turns the tap off and the shower's jet stops. There is just the soft falling of the last stubborn drips around the ring. He feels for the towel over the rack, wipes his eyes. He goes to the basin and bench, leans on the Formica top, looking at his faint reflection in the steamed mirror glass. He scrapes a finger across the glass, then uses the four fingers of his left hand to draw a pattern like falling rain, down over his face to his waist.

He stands with a cup of coffee, looking through the window of his bedroom to the ocean. He turns and takes a crayon from the top of his writing desk, draws on the moist glass.

$$D + D \to {}^3He + n$$
$$D + D \to T + p$$
$$D + D \to {}^4He + gamma$$
$$p + D \to {}^3He + gamma$$
$$p + T \to {}^4He + gamma$$
$$D + T \to {}^4He + n$$

He knows already that nuclear fusion reactions occur in two separate stages. Stage one: the reactants fuse into an excited intermediate nucleus. The product of stage one is called a compound nucleus. In stage two the nucleus de-excites by decaying into another product such as helium three or four, plus a proton or neutron. These reactions are routine in hydrogen bombs, but they occur only at several million degrees.

He sits on his bed, looking up through the formulae to the sky.

A few days later Troy sits in the grass, looking up at the old clock tower. When its hands move to two o'clock he stands and walks to the auditorium. He leans against the metal rail shadowing a set of steps, watches the students emerge and walk off across the quadrangle. When no one appears for a couple of minutes he goes through the foyer and into the dark.

She sits on the stage, wearing leggings over her tights. Her dancing shoes are beside her. She sits with one knee raised and her chin resting on that knee, her eyes looking away into the dark, empty rows. He walks down the steps. She looks up.

'Part of me was hoping you wouldn't come,' she says.

He looks up into the racks of lights, only a few switched on, bright holes in the darkness. He stops at the edge of the stage, then walks on. When he reaches her he sits, not wanting to loom over her.

'Everything that happens on this stage happens for a reason,' she says. 'Every inch of it is an inch of me.'

'And the world outside?'

'Is the world outside. Have you come to ask me your question again?'

'No.'

'Aren't you curious any more?'

'Yes.'

She smiles.

'I can see I'm going to have to just push my way into your endless monologue,' she says.

He smiles this time. She grins, then stands and goes to the

edge of the stage and retrieves a string bag and her boots. She lifts a pair of jeans from the bag, slips them on over her tights. Troy watches her, the delicacy of the movement, her fingers reaching to flatten out the material of her tights where it bunches up with the pull upwards of her jeans. She glances at him, her eyes widening in mock admonishment and he looks away, squints into the lights. She walks towards him then pauses, balances on one leg, slips a boot over her toe. He steps to her and she uses his shoulder to balance while she puts the other one on.

'When's your next class?' he says.

'Tomorrow.'

'I was heading down to the water. Get some sea air.'

Akiko puts her point shoes on the back seat of her Mini and they walk to the Chev. Troy heads down to beach road and under the railway bridge to the waterfront. He swings into the car park at Mission Bay. A squall comes in from the harbour, rendering North Head little more than a sketch, Rangitoto almost a mirage. The windscreen begins to steam with the unexpected chill. Troy reaches into the back for his leather jacket, then opens the driver's door.

'Be back in a sec,' he says.

Akiko sits looking through the rain at the trees. A few minutes later Troy's voice appears beside her.

'Hey,' he says, 'you're getting wet!'

He has his jacket as a cape over his head. He passes her two polystyrene cups of hot tea, the rain unsettling the tea's surface. She takes both cups inside and then he runs around to the driver's side and steps in.

She winds the window up two-thirds of the way. The tea is still warm with his sprint across the grass. She sips from her cup, leans back in the seat, looks out at the slopes of Rangitoto rising through the rain.

'Did you know that Rangitoto means fire in the sky?' says Troy.

'No. I didn't.'

They both watch the showers drift.

'When was the last time it erupted?' says Akiko.

'Dunno. How long have you been in New Zealand?'

'Seven years.'

'Where are you from?'

'Nagasaki.'

She sips again from her tea.

'One more question,' says Troy.

She turns.

'Do you like old silent movies?' he says. 'There's some sort of festival on at the Imperial.'

'Are you asking if I'd like to go with you?'

'Yes.'

Akiko finishes the last of her tea. She looks back through the windscreen

'Yes,' she says. 'I do like silent movies.'

'I'm on the night watch until the weekend,' says Troy. 'But how does Saturday night sound?'

She nods, looks back up at him. She fumbles for something to do with the cup. Troy holds out his hand and she gives it to him and he sits looking at the polystyrene, runs his finger across it.

'What is it?' says Akiko.

Troy looks back up.

'Saturday night it is then,' he says.

Caleb sits among a pile of notes, writing in his rough scrawl. Jotting down jagged half-sentences on a page.

D2 gas molecule, bond distance 0.074 nanometers
Cold fusion rate (in theory) 3×10^{-64} sec^{-1}
Crap
One fusion a year in an amount of deuterium equal to a solar mass
Muon catalysed fusion two deuterium nuclei = 207 times smaller separation distance

The silent movie retrospective features shorts from Charlie Chaplin, Buster Keaton, Harry Langdon, Fatty Arbuckle and Harold Lloyd. Troy and Akiko sit by the aisle, Troy in a checked shirt and jeans. He and Akiko smile all the way through, laughing out loud a couple of times when Harold Lloyd battles to keep a turkey he won in a raffle secret from the rest of the passengers on a tramcar that doesn't allow animals on board. One stunt sets Akiko forward in her seat. Fatty Arbuckle strikes a match against a passing train then reaches with nonchalance to grab the handrail of the caboose and is flung through the air, landing with ease on the rear deck, standing smoking his cigarette. She half turns to Troy, the flickering screen lighting his curly hair. He shifts in his seat, reaches to brush his palm against a thigh. She feels his glance move to her and she looks back to the screen.

At intermission they sip Earl Grey in the theatre foyer, 1920s movie posters staring down from the walls around them. She leans against the leather seat, looking up at a poster, tracing the lines of Lon Chaney's clown make-up with her eyes.

'His parents were both completely deaf,' she says.

Troy raises his eyebrows.

'Lon Chaney,' says Akiko. 'They never spoke to him and he never spoke to them. So he grew up in a world of silence.'

'So silent cinema was the perfect place for him.'

'It would have seemed like home.'

The lights in the foyer dim. She looks towards the theatre entrance where the usherette stands in the doorway.

The session finishes with scenes from a Chaney film, *He Who Gets Slapped*. Chaney's clown stands with his face contorted in anger, spinning a globe, watching the earth and its continents and oceans spin out of control. Akiko slips a hand beneath Troy's on the wooden armrest. He squeezes it once, without looking away from the screen.

After the movie they sit at a traffic light. He lifts up his arm, glances at his watch. There is a faint red glow from the traffic light on the skin of his cheeks. The light changes and he drives on. He leaves her at her gate, easing it open with a hand then stepping aside.

'I may never have the answer to your question,' she says.

He stands still for a moment, then nods.

Wednesday, Akiko phones for Troy at the station. The guy who answers says that Red Watch isn't rostered on again until Thursday, but the bloody mob will probably be in the back bar at the Fisherman.

She drives downtown and goes into the Fisherman's public bar. The room is full of white-shirted men, some with ties dangling from collars pulled open with rough hands. Some of them look up from their beer glasses. For a few seconds there is a slight drop in the volume of voices, the knock of beer jugs on the tables now audible. She asks the barman about the back bar and he points to a corridor.

Monty looks up from a crowded table. He stands.

'Yikes,' he says, 'you've found our den of iniquity.'

'Your secret's safe with me,' says Akiko.

He points towards the rear of a trellis frame where Troy sits in jeans and a black T-shirt, his legs and feet raised up on the plastic chair next to him. Though the outdoor area is crowded with people, Troy sits alone. She stares through the cigarette smoke, between the leaning profiles of chatting faces. When she taps against the tabletop he looks up, surprise in his eyes.

'I fancy a movie,' she says. 'Something with sound this time.'

At the theatre he orders a tub of ice cream and two red plastic spoons and they both sit delving into it throughout the film. By the mid-point it's as liquid as cream. Akiko winces as James Bond dodges bullets. She takes the empty tub from Troy's fingers and sets it on the seat next to her. She puts her hand in his, smiling when she realises that both times she has touched him it has been within the flickering glow of a cinema screen. After the movie they walk back down Queen Street and cross to the wharves. The ship-berthing bays stretch out into the darkness. Troy looks down at the water, the first few yards glittering in the streetlights.

'I haven't mentioned to Caleb that we've met,' says Akiko. 'I'm not sure why.'

They walk along Princess Wharf. Hawsers hang down from a small ship, the rope creaking. There is a low hum from the engine. They walk between boxes and around to the empty side of the wharf. She brushes some grit from one of the metal bollards and sits. Troy sits on a wooden beam.

'You two aren't at all alike,' she says.

'Should we be?'

'I don't know.'

He kicks at a stone.

'Caleb said you've been in Vietnam,' she says.

'I did three tours.'

'But you were a soldier before that.'

He nods.

'I'm in the protest movement,' she says, 'against the war.'

His face shows no reaction. In fact it shows nothing at all. He looks out over the water to the far shore. The scarf of lights on the harbour bridge rises and falls in a huge arc.

He drives her back to the Fisherman, pulls into the kerb behind her parked Mini. He doesn't switch off the Chev's engine. Akiko reaches for the handle and opens the door, pauses with her hand resting on it, the scent of night air joining them in the car. Troy looks at his watch.

'Are you on duty soon?' asks Akiko.

'No, there's somewhere I've got to be.'

'At this hour?'

He nods. She looks at him.

'If you don't want me to be here,' she says, 'just say so.'

'I do. But like I said.'

She stays in her seat, draws the door closed.

They cross the harbour bridge, stop at a burger bar in Devonport and carry on north. Troy drives in silence, now and then reaching for a chip from the parcel sitting in Akiko's lap. She breaks off pieces of fish and dips them into tomato sauce for him. They pass beyond the last of the city lights, head up the coast highway.

A crowd gathers between the streetlights at the waterfront at Orewa, the wind off the bay billowing their jackets and jerseys. Salt spray splashes across the boulders. Heads turn as the Chev swings off the main road and into the beach car park.

'Is this the somewhere?' says Akiko.

Troy runs down through the car's gears and glides to a

stop. He turns to her.

'I won't be long,' he says.

'What?'

'If you just wait here. I won't be long.'

'I don't understand.'

'I won't be.'

His eyes are shadowed by the car's roof. They sit with the rumble of the engine making the seats beneath them shiver. Akiko steps out, watches Troy ease his car forward, next to another. She pushes through to the front of the crowd of fifty or so people, pulls up the collar of her suede jacket against the wind.

Troy flexes his fingers. The other car is a new Holden Monaro, its driver in his forties at least. The Monaro driver puts on his leather driving gloves, regards Troy with diffidence, though he looks with interest at the Chev. He pulls his keys from his pocket, reaches through the window and starts the Monaro's motor. He opens the door and slides in. Akiko stands against a tree. Troy glances once at her, then gets behind the wheel. A girl in jeans with a butterfly stitched onto the rear pocket walks between the cars. Troy hands her his money and the other driver does the same. She walks a few paces ahead and lifts off her sweater and raises it in her arms. Troy flicks the key in the ignition. He runs the wipers a couple of times, looks across at the Monaro and nods, his hand closing over the floor-shift handle.

A flicker of movement as the girl's sweater falls. Troy crunches the accelerator pedal, letting first go all the way up, then into second, third. Focusing on the bend approaching. Into fourth, the Chev easing away now. He stares at the power pole at the apex of the approaching corner, calculates his best line. Then he feels a shudder, glances in the mirror to see the Monaro angled towards him, then away. Then back again as the driver yanks hard on the wheel to try and run into his rear guard. He pulls hard on the Chev's steering wheel, in front of the Monaro now. He slams the brakes and the other driver does also, but locks up. Troy accelerates away again, a last glimpse in the mirror as he rounds the bend, the Monaro trying to get back up to speed, but his revs shot to hell. Troy swings wide, cutting off the Monaro's driving line. There is a squeal of brakes from behind him. Troy goes into the corner, hands gripped so hard on the steering wheel that his fingernails dig into his own skin. The Monaro driver tries to correct, but skids on the sea-wetted pavement, travels up over the curb and into the sea wall. Troy doesn't hear the crash over the roar of his engine, just sees the scattering glass in the street light's glow.

He slows, turns halfway round in the street. His fingers are ice on the steering wheel. Lights begin to go on in the houses looking out over the water. He sits, breathing hard, then slams into reverse, swings around, shifts the gear lever into first and floors it. The Monaro is crumpled against a power pole. The driver leans against the sea wall, half-toppled like a midnight drunk. A couple of running figures appear in driveways. A torch beam skitters. The Chev passes them all in a blur, crossing the centre line when he sees the youths gathered at the race's starting point. His tyres slip on the wet stones. He sights the girl with the butterfly pocket.

'Hey!'

She runs over, hands him a wad of money. He doesn't have time to count it. Akiko runs from the grass berm beneath the trees, gets in beside him and slams the door.

'Shit!'

'What?' says Troy.

'I couldn't tell from here whether it was him or you!'

She punches his shoulder, then folds her arms, looks out at the darkened sea. The sound of a siren whines, getting closer. The crowd that stood watching only a few seconds ago has vanished. Troy takes a side street, then heads back up to the highway. He can sense her seething beside him.

'I won't watch you kill yourself,' she says.

'I'm not interested in killing myself.'

'Does that make a difference?'

When she turns to him her eyes are wet. Even in the darkness, he can see them. He shouldn't be able to, but he can.

'If you even attempt to make some bullshit promise,' she says, 'I'll hit you.'

'I've got nothing to promise you.'

She stares out the window. He bites down on his bottom lip, blinks hard as he begins to speak.

'Look –'

'Don't,' says Akiko.

He tries to reshape his words, but she raises a hand against the flicker of streetlights. He looks back to the road.

He could head straight back across the bridge to town, but he doesn't. Instead they track the full moon's path in the sky, clean across the country to the wilds of the west coast. In the sweep of headlights from a passing car he notices her leaning to one side, away from him. Asleep, he guesses. Part of him hopes she is. He slows, eases to the side of the road and stops, leans forward and takes off his leather jacket. He drapes it over her chest, feeling her move as he raises the edge up beneath her chin. He drives on, avoiding each road he knows will hasten her home, takes other winding paths instead. He glances down at her in the glow of each passing set of headlights, grateful for once for oncoming traffic. He drives on for an hour, finally pulling up at a gravel turnaround above a sweep of black sand. He steps from the car, looks down at the huge chunks of driftwood. Even in the pale moonlight the logs sit white as glacial ice against the crashing waves.

A crunch of stones. Akiko walks to him, then away across the shells, the wind rustling her hair across her face. He watches her pass across the moon-dusted sand, her figure breaking the line of the horizon. She calls and he goes to where she stands with something in her hand. He opens his palm beneath hers, raising hers up against the moonlight. A pāua shell, its iridescent centre hidden in shadow. He guides her hand to just above the apex of her collar bones, as if the shell is a pendant. She offers it to him, but he flips it over, still in her palm, closes her hand around it.

He is too tired to drive back to the city. He gets a blanket from the boot. In the night she lies curled on the back seat, wrapped in the blanket. Troy sits with his jacket over him, leaning against the door frame. Glass against his cheek.

In the faint dawn light he turns, taps the leg of her jeans, but she is still asleep. He walks up into the dunes. He watches the east turn grey, the grass coming alive yard by yard in the new light. He goes back to the car and sits blinking the sleep from his eyes, looking up at the pāua shell sitting on the dashboard, like the hull of a tiny boat.

In full light they walk down to the water, stand in the lowest of the waves, Troy running his sea-wetted hands over her cheekbones. He flicks at the wisps of hair trapped within her scarf, freeing them to the wind.

'What does Akiko mean?'
'One meaning is autumn's child.'
'Were you born in the autumn?'
'No. In the summertime.'
He waits for her to explain but she doesn't.

'I don't need saving,' she says. 'Not when you stepped up onto my stage and not now.'

'Neither do I,' says Troy.

'I just need you to know that.'

He nods.

'Don't think I'm not still angry with you,' she says.

He looks at her for a moment, then lifts the pāua shell from his pocket and blows a breath into it, closing her hand around it.

'I guess,' she says, 'I'm just not sure I want to love someone who could die at any minute. That's all.'

'Then you'll never love anyone,' says Troy.

IX

Puff, the Magic Dragon

Rangimoana
April, 1989

Rai stands at the arrivals gate of the international terminal. Behind her the individual panels on the flight information board click over, numbers changing as new information supersedes old. She takes her diary out of her kete and checks Etta's flight details again, then takes an elastic tie and draws her hair back, setting its length through the tie, glancing forward again when the first figures come through the gate.

Etta also has her long hair tied back in a pony tail, though unlike Rai's it is grey fading to white. Rai smiles, watching the flicker of Etta's figure ripple between the other passengers. She watches her grandmother for a good ten seconds before Etta notices her and stops, her eyes wide.

'You're not gawky any more, kid,' says Etta when they meet.

They hug.

'Let me look at you,' says Etta, leaning back. Etta's eyes are still green, greener still perhaps for the fading of the skin around them. Etta talks about her flight, about the crappy coffee and crappier food. Rai says nothing.

'Am I going to get a word out of you?' says Etta.

'Watermelon,' says Rai.

Etta laughs. They hug again, then go to the luggage carousel. They drive in Rai's old Volkswagen, towards the Manukau Harbour, the obelisk on One Tree Hill beckoning out of the pale blue sky.

'I've been sprucing the old place up a bit,' says Rai.

'Will I recognise it?' says Etta.

Rai looks across at her, thinks to answer, but doesn't. Twenty minutes later they are still locked in the suburbs, with traffic lights and queues clamping them to the city. When at last they strike some green, leave the western suburbs behind, Rai notices Etta has her face against the windowglass, her eyes closed.

Rai takes the road out to the coast. When they crest the hill above Rangimoana the sweep of the bay opens up.

She has one bag of clothes, and two camera cases that look like they've been dropped from a skyscraper. Battered and peeling and scarred. But the locks still sit tight and Etta seems to pay their worn skins no mind. The two women lug the cases inside the house and Rai makes sandwiches. From the kitchen she can hear doors opening and closing, Etta's footsteps around the house. She debates for a moment going with her, but then decides to leave her be.

Etta sits, leans back on the couch.

'You can have your old bedroom,' says Rai, handing her a plate.

Isaac walks down his railway carriage's rear steps, onto the dew-soaked grass. He grips a plastic bag in his hand, his jandals clack-clacking against his bare feet as he walks into the marshes, where he climbs a small grass mound edged with toetoe. He opens the plastic bag and scatters pieces of bread onto the grass. By the time he is halfway back to the carriage he can see the shadows of gathering birds arrowing across the grass.

He puts the kettle on. When it boils he walks over to the bench, pausing when he glances up and sees his thin face in the mirror, through a shroud of steam.

Rai makes a breakfast of tea and toast and sits out on the deck with Etta. Etta reaches for the margarine, spreads some on her slice. She has left her hair untied this morning and it strays across her face. Rai glances down to where its tails reach to Etta's waist. The tips are whiter than the smoke-grey roots.

'I let it grow long when I stopped climbing in and out of helicopters,' says Etta.

Rai takes a bite of toast. 'What was the shoot in the States?'

Etta looks up. 'New Mexico,' she says. 'The Trinity site.'

'Trinity?'

Etta looks away off the edge of the deck, towards the dunes. 'Where they tested the bombs they dropped on Japan,' she says.

'Why do they want photos of that stuff now?'

'A revisiting, I guess.'

'What's there now?'

'Nothing much. How are your studies?'

'Hard work. Fitting in my lectures and assignments with the part-time job.'

'Are you managing?'

'Sort of.'

Rai leans back in her wooden chair, her elbows on the armrests. She could tell Etta about the time that she's been spending with Isaac, of her regrets at all the time she hasn't spent. But there is something different about Etta now.

Something different in the Etta she picked up from the airport than the Etta she had stood at the departure gate and waved to four years ago, or the Etta who stares out of the sole photograph of her among the hundreds on the walls of the house at Rangimoana.

Something in her eyes.

Isaac sits on the edge of a chair out on the grass, bending to polish the Indian's rear wheel fairing. He stares into the guard's faded teal-blue paint, seeing in it the miles of ocean and land it has travelled to get to this point. Seeing also his own miles of ocean and road and rail and desert.

He sits running cloth over metal until his hand begins to ache. He looks at it, shakes his head at the advance of age. He leans back, drops the wet cloth back in the plastic bucket. Droplets splash his bare legs beneath the frayed fringes of his cut-down trousers. The Indian shines in the afternoon sun.

December, 1969

Caleb sits among the children on the lawn, handing out little paper folds of coloured chalk dust. He moves them back into a circle, leaving an empty ring of grass in the middle. He leans forward and opens his paper fold then blows a breath across it. A tiny cloud of sky-blue dust stretches then fades. A couple of the children pick up their little sachets and do the same. Smaller clouds form and fade. The children laugh, all raise their paper folds.

'No, not yet,' says Caleb. 'When I signal. Remember the song?'

They sit nodding, then begin to sing.

Puff, the magic dragon lived by the sea
And frolicked in the autumn mist in a land called Honah Lee,
Little Jackie Paper loved that rascal Puff,
And brought him strings and sealing wax and other fancy stuff,
oh

As they sing they watch Caleb.

Oh Puff, the magic dragon lived by the sea
And frolicked in the autumn mist in a land called Honah Lee,

'Now!' says Caleb.

All the children blow and clouds of coloured dust hang for a few seconds, then vanish. Red, orange, yellow, green, blue, indigo, violet.

A rainbow among them.

While he sings the next verse the children pick up more powder, ready for the next chorus.

Akiko sits in her yukata, cross-legged on her couch. Troy lies on the floor beside her. Two candles burn in small, round dishes, beneath ornate stands with cups of oil-scented water. Troy glances up at the scissors she holds. She moves closer, lifts the scissors and begins to snip off a few singed strings of hair. He blinks.

'That should do it,' she says.

She touches the faintest of fingertips against his eyelashes, then leans back, puts the scissors up on the little table. She drops the strands of burnt hair in the wicker wastepaper basket.

'You look tired,' she says.

He glances at the wicker basket.

'Too many crazy hours,' she says, 'getting up to fight fires.'

'I'll be on day watch again next week,' says Troy.

'When you're on nights you should sleep during the day.'

'I can't sleep in daylight.'

'You don't sleep much in darkness either.'

He stands and walks to her mantelpiece.

'Is that the pāua shell from the other night?' he says.

'Yes.'

'Where'd you get so many shells?'

'Just picked them up, whenever I went to the beach. How could you tell that one from all the others?'

'Just could.'

He flicks at a foolscap-sized box on the mantelpiece. A rip in the cardboard box reveals coloured paper beneath. He lifts it out and opens it, leafs through the various sheets. Crimson, jade, aquamarine. He glances along the bookshelf at some of her handmade books.

'Do you use this for them?' he says.

'No, it's origami paper.'

'Can you make stuff with it?'

'Yes.'

He brings it over, sits on the floor in front of her.

'Now?' she says.

'I'd like to see some.'

Akiko slides out the page of crimson, runs her fingertips over the paper's face. Smooth, alive, like a leaf's skin.

'Try it with me,' she says.

Troy takes the yellow sheet. Akiko begins to fold one corner, reshaping it. She looks up at Troy, guides him on with her eyes.

'What's it going to be?' says Troy.

'You'll find out,' says Akiko.

She folds another line, gestures for Troy to follow, to mirror her movements. He fumbles for a while, his fingers rushing.

'Slow down a bit,' says Akiko. 'It's not a drag race. Just feel your way.'

She makes the next fold then lays her hands close over his, but not touching him. They work in silence. Akiko makes one last fold and she sits back, lifts her hands away from the figure of the origami bird.

Troy sits looking at what he has folded.

'It's a duck,' says Troy. 'I've made a duck.'

'Mine's a crane,' says Akiko.

'Like I said. It's a crane. I've made a crane.'

'They're considered lucky. A symbol of a long life.'

She lifts her paper crane up to eye level, then sets it down in the open palm of her hand. Troy holds his up, so the two figures mirror each other. He leans forward and blows a breath across her hand. The paper ripples in the tiny wind.

Two days after Etta had photographed Troy and the children in the river, he'd hitched a ride with an Australian helicopter. When he returned to the New Zealand infantry camp an officer stood in the doorway.

The officer glanced at Troy's empty ammunition belt, then down at his rifle. 'You got anything left in that?' he asked.

'I always keep a few,' said Troy. 'At least one.'

The officer ran his tongue across his lips, swatted at a couple of flies with his hand. He looked over at a rough fence of stakes, beyond which three figures stood in the rain, hands in their pockets.

'Keep an eye on them,' he said, 'until I figure out what the hell to do with you.'

Two of the prisoners were teenagers. The other was an old man, balding and bow-legged. All were dressed in black. The old man kept talking to the boys. The guard Troy relieved said he'd told the old man several times to shut the hell up, once even entering the holding pen to crack him over the head with the butt of his rifle. When he stepped beyond the stakes again the old man had reached up, touched his fingertip to his bleeding forehead, then began talking again to the boys.

Troy didn't bother to tell him to be quiet, just stood watching him for a while, noting the increasing anger in his voice, the quiver of spit on his lips.

The rain began to ease. Night fell, quiet.

Troy upended an old drum and sat. He raised his chin to the old man and asked him in his bad Vietnamese how old he was. The old man stared. Troy asked him again, this time in his even worse French and the old man narrowed his eyes and asked him, in French, why he wanted to know. Troy shrugged. The old man looked with disdain at the two boys, then back up through the vertical lines of green between the stakes at him.

'Sixty-two,' he said in Vietnamese.

Troy nodded, asked him in Vietnamese how, with his creaking bones and bow legs, he'd expected to stay free and he laughed and said he'd never been free but he was looking forward to it. Troy told him he might not recognise freedom if ever he found it, but he smiled again and said he would. Or his children or grandchildren would.

'Are they your boys?' said Troy, nodding at the two others.

The old man spat into the ground, shook his head. Then he said he had fought the French and he had fought the Japanese and now the Americans and their criminal friends and if men with three heads and fiery wings dropped from the sky and landed on his soil he would fight them too.

'My father was killed by men who dropped from the sky,' said Troy, in English.

The old man's brow tightened, he shook his head, so Troy repeated what he'd said, in Vietnamese. The old man nodded, asked Troy if his father had died on his own ground.

'No.'

The old man turned away, his body so thin, dirty clothes sticking to his withered bones. The skin of his hands seemed to be peeling in the net of moonlight coming through the trees.

'E hoa,' said Troy, 'ka whawhai tonu mātou. Ake! Ake! Ake!'

The old man looked back, raised his eyebrows. He asked Troy what he'd said.

'Friend, we shall fight on forever and ever and ever,' said Troy in Vietnamese and with that the old man smiled. Troy stood and raised his rifle and the old man braced himself, spoke to the boys and told them to stand also. Troy looked down at the barrel, all three of the figures in the pen also staring at it. He took the safety catch off the rifle and pointed it into the pen. The old man's eyes widened and he took a deep breath, his shrunken chest expanding an inch at most, in shambling defiance. He glared at Troy. One of the boys began to cry. A loud fart came from his friend and a dark trickle appeared over his bare feet. The old man still glared. He said something in Vietnamese that Troy couldn't understand. Troy leaned forward, pulled the rope from the gate and eased it open. The old man looked at the gap, large enough only for his frail silhouette. Troy nodded and the old man stepped past him and he closed the gate again, the two of them standing in the mud. Troy stepped back and the old man walked, then crept towards the trees, glancing back every other footstep. At the forest's edge he turned full to face Troy and nodded and Troy nodded too and then the old man glared at Troy one last time and spat into the dirt and was gone.

Somewhere a toad bellowed, leaves swished against sodden branches. Troy closed the gate, sat back on the drum, looking at the two boys.

Troy.
Troy, says the photographer on the riverbank.

'Troy,' says Akiko.

He looks up.

'Sometimes I wonder if I have to send out a search party to find you,' says Akiko.

He smiles, then senses his smile fading.

'I should go,' he says.

'Should you?'

'Yeah.'

'That's the second time you've said that to me.'

He looks into her dark pupils, sensing her standing alone on an empty stage. The sound of his boots walking towards her.

'I should,' he says. 'I'm just tired, that's all.'

He walks out into the rain, holding his leather jacket up over his head as he dashes down the path. He sits in the Chev, the motor running, watching the raindrops vanish in the wake of the wiper blades. He turns to where she stands in her doorway, her face backlit, hidden. Maybe it was just curiosity at first, how he followed not his brother but the woman who was with him. She was a stranger until that moment when she stood alone on the stage, moving neither forward nor back. The moment when he realised that even though the last five years of his life have been lived at light speed, in reality he too was standing still.

He slips the wheel through his fingers, eases down the driveway and out onto the rainswept street.

She stays in the doorway, watching the rain cover the dry patches where his car's tyres passed. The pitch of the engine rises, falls and rises again. Begins to fade, but doesn't vanish.

It seems, with the wind, to come from all directions, then settle into a circle around her. Around her driveway. She steps out to the edge of the verandah, listens to it, realising then it *is* circling. She walks full out into the rain, turning as the engine grows louder to look to the left of her gate where the headlights appear and the car turns back in and stops in front of her. She looks down at her clothes, the beams washing over her, then dying in an instant. The engine stills.

'I was wrong,' he says as he steps out. 'I don't want to go.'

'You didn't say you wanted to go. You said you should.'

In her bedroom she undoes her yukata's strap, slips into the sheets. He flicks off the light, undresses and moves to get in beside her.

'Can you turn the light on in the hall,' she says. 'Leave the door open a little.'

'Sure.'

Her eyelids close against his chest, then she looks up. His face is lit by the light around the edge of the door. A hand touches against her hair. Fingertips circling.

'If you weren't born in the autumn,' says Troy, 'why did they call you autumn's child?'

'Shhhhh.'

'It's only a question.'

'Shhhhh, Troy. Just sleep.'

'I haven't slept for years.'

The next day he hunts the shops for origami paper. He gets some blank stares.

'Won't just any coloured paper do?'

'I don't think so,' says Troy.

At the third shop the woman smiles and goes into the back, coming out with a box just like the one on Akiko's mantelpiece. Troy reaches into his pocket for his wallet.

'Is there, like, a book on how to do this stuff?' he says.

The woman squints her eyes for a moment, then leads him off down one of the aisles.

He spends an hour parked in the Chev in the little lay-by next to the rose gardens in Parnell, glancing up now and then at the forklifts moving about on the wharves below. He folds four figures, each one less fumbled than the last, following the instructions in the book for the first two then working from memory and instinct after that. He folds one more, his movements quicker this time. His mind goes through the instructions from the inside, as if he is teaching an invisible student. He sits the last one at the end of the line, then sits back, looks along the row of figures.

'Duck. Duck. Duck. Duck …'

He looks long at the last one, then takes the others off the dashboard top.

'You, my friend,' he says to the folded figure.

He drives to Akiko's flat, sets the last paper crane on the front door mat and leaves.

In the evening Akiko sits sketching choreography routines, her hands adept at movement, her lines always between one state and another. She cannot draw portraiture – her eye loses touch with figure and features if they remain still. She can capture instants only, not minutes. The features on still figures – a leaf, a twig, a stone – slip back into the weave of the paper like insects whose camouflage renders them part of the landscape. It is only when they move that they come alive to her eyes.

Tonight she draws a male figure, moving from step to step, in one continuous line from her pencil. She takes the front of a foot of one as the cue to begin the rear of the foot of the next, each giving birth to another. She angles her head, stands and walks around the page, stilling the figure and transferring his movements to her own feet.

Troy arrives again in darkness. This time she hears his car in the street and opens the door just as he raises his hand to knock. She takes his hand and unwinds his balled fist against her lips. Finger by finger. When he blinks into his momentary sleep she is with him now on the page, even though he is still and it is she again who is moving. In her dreams she steps around him, her toes tapping out the architecture of a circle, a moat around him. In the night she rolls over, again and again, sensing even in her sleep that he will not let his arms slip from holding her.

He wakes at dawn and walks naked down her hall to the bathroom, pausing to look out the end window, through the stripes of the venetian blinds to the tree-fringed gully. He hears bathwater begin to run behind him, looks down into the nīkau leaves on the slope, turning only when she steps against him, eases her arms around his waist. Her hands crossing one over the other at his navel.

'Don't leave me today,' she says. 'I don't care if the whole world is on fire, don't leave me.'

They step into the steam, Akiko fumbling for the taps. She touches against the edge of the bath with her toes, is about to step into it when Troy snatches her off her feet and she explodes into laughter. He raises her so her head is almost to the ceiling, then steps over the rim of the bath and in, sitting back against the cool, wet enamel then letting himself slip into the hot water, Akiko tight against him. Inch by inch they break the surface, the water lapping at the top edge of the bath. Two pairs of eyes stare at it, waiting for it to overflow, but it doesn't, it just vibrates, oscillates. Waves and troughs, then quiescence. He runs his fingers up over her breasts and collarbones, up her cheeks to her eyes. He feels her lids close against his fingerprints. Her lips are against his wrists, as if she wishes to plug into his veins.

They sit stock still, photograph still, for a dozen sweet breaths, then he moves his hands again. Up and over her, feeding strands of her wet hair into his mouth. He bites against them and she laughs and he lowers his hands into the water, cups them then raises them, releases the water over her hair. She leans back against him, her breathing seeming as deep as the gully beyond the window. Deep enough to swallow the trees and soil and rainwater in the leaves. He washes her hair, strand by strand. Not with soap, but with the touch of his lips.

Against the swirls of history in the skin of his fingertips, he can feel her smile.

The sheets are wet within seconds of the two of them slipping within their folds, the towel let fall on the floor. They roll over and over like the circles of a scroll, then he lies on his back, pushing himself up the sheets until he is against the headboard and she lies on top of him. He raises her so she straddles him, her hair dancing over her breasts and tummy, sweeping from side to side as she angles her head. Her eyes look into him. His own eyes widen with an electricity that she feels; she grabs his hands, rubs the palms hard over her nipples. Then gentler, Troy lifting his hand a few hundredths of an inch away from her so she has to stretch to reach him.

He raises her, slips further down the bed and tastes her, her legs forming a bay for him to shelter in. Her secret waters. His lips, then his whole body anointed. In the midst of her he finds he wants to talk, now, of all times. Tell her everything. But he will not, he does not. The only sound is the rustle of her scarves shimmering in the wind. *What do you see when you dance*, he had asked her, and he senses now she will not tell him with words. He rolls her over, rises above her, looks down for one last moment, knowing his eyes carry the question, in the way the outline of her body carried a question that first time he had seen her dance. She blinks and he leans to her, clears the hair from her eyes with his lips, lets it fall on the sodden pillow.

The last thing he sees before he closes his eyes is *her* eyes falling closed.

When she wakes it is afternoon. Her cheek is against Troy's hip, their figures are an X on the rectangle of the bed's frame. The bittersweetness of their scent clothes her. She kisses his bare skin, then again. She runs her tongue over the ridge of his hip-bone, taps him with a fingertip to see if he is awake. He doesn't move. She rolls over, looks up at the ceiling. The shadows of the leaves on the trees outside are like a pulse of veins beneath skin. She raises a hand, wonders if her faint shadow could leave an imprint amidst so many. A stir in his muscles, tendons flexing, and he sits up. His face over her. She looks up.

'Hello, stranger,' she says.

'Stranger?'

She crinkles her nose and pushes him back down onto the mattress and straddles him. Insisting on his hardness with the pressure of her body against him. Her taut tummy is against the cut steps of his midriff. She leans over, bites him on the end of his nose and he melts into laughter for a moment, then tenses again. She moves against him to guide him into her and then just lies still, full with him. Neither of them move for a long time, then she lays her head on his shoulder and glances to where her tree of scarves shimmers like the current she can feel in every muscle. Every sinew.

A few days later Troy goes to pick Akiko up from university. He looks at his watch. He's early. He parks at the kerb on Princes Street, sits looking up at the people coming and going. Then one catches his eye. Not Akiko, Caleb. Caleb walks over the pedestrian crossing towards a few motorbikes parked on their stands. Troy pulls out, drives towards him. When the Chev is level to where Caleb is setting his satchel in the Indian's carrier bag Troy stops, reaches over and pushes open the right-hand door. He touches a hand against the horn. Caleb looks up, then buckles the carrier bag closed and walks towards the Chev.

'Li'l brother,' says Troy.

'Not so little.'

'Yeah,' he says, 'it's been a while.'

'Nice wheels,' says Caleb.

'They'll do.'

'When did you get back?'

'A while ago.'

'On leave or for good?'

'For good.'

'Good.'

'Yeah.'

Caleb crouches, one hand on the open door. Troy looks into his eyes, seeing for a moment the tiny eyes that had looked across from him from the other small bed in their room when they were kids. Open wide, considering, questioning.

'What are you doing these days?' says Caleb.

'I'm a fireman.'

Caleb chuckles.

'What?' says Troy.

'You said you would.'

'Yeah.'

'Yeah.'

A car behind Troy beeps its horn. He looks up in the rear-view mirror.

'I better move,' he says.

Caleb stands, pushes the door closed. He bends down to the window. 'I'm still out at the house,' he says. 'You know where to find me.'

'Yeah,' says Troy. 'Okay.'

Caleb steps back, his face hidden by the ceiling. Then he walks back to the Indian. Troy is about to move when he sees Akiko come round the corner from the library. He watches Caleb ride away, then moves forward, slowing when Akiko waves.

Caleb takes a bottle of sparkling wine from the larder, opens it. The cork hits the ceiling. He ducks as it comes back down but it still hits him on the head. He crouches, laughing. Akiko calls out from the other room.

'Nothing,' he says. 'Just some target practice.'

He takes the bottle and two glasses into the lounge and they sit sipping until he notices a numbness in his hand. He sets the glass back down, flexes his fingers.

'Pins and needles?' says Akiko.

'Sort of.'

'Perhaps your hand is drunk.'

He raises the glass again, but his grip ebbs and he drops it on the floor. Wine splashes on Akiko's bare feet.

'Shit,' he says.

'Are you okay?' asks Akiko.

She lifts her foot away from the broken glass. Droplets slip down from her foot onto the floor.

He reaches down for the biggest glass fragments, his fingers fumbling.

'Don't do that,' says Akiko. 'I'll get the dustpan.'

They clear the broken glass, wipe the floor clean. Akiko puts on her shoes, just in case. She sits watching him sip from a new glass.

'What's the occasion, anyway?' she says.

'For what?'

'The wine.'

'Nothing. Just felt like it.'

They sit sipping, watching the day fade. Akiko leans back on the couch. Caleb sits forward.

'I saw Troy yesterday,' he says.

She sets down her glass.

'What did he say?' she says.

'Not much.'

'Not much?'

'No. Just, hello. That sort of stuff.'

'Nothing else?'

'He's left the army, got a job as a fireman. He used to talk us to death when we were kids, talking about how he was going to be a fireman.'

'But he became a soldier instead.'

'Yeah.'

Caleb raises his glass, drinks.

'Yeah,' he says, 'he became a soldier instead.'

A week later Troy knocks on Akiko's door.

'Have you just come from a fire?' she says.

'Yeah, sorry.'

She reaches up and bends his head forward and kisses him on his forehead. He guesses the scent of smoke is still in his hair. He hasn't thought about that until now.

She runs a bath and they sit, still clothed, on the edge of it, Akiko on his knee. Balancing. Her feet stretched against the tiles, arched.

'Don't apologise,' she says.

In the bath he soaps her. His fingers slipping down across the planes of her cheeks, the shelf of bone so sharp, as if carved from teak or sandalwood. But her eyelids are soft, her lips softer still and moist as she tongues his fingertips then turns around in the bath and he opens his own lips. Steam against his skin, her own wetness in this world of water. He stands and lifts her into his arms, and she shrieks as they bisect the doorway with a fraction of an inch to spare. He walks, oozing water, carrying her, dripping, down the hall to where they swim on her sheets. He wraps her in their cocoon, rolling her over like a breaking wave.

In the night she hears him stir, get up and go to the kitchen. The creak of taps running. He comes back but doesn't get back into bed. He stands by the window in the light from the streetlamp, filtered through the trees as if through gauze.

'Hey,' she says.

He turns around and the light shifts with each touch of wind in the branches, brighter now at the base of his throat. He moves and it moves, inch by inch, until it is over his heart.

Caleb sits in the doctor's waiting room, one arm and hand flat on the armrest of the couch, the other across his chest. He tries to blink away his tiredness, but doesn't succeed. The doctor arranges some blood tests and Caleb sits watching the nurse arrange the five vials into a kidney-shaped enamel dish, then look at him. He watches also as she slips the needle into his arm, curious at the pressure within him that feeds the blood into the glass vial like water from a tap.

'When will I have the results back?' asks Caleb.

'Not until after Christmas.'

He nods, presses with a couple of fingers on the needle's insertion point.

On Christmas morning Caleb sleeps late, sits up blinking hard at the sound of Akiko's voice in the hall. He walks out, stands in just his beach baggies, squinting into the bright sunshine through the kitchen windows.

'Hard night?' she says.

'Something like that.'

She has made a trifle. She opens the refrigerator door and puts it in among the stale bread and a ragged sheath of paper with chips spilling out of it. She steps back, frowning.

'You should look after yourself better,' she says.

'Too true.'

He makes her some ginseng tea and they sit out on the deck.

'When are you going to see your dad?' she asks.

'Tomorrow.'

They go for a walk on the beach.

'Are you happy, Kiki?' he asks over the roar of the waves.

She doesn't answer. She picks up a shell and skims it towards the surf where it vanishes without bouncing.

'I have never been good at that,' she says.

Caleb picks up a shell, bends and throws it. It also vanishes without bouncing. Akiko goes to pick up another shell but stops. She takes a couple of paces further up the beach and stands holding a large pāua shell.

'Cool,' says Caleb. 'Add it to your collection.'

She stands holding it for a moment, as if weighing it. She looks up at him, then sets the shell back in the sand.

The next day Caleb rides out of Auckland and heads to Mount Iris. The roads are quieter than normal, with a few caravans and boats on trailers dotted among the cars. He puts the Indian on its stand in the car park and lifts a plastic box and a giftwrapped package from a saddlebag. He checks through the guard house and walks up the concrete driveway towards the front entrance, his head turning when he sees a hand wave. He steps onto the gravel path winding among the trees, nods his head as Isaac lowers his raised hand.

'Happy Hanukkah,' says Caleb when they greet.

Isaac opens his arms and the two men hug. Caleb steps back, hands Isaac the wrapped book. Isaac loosens the wrapping with his fingernail, peels the top of the giftwrap back. He clears the paper, lifts the book up into the light.

Feynman on Physics.

'Did you know Feynman?' says Caleb.

'I worked with him at Los Alamos, heard him play the bongo drums.'

'Was he any good?'

'Not on the bongos.'

Isaac puts the book down on the wooden bench and they sit taking the sun.

'I like the sound of the birds here,' says Caleb.

'So do I. Only reason I come here.'

Caleb bends and opens the box and takes out the trifle. He reaches into the pocket of his denim jacket, lifts out two plastic forks wrapped in paper napkins. Isaac glances down at the trifle.

'Akiko,' says Caleb.

Caleb shifts sideways, making some room to set the box between them.

'Christmas,' he says.

'A choir visited, to sing carols,' says Isaac. 'They set up in the common room. Formed into a semicircle and stood bellowing, staring wide-eyed at us. I don't know who was more wary, the choristers or the patients.'

'Yeah. We had the RSA band out on the beach at Rangimoana on Christmas Eve. Trombones and trumpets. Remember that tiny old guy with the tuba as big as he is? "Silent Night" against the surf. "Wenceslas" against the westerly.'

He and Isaac sit scooping at the trifle until it is two-thirds finished, then Caleb drops the forks into the box and snaps the lid back on.

'I've nominated cold fusion as my thesis problem,' says Caleb.

Isaac lifts a handkerchief from his pocket, touches it against his lips.

'Good for you,' he says. 'Put me to shame.'

'I intend to. Thanks for the idea.'

'It wasn't my idea.'

Caleb sets the box down on the seat next to him. He glances down at the gravel of the path through the gaps between the fading green-painted wood of the bench. He picks at a flake of paint with a fingernail, looks back up into the trees.

'Tell me about Antarctica,' he says.

A shift in the breeze sets the poplar leaves glistening.

'Why?' says Isaac.

'I need to know.' Caleb gestures with a hand at the pristine grounds, at the hospital building. 'I need to know where all this began,' he says.

'It didn't begin in Antarctica.'

Caleb turns to Isaac.

'Then tell me where it did,' he says.

Isaac stands and walks to the garden and comes back with a twig. He leans and scratches a couple of lines into the gravel. Then more, until a drawing of a Hanukkah candle emerges from the dust.

'A while ago,' he says, 'one of the other patients, my room-mate, tried to hang himself. He tied his socks together, looped one end around his throat and tied them to the light fitting. He stood on his bed and jumped.'

'What happened?' says Caleb.

'The knot unwound. He tried again and again, but the knot kept unwinding.'

'So what did he do?'

'He started to cry.'

'What did you do?'

'Nothing.'

'You didn't try to stop him?'

'I was curious. He'd only tied the knot once. It was never going to hold. I wasn't watching him die.'

'So what were you watching?'

'I was watching the knot. Not the person. I've always been curious about knots.'

Isaac reaches down with the stick, draws a circle in the middle of the candle, then rays radiating outwards.

'You don't need my ghosts inside you,' he says.

'I already have them.'

Isaac scratches out the shape of the candle, leaving the radiating sun. A tiny cloud of dust rises.

On the last day before the Nuclear Age began, the plutonium bomb sat on its one hundred foot high tower above the floor of the Jornada del Muerto in New Mexico. Jornada del Muerto – the journey of death – had been named by sixteenth-century Spaniards after a party of travellers had perished there for want of water.

To hide the inhabitants of the Manhattan Project laboratories at Los Alamos from prying eyes, the military had given them all one address. PO Box 1663, Albuquerque, New Mexico.

The day before test day Isaac sat in a jeep, looking up at the tower etched against the desert sky. The bomb's platform still now, after all the hubbub of the previous days with physicists and engineers crawling over its framework. A few had posed for final photographs next to the gadget, then the last of them climbed down the snakes and ladders board of tubes and scaffolding and stepped into the desert dust.

Outside of a small circle, the rest of the world was unaware of not only the event but the years of work that had gone into planning for this moment. In the pre-dawn darkness of test day a gathering of thunderstorms inched closer to ground zero, threatening to make the generals postpone the test. It was as if nature's own agents of destruction were moving in to examine this stranger, this brother arrived among their fraternity. A device using forces that had lain dormant, beyond mankind's grasp until now.

July 16, 1945.

A month before the designated physicists left Los Alamos for the test site, Isaac had taken an afternoon off, signed out a couple of jeeps and gone exploring with a group of the Los Alamos scientists and their ever-present shadowers from military security. It was the scientists' first outing in weeks.

Enrico Fermi, who had supervised the building of the world's first nuclear pile, was a keen hiker. He brought along a map and hikers' guide book. Isaac sat with one foot up on the jeep's passenger step, the map raised to shield his face from the sun. Every now and then he unfolded it and called out directions.

An hour's drive south of the mesa he signalled and the first jeep stopped. Fermi flicked the key to quiet the putting motor and the silence rose about them. Isaac sat listening, but there was no sound. No leaves to swish in the wind, nor even wind. The first sound was a crackle of boots on dirt.

'It says that there is a lake here?' said Fermi. He lifted the map from Isaac's hands, searching its crumpled and dusty paper.

They took their hats and army issue packs and water canteens and walked up the slopes between the giant saguaro cacti. In a slight valley beyond the first rise an arroyo showed the paths of rain floods past. None of the rocky draws held any water. Columns of basalt and sandstone rose like giants' tombstones. They walked on down the valley, then turned at Isaac's signal to head up a rise, head for a treeline.

'You sure that's not a mirage,' said one of the Americans, looking up at the trees.

Isaac turned. 'Who sees the trees?' he said.

Everyone nodded, even the army security men.

'Mass insanity?' said one of the Brits.

At the foot of some cliffs stood the crumbling walls and ramparts of an ancient Indian settlement. Fermi began to read from the guide book. *The fort is probably a thousand years old, made by builders of unknown origin.*

They crested the rise, pausing in the treeline to look down to where the small lake lay. In effect the lake was a pond, about the size of an Oxford University dining room, fed from an underground spring. It sat amidst a glade of old cottonwoods, their bark ribbed and flaking, their reflections like photographic likenesses on the still water. Isaac lazed for a while with the others at the water's edge, smoking a cigarette, eating beef jerky from greaseproof paper. Then the others stripped down to their swimming trunks and headed for the water. Isaac couldn't swim, so he took his pack and walked back over the hill to the ruins.

A huge cliff face stood over the edge of the valley floor. In the sheltered lee of its overhang lay carved stone huts, alleyways, several sets of steps. Everything, including the cliff, had an air of impermanence, as if the vast rock cliff face could fall at any moment. But, if the guide book was to be believed, the stone village had sat snug for a millennium. Isaac crouched, turning over pebbles, scratching in the dust, intrigued with the idea of a hidden history to decipher. Physicists are a form of archaeologist after all. He knelt, digging with his pocket knife, flakes of red dirt dotting the cuffs of his khaki pants. After a while he found a wedge of coloured clay, the pigment burned and glazed, as if in a kiln. The next scrape revealed another sliver, then a piece of blackened diamond-shaped stone. He raised it against the light, turning it over in his fingers.

He searched the desert floor for hours, the air turning cool in the canyon shadows. A jeep horn sounded, then again. Isaac carried on digging until he found a tiny cup, perhaps half the size of a teacup. On one side was the unmistakable thumbprint of a child who must have clasped hold of it just before the cup ossified forever in the blast of the kiln fire. He turned it over in his hand.

There was a crunch of boots on the stony dirt. Isaac looked up to see Fermi peering down. Isaac stood, the child's cup in his palm.

'What do you have there?' said Fermi.

Isaac crouched again, dug a hole in the earth with his knife, set the tiny cup back in and covered it over.

When they walked back down through the saguaro, the limbs of the cacti cast long shadows in the slanted light.

A month later Isaac stood on the desert floor, the night chill settling on his skin. Looking up at the bomb platform with its canvas awnings. The bright light from the oil lamps on the platform cast the jagged shadows of those engaged in the bomb's final assembly against the canvas. The fabric ruffled in the breeze, giving the shadows the jerky movement of marionettes. Two months later he saw those shadows again, ghost signatures burned onto the surfaces of buildings and bridges and pavements in Nagasaki. Where the figure in front had shielded the surface behind from the A-bomb's heat wave. Just for a fraction of a second before the figure vanished.

A ladder, a guard rail. A human body...

Fermi was one of those gathered at the Trinity site that July morning to witness this new theatre, whose rising curtains would open to the possibility, for the first time ever, that someone could destroy not inches or miles of the world, but *all* of it. Fermi himself was unmoved by the solemnity of the occasion, speculating in dark mischief at one point on whether the explosion would ignite the earth's atmosphere and set the whole sky afire. The generals scowled beneath the brims of their caps.

Isaac watched the test from Campania Hill, twenty miles from ground zero. Sitting in the pre-dawn dark with his knees up, trying to stop his boots from slipping on the dusty ground. He reached beside him, searching for something he could throw when the bomb's shockwave hit so that he could gauge the force of the wave. He scratched about in the sand, following his torch beam to where a few fragments of desiccated bone lay half-buried. Some creature that had died of thirst. He took them like child's marbles into his palm.

For a while he echoed his colleagues' mantra of counting off the minutes but lost track amid an image that came to him out of the desert dark. A small boy in a wood-panelled classroom, standing on tip-toes, chalk dust on his woollen vest, his five-year-old arms stretching to reach over the lip of the blackboard to write out all he knew of the three times-table. The boy reached, stretched as hard as he could with the chalk to complete the loop on the nine with its tail like a tadpole, but in stretching the chalk slipped from his grasp. He snatched at it but missed, seeing it bounce off the ledge and tumble spinning to the floor, just as the flash of light from the bomb's tower tore his adult head to the left. He turned away, grabbed the visual filter, raised it over his eyes. His fingers held the bone fragments clasped tight. When the shockwave hit he tossed the bones high above him. They vanished in an instant. He lifted the slide rule from his pocket. The numbers flickered red and blue and violet in the strange new light. The straight edges of the slide rule crackled like sparks, then faded to the soft glow of embers.

Caleb glances down at Isaac's carved sun radiating on the gravel path.

'Were you frightened by it?' he says.

'No. Not then.'

A man, a woman and a couple of children come from the hospital building and sit on the sunlit grass. They are all wearing party hats. With them is a young woman Caleb had seen once wandering the corridors of the hospital, the shoulder of her regulation frock hanging loose. Her pale skin tattooed with old bruises. Today she is fully clothed and wears a pink crepe-paper party hat.

He turns back to Isaac.

'The last bomb dropped on Pearl Harbour in 1941,' says Isaac, 'missed and landed instead on Nagasaki in 1945.'

The family in party hats begins to sing. All except the young woman. She sits stone still, eyes staring, the only movement the breeze flicking the paper tips of her hat.

A month after the war ended, the Manhattan Project Atomic Bomb Investigation Group flew into Japan in a converted B-29 bomber, much as the bombs themselves had. It was only a few weeks after the hundred or so dignitaries had stood on the deck of a warship in Tokyo Bay, scribbling their names on pieces of paper, as if cheques to reimburse the world for what it had lost in the slaughter. On the outskirts of Nagasaki there were American soldiers, armed but not menacing. In the city itself there were almost no soldiers, as if such trappings were unnecessary, which was almost true. There were few people left in the city to point a gun at.

An investigation party – Isaac, a corporal, two GIs and a publicity officer – left the temporary military barracks in a jeep, drove down streets deserted of all but a trickle of hand-pulled carts, people looming out of the dust with masks over their mouths. A few glanced now and then towards the jeep as it passed with its tail of grey dust, downcast eyes rising just for an instant. Isaac had a map and was looking to calculate the blast radius. The map more resembled a city than the city did. There was a desert sense to it. Centuries of human works had been swept up and sucked back into sand. He could pick out a bay on any empty coast where no one had ever built and say, there, there was once a city there, and the listener might shake their head and laugh and call him a liar. But that's what it looked like. Like the existence of the city had been a lie.

The corporal steered Isaac's party on up a slope. The jeep's wheels snagged and bounced in the rutted dirt, like a kite in a skittish wind, careening around roads that seemed to possess little logic to them, weaving in and out of the rubble. The corporal nudged the horn when they'd chanced upon a pocket of people who'd sifted through the debris and walked with meagre belongings in a cart. The visitors stopped several times, lost, in disbelief that they *could* be lost in a place where one could see for miles in any direction. Streets and alleys and lanes would meander then just stop at an open lot or a small cairn of ashes, as if built to lead nowhere.

They crossed the Urakami River, heading northwest. Isaac held the map, lifting it every now and then to shake it free of ash and dust. The wind rose up the valley and they had to hold handkerchiefs or a rag over their mouths. On one street up in the hills, well away from ground zero, the road had acted as a fire break. Blazes had swept up the slope, annihilating all before them, like the Trinity blast wave that had carried away Isaac's tossed collection of bone fragments. The land on one side of the road was burned naked, while on the other the houses were little touched. In the unburned houses women stood sweeping ashes from stoops. Men perched on ladders, scooping bucketfuls of ash and grit from their roofs.

Isaac signalled for the corporal to stop. He stepped from the jeep and walked a hundred yards over into the glazed soil, looking for some structure, something solid to bar his way. But there were none.

When he returned to the jeep, the GIs were into their midday rations. The corporal sat chewing on a tiny bread roll, squinting up into the warm sunlight. Isaac's approaching shadow crossed his body and he looked up and smiled. Isaac returned his smile, knowing that this soldier sitting chewing among the wreckage would have been among the first to land – and perhaps fall – in the invasion the bomb had rendered unnecessary. Amid all this destruction, he was just glad to be alive.

They moved on, tracking the path of the river, its choked and blackened water the only constant in suburbs that looked like they'd been eaten away by moths. Isaac thought of the brief lecture they'd been given on arrival, sitting in a room with an overhead fan circling, its blades sending ripples of shadows over their faces. They'd been told of the thousands of scorched bodies dragged from the river's toxic vein. Of the corpses piled by the riverside, taken away by soldiers or locals press-ganged into mortuary service. Of men perhaps carting away wives or sons or daughters without even knowing, so burned were they.

They stopped at an old cobbled lane which Isaac supposed had once run between a honeycomb of houses. It was just open land now. Windswept. A woman's sandal lay among the ashes, sitting amid a circle of prints. They were hasty, willy-nilly, as if an invisible figure was still running around in circles. Spinning. The scuffed tread marks were still visible in the dirt.

A sandal, a circle of footprints, everything but the woman.

He turned at the sound of footsteps. One of the American soldiers was standing next to him, holding a toy train. He passed it to Isaac and they both stood looking at it, perhaps sharing a history of tinkering with train sets as boys. Isaac set it down in the dirt, tried to push it a few inches, but its burned wooden wheels wouldn't turn, its workings clogged with dust. He looked up again, just as the publicist's camera clicked. Two men, a child's toy train. Half-burned wooden wheels, a blackened toy smokestack. Its sole carriage scalded – the paint stripped away – but whole. The military publicist lined up another photo. Isaac raised the toy engine to him, but the publicist turned away to capture something else, so Isaac stood holding the train, a fingernail clearing away the clogged ash to allow the wheels to spin. He sat down on a fire hydrant, listening to the squeak of the wheel revolving on its blackened axle. When it stopped there was silence. The faintest sound was discernable. A gull's cry from a hundred yards away. A slip of ashes from an overturned roof. Then silence. He had never known such silence before, not even in the desert. At least not since the last seconds before they detonated the Trinity bomb.

'How many died?' asks Caleb.

'I don't know,' says Isaac. 'But we shouldn't use the past tense. With the effects of radiation, they'll still be dying.'

The group of people on the hospital lawn sit singing, the older woman prodding the younger woman, mouthing the words in an exaggerated gesture, waving her arms in a slow arc in front of her, trying to get the younger woman to sing. But the younger woman sits in silence.

Caleb watches her, looking in his mind, through her dress's bright fabric to the bruises he had seen on her skin.

'Trinity didn't stop me,' says Isaac. 'Even Nagasaki didn't stop me. *There is a war on* was the phrase seared like a branding iron into our minds. At Los Alamos, it was true. But the phrase outlived the war, the armistice. On the Hill sometimes when I'd draw my stare back from slide rules and charts and protractors for my coffee mug, I'd see men crouching in the weave of the paper or the chalk-dust on the blackboard. Crouching in trenches or in the hulls of landing craft, the tips of their rifles unsteady as their hands gripped the stocks too hard, their minds counting the seconds to the moment the offensive would be launched and they would be swept up in its surge.

'Above the physicists towered an immense set of scales. Conscience or victory. Conscience or victory. I never answered the question before Nagasaki, in fact I never even *asked* it until I saw the goats chewing.'

Caleb turns to him.

'Goats?' he says.

A gust blows through the sycamores. One of the children on the grass loses her party hat. She clambers up and runs and snatches it back from the wind.

'Bikini Atoll, after the war,' says Isaac. 'I sat in the viewing room set up for the physicists and military brass and reporters. We watched the film from the Able bomb test, the first nuclear test in peacetime. Bikini Atoll, July, 1946. The event itself had been preceded with much fanfare, the strangeness of the sudden swell of publicity not lost on us. We'd worked for years at Los Alamos cloaked in silence and invisibility.

'At the Pacific tests our photos were taken, not for security passes but for newspapers and newsreels. Cakes were baked in honour of the atom, nicknames were given to the bomb, its builders, the ships in the Bikini lagoon, even the dozens of test animals loaded onto the otherwise empty ships. All captured within the serenity of the atoll's palm-dotted borders. But the reporters had been disappointed, expecting Armageddon-on-demand. One report described the bomb as *ZZZ-ZZZ-Pfffffz-Zzzz*. They wanted more bang for their buck.'

The young woman in the pretty dress still doesn't sing.

In the large Quonset hut used as the viewing room at Bikini, Isaac slouched in the tropical heat, his feet up on the empty seat in front of him. He had a banana in his hand, from a bunch bought from a vendor standing up out of a canoe.

The screen flickered, and in its staccato light Isaac reached down and unpeeled the banana, stripping away the soft skin. He looked back up at the screen just as two goats appeared in frame, tethered to small metal rails on the deck of the vessel *Niagara*. Both were munching on a scattering of hay, standing with their alien eyes dead still, only their jaw lines moving. One leaned forward, pulling against the strain of its collar tethered to the ship's rail, its tongue poked out to drink from its water bucket. It raised its head again, bent for another mouthful of hay and began chewing.

The screen went white.

When it cleared, the goats came back into frame, the forward of the two still chewing. The sky and ocean boiled behind it, dark flashes rising and falling like drunken birds. The sea began to tremble and the deck rose, then fell again. The front goat kept on chewing. The second one was gone, only twisted strands from its metal tether remaining. The chewing goat leaned to the bucket again, but the bucket skidded away. Flying pieces of the ship's deck and superstructure blazed by, the bomb's shock wave scouring a destructive circle, tiny in the vastness of the Pacific, a hole in the future. The goat's indifferent eyes appeared once more, its pupils wavering only in time with its chewing. Then it too vanished.

Most of the ships at the Able test had survived, though some sank. There were no human fatalities. Ten percent of the test animals died in an instant, vaporised or torn apart. The survivors were feted. A pig locked in a toilet for the blast appeared the next day swimming in a lagoon. It lived in celebrity for another five years, though – it was noted – it was sterile. A rat gave birth, perhaps even as the bomb went off, to three baby rats. The baby rats were given the names Alpha, Beta and Gamma. But even the goats that lived through the test didn't do so for long.

Cancer.

When he came to New Zealand Isaac let the envelopes from the British Ministry of Defence yellow and tatter and curl in bottom drawers. He didn't want to be part of their larger, lethal envelope of research and testing. He had read the first all the way through. The second got a cursory skim. He stopped reading the third at the end of the first line. They all said the same thing, though with increasing force. Another testing program, for another war that had been searched for and sighted just over the horizon, like a landfall.

Christmas Island was the new Bikini. He missed that one. He missed them all after that.

The people on the grass begin another song.

God rest ye merry gentlemen...

'The Able bomb's yield,' says Isaac, 'was the equivalent to 23,000 tons of TNT. About the same as the Nagasaki device. In around one ten-millionth of a second it annihilated less than one gram of matter, converting it to energy. A few years later, a few miles from this same spot, the first hydrogen bomb, codenamed Mike, would be detonated; yield 10,500,000 tons.'

Isaac turns to Caleb.

'When you were a baby,' he says, 'you had blue eyes. Well, almost blue. I missed them changing to grey. On your first birthday we had a party, just a little do out on the beach. You were the only one unaware of it. It's funny when I think I was unaware, later, of so many of my own birthdays. On your first birthday, Troy and I played cricket, with a metal bucket as wickets. Etta sat with you on a driftwood log. Your face peeked out from between the blankets. In the afternoon it turned cold for April and I stood holding my cricket bat, shivering. I couldn't see Troy's last bowl for sand being whipped up by the wind. The wicker picnic basket blew over, the serviettes rolled in the sand. All I heard was the ball hitting the metal bucket.

'Etta was freezing, and worried about you. Troy didn't want to come inside, he wanted his turn at bat. "Let's go in," said Etta.

' "No!" said Troy, "I bowled him out!"'

' "It's freezing out here," said Etta. "I'm taking Caleb in."'

'We followed, Troy cursing under his breath. I ran my fingers through his hair.

' "You got me fair and square," I said.

'Halfway through tea you began to cough. By mid-evening you were sweating. We kept you warm overnight, but I could feel you shivering even through your blankets, your eyes weeping a sticky mess. Before dawn Etta rushed over to the neighbour's with Troy. I picked her up from there, riding the Indian and carrying you in a duffel bag on my back. She took the bag from me, nestled you deeper in your towel and blankets. I glanced up at Troy standing in the neighbour's window, his hands raised against the glass. Then we set off over the hill.'

Caleb reaches and fastens a couple of buttons on his denim jacket.

Isaac leans forward, clasping his hands together. The palms pressed hard.

'I changed down a gear on the Indian,' he says. 'The headlights illuminated the edges of the road as we cut up the hillside. The pre-dawn darkness hid the sheer drop to our right. Etta was pressed hard against me, you against her in the bag on her back. She couldn't see you but she would've felt you, though perhaps your shivers were lost in the pulse of the motorbike. There were five or six miles of bush to get through before we'd even see a streetlight.

'The hospital was another five miles after that.

'After the *Life* magazine article and photos Etta's stock rose. The turned up noses of the local defenders of social morals stayed that way but she didn't care any more. I'm not sure she ever did. She began traveling, shooting photos for articles wherever she could get them. I deputised as the world's worst mother. She photographed everything from cakes to car accidents, though I knew there was only one thing she wanted to photograph. Faces. I was a man who had once whittled a figure from driftwood, giving him limbs and the outline of clothes but no face, but there were expressions at the edge of eyes that Etta could capture that I couldn't even see until she pointed them out.

'The headlight beam cut across trunks and branches, an atomised scythe. On the corners Etta gripped her arms harder around my waist and I tried to speak to her in my mind, as if she could read me. The rest of the time I just counted the minutes, counted the miles.

'We'd go now and then to the pictures when you were old enough, short films would come on among the Donald Duck and Goofy cartoons. Shots of air-raid shelters, children leaping under desks at the sound of a siren. You used to ask later, what game were they playing, Dad?'

'Yeah,' says Caleb. 'I remember that.'

'There'd be shots of an old codger in England posed beside a corrugated-iron hut in his backyard, a World War One gasmask over his face. People began stockpiling tinned food in the basement. Even in New Zealand, lunchroom conversations turned away from movie stars and rugby results to how far you'd have to be from the epicentre of a blast for the burns to subside from third degree to first degree. Which would last longer, tinned peaches or beans.

'While those kids were practising diving under desks, we marched. Just a trickle at first, like a leak from a cracked cup. A new phrase had entered the lexicon. *Nuclear Disarmament*. But it turned out that disarmament was a terrifying word, much more terrifying than armament.'

Isaac steeples his fingers in front of him. Caleb thinks for a moment to touch a hand against his, but he doesn't.

'About a hundred years after we'd left Rangimoana,' says Isaac, 'the lights of Auckland appeared through the trees. I felt Etta tap her helmet against mine. I nodded. Yes, I see them, I said to myself.'

Isaac reaches down again, picks up the twig and begins to scratch a shape beneath the carved sun. A boat.

'The men who went to the Christmas Island tests,' he says, 'had to stand on the deck with their backs to the blasts. They had welders' goggles on. A few seconds after the first flash they were told to turn to look at it, through watering eyes. An hour later some of the ships' crews watched the bows of their vessels turn towards the gap in the air right beneath where the last of the mushroom cloud rose into the stratosphere.'

The twig breaks off against the hard path. Isaac doesn't raise his hand. It hovers above the gravel, trembling.

'One by one, house lights came on,' he says, 'all across West Auckland. It struck me then that I didn't know if you were even still alive or if we had already become a high-speed hearse.'

Isaac stands, lets the last of the twig fall.

'We marched down Queen Street,' he says. 'We marched on Parliament. I was just one of the crowd at first, until word spread of who I was. Or who I had been. There were trade unionists, conchies, doctors, the occasional ex-soldier, even a couple of my physics students. Bertrand Russell was one of our patron saints, but also young mothers who wanted their kids to live to make them grandmothers.'

Caleb stands, touches a hand against Isaac's arm.

'Dad.'

Isaac turns to him.

'When I rode wondering if you lay dead against your mother's warm back it struck me,' he says, 'that all I could do was ride faster, travel faster. That was the only way I could help you. Even all my science couldn't negotiate you one single extra second of life. I knew how distant stars grew from proto-star birth clouds, what isotopes of hydrogen would fuel a bomb, how under enormous pressure and heat lithium would move along the periodic table into tritium, but I didn't know, beyond the basics, what made my son breathe. Einstein said that no speed beyond the speed of light was possible, but I would've settled for a tiny fraction of light speed. I needed to go only fast enough to get you to the hospital before that breathing stopped.'

'Dad,' says Caleb, 'let it go. I'm here.'

'All I could do was ride, Caleb. All I could do. Like any numbskull with five minutes of lessons. We scoured the streets, our shadows in the streetlamps made jagged by frantic gestures. Is the hospital this way or that? In the end I let Etta lead me with pointing fingers. Then the first rays of the rising sun caught the pale block figure of the hospital building in its grey light.'

Caleb takes Isaac's arm, draws him close. Isaac's body is taut, cold against him.

'Dad,' he says, 'let it go. I'm here now, alive, and so are you. We're safe.'

Isaac stares at him. His bristled cheeks hollowed, the late afternoon shadows darkening his eyes.

'On your second birthday I gave you a little wooden

train,' says Isaac. 'Do you remember?'

'Not the birthday, but I still have the train.'

'For your third we gave you a tricycle I'd built from discarded parts. Do you remember what I gave you for your sixth birthday?'

'Sure. A slide rule. Books of mathematical puzzles.'

Isaac turns. His blinks a few times, fast, then looks away into the blue sky.

'I would never have found the hospital, Caleb. Without your mother. Don't you see? Never. My world existed in places I couldn't see with my eyes, only in my mind. That was my home. The world I *could* see was a mystery to me.'

Caleb draws Isaac back down to the bench. They sit in silence for a long time. After a while the group with the party hats gets up and heads inside. The little boy stares up at the young woman's impassive face. A little while later, all minus the young woman come back out, walk down the path to the main gate and, one by one, take off their crumpled hats as they get to the gate-house.

'You know what I miss?' says Isaac. 'Time. There's no time in here. Not in a usable sense. No differentiation of time or days. Someone could appear in July and say Merry Christmas, and those who remember Christmas would smile, laugh, join in the celebrations. Concepts such as Tuesday, or September have no real meaning. There is warm, cold, light, dark. Nothing else.'

The oncologist makes an appointment during the Christmas holidays to see Caleb, leads him into a small room, the décor a pale, almost antiseptic blue. Caleb takes off his shoes and clothes, puts on a white gown that opens only at the back, wondering if he looks like either a Roman senator who perhaps suffers from incontinence, or a chip wrapper.

In the midst of all this colour neutrality is a picture, a ragged outline of a single flower. There is a name beneath it, in a child's hand. He can't make it out – can decipher only the small addenda next to it: '... aged 5.'

'That picture,' he says, 'I guess –'

'Yes,' says the doctor.

The nurse ushers Caleb in to a small room filled with gadgetry. A desk sits in a corner, a jumble of notes sprawled on its top. One machine has a seat in front of it, as if the sitter pilots the contraption. The doctor and nurse stand for a moment behind a screen, then leave the room. Caleb closes his eyes to the whirring of the machine.

A couple of hours later he eases the Indian over to the kerb, glances at his watch. He silences the motor and sets the cycle on its stand and takes the strap of his satchel and lifts it from the carrier bag. When he knocks on the door of number 27, Weston is already standing in the doorway, glancing past Caleb's shoulder out into the empty street.

JK looks up when Caleb enters.

'You look like shit,' he says.

A couple of the group sprawl on couches, a couple sit on the floor, like kindergarten kids, their faces old before their time. All except Weston, who prowls the edges of the room, no more than an inch from any given wall at any given moment.

'They're ignoring us,' says Weston.

'Maybe we need to be more visible,' says JK.

'We're blowing things up,' says Weston. 'How could we be more visible?.'

'No,' says JK, 'like statements to the press and stuff.'

'Like the usual university mob?' says Weston.

'They get noticed,' says JK.

'Sure,' says Weston, 'we could fart around like Bill and Ben.'

'Bill and Ben?' says JK.

'The flowerpot men,' says Weston.

'I know who they bloody are,' says JK. 'I just don't get the connection.'

'The Vietnam war protestors,' says Weston. 'Sitting in the middle of the road, holding hands. Singing "Kumbaya." '

'And your alternative is?' says JK.

'You don't fight guns with flowers,' says Weston.

'We're not fighting against guns,' says Caleb. 'We're against bullshit politics.'

'Which always ends up being enforced with guns.'

Caleb looks at the others, aware now that some of them are wavering. He can see it in their eyes, the slight crack in their voices, like a hairline fracture in glass.

'It's time we got moving again,' says Weston.

'So they can ignore us again,' says JK.

'Not this time,' says Weston.

Caleb raises a hand.

'What we need to do now,' he says, 'is decide right here who wants to go on and who doesn't.'

'Young Master Simeon is right again,' says Weston.

'A vote?' says JK.

'No,' says Weston, 'not a bloody vote. This isn't the city council.'

He takes off his watch and unclasps the leather cover.

'It's two minutes to four,' he says. 'When it's four o'clock we'll carry on this conversation. Anyone who doesn't have the stomach for it won't be a part of it.'

'Two minutes?' says Michael.'

'One minute forty-seven,' says Weston.

No one moves for a moment. Then Michael stands and pushes past the others' legs. JK takes his guitar from the metal stand and follows him out. Leaving Dominic, Weston and Caleb.

'No need to wait for four,' says Caleb, 'agreed?'

'Agreed,' says Dominic.

Weston clicks shut the clasp on his watch cover. He reaches around behind him and pulls out a wad of papers from a leather satchel.

'There's a military base in Papakura,' he says.

'We're gonna attack an army base?' says Dominic. 'Shit!'

'No. We're not the Green Berets. There's a pub the off-duty guys drink at. Out in the wop-wops.'

'No,' says Caleb. 'Wives. Kids playing tag in the car park.'

'After hours,' says Weston.

'How long after hours?'

'Three am maybe. There's a big rubbish skip against the back wall of the pub. Massive thing. A fire there would set the whole place going.'

'Streetlights?' says Dominic.

'Bugger all,' says Weston.

'Houses?' says Caleb.

'Too far away to see anything until the flames go up. There's a car yard next door. A garden centre on the other side. Low fences. Hiding places.'

'You love this stuff,' says Dominic.

'Do we want to make a point or not?' says Weston.

'I don't like it,' says Caleb.

'You had your chance,' says Weston. 'You were to come up with the next target, but you sat on your hands.'

'I've been preoccupied.'

Weston shakes his head.

'The door's still open,' he says.

'No it isn't,' says Caleb. 'We're in this now until the end.'

In Akiko's bedroom the scarves dance in the wind as Troy seeks to know every shudder of her body. Her head now on the pillow, now on the bare sheet. She feels herself rise towards him, her nipples tugging her as he finds them with his lips. She closes her eyes, her whole body travelling the same circle, the same swirl as his tongue on her skin. Her fingers clawing against his back as he slips down her length and she draws his weight against her, needing it, needing to be gripped between his body and the bed, between this world, this moment, and all that has come before. His breaths now against the private pores of her inner thigh. She takes a curl of his hair between the forefinger and thumb of each hand and rotates it again and again, draws him closer still. Deeper.

There are moments, just moments, when time staggers for him. Here, now, her sleeping face against his chest. Beyond the window glass the rainy afternoon fades into a rainy dusk and he looks up through the highest branches at it. A water sky. Water time. Knowing now that those months without more than an occasional troubled blink of sleep are beginning to slip back into the trouser pocket of the uniform he shed the day he left the army. The fire alarms silent, everything quelled, quenched, by the rain·that is she. He reaches up, touches the window latch. There are wisps of raindrops on his wrist. He eases further down into the sheets, draws her closer, her leg across his, her arm across the full width of his body. Her ear over his heart.

In his sleep he opens his eyes to where he swings in the

hammock on the deck at Rangimoana. He looks through the string squares at Caleb's face.

'It's raining,' says Caleb.

'I noticed.'

'You'll get soaked.'

'Piss off.'

'Go ahead. See if I care.'

'What did I just say?'

'You'll be the one sneezing and wheezing.'

'Am I talking to myself?'

'Troy?'

'Piss off!'

'Troy.'

He blinks again and Akiko's face is above him.

'Troy,' she says, 'it's me.'

'Hi.'

'Hi? Hi? You just told me to piss off!'

When the first fire bells of the day go Troy looks up at the sky, thinking if it was raining harder they might not have to go at all. Monty glances across the engine's cab at him.

'It never rains quite that hard, brother,' says Monty.

'What are you,' says Troy. 'A mind reader?'

'We've all been there.'

The traffic is slow, the streets clogged with people making a dash across the tarmac with umbrellas, or briefcases held over their heads.

'You know,' says Monty. 'The worst guys to have on the shift are young, just-married guys. They've got too much to lose.'

Jimbo and Tank turn to look at Troy. Geronimo glances up into the rear-view mirror.

'I'm not married,' says Troy.

'Just a theory of mine,' says Monty.
'Screw you *and* your theory,' says Troy.

Caleb looks over the trees in the family's yard, up to where the Waitakere Ranges rise against the sky. The grass is still a touch damp from this morning's rain, but he doesn't mind and neither do the kids. They sit chewing on birthday cake, supping from paper cups with fruit drink or milk. He does some mime, then his balloon animals. He sits in the grass, lifts a large, misshapen balloon from his red sack and pulls and prods at it, the rubber making rude noises. The children can see the balloon is pulled over something.

'Can anyone guess what it is?' he says.
'A book?'
'A rolling pin?'
'A horse?'
'A horse?' says Caleb.
The children break into laughter.
He puts his lips to the balloon's opening blows, making straining faces as he goes. The balloon's edges spread and it grows further and further, until he reaches into his pocket and pulls out a pen and uses the nib to pop it. The children jump, then laugh again. They sit looking at the ukulele, bits of destroyed rubber hanging off its wooden body.
Caleb begins to strum and sing.
Puff, the magic dragon lived by the sea ...
The children sing along with the chorus.
And frolicked in the autumn mist ...
Caleb sings the next verse alone.
A dragon lives forever but not so little boys
Painted wings and giant rings make way for other toys.
One grey night it happened, Jackie Paper came no more
And Puff that mighty dragon, he ceased his fearless roar.

Some of the parents amble over from their conversations, begin to join in. The children cheer at the song's end. He sings two others, plays a couple of instrumental pieces on the ukulele, then leads them in one last song.

Rocking, rolling, riding, out along the bay,
All bound for Morningtown, many miles away...

He gets the children to stand, follow him in a pied piper's trail across the grass. He swings the ukulele from side to side as he plays, glancing back to watch the children's footsteps stream away behind.

Maybe it is raining, where our train will ride,
All the little travellers are warm and snug inside ...

Caleb sits in the oncologist's waiting room, debating whether the flowers on the coffee table are real or plastic. The receptionist looks up at him a couple of times. The door to the surgery opens. A woman and child come out and the oncologist says something to the receptionist. The woman fidgets in her handbag while the child runs his fingers against the wall. She fumbles with some keys and a pen, then loses control of the handbag and it drops to the floor. The child jumps, his eyes staring. The woman curses, bends to pick up her glasses case, a comb and small purse. Some coins roll across the linoleum.

'Mr Simeon,' says the oncologist, standing with a file in his hand.

They sit in his office and he preambles for a while, then sits up and tells Caleb the results. They discuss it for a moment,

Caleb losing the thread while he thinks again of the woman dropping her purse, her things rolling on the ground.

'Why plastic flowers, doc?' he says.

'Excuse me?'

'Plastic flowers in your waiting room. Why plastic?'

'They last longer.'

'What's this thing called again?' says Caleb, pointing at the oncologist's notes.

'Acute lymphoblastic leukaemia.'

'Tough to spell. You any good at spelling, doc?'

'Look, we need to –'

'Explain it to me.'

'The cancer?'

'Yes.'

The doctor leans back in his chair. He clicks his ballpoint pen a couple of times.

'The bone marrow produces two main types of white blood cell,' he says. 'Lymphocytes and myeloid cells. They work together to fight infection. As some myeloid cells and some lymphocytes live for only a short time, a few days perhaps, the bone marrow is always producing more.'

He stops, clicks his pen again.

'Go on,' says Caleb.

'When they are mature enough to leave the bone marrow, the white blood cells are released into the bloodstream to circulate around the body. Acute lymphoblastic leukaemia is when there are too many immature lymphocytes, lymphoblasts, sometimes called blast cells. They fill up the bone marrow, prevent it making the replacement mature cells that the blood and the body needs.'

'So I'm open to any and all infections.'

'Yes.'

Caleb nods his head. He looks out the window. A

bumblebee hovers a few inches from a flower.

'What's the treatment?' he says.

The oncologist leans back in his chair. He takes his glasses off and wipes the lenses with a cloth.

'The treatment I recommend is radiotherapy,' he says.

'Radiation?'

'Yes.'

'You're kidding.'

'It uses high-energy rays to destroy the cancer cells.'

Caleb goes to the window, feels himself begin to smile. He turns back towards the desk.

'I'm not sure I see what's humorous,' says the oncologist.

X

Ashes and Eggs

January, 1970

Akiko and Troy celebrate New Year's Eve with a bonenkai party to honour, and consign to history, the departing year. The following day, shogatsu, she cooks traditional o-zoni soup from chicken, carrot cut in the shape of a plum blossom, fish paste and mushroom, with a piece of citron leaf for extra taste. They sit on the sand at Mission Bay, spooning the soup and noodles while they watch the first sun of the year set. The following day she drives out to Rangimoana, carrying New Year gifts for Caleb in lacquered boxes. Sweet beans, sweet mashed potato, grilled fish, sweet omelette, vinegared fish, taro, carrots and mushrooms. Caleb isn't at home when she calls. She takes the boxes in and sits, waiting for him. When he hasn't appeared mid-afternoon she goes swimming at South Bay where the summer crowd swells with the heat. She walks the length of the beach and back but Caleb still hasn't returned, so she leaves him a note and heads back to the city. She phones twice from home, but he doesn't answer. Then, as she's getting ready for bed, the phone rings.

'Hey, Kiki,' says Caleb.

'Hiya.'

'Thanks for all the presents.'

'You're welcome. I waited but...'

'Shame I missed you. Had things to do.'

When he hangs up she lies back, closes her eyes. There's a faint sound of crickets. She sits up, opens the window wider so she can hear them better.

The thing to do Caleb mentioned was the radiation treatment. Each day for two weeks he lies on a bench in a hospital gown, listening to the clicking and whirring of the machines, the footsteps of the doctors and technicians. He asks no questions, strikes up no conversations, his eyes finding a particular point among the rectangular panels of the ceiling where four of the pockmarked tiles meet in a cross pattern.

He lies back, imagining the straight lines amid the tiny craters like a series of breakwaters or walking paths. Just wide enough for him to amble along. Each day when he is undergoing treatment his eyes choose a different route. Shall I go north or east or west? He passes sunlit doorways, drinking fountains, trees in huge terracotta pots, fields of yellow strawflowers or paths of drifting sand that lead to ocean waves higher than a house. He sits among all these things, takes the sun and wind on his face. Sometimes the sun is so hot that it starts the tall grass burning, and ashes stain his face. Sometimes the wind is so cold that it brings snow.

Then one day the strawflowers turn out to be plastic. He lifts his hand away, rubs his fingertips together just as the doctor comes back into the room.

At the house at Rangimoana Caleb sits doing some calculations for his thesis. Akiko has a small wicker basket beside her. In it are three eggs she has drained through a pinprick hole in the top, transforming the surface with a thin bristled brush, painting lines and swirls, dappling cross-hatched honeycombs of colour. She had set two of the eggs' contents in a cup in the refrigerator. The last she raised above herself, let the liquid and its yellow centre slip into her open mouth.

She sits etching the edges, then the bright yellow petals of the fukujuso flower that she has seen grow in winter, even in snow. She rounds the flowers with a touch of the muhyo, the white frost. One she bathes in the sunset orange of autumn persimmons, ghosts faint feathers of susuki grass against it.

In the morning she goes up into the bush to collect grasses, pine needles and cones to assemble as a display base for the eggs. When she gets back Caleb isn't home. She sits out on the deck, working on her tutor's notes for the coming first university term for the year. The air is sultry, the breeze shy. When Caleb comes along the road he turns left instead of right and rides out onto the beach and sits on the bike, staring out to sea. She watches him through the wood slats of the deck palings. He leans back on the seat, a new gauntness to his profile.

She crosses the road to the dunes. She is only a couple of paces away before he half-turns towards her.

'Hey,' he says.

Even in the afternoon heat he is wrapped in his denim jacket, two layers of T-shirt and a woollen scarf. She slips a hand beneath his jacket, goes to glide it up his torso, but he leans away. She raises a finger against his cheek.

'No matter how many times I've seen this view, it still takes my breath away,' he says.

She follows his stare to the waves.

'Funny expression that,' he says, 'takes your breath away. Not pauses it or disrupts it, but takes it away.'

He stands on the pedals, kick-starts the bike and works the throttle with his palm. Akiko grabs the sleeve of his jacket, then his arm. He glances down at her hand. Without letting go of his arm she swings her leg over the seat and sits behind him. He shifts forward and steers them down the gentle slope of sand, each inch darkening as they approach the sea. Caleb straightens their path, heads on down the beach, stands once on the pedals to look out over the first rows of waves. They ride all the way down to Koroheke, fording a couple of glistening streams. Beyond Koroheke they keep riding, past the old shop wagon. Akiko sets her chin on his shoulder. There is a scent of leather, of sea spray and engine oil. And in that spray she sees Troy's eyes also, turning to glance at her from out of Caleb's face. Half-brothers, a tree split down the centre by a single axe blow.

He rides past the village, past the road that leads down to the blowhole and on up the hill. The bike now riding over the shadows of trees that are to the left, and the ocean opens up to their right.

She taps him on the cheek and he half-turns. She speaks into his ear, but the sound is lost amid the Indian's hum. He shakes his head, his long hair washing across her face. She extends a hand, pointing to the edge of the road. Caleb winds down the throttle and pulls onto the dusty verge. He flicks off the motor.

'Sometimes I wish I could just carry on riding out to sea,' he says.

'Might be a problem on the motorbike.'

'Nah. I'd just need to replace the rear wheel with a gear assembly, where the teeth turned another gear wheel, rotating at a ninety degree angle.'

'Um, okay.'

'The assembly would be attached to a shaft that rotated a propeller. The whole thing would be attached to a hull. Here, I'll show you.'

She smiles.

'It'd work,' he says.

He lifts a small notebook and pen from the pocket of his jacket, begins to sketch.

Akiko looks at the sketch, she puts her hand on top of Caleb's.

'I believe you,' she says.

He puts the notebook back in his pocket. He guides the kick-start lever out with the toe of his boot and stamps it down. The engine sputters. He does it twice more and it starts the third time. He closes his hand around the throttle but Akiko taps his arm and steps off, motions for him to slide back. He lets go of the handlebars and shifts to the back of the seat and she steps over onto the bike. She works the clutch and puts the bike in gear and turns around in a slow arc across the asphalt. She changes into third and then fourth as they hit the flat and the bike roars towards the corner around the estuary. She feels his grip tighten around her waist, loosen again when she guesses he senses that he might be hurting her. She slows as they cross the bridge and take the last corner, then accelerates to almost the end of the road. When Akiko steps off, Caleb's eyes are closed.

After eating, Caleb pours a glass of wine out on the deck, spilling some onto his fingers. He flicks them dry above the glass's rim, gestures the bottle towards her. She shakes her head.

They spend most of the rest of the evening in silence. Akiko goes over some choreography sketches and Caleb doodles on a pad. When he goes out for a few minutes to stare into the dark beyond the dunes she stands and leans over the pad, expecting some of his maths or the cartoon characters he likes to draw. Crazy animals and dragons and creatures that have never had a name. But instead she finds a single word written over and over.

Radiation.

In the night she wakes, hearing the screen door rattling in the wind. She rolls over, clamps the pillow over her ear, but the sound still clutters her sleep. She stands and puts her robe on and walks out into the darkened hall, the wooden boards cool beneath her feet. The front door is open and Caleb sits naked out on the deck, his back up against the railing.

'Hey' she says, 'what are you doing out here?'

He stares at her.

'Caleb, you're shivering.'

She reaches down, touches her palm against his hair, runs her hand through it. He turns his face side on to her and blinks, and she sees an old man's gaze. The horizon and its foreground of ocean seem to come from his eyes as he blinks again and again, unsettling the waves miles away.

'Caleb, what's wrong.'

Now his face is a boy's face again, as if going through the stages of his life in seconds. He turns to face her, a wide grin ushering the years away over the ocean.

'What are you doing out here in the middle of the night?' he says.

'Me? What?'

She undoes the belt of her robe and slips it off. She raises it over his shoulders. They walk inside, Akiko naked now. Caleb steps into the bedroom doorway and slips the robe from his shoulders and hands it back to her. She puts it on. He lies on the sheets, draws the blanket over him like some sand creature avoiding the eyes of the world.

In the dark she can draw a dozen different expressions on his face. An identikit man. She touches the door closed with her heel and slips in beside him. He lies looking up at her, and part of her wishes for a light on his face and part of her doesn't.

'You're still trembling,' she says. 'Are you still cold?'

'No.'

'Caleb —'

'No. I'm not cold.'

He props himself on one elbow and she lies down against the sheet, her head on the edge of the pillow. She moves close enough so their noses touch. He reaches with a hand, brushes it across the first inklings of hair above the skin of her forehead. A fingertip brushes a cheek, another closes an eyelid.

'Remember the day we met?' he says.

'The invisible kite?'

'Yeah. And the other guy's kite I wouldn't let go of.'

'You wanted to fly.'

He rolls onto his back. She moves against him, a leg across his, her cheek against his shoulder.

'Yeah,' he says, 'fly.'

In the night she wakes to his body shuddering. His eyelids are closed but flickering, storm filled. She pulls tighter against him, hoping her warmth will still him. And it does. In the first grey of dawn he wakes, runs his hand across her neck.

They spend the morning on the beach. She wants to drag the inflatable mattresses out, go swimming, but he doesn't. He just walks on the wet sand in his multicoloured beach baggies, watches her swim in the low waves. They spend the night with Akiko lying against his back, waking a couple of times to still his shivers, or to glance towards the door where he vanishes then comes back with a tall glass of water. He sits gulping, then lies back down.

Neither can sleep. In the night dark he sets random sails from his memory afloat on the humid air. Diving off an old wooden jetty at Opononi, climbing dunes fifty feet high and rolling, spinning, over and over down their slopes. Standing in the shallows holding a wooden pole, a knife fastened to its tip with raupō twine. Watching fish among the harbour's ripples. Feeling the tiny waves radiate from where his spearpoint pierced the surface, then the fish or its turbulence or its wake beneath the water touched against him as it passed. He looked for droplets of blood in the water but never saw any. Just sand, beach pebbles set rolling in the current.

On the third night, the evening before she has to go back to the city, he sits on the floor watching her working on one of her egg paintings. She overlays leaves of blue, green and black on the egg's surface in strokes bold enough to shine but delicate enough not to break or even dent the eggshell. He goes into the kitchen, fetches himself a glass of water. Akiko looks up to where he stands at the open refrigerator. He takes out an egg and weighs it in his hands.

In the night she wakes. He is propped up on one elbow, looking towards the window. The curtains sit open at the windows' edge, the night so dark with a missing moon. She sniffs something familiar, glances at his hands, a couple of fingers afire with paint.

'What have you been doing?' she says.

He leans back, takes an egg from the sheet beside him and raises its painted body over himself.

'Can I see?' she says.

She opens her hand, but he moves it instead in front of her eyes. Turns it around in his fingertips.

Toetoe plumes, tiny sand dunes. A sweep of sea.

'Not bad,' she says.

He taps the egg's top with a nail, then harder. It breaks. He smiles at her and she stares for a moment, then he tips it over, a finger held beneath the opening. She lies back and he takes his finger away. She takes the bounty against her tongue, swallows it. He raises a hand, wipes her lips.

'Yeah,' he says, 'I wanted to fly.'

He runs a hand across her tummy, cups a breast beneath her T-shirt.

'No,' she says.

'Kiki –'

'Caleb, I can't.'

He begins to move against her, his body trembling, his breaths sharp.

'Kiki,' he says. 'I need to fly.'

She shifts sideways on the bed and he follows her, naked now. He moves against her but makes no attempt to hold her with his arms. His body is hot, she can feel sweat on the skin of his chest, taste it on her tongue. His hardness moves against her pyjama bottoms, across the sensitive skin above her pubic hair. She takes his face in her hands.

'Caleb, you know I love you. You know I'd do anything for you, but we can't be like this. I can't do it.'

'Why?'

'I can't. You have to let me go, Caleb.'

For a moment he doesn't, then he lifts his body away, falls beside her, still against her. She turns, kisses his cheek. His eyes are closed. He presses against her. His body jerks, his breath catches, then he shudders.

Not from the cold.

The skin of her hip is wet.

He shakes his head, his teeth gritted tight. And in his trembling she senses both his orgasm, and his heart breaking.

The new university year begins, the days shortening, the light slipping away earlier as Akiko drives up K Road towards Ponsonby in the evenings. Two weeks after the term starts she stands looking up at the proscenium arch over the auditorium's stage, the cyclorama running away from her into blue sky and white clouds from floor to ceiling, the blue segueing into darker hues, then darker still until a night sky rises far above their heads.

She watches the dance class go through the routine once, then looks back at her bag. She tells the class to keep going and takes her ballet shoes from her bag. She puts them on and stretches a few times and the dancers part for her. She moves among them and calls for the routine to start again.

One of the lighting technicians changes the setting, and blue lights flick on, then move to green with different filters on different lights. They go through the routine once, overhead light burning the dancers' stark shadows on the floor. Akiko senses a slight stiffness in her limbs. There is a hint that, though she still practises every day, her fluidity is a touch off-cue. She wills herself on, opening her eyes wide when the shadows beneath her begin to merge and the light fades and she misses a step change for the first time in years. It all happens in a slow, theatrical gesture. The proscenium seems to rise straight overhead like a giant arm. She blinks, trying to clear her head, but it's too late. When she blinks again she is sitting on the floor, staring up at the puzzled faces.

She stands, still dizzy, appoints one of the class to lead the practice and goes down the hall to the changing rooms where she sits for a moment among the lockers and coat hooks then stands and staggers to the toilet and vomits.

She can still see the proscenium rising above her the next day when the doctor sits down at his desk and folds his arms, and says, 'Congratulations.'

When Troy gets to Akiko's he drops his gear bag on the kitchen floor. She comes from the bedroom and they kiss and when he lets her go she doesn't move away.

'Three,' she says.

'Hmmm?'

'Three. We're going to be three.'

Stillness.

Silence.

He raises his hands to her face, one each side of her cheeks. Then slips them down across her collarbone, down over her breasts to her midriff, where they meet again.

In the night she wakes in the rain and sits up, watching the scarves play in the breeze. A faint moonlight, the orb itself lost somewhere out beyond the reefs of cloud. Troy sits up, draws the sheets away from Akiko's naked body, looking down at her belly. He reaches over her to where a paper crane sits on the windowsill, lifts it down and sets it atop her, over her navel. She chuckles and the paper crane begins to slip away. Troy lifts it to his lips and kisses it, then sets it back atop her.

Caleb stands at the street corner, leaning against a concrete telephone pole. He looks up to where its tip vanishes into the night. There are streetlights up and down the road from where he stands but his figure is in darkness. It is so dark that when Dominic pulls up to the kerb in the stolen van he drives right on by Caleb, then stops. Caleb whistles and the passenger door creaks open.

'Could you be any harder to spot?' says Dominic from the driver's seat.

'I should've worn fluorescent clothes,' says Caleb, 'maybe a neon sign that says *bomber*.'

'Yeah, all right.'

'Where's Weston?'

'Nursing his baby.'

Caleb slides open the rear door and stands peering into the back of the van to where Weston sits with the drum and a box of detonators. They drive for a while, Caleb pointing the way until the pub car park appears across the street. There are no lights on in the pub's frontage. Dominic drives past once, carries on around the block then back to where he pulls into the car park. They sit looking at the rubbish skip.

'Looks like the commandos have gone off home,' says Dominic.

'Indeed,' says Weston.

'Are we nuts?' says Dominic.

'No. The war is nuts. We may be the only sane people in the debate.'

'Debate?' says Caleb. 'We blow stuff up!'

'Strictly speaking, yes,' says Weston. 'But is that not a form of dialectic?'

'Dia–what? says Dominic.

'You should've listened more in class,' says Weston.

'You sure there are no cleaners or anything?' says Caleb. He looks through the wire fence at the used-car lot next door. The handpainted price signs are stark in the deep blue light. Dominic steers the hand-cart out of the back of the van, then lays down two lengths of four-by-two timber tight against each other. The three of them manoeuvre the drum down the timber ramp. Weston lifts the kid's plastic lunchbox with the railway detonators, the electrical switch and wiring and holds them flat against the drum's side while Caleb fastens them with masking tape. They push the cart and drum over to the rubbish skip and set it flat on the ground. Caleb taps a knuckle against the drum, the sound deadened by forty gallons of kerosene mixed with polystyrene, congealed and frozen into a rubbery paste. A jelly. Weston completes the wiring, connecting the circuit of the switch to the detonators.

Weston walks back to the van, ducks behind it when a white Ford Zephyr passes from streetlight to streetlight. Dominic and Caleb crouch behind the skip. When they come out Weston has an aerosol can in his hand. He goes over to the concrete wall, shakes the can and begins to spray. The others watch him.

'Boom boom,' says Dominic. 'Appropriate.'

'That'll send the cops out looking for Basil Brush,' says Caleb.

Dominic laughs for a moment, then leans and spits onto the pavement.

'And with that coda we'll take our leave,' says Weston.

Caleb and Weston get into the front seat and Weston lifts a leather bag from beneath it and takes out the radio control. Caleb drives out of the car park and on down the street to the corner where they park among a pile of fallen leaves scattered in the gutter. Weston glances up at Caleb and grins and turns the switch. The crack is sharp but not deafening but then is lost in an instant, swallowed by the huge wooosh as the incendiary fuel ignites. Pieces of the metal drum fly like shattered glass, the pub's roof soon punctured with shards of fire. The drum's burning lid goes spinning off across the concrete, landing amid the cars in the used car lot next door. Flames run down windscreens and door panels. Other droplets, larger globules of liquid fire fall on bonnets and roofs.

Caleb glances at Weston's face in the glow from the flames. Weston turns to him, their two pairs of eyes meeting in the sudden sunlit shadows.

'Shall we away?' says Weston

But something catches the edge of Caleb's vision. The rear door of one of the burning cars opens and a figure falls out.

Caleb steps from the van, ignoring Dominic's hisses at him. He starts to run back toward the car park, his eyes focusing on the flailing figure caught like a blown ember between the jagged blades of fire. Caleb sprints, takes off his denim jacket as he runs, throws it over the man before he reaches him, drags him away across the burning pavement. The man flails at the air and Caleb tears away his jacket and starts whacking the man's clothes with it, tearing his burning duffel coat off with one hand. The man falls again, curses Caleb. Caleb shakes him; rheumy eyes, a wild graze of stubble. A derelict finding a sleeping spot in one of the cars. He falls slobbering to the pavement and Caleb drags him again, all the way across the street and up against a small brick wall. The road is sticky now with blobs of the jelly. There is a screech as the van pulls up. Caleb grabs his own jacket back and Weston slides open the side door long enough for him to dive headfirst onto the metal floor. Dominic guns the motor, takes the next right-hand turn and heads towards the motorway.

'Did you tell him your life story to go with the good look at your face he got? says Dominic.

'He's too pissed to identify his *own* face,' says Caleb.

Dominic begins to laugh. Caleb looks up.

'What's so funny?' he says.

'Must've been a bit of a rude awakening,' says Dominic.

'Whoops,' says Weston, 'there goes the neighbourhood.'

Troy is halfway through a bowl of cornflakes at the fire station the next morning when he hears the report on the radio. At the phrase 'incendiary device' he stands and walks over to the radio and turns it up. After his shift he drives down the motorway to Papakura. It doesn't take him long to find the site, the investigators wandering around with clipboards, handkerchiefs over their noses. The stench of kerosene still haunts the air. Troy steps out of the Chev and walks to the edge of the burnt concrete. He raises a boot to step within the scorch marks, but an outstretched arm stops him.

'I'm on the crew at Central,' says Troy, showing the fireman his own badge.

'Bit far from home aren't you?'

'We've had some hassle with this stuff.'

'This stuff?'

Troy sniffs the air, looks across the scorched parking lot at the cars turned grey and black with the fire.

'Anyone hurt?' he says.

'One. He's in Middlemore.'

Troy stares for a moment then walks the length of the scorch marks. The main sweep of the fire ends about thirty yards from its epicentre, fading then into small blackened islands here and there. In the middle of the road there is a set of skid marks, wheels locking under sudden braking. He crouches, touches a finger against the tiny strands of shredded rubber. He looks across the asphalt where a faint trail of footprints in the sticky jelly leads to the skid marks. Ending a few yards from them, the pressure of the bodyweight on the front of the feet. As though the walker – or runner in fact, judging by the lengthening stride – had made a leap. A man in an awful hurry.

He nods his farewell to the fireman standing guard and walks back to the Chev.

Caleb dials, stands looking out the window, the phone receiver in his hand.

'Lunatic asylum,' says Weston.

'Not funny,' says Caleb.

'I'll fire my scriptwriter.'

'We should lay low for a while.'

'Agreed.'

When he hangs up, the phone rings. It makes him jump. He picks it up.

'Hi,' says Akiko.

'Hi, yourself.'

Silence on the line, then, 'I'm pregnant,' says Akiko.

He takes a long breath, swallows, hard. He looks back out the window, then at the clock on the wall. At the dust on top of the stereo speakers. Her words echo in his head.

'Hey,' says Akiko, 'are you still there?'

'That's great news.'

'Yes. Yes, it is.'

A pause on the line. The sound of Akiko breathing. Then Caleb hangs up, the bell receiver making a loud ping as the plastic hits the two little metal lugs with the bell attached. He stares at his hand still on the receiver. Sees for a moment the bones through the skin, as if the phone has the power of an X-ray.

The phone rings again, but he doesn't answer it.

The oncologist looks up from his desk.

'Three good tests in a row,' he says.

'I was always good at tests,' says Caleb.

'The abnormal, immature white cells are no longer showing in your blood or bone marrow.'

'So normal bone marrow is developing again?'

'That's what they indicate.'

The oncologist writes some notes on the file. Caleb watches him for a moment, then drifts into those fields of fantasy that he conjured up during the radiation treatment. This time the snow has gone, the fields blaze with grass as high as his shoulder. The oncologist's voice drags him back.

'There may be a small number of the abnormal lymphoblasts left,' he says. 'To get rid of these I'm going to put you on some medication. You'll need to take it for the next few months, maybe longer. Have regular check-ups.'

'Remission,' says Caleb.

'Well,' says the oncologist, 'the data looks promising.'

Akiko works on through Easter and on into winter, her shadow on the stage floor becoming fuller. For the first five months she continues to walk between the rows of dancers in the warm-up, glancing up into the mirror at her cheeks softening. After that she takes to sitting on a round-top stool, turning herself in a slow circle to watch her class move around her.

Troy alternates between Blue and Red Watch, between day and night shift. He neither sees nor hears of any more incendiary attacks. He sits with Akiko whenever she goes to visit her doctor, a hand holding her hand across the gap between the two plastic seats.

One morning he wakes early and draws the sheets down over her sleeping form. Her breasts are fuller now, her belly round like the first half of a rising sun. He runs a fingertip up the length of one leg, then over her soft tufts of hair and up over her belly. One of her fingers moves, taps against him. He looks up into her open eyes.

'And what are you doing?' she says.

He laughs, leans over and kisses her.

The twenty-fifth anniversaries of the bombing of Hiroshima and Nagasaki pass with little fanfare. Akiko and Troy sit one night watching a documentary on television. Troy has to stand every couple of minutes to fiddle with the rabbit's ears aerial whenever the picture begins to dissolve into a fine dust.

He looks back at her.

'How's that?' he says.

She doesn't answer, just stares at the screen. He steps back. A pale cloud rises over a city. Then the picture begins to break up. He moves the aerial again, but the images just flicker. He thumps the top of the television with his fist, turns back to where Akiko sits with her hands closed one over the other on her belly. He hears the word Nagasaki, then there's nothing but static. He walks back to the couch, holds on to her in the darkness.

He still bathes with her, Troy sitting with his back against the slope of the bath, Akiko snug against him. He soaps his hands and slips his palms up and over her fullness, all the way up to her eyelids, massaging her temples in his fingers' path all the way to the ends of her long hair. At the beginning of October she leaves work and his Chev is parked outside her house every night. The fires begin to scare him now, not the individual flames, but their collective ferocity, their unknowing accedence to the laws of physics now a knife's edge to him, to this him that is now more than a him, a two, soon a three. There are times when he works the pumpers' hose reels, twists the handle into a hydrant or even stands at a verge of flame, when he thinks of her. That sunrise roundness to her, and his fingers slow, stop what they're doing. She is with him, like a wallet photograph. *Her* eyes looking into *his* fires.

'Tell me,' he says to the flames. 'What do you see when you dance?'

XI

Tin Men

Rangimoana
April, 1989

Etta looks to where the hills rise like the walls of a cathedral above her. She knows that these are more cliffs than hills, though their greenery betrays their sharpness. There's a little car park here now, some stained logs set up as rails to separate the dunes from a barbecue area. A handful of houses rise through the leaves, real-estate signs dot the blank sections. She cuts through the dunes, over jandals tracks, dogs-paw markings, down to the slight tip of the beach towards the ocean. Nothing of the shape of the dunes is as she remembers, but the sea is as it was yesterday and probably a thousand years ago. She moves on, careful of step, the sand moving beneath her naked toes. Her backpack tapping against her spine.

She takes a few photos of the beach: a couple of joggers, a wagging-tail dog, the trail bike the lifeguards use. Passers-by nod to her, some say hello. She walks until her feet ache, then sits. A small boy wanders past and she follows him with her lens. He narrows his eyes.

'Can I take your photograph?' she says.

'No.'

'It won't hurt.'

'No,' he says.

She smiles.

'All right,' she says and lets the camera sit back against her chest.

His eyes narrow again, then he looks away. He crouches next to the thin stream of water leeching from the lagoon. It glistens like cutlery. He reaches with a finger, touches the water and squeals, and she laughs. He turns round to glare at her.

'Cold?' she says.

'No.'

He stands and dips a toe in this time, but his leg recoils. He turns and runs back up the sand. Etta walks to the stream, reaches with her own toe, the cold water stinging her tired soles. She hisses for a moment, walks on through it.

Rai and Etta sit at each end of the couch, Etta writing in her journal. When either of them moves, the couch frame rocks. Etta looks down at the couch's chipped legs. One foot has broken, half collapsed. A couple of old beer coasters sit beneath it.

'Happens to us all,' she says.

Rai smiles.

'I need to go and see the guy at the museum tomorrow,' says Etta. 'About the layout of the exhibition. Can you take me?'

'Sure.'

'Thanks.'

Etta bends to her backpack and lifts out a long plastic box and flips the lid open. Rolls of film sit like ice cubes in the indentations of the tray. She takes a couple of rolls out and examines the markings she has made in black felt pen. She jots some numbers down next to notes in her journal.

'And thanks also for not asking,' says Etta.

'Asking what?'

'How long I'm back for.'

'I almost have, a dozen times.'

'Yeah, I know.'

Etta closes the lid on the tray.

'What made you want to become a war photographer?'

Etta looks down at her writing.

'I never set out to,' she says. 'The first photograph I ever took was of a soldier, though it was the man I photographed, not the uniform or the flag or even the ideal. The human being. I've been doing that ever since; photographing human beings. In inhuman moments.'

'The things you've photographed, must've been hard to keep going.'

Etta shrugs. 'I suppose so,' she says, 'but it would've been harder to stop.'

She sits back, her fingers resting on the tray.

'The day after the last helicopters got us out of Saigon in 1975,' she says, 'we were on the aircraft carrier, the *Blue Ridge*. Heading for the Philippines. Some of the journalists and photographers had somehow sneaked a couple of bottles of bourbon into their meagre luggage, though they'd left all their clothes in Saigon. One of the photographers, an American, stood up drunk and proposed a toast to the Bo Dar café, then the Caravelle Hotel where a trail of Vietnamese bar girls used to knock on his door and leave with a few crumpled US dollars. Those dollars would help feed the girl's family, when the paddy their village worked had been bombed into a swamp, or their brothers and cousins and uncles snatched away by one army or another. He proposed another toast, everyone threw peanuts at him. A couple of officers came and went. The drunk guy saluted, then farted and saluted again. Then he pulled a rifle cartridge from his hip pocket, held it up in the air. I remember that it flashed like a firefly in the harsh fluorescent light. He said that one day one of us, one photographer, would photograph the last bullet. He staggered and fell, drooling. He looked at me through glazed eyes, handed me the cartridge, then passed out. He spent the rest of the evening snoring, being used as a table to hold glasses. In the morning, while most were nursing hangovers, he shot himself.'

Rai swallows, hard. 'Do you believe what he said?' she says.

'About the last bullet?'

'Yeah.'

'I believe I'd like to be that one photographer.'

'What did you do with the cartridge?'

Etta reaches under her denim shirt. She has a black T-shirt beneath. Dangling on a thin metal chain is a rifle cartridge, the chain running through a hole in its centre. The bullet is missing. She holds it up.

'Jesus, Nan,' says Rai. 'Sometimes you freak me out.'

'Sorry, kid.'

'Can it go off?'

'I had the charge taken out.'

Etta puts the cartridge back beneath her shirt.

'Do you have a contact for Isaac?' she says.

Rai stands and walks to the window. She stares into the dark, though in fact all she can see are the reflections from the room. Herself, Etta sitting looking at her from the couch.

'Yes,' she says. 'I visit him.'

Etta's eyes widen.

'I didn't know,' she says.

'You wouldn't.'

Etta closes her journal, leans back against the couch.

In the morning Rai drives them up through the Auckland Domain to where the stone mountain of the museum rises through the leaves. Someone throws a Frisbee, three women sit clinking champagne flutes above a blue and white gingham blanket. A young oriental man takes a photograph of his girlfriend. After Etta clicks the passenger door shut the silence circles, drawing their eyes to the cenotaph, to the high doors beyond.

They ask at the front desk about the exhibition, then walk through the Polynesian display, glancing down the walkway to the wharenui sitting on the cold stone tiles. Even children's footsteps echo here, their reflections bouncing off the squared glass of the display cases. A man in a dark blue suit approaches, shakes Etta's hand, both his hands closing over her weakening grip until he sees her grimace.

'Sorry,' he says.

The rooms are white-walled, anaemic. The taste of paint sits in the throat. Men in paint-splattered overalls command step ladders, spray cans in their hands, the fabric of their masks moving in and out over their mouths as they breathe. The curator asks them to stop for a moment as he leads Etta and Rai past the empty display walls to a room in the rear where whiteboards are laid out on tables around the room. Hundreds of photographs fixed to them by magnetic holders.

'We were tossing and turning over which ones to put in,' says the curator. 'But with you here now, well.'

He lifts up the boards one after the other and wedges them between a tabletop and the wall.

A SINGLE FLOWER SITTING IN THE MUD, BETWEEN A DISCARDED ARMY BOOT AND A STEAMING SHELL CASING.

A SOLDIER WITH THE DARK SMUDGES OF BOOT-BLACK ON HIS CHEEKS FOR CAMOUFLAGE, WEARING A BADGE THAT SAYS I LOVE LUCY.

A SAFFRON-ROBED MONK PRAYING AMONG SHELLFIRE AND FALLING MASONRY.

Etta says yes, no, maybe. Sometimes she just nods or shakes her head. She agrees with many of the museum's choices and the layout, now and then lifting the magnets and shifting the order.

'Can you enlarge this one?' she says.

'Yes, sure.'

'And this one, and this.'
'Yes.'

Rai walks around the room, leafing through the photos.

A SKELETON DRESSED IN A HAWAI'IAN SHIRT AND TEN-GALLON COWBOY HAT.
RIFLES STACKED AGAINST CRATES OF COCA-COLA.
A COCKROACH WALKING BENEATH STRANDS OF BARBED WIRE.
A YOUNG WOMAN IN A MINISKIRT, EYE SHADOW AND FALSE EYELASHES APPLIED WITH CARE, LYING IN THE STREET WITH HER THROAT CUT.

She looks back at Etta, sitting on a plastic chair with a photograph in her hand. Her head is still, her eyelids blinking. Rai walks over to her. The photograph is of a soldier with his face a few inches out of the water of a river, the faces of two children lying against him. Etta looks up at the curator.

'Not this one,' she says. 'Thanks.'

October, 1970

The crowd mills in the spring rain, keeping beneath the awnings of shops, watching the street theatre. The fire-eater walks across the wet pavement, garbed in his lizard costume. He passes the half-dozen mannequins, all dressed in baggy 1940s suits and dresses, limbs in various raised-arms poses that speak of sudden revelation. Perhaps a frozen moment, photographed mid-gesture. Halfway across the path one of the mannequins swivels its eyes, so its gaze follows the fire-eater's footsteps. A couple of children shudder and one leaps back, startled at the mannequin's sudden life. He steps forward, only his legs moving, the rest of his body still, his gaze not moving away from the fire-eater's shadow.

The fire-eater takes a metal spike and dips it into a small drum, then raises it, revealing then that his other hand carries a wooden match. He stops by a lamp-post, strikes the match and lights the end of the spike. Flames rise above his upraised arms, the mannequin now following his gesture, both figures statued for a moment, the gathering crowd of spectators silent. Then the fire-eater passes the burning spike in front of his lips and blows. A flame jets out over the wet pavement. He does this several times, each time the flame rising higher, people stepping back at the edge of its heat. The mannequin sneaks behind him, to where a tarpaulin covers a few vague shapes on the ground. He reaches beneath it and emerges with a giant balloon hammer and runs to the fire-eater, begins attacking him with the hammer and the fire-eater drops the flame, cowers for a moment, then runs away up an alley.

The burning spike is now at the mannequin's feet. He turns to face the crowd, breathing hard, the stillness of his face beginning to crack, move into a scowl. The children stare, not moving. He raises the hammer high above his head, the flame still sputtering at his feet. Parents grab their children by their raincoat collars, pull them away. The mannequin's face paint begins to crack as Caleb allows himself a smile.

Caleb walks to the high tide line where he sits among the shells, rubbing at the cooling sand with his thumb. He is still sitting there when a shadow finds him and he looks up to see Akiko, her hair ringed by the twilight.

'A swim?' he says.

She crinkles her nose.

'I'm not in the perfect shape for swimming,' she says.

'Come on,' says Caleb, standing and lifting off his T-shirt. 'Just a paddle.'

She looks out across the wave tips. He raises a hand. She reaches for it, weaving her fingers between his.

'Last one in,' he says.

He peels off his jeans and walks down into the tide, turning to see her head tilted to one side, a finger fidgeting with her dress. She walks into the shallows, still in her dress. Her eyes widen as each spray of cool water hits her. Her mouth forms a silent O. She closes her arms around him.

'Am I going to get to meet him?' says Caleb.

She looks out to sea, shakes her head.

'Why do you want it that way?' says Caleb. 'I don't understand.'

'I don't.'

'But he does?'

'Yes.'

'You've never let anyone tell you what to do.'

'I'm not.'

'Then what are you doing?'

'Don't, Caleb.'

'Kiki –'

'Just don't.'

She lets out a long breath against his neck and he closes his eyes to it, takes her warmth into his pores. Then he steps back and shapes to splash her, but she waggles a finger and he folds his arms with all the ceremony of a gentleman's club doorman. Then she splashes him. He doesn't flinch, not even when she splashes him a second time. He steps close, makes as if he's about to splash her, but doesn't. The outline of her breasts and full belly taut beneath the wave-wetted fabric of her slip. She looks down at the surf gathering around them, foam breaking in whispers.

'We'll always be friends,' she says. 'You know that.'
A wave breaks against him. He closes his eyes to it.

Akiko stands in the shower, eyes closed to the droplets. Her figure so much larger now. She wipes some water from her face, opens her eyes and looks up at the circular shower head faucet. She raises her hand, pushing her small fist against the metal in the middle of the faucet so rings of water spin and fall around her. She closes her fist tight, closes her eyes also. Still seeing in her mind those rings of water.

Troy, she has come to know, has also drawn a ring, a circle around himself. Sometimes she thinks she has entered that circle and sometimes she thinks he just moves beyond it now and then to be with her. He has kissed the scars on her throat, the scars on her legs but she hasn't said anything about them and he hasn't asked her. It's curious, how their own histories have remained at the edge of the moments they've spent together, like an audience at one of her dance performances. Just beyond the rim of the stage lights.

In the nights his sleep is often jagged. Sometimes he tells her random things, it seems, as they come to him. But only when they lie against each other in the dark. In daylight he will not move out of the moment. She lies now, her eyes closed, listening to the low, soft hum of his voice. He tells her of water-filled terraces that sound to her like Rangimoana waves. Of temples with overgrowing vines like green arteries, inhabited only by monkeys who bombarded the soldiers and their mechanical weapons with hard nuts that left red welts on the skin. Of a flax-roofed A-frame hut filled with monks in saffron robes, chanting to the accompaniment of a single bell chiming. A bell the size of a fingernail. All while automatic rifle fire echoed amid the pandanus palms. Of villages with pale-skinned babies, black-skinned babies, discarded by their foreign soldier fathers like cigarette butts. Through it all she lies, showing no reaction, sensing perhaps that no reaction is called for, no more than the instant a tear slips off a cheek to dissipate in the air or in the dirt requires a reaction, a catch from a hand. She offers him nothing at all, save a squeeze of her hand, and that draws no reaction from him. The words are soon gone, without applause or comment.

In fact she offers him little, sometimes only her tired feet at day's end, after the weight of their child has made her ankles ache. He wipes them down with a sponge-cloth or sets a plastic basin with warm water beneath her. His large hands feather-soft against her small toes.

She leans forward, kisses his cheek.

He eases off the accelerator as the Chev dips and rises on the winding road through the bush-lined gullies where the leaves grow right to the road's stony edge. The first glimpse of sea is a revelation, as always. But there's more to it today. After all he has made this journey a hundred times. But he is accompanied now. A woman, a child to be. Back to the house his step-father and mother built over the former marker place where a Fibrolite and corrugated-iron bach had stood. The bach he was born in. Where his own afterbirth is buried beneath the trees, part of the soil now.

He glances across at Akiko and she smiles at him and drives on. But there is weight in his fingers. A weight in each turn he makes, each small gesture. He senses it more each day. Senses that Akiko is not the only one carrying.

'A bloke in love is a danger,' Monty had said, and Troy had scoffed. He has thought about it since though, squeezing the words in his hands until they break and reform. A danger.

A bloke in love has something to lose, and that makes him hesitate. He'd always thought a man with nothing to lose was free, and in a way he was right. But it goes deeper than that. A man with nothing to lose has nothing to value, perhaps nothing to be free for. How does such a bloke tell the difference between a pile of clothes in a burning room, and an unconscious figure on a bed. Or between the casing of the sniper's bullet and the hand that strokes his back when she thinks he is asleep.

Maybe the man who *isn't* in love is the real danger.

Caleb leans back in his chair, against the basement café's walls. He takes a sip of his Turkish coffee and looks through the rims of Weston's glasses.

'They might pull out of Vietnam,' says Caleb. 'Soon.'

'Based on what?' says Weston.

'The debate's in the papers.'

'The debate's been in the papers forever,' says Weston. 'They need reminding.'

'Sometimes I wonder if the war has anything to do with this.'

Weston reaches mid-table to where a small ceramic cup sits with a stick of incense burning. He taps the stick halfway up, and a few tiny drops of ash fall.

'How old are you, Caleb?' he says, looking through the smoke.

'What?'

'How old are you?'

'Twenty. What the hell does that have to do with anything?'

'You're talking like you're ready to be put out to pasture.

What's next, bowls? Housie?'

'Nice try, but no cigar.'

Weston leans back in his chair.

'We're not going to give up,' he says. 'You might.'

'Let's just say I have more to think about now. More to lose.'

'That's all it comes down to?'

'Shit. Last time you almost fried someone. Who's next? Another wino, maybe a kid in the wrong place. A cop come to check it out. Tell me, did the attacks get through? Did you notice the machine spluttering at all? We were sending them a message, a protest. Tell me, has one less bullet been fired?'

Weston takes off his spectacles and puts them in his string bag and takes out his sunglasses instead.

'Each action generates an equal and opposite reaction,' he says.

'Bargain basement physics now?'

Weston lifts a cigarette from a soft-cover packet, touches its tip against the incense stick's glowing tip. He takes a draw, looks across the tables at the café's other customers.

'We can of course rely on you,' he says, 'to keep your mouth shut.'

Caleb sits looking at him. Noticing the tautness to Weston's features, the age in his face even though he is only two or three years older than Caleb. He doesn't answer Weston's question, if it was a question.

He watches Weston go, knowing Dominic will be waiting somewhere outside, watching the traffic pass by.

He finishes his coffee, swirling the last of it around in the bottom of the cup. He nods to the cashier and walks up the stairs towards street level. Halfway up, his limbs begin to flag, fold, and he feels himself crumbling to the concrete.

The whack of his joints on the hard, sharp steps is not even painful. Just inevitable. He reaches with an arm, stretches out as he slides from step to step back down to the doorway. People come from the tables, help him up. He thanks them, spiked wheels now turning within his bones, as they had a few months ago. He struggles up the steps and sits at the top, the wind down Queen Street cold on his tingling skin.

The oncologist sits looking over the test results.

'Remind me, doc,' says Caleb, 'what does remission mean?'

'That was then.'

'And this is now?'

'I wish I had a reason for you, Caleb. Beyond anatomy, pathology.'

'You don't have to, it's not your job. Your job is just to tell me yes or no.'

'What would "yes" signify?'

'That we got all the cancer,' says Caleb. 'That it hasn't come back.'

'Then – no.'

Caleb glances down at the desk. The curled edge of a desk jotter, a couple of crumpled pieces of notepaper.

'This treatment is still in its infancy,' says the oncologist. 'There's so much we don't know.'

'Infancy,' says Caleb. 'I like that. A friend of mine's going to have a baby. There's a little corner in my mind, a place the cancer can't get to, that wanted to whisper my name over the baby's head.'

'I don't understand. You have a child on the way?'

'On the way? Yes. Me? No.'

'Look, Caleb, I –'

But Caleb is already halfway through the door.

Caleb sits on the Indian's seat, raising his face to the sun. He pulls in at the nearest service station and fills the tank and rides south, down to the motorway's end, then takes an off-ramp and crosses beneath the overbridge and rides back north again. He doesn't take any of the city exits, riding instead over the harbour bridge and heading further north. He turns left onto the road across the upper harbour, glancing up at the stark sun, imagining it highlighting his dying bones.

As he heads west, clouds begin to roll in off the ocean, cutting the light. By the time he hits the coast the clouds are shedding their water. When he reaches the West Coast road it is raining hard but he keeps riding, his T-shirt more water than fabric now. His hair is a single stripe down his back. A centreline on the road to the ocean. Down Rangimoana hill he slows, raises a single arm into the rain. His hand opening, a cup for the rainwater.

The fire is well advanced when the Red Watch crew get there, just on dusk. They leave the fire engine's headlights on, centring the burning prefab building in their cross-hairs. High-rise office blocks loom around them. Troy smelt the kerosene even as they were pulling over to the kerb. The black smoke rushes away in the suck of air between the buildings. When it's clear the back-up crew is needed to fight the fire itself another is called, then another. The blaze's edges are localised, the open construction pit isolating it. But there are a couple of mechanical diggers and a bulldozer within a few paces, likely to have petrol in their tanks. The overhang of other buildings are within a spark's reach. The crews struggle down into the hollow and train their hoses on the fire.

Tank and Jimbo edge closer to the fire. Troy looks through

the heat haze to where the blurred figure of a squat black shape sits within a wire cage fence. A white sign shines, red lettering for danger.

'Hang on,' he calls over to Monty. 'There's a transformer there.'

'What's that prefab office thingy made from?' calls Monty back. 'Can you see.'

'Aluminium!'

Both men shout but it is too late. The spill back of water from Tank and Jimbo's hoses has reached their boots. The sparks from the live cables arcing draws everyone's stare. There's a crunch, like stepping on a snail in the darkness, then Tank and Jimbo totter backwards into the water, Jimbo's arms jerking. Troy runs to the edge of the water, knowing he can't reach either man, knowing that stepping into the water will see him electrocuted.

He looks across to where the bulldozer sits, then runs to it and climbs up into the metal seat. He fumbles for the ignition, shouting when his fingers tell him the keys are still in it. First lucky break. He starts it, the smokestack puttering beside him. He works the throttle, then tries each of the control knobs for the scoop adjuster, finding it when he is halfway across the building site's width. He digs the scoop into the dirt, ploughing up topsoil and clay. Monty and Geronimo walk beside him, all of them staring at the prone figures in the crackling water.

Monty leans to Geronimo.

'The rubber gloves,' he says.

Tank runs back to the fire engine. Monty shouts into his walkie-talkie.

'Get someone to get the bloody power switched off!'

Troy aims the bulldozer's huge metal snout straight at the fallen firemen, raising a tide of dirt before him. The ring of electrified water hasn't grown, the others turning the pressure off at the source. Troy knows if he strays into its circle the metal tracks and frame of the bulldozer will suddenly become a conductor. Live. He ploughs on, Monty shining his torch at the water's edge, calling out distances foot by foot. When it is down to six feet Troy works the scoop up, fetching the dirt forward over the water's reach, over the firemen. Entombing them in a yard-deep mound of dirt. Geronimo puts on his rubber gloves, throws a pair each to Monty and Troy. Geronimo then starts towards the fan of dirt, but Monty grabs him.

'No!' he says, 'it isn't deep enough. Your feet'll go all the way through to the water. We have to do another go.'

Troy is already backing up. He sets the scoop lower this time and moves forward, conscious he could dig too deep and the bulldozer could become marooned. But it doesn't. He drives another few cubic yards of earth over the water, over the men, then stops the dozer and jumps off. Geronimo is on his hands and knees in the dirt, reaching down with his ·gloved hands for a grip on the buried firemen's jackets.

'Got one!'

Monty joins him, then Troy. Monty grabs an arm, and he and Geronimo pull Jimbo out, Jimbo's face pale. Troy drags him to flat ground, leans over him and begins the resuscitation procedure from rote. Two men from the Ponsonby crew help drag Tank out and they lie him flat also, breathing air into his lungs.

'He has a pulse,' says Monty. 'Bugger all, but it's there.'

'Nothing here,' says Troy.

The ambulance crew is there now, and Monty, Geronimo and Troy help them stretcher Tank and Jimbo up through the ambulance's open rear doors. The third crew on the scene puts out the fire. The power-board maintenance men have shut off the power to the whole city block. When the men get back to the station Geronimo begins to attack his locker, kicking at it with his boot. He tears the wooden door off its hinges and smashes it against the bench top. Troy walks to him, puts his arms around him, locking Geronimo in his grasp. Geronimo leans against the wall, nods his head.

They sit at the table, still in their full call-out gear. Monty looks up.

'It was my fault,' he says. 'Should've reccied the place better. Clocked that substation.'

'There wasn't time,' says Troy.

'Should've made bloody time,' says Monty. 'Two men down. Jesus, what a mess.'

'Did you smell the kerosene?' says Troy.

'Yep,' says Monty. He bows his head.

Geronimo leans back in his chair, stares out into the new day's light. Troy takes a sip of water from a cup, tips the rest over his hands.

Caleb raps the back of his hands against the doorway, looking through the smoke-glass at the rectangular shadows of the hallway. A shadow grows.

'Yeah?' says a voice.

'It's Caleb, let me in.'

The door opens a fraction. Dominic stands blinking into the new day's light, a bowl of rice bubbles in his hand. Caleb pushes the door open and steps inside, stopping only when he gets to Weston's room and the figure sitting on the bed looks up.

'To what do we owe this pleasure?' says Weston.

'Why start up again?' says Caleb.

'What business is it of yours? You look like shit, by the way.'

'That construction site. Two firemen ended up in hospital. One's on life support.'

Weston turns to the window, pulls the curtain back a few inches, blinks at the day. He lifts the pack of cigarettes from the small table next to the bed, lights one and sits back, looking through the smoke at Caleb.

'Well?' says Caleb.

Weston takes another draw on the cigarette, coughs.

'How long are we going to do this dance?' says Caleb.

'You forsook your right to anything when you bailed,' says Weston. 'Including information.'

'You poseur,' says Caleb. 'You think this is a James Bond movie don't you?'

'Inappropriate analogy.'

'It has to stop.'

'Thank you, Moses. Can I have a copy of the stone tablet?'

'Now.'

Weston gets out of bed, wearing only his underpants. He reaches for his glasses and puts them on. Being almost naked, the frailty in his frame and movements is a shock to Caleb. Dominic appears in the doorway.

'Maybe you should go,' says Dominic.

Weston puts his sunglasses on.

'I mean what I said,' says Caleb.

'You don't have any pull here anymore,' says Weston. 'Unless you have some sort of chip to bargain with?'

'Happens I do.'

'We're all ears,' says Weston.

'There's a protest rally, in the park.'

'Yes,' says Weston, 'I know. Strumming guitars and rattling bangles.'

'Just people who want change.'

'Singing won't change anything,' says Weston.

'Nor will electrocuting firemen.'

'This has been sixty seconds of my life,' says Weston, 'are we coming to the part about the bargaining chip?'

Caleb steps full into the room for the first time. He walks to the window and pulls back the rest of the curtains. Old-world suburbia: an elderly couple out walking, a woman with a little boy. A couple of kids passing a Frisbee back and forth.

'But you have to commit,' he says, looking out the window. 'You have to commit to ending it.'

'Well, for that, this idea would have to say it all.'

Caleb watches the Frisbee fly, rotating faster than the eye can count. It hovers over the rough hedge fence bordering the footpath, lands on the mangy grass fronting the old villa. He looks down at it, a tiny circle of pale yellow amongst the weeds.

An hour later he stands at his doctor's window.

'For what it's worth,' he says, 'I don't feel that bad.'

'Some days you will,' says the doctor, 'some days you won't.'

Caleb glances down at the prescription pad, the doctor's illegible scrawl. He smiles. The doctor looks up.

'Do they give chemists lessons in deciphering hieroglyphics?' says Caleb.

He picks up his pain medication and walks out into the humid air. The spring is turning over into summer. He shakes the bag, the pills rattling in the plastic bottles. He takes two bottles out and raises them each side of his head, like a set of maracas.

There are times now he rides to the blowhole above South Bay. Among the rock cliffs as high as a three-storied building. 'The Mausoleum', the surfers call it, where the unwary go in, but might not come out. The swirling currents twist in the circular bay below. He thinks of Dominic's face through the doorway, Weston sitting like a small boy, peering through dark sunglasses in his own bedroom. Every few seconds, when a big wave enters and rages at its capture, the blowhole erupts, drenching him. He lays back, the sharp stone not as uncomfortable as the stinging inside his veins.

He could have acceded to more radiology, but he won't. He won't spend his last days amid the metallic whirr of electric motors and gauges and scopes. That awful plasticy noise that the wheels of the drugs trolley makes on the linoleum floor. He won't die vomiting. He could just lie here amid the blowhole's trumpeting or even just slip down off the rock's face and join the smoke-glass water. But he doesn't think he'll do that either. He has made a promise, a promise to people he doesn't even like, cannot now (if he ever could) call his friends. But his commitment to them is secondary. He has a more binding commitment to the face on the magazine cover, looking up out of the water, past the scalded faces of the two children.

Yeah, he saw the photo. Troy in the river.

No, he doesn't want to see it again.

Akiko opens the door to the house at Rangimoana, drops her bag in the sitting room. She goes through the hall to the main bedroom and out to the deck where Caleb lies in the hammock, looking over the top of the rails to the ocean.

'Thought I'd find you out here,' she says.

He doesn't answer.

'You okay?' says Akiko.

'No.'

Akiko touches a hand against his chest.

'Caleb.'

'There's something I have to tell you,' he says.

Akiko steps closer and he reaches out of the hammock and takes her hand in his. The hammock rocks against her.

'What is it?' says Akiko.

He takes a deep breath, the only sound now the creaking of the hammock's ropes.

'Caleb, what is it?'

'It's called acute lymphoblastic leukaemia.'

'What is?'

'What I have.'

'I don't understand.'

'Bone-marrow cancer.'

Her hands are suddenly cold, though Caleb's are still warm. She closes her eyes.

'Those mysterious vanishings,' she says.

'Yeah, I was having radiation treatment.'

'Are you cured?'

'I thought I was.'

'Thought?'

She moves closer still, laying her hands across his chest, every slight movement of either of them setting the hammock swaying.

'I need you to make me a promise,' says Caleb.

Akiko swallows, her eyelids shut tight.

'No one else is to know,' says Caleb.

'I don't know if I can.'

'No one.'

She opens her eyes just in time to see his fall closed.

'I'm going to grab a nap,' he says.
'Caleb –'
'Please, Kiki. I'm so tired.'

Troy walks down the long corridor to the nurse's station and asks the woman about Jimbo and Tank. Jimbo is still in the critical ward and can't have visitors. Tank has been moved to the burns unit. Troy sits at the foot of Tank's bed, leaning forward with his hands clasped between his knees, looking up at the bandages wrapped around Tank's arms and legs. His face, though tinged a slight yellow, isn't burned. To his left the monitor beeps. Troy watches the electric ticks crackle at each heartbeat. He stands and walks to the window and looks down at the trees in the domain.

A nurse comes in, adjusts Tank's pillow and checks the chart at the foot of his bed. She doesn't say anything to Troy, nor he to she.

He cuts through the domain, the Chev's driver's window open to the cooling wind. After a while he notices some of the lamp-posts have large pieces of paper stuck to them. He stops next to one. Orange paper, handwritten lettering.

Stop the War Now!
Rally for Peace.
Auckland Domain. Armistice Day, November 11th
An hour after he gets home Monty phones to tell him Jimbo died without regaining consciousness.

In the night they lie in the dark, Akiko listening to the ticking clock in the hall.

'Had you known him long?' she says.

'I thought you were asleep,' says Troy.

'I was.'

The clock ticks.

'A few months,' says Troy.

'Were you good friends?'

'Workmates.'

Her mind lets go of the clock, listens instead for Troy's breathing.

'You know,' says Troy, 'when I went to ask about Tank, the nurse asked me his real name and I didn't know.'

Akiko shifts in the sheets, rolls over onto her right side.

'That's not a crime,' she says, 'if that's what you were thinking.'

An hour later she is still awake.

'Troy?' she says.

He mumbles something.

'There's something I need to tell you,' says Akiko.

He rolls over, flicks on the light.

'What is it?'

She turns to him, looks into his sleepy eyes.

'Kiki, what is it?'

She shakes her head.

'Nothing,' she says.

November, 1970

Caleb checks his watch, glances up at the late afternoon sun. He goes to his bedroom and eases the dresser out and reaches into the hole that he has knocked in the wall. He lifts out the plastic bag with his medication and spreads out a half-dozen pills on the dresser top. Painkillers, vitamins, antacids for the wear on his stomach caused by taking all the other pills. He has grown used to the moments that can turn to hours when his body flops into a chair or his bed and the act of getting up to go to the toilet requires a half-hour's motivation, lying staring at the ceiling, drawing the path down the hallway in his head. Sometimes, if he takes enough meds he gets a couple of hours' respite, if not from the stiffness, at least from the pain.

He rides out alone often now, not wanting to be in the midst of a conversation when he begins to sweat for no reason. Not wanting to fall asleep while chewing his meagre meals.

Clearings in the hills, empty nooks in the rocks above the blowhole or beyond the boulders of South Bay. He has known it all in just a few months. The night sweats that turn his sheets sodden, the weight loss that scours his frame like a desert wind. Pain in his bones, bruises that appear without prompting, turning his legs and backside into a patchwork of lethal purple just by something as minor as the mere act of knocking against a door jamb.

He looks at his watch again, then opens the lid of his bottle of painkillers. He needs a couple of hours' grace.

The salt spray hazes in the open doorway, spicing the air. Etta finds a seat just off the aisle, takes the battered straw hat from her head and sits it in her lap. She turns to watch the townspeople file into the hall, but makes no direct contact with them. She can't recall names, but there are hints in faces, the timbre of a voice or the angle of a stare that opens little pockets in her memory. A hum of conversation encircles the hall until a small woman steps from the folds of a makeshift stage curtain and walks to the edge of the platform. She is dressed in a frock that predates World War Two. There are a few hisses from schoolboys, silenced by smacks on the back of the head from their fathers. By the verbal farts and jeers from the audience Etta guesses the woman must be the local schoolmistress, as she herself once was. The woman stands guardsman straight and announces the first act and a small boy with a ruddy face and glasses appears, sings 'Jerusalem' in a tone that is as close to whistling as it is to singing.

After a couple of songs from individual children – with the occasional falter as words are forgotten – three girls and three boys appear in animal costumes, the boys dragging a wagon with an old tea chest sitting on it. They offer a rendition of 'Old MacDonald had a Farm' that bears little resemblance to the original, accentuated by the inclusion of lions and elephants. The song ends with the girls losing all coordination of voices and movements, to the amusement of the audience.

The box's lid bursts open and a large figure somehow climbs from it, limbs unwinding. Silver trousers and baggy silver jacket. His sleeves balloon from his sides, from which long fingers reach up to push a silver hat back on his head. His face is also silver, fixed in an exaggerated smile. A patchwork cousin to the *Wizard of Oz*'s Tin Man.

Etta sits forward as the silver figure moves amid the children, their tiny feet jumping away from his jerky movements. But there is something in his disjointed gait that hints at a grace beneath. A sudden pirouette which seems doomed to end in a clatter of limbs to the floor is saved by an elastic pull of his legs back upright. He crouches, looks out at the audience, some of the seated children booing, some clapping. A toffee paper sails towards his face and he catches it, holds it aloft like treasure. A shrug of the shoulders, a roll of his eyes to the gallery. Music starts through the loudspeakers, a jaunty 1920s rag, and his limbs suddenly assume the ease of a bird's wings and he begins to dance.

Etta is startled to hear that his shoes are fitted with metal taps. A few elaborate steps, another pirouette, then the music slows, a drawn-out moan from the loudspeakers and the children dissolve into giggles. Someone is playing with the speed control on the gramophone. Sixteen rpm, then back to thirty-three. Then to forty-five, his limbs splaying to keep up with the sudden speed changes. A leap and he is atop one of the speaker cabinets, hands on hips, legs braced. A moment of triumph, but with one foot slipping past the speaker's edge, hovering in emptiness. For an instant he stands staring over the heads of the audience at something an infinity away. Then he clasps his hat to his head, and the other hand – seeming almost disembodied – reaches up to pull his collar, drags him backwards off the cabinet and back across the stage, the rest of his body jerking in argument. The audience shrieks with laughter. Up and down goes the speed of the music. Slower, faster, the Tin Man in a desperate struggle to keep to the rhythm.

Etta realises she is no longer laughing, though the rest of the hall is in uproar. Amid all the slapstick mayhem there is a fixed numbness in his eyes, a scarring, like moth holes discovered in a favourite piece of fabric. She turns away, looks to the window and the dusk beyond, the jolt of the changes in the music's speed like blows against her body. When she turns back the Tin Man is collapsing piece by piece to the floor, stray limbs fighting to stay upright. A shoe comes off, revealing a holed silver sock, toes wiggling. He struggles to stand one last time, but his hand reaches up again, drags him by the collar back towards the box and he tips backwards into it, a single hand raised.

The lid shuts.

The children grab the wagon's handle and pull the box away offstage. The music comes to a sudden halt and a voice announces an intermission. Etta stands and pushes past a couple of outstretched legs, batting away clapping hands. She walks up the aisle, out over the road and into the scent of the harbour, stopping only to steady herself with a hand against a telephone pole.

She lifts a cigarette from her bag, grips it in her fingers. She lifts out a matchbox, strikes a match, but the wind blows it out so she lights another. Again the wind blows it out. Then another.

A crackle on the stones outside the hall turns her head. Footsteps. Her eyes discern a figure moving from shadow to shadow, lit now and then as someone comes from the side entrance of the hall and sends a spray of light into the darkened courtyard. The Tin Man. He walks over to the fence alongside the hall and crouches, retching. The hall doors close and he is lost in the shadows again. Then his face appears in the tiny circle of a burning match he holds in front of his eyes. He looks past the flame, either to where Etta stands or out to the darkened ocean, she cannot tell which.

Etta drives her rental car to the end of the road and steps out. She looks up at the hillsides above the town. They are speckled with lights that were not there the last time she stood here within the sound of the surf. She lifts a torch from her army bag and goes through the trees and sits on the sand, the collar of her jacket pulled up. She flicks her torch beam on and off, breathing in the sea wind. Somewhere amid the torch beam's moments of life the voice comes to her.

My apologies, it says, I didn't know there was anyone here.

She reaches down, takes her boots and socks off and sits barefoot, the sand smooth, cold. She stretches her legs, feeling a couple of shells make way. Then she stands, her boots in one hand, the torch in the other, and walks through the trees and crosses the road. When she hears the creek to her left, even in darkness, she knows where she is. She crosses the swingbridge and carries on up.

Loud music comes down through the trees. A howl of electric guitars and driving drums. A single light comes from the house.

She crests the staircase, drops her boots at the front door and goes beneath the arch of the trellis to where the music blares, the vibrations buzzing through her skin. The Tin Man stands at one of the blackboards nailed to the outside wall, a piece of chalk in each hand. Writing lines of numbers and symbols – with both hands – at the same time. His eyes glance from one line to the other. He pauses, then begins to write anew, faster this time. The figures appearing in a blaze, like bullet holes. A scattering of moths circle the bulb above his head. Etta sits on the wooden bench. Then the chalk drops from his fingers and he curses. It bounces on the floorboards, then stills. He reaches for it, flexing his hand, pausing when he sees Etta's bare feet at the edge of the circle of light from the bulb. He looks up.

'Hello, Caleb,' says Etta.

He stands staring for a moment, then takes a couple of paces towards her, reaches and lifts the straw hat from her head and sets it – half askew – on his own head. His silver face is thin, cut with shadows. He lifts the hat away, twirls it on a finger then flicks it in the air and catches it again and sets it back on his head. She looks through the silver make-up and into his grey eyes. He holds her stare for a moment, then turns back to his blackboards, to his wild scrawl of numbers in chalk-dust. In the glare of the electric light the figures hang as pale as the whitecaps of Rangimoana's waves.

'You kept hold of Dad's old hat,' he says.

'It's been around the world a few times. It was the only thing I had of his.'

Caleb turns away, looks across the lines of numbers, out into the dark.

'That's not true,' he says. 'You had his heart.'

Troy and Akiko go late-night shopping at the supermarket. They are halfway back home when Akiko winces, takes a sharp breath. Troy glances over at her. Her expression is fixed. He looks back at the asphalt, the white marker lines melding into a single line. Her hand slips over his wrist. He slows, changes down through the gears, the Chev's motor rising and falling in pitch.

'The hospital,' she says.

She looks up at the hospital's pale walls rushing by. The faces above her. A nurse, a doctor. Troy takes her hand and she closes her eyes to everything but his touch, her grip tightening whenever the pain coils within her.

Troy stands alone in the waiting room. The streetlights shine beyond the windows. He turns and looks through the double doors and down the long corridor to where other corridors lead away. The quiet is overwhelming. He longs for noise – engine noise, street noise, voices, anything – but there is only silence.

The door opens and the doctor appears and takes off his mask.

'You have a baby girl,' he says.

Akiko lies swathed in blankets. Her hair is wet, streaked over the pillow. Her face so pale, a redness at the corners of her lips, in her eyes. She has the baby bundled in blankets against her. A mess of dark hair, a pink forehead. Eyes shut tight.

Akiko smiles. Troy sits against the edge of the bed, takes Akiko's face against his cheek. The baby nuzzled between them.

'What do you want to name her?' he says.

'Rai.'

'Rai. What does it mean?'

'It means trust. Trust.'

Etta spends the night curled up on the couch. In the morning she rolls over and looks at the thin slice of sunlight in the gap between the drapes. Dust swims in its path. They had not spoken for long after she found Caleb writing on the blackboards on the deck. Her eyelids felt weighted with stones. Caleb slept in the big bedroom Etta once shared with Isaac's. Etta had glanced towards the boys' old room, but Caleb shook his head, so she bunked down on the couch.

She showers and dresses and comes back down the hall to the lingering smell of toast. She wanders down the hall to the master bedroom, raises her hand to the tap. A motorbike's engine rumbles on the path outside. She walks back through the kitchen and out onto the path where Caleb sits on the Indian, slipping a leather satchel into the saddlebags. He looks up at her, fastens the saddlebag's clasp.

'I'll head into town,' says Etta. 'Your fridge looks a bit bare.'

He shrugs.

'Are you a tea or a coffee drinker these days?' she asks.

'Why are you here?'

She glances at his hand gripped hard on the motorbike's throttle. Caleb turns forward, manoeuvres down the drive.

Etta watches until he vanishes, listens until she loses the sound in the trees.

She leans over the bathroom basin, blinking her eyes within the falling water. She washes her hair, lets the water keep running until all the soap has been rinsed away. She puts a load of washing through the old wringer machine then goes for a walk along the beach, stopping now and then to take photographs; Koroheke, the stalks of spinifex leaning away from the wind, gulls diving in the waves.

She sleeps on and off all day, jet lag stealing her concentration. At one point she wanders into the main bedroom and sits on the bed. Notebooks are stacked in what she guesses is precise order, clothes are also stacked. On the dressing table stands a small statue of the Tin Man, standing upright, axe over his shoulder. The figure stares across the room also. His other hand is raised beneath his hat brim, as if something in the distance has caught his metallic stare.

Dusk finds her out on the stones arranged in a rough half-circle at the head of the driveway. She is listening to the sound of the motorbike for a good half-minute before she realises she is. Her mind elsewhere. It comes up the drive and stops. Caleb turns off the motor and looks over the handlebars at her.

'Do we have to be strangers?' says Etta.

He steps off.

'You're asking *me* that question?' he says.

He turns towards the house, takes a couple of steps.

'Caleb,' says Etta.

He stops, but doesn't look at her.

'Do you know where Troy is?' says Etta.

He turns, then keeps on walking.

'I saw the photo,' says Caleb, still walking. 'How could you do that?'

'It's what I do,' she calls.

He looks at her for a moment, then goes on inside.

The men of Red Watch clap Troy as he climbs the stairs to the locker room with his bag. Troy notes the two new faces amongst them, to replace Tank and Jimbo. Monty hands him a cigar in a plastic wrapper.

'A fireman or an accountant?' says Monty.

'We have a daughter.'

Monty smiles.

'Good on ya,' he says.

It is a quiet day; a scrub burn–off that gets out of hand, a chainsawed tree that falls the wrong way and takes the edge off a corrugated-iron verandah, a fire in an abandoned shop that extinguished itself before the crew even arrives. In the afternoon Troy steps from the fire station door and heads towards the Chev parked at the kerb. But another shape intrudes. Propped on its stand. The Indian.

'You know,' says Caleb, from where he leans against a wattle tree, 'you never answered my question.'

'Which was?' says Troy.

'Is it true, that you can hear a train approaching from miles away, by putting your ears to the railroad tracks?'

Troy's stare slips from the present, seeing a child's body turn towards him. Caleb's grinning face as he pointed his little kid's penis at the steel horizons of the railway tracks. The stream of pee jiggling as the boy erupted in giggles. Steam rising from the wet grass.

'Yeah, I followed her,' says Caleb. 'And you. I had to know.'

Troy looks down at the pavement for a moment, nods his head.

'Congrats, by the way,' says Caleb.

'Thanks.'

Caleb steps away from the tree, his body so thin, cheekbones like razors. He walks towards the motorcycle and swings his leg over and sits and glances back.

'Ma asked after you,' he says.

Troy's body stiffens.

'Yeah,' says Caleb, 'she's in town.'

Troy looks up into the greying sky.

'Hey, Troy.'

'Yeah?'

'Don't ever answer my question. I believe I want to go on wondering.'

Troy thinks to say something, but nothing comes out. He turns to watch the motorcyclist circle around him and go to the edge of the driveway and sit waiting for a break in the traffic. When he is gone all that's left is the Chev, its yellow panels stark against the grey concrete.

Caleb hand-washes his clown outfit in the tub, then pegs it on the line. Waistcoat and baggy pants, ring-striped socks. He spreads the sleeves against the clothes hanger wire, stopping cold when he sees Etta standing a few feet away, staring at the empty clown's shell swinging in the breeze.

'I told Troy you were here,' he says. 'For what it's worth.'

'It's worth a lot,' says Etta. 'Thank you.'

Troy wakes to a faint, slatted sun, looks through the venetian blinds to a lightening sky. He glances down to where Akiko lies with her eyelids flickering against the skin above his collarbone. He reaches around, parts a few stray hairs with a fingertip, looking over her to where Rai sleeps in her bassinette. He draws himself away from Akiko, eases her head back down against the pillow and stands and goes to the child and crouches watching her. Rai's eyelids flicker also. He touches a finger to his lips then against her forehead.

He walks the shadowed hallway to the bathroom and slaps some water over himself then goes back to the bedroom for his jeans and car keys.

He works the clutch and changes down to third then accelerates up the hill, the Chev the only car on the road at this hour. He winds it out up Kepa Road to the brow then slows, houses now dotting the hilltop to his left, the grass bank falling away to his right, down the steep slope to where the Orakei basin's water shimmers. He takes a couple of side streets down the hill towards the harbour and pulls out onto Tamaki Drive. A couple of people walk, a dog trots by itself along the footpath above the sea wall. He stops, steps out and looks over at Rangitoto. He had read once that the volcano isn't in fact extinct, isn't dead, but is dormant. Sleeping. He looks across the path of water out to it, as if he can see beneath it, see into its workings like he can the Chev's. What simmers beneath and why. But all he can see is water.

Then his mother's face.

When he sits back on the edge of the bed Akiko and Rai are still asleep. He taps the edge of the plate, watches Akiko's eyelids rise as her nose senses the hot-buttered bun and the cup of herb tea. She smiles.

'Couldn't sleep?' she says.

He doesn't answer, just leans and kisses her on the cheek.

It is mid–morning before Troy leaves. And when he does, Caleb sits watching the Chev pull out of the driveway, watches the brake lights and indicator flicker at the end of the street. He pulls out of the sidestreet. When Akiko answers the door she tucks the inner edges of her robe in tighter and shows him down the hall. Upstairs he turns from her sleepy eyes to the tiny face above the folds of the cot's blankets.

'You can pick her up if you'd like,' says Akiko.

Caleb crouches, looking through the vertical wooden slats of the cot at Rai. He senses that his stance is wobbly, his hold on the earth tenuous. He touches his palm against the pastel pink of her jumpsuit, closing his eyes to her warmth. He stands and slips his arms around Akiko, holding her tight even when the pain in his withering body stabs him. Breathing hard through his nose. She winces at his tensed jaw line.

'I'm sorry, Caleb.'

'For what?'

'For everything.'

'Everything?'

'For it being Troy.'

Akiko sits on the bed, looks through the window at the trees. Her hands tighten into fists. She shouts, wordless, her eyes shut tight.

'Kiki,' says Caleb. 'Don't.'

She glances at the cot.

'Half of me is happy,' she says, 'but the other half is dying with you.'

When she looks up her eyes are damp. Her voice quivers.

'Screw your dad and screw all the others out there, tinkering away with stuff that poisons everything it touches.'

'None of this is Dad's fault.'

'Oh, really?'

Caleb shakes his head.

Akiko closes her eyes, takes a long breath.

'You think I don't recognise you?' she says. 'You think I haven't seen you before? Hundreds of you, stumbling to death? I went into hospital once in Nagasaki when I was a child, to have a broken finger reset. I'd fallen while dancing. While I was in the waiting room I wandered off, down corridor after corridor, realising after a while I was lost among all that sterile whiteness. I had the feeling that the more I tried to go back to where I was supposed to be, the further I wandered away. At one end of the building there was a ward just for them. Even those who had survived had had their names wiped away, by my people, by the Americans. The great, collective forgetting. United only by their bandages. Only there's no bandage for the crater beneath my feet.'

'Kiki.'

'And now you're falling into it. Don't you see? I've spent my whole life dancing on a tightrope above that crater. Trying never to look down.'

'Kiki.'

'Never.'

Her arms are folded tight across her chest. Caleb takes a step towards her, but his limbs stiffen. He closes his eyes, feels his way to her, stands with his chin over her head. He leans close to her, his lips against her ear.

'Remember when I asked you,' he says, 'if a man did something wrong but for the right reasons, would that man get forgiveness or damnation?'

'Yes.'

He reaches and draws back her hair and kisses her on the temple, his lips against the tiny pulse beneath her skin. She closes her eyes to his touch.

'I need to believe in forgiveness,' says Caleb.

At the fire station Troy walks up the stairs. Monty looks up from where he sits wiping some grime from his boots.

'You forget you're not on today?' says Monty.

'Nope. Just come in for something.'

Troy opens his locker, shifts his toiletries aside to reveal the two photographs on the back wall. One faces towards him, one faces away. He pulls both away from the wall, the sticky tape coming apart. He peels it all off, puts both photographs into his shirt pocket. He walks back to the smoko room. Monty puts his boot and the rag down on the floor and sits back on the couch.

'You coming back?' says Monty.

'Like you said, day off.'

'No. I mean ever.'

'Why?'

'The look on your face.'

'Will the fires stop?'

'Nope.'

Troy doesn't answer. Monty smiles – not his usual smirk but something deeper, deep enough to turn his eyes away for a moment. Then back. Troy raises his chin to him, turns and walks on out the door.

The oncologist looks up from his notes, sets his pen down on the page.

'Two or three months, perhaps,' he says.

Caleb nods. The wind from the open window to his left tweaks the edges of the pages of notes. Flips one over, then another. The oncologist lifts his pen out of the way, draws the cover of the manila folder closed.

'A hell of a lot of pages, doc,' says Caleb. 'None of them had the answer.'

'You've chosen what to do and what not to do.'

'That's not in dispute.'

'Well then.'

'What will the end be like?'

The oncologist leans back.

'Lethargy, anaemia.'

'I'm pretty much there already.'

'Then an infection, something that would, for a healthy person, be quite minor. There are any number of ways.'

Caleb looks up at the bare walls. An out-of-date calendar, a couple of photos of a dog. A hessian board with small notes tacked to it. The desk is chipped at the edges, the painted walls faded.

'You should get this place done up, doc,' says Caleb as he stands. 'You said perhaps. How big a perhaps?'

'It could be longer. Could be sooner. We still don't know that much about it.'

Caleb nods.

'See you, doc,' he says, 'look after yourself.'

Caleb meets Weston and Dominic in Victoria Park. Caleb stands looking up at the cars on the flyover, listening to the clackety-clack of their wheels over the concrete joints.

'Nice choice,' says Weston, glancing across at the spot where the first napalm explosion had burned a circle in the grass.

'If I do this,' says Caleb, 'it has to stop with this.'

'If?' says Weston.

'When,' says Caleb. 'But you have to promise.'

'Cross our hearts and hope to die?' says Dominic.

Caleb stands for a moment, then balls his fist and punches Dominic, high on his cheekbone, at the corner of his eye socket. Dominic staggers, regains his balance. The shock in his eyes is burned away by his snarl. Weston steps between them, raises his arms.

'We're not brawling in the playground like bloody kids,' he says.

Dominic raises a hand, touches it against his eyebrow. Caleb stares at him. Dominic turns and walks away. Weston takes a packet of cigarettes from his jeans pocket, then a box of matches.

'Dramatic,' says Weston, as Caleb takes a cigarette from the pack.

'You have to promise,' says Caleb.

'And you trust my promises?' says Weston.

'I guess I'll have to.'

Well past midnight Isaac wakes in his hospital bed at Mount Iris. There is a steady sobbing coming from one of the rooms. Every now and then he hears doors open and close and voices, and the sobbing stops. Then the doors bang again. After that, the sobbing begins anew. He stands and walks barefoot out into the corridor, the white fluorescent lights blinding. Down the passage, stopping when he glimpses the nurse's station, waiting until the nurse turns and goes into one of the other rooms. The sobbing stops. He moves past the deserted station to another corridor. He stands looking out through the wire mesh at the dark.

The sobbing starts again.

When the Tin Man rises up out of the crate the children jump, then break into laughter. Caleb stares through the silver eye make-up at them, a tiny smile hidden by his painted grin. He reaches down, opens up a drawer in his mock-tin belly and begins to search, letting things fall out as he does so. A black-faced gonk, an old crier's bell, a slithery rubber lizard, a clutch of fake dollar bills. He draws around a ukulele attached to his back with a string, begins to warble in a broken falsetto. One of the children picks up a dollar, curls it into a ball and throws it at him. He accepts it, puts it in his mouth and chews and swallows it.

He blows up a couple of balloon animals and gives them away, but the older boys snatch them out of the fingers of the younger kids and burst them with their hands or crush them beneath their feet. Caleb stares.

'Don't do that,' he says in his normal voice.

'Says who?' says one of the boys.

He makes another balloon, a giraffe, hands it to a little girl. A boy seizes it from her, stomps on it. The loud bang sends a shiver through the younger children. A couple cry.

'I said, don't do that,' says Caleb.

The boy gives him the fingers. Caleb stands and chases him, raising his ukulele like a hammer. The boy squeals, begins to wail. Caleb stops, stands, breathing hard, the ukulele still raised. The boy runs out of the room to where the adults are gathered. Caleb sits cross-legged on the floor, looking along the wooden boards at the snatches of sunlight igniting the wood grains. Igniting the dust. He cradles the ukulele and begins to sing.

When a man's an empty kettle
He should be on his mettle
And yet I'm torn apart

The boy appears again, dragging his father by the hand. They approach, the father stern of face.

Just because I'm presumin'
I could be kind of human
If I only had a heart

'What's all this about?' says the father.

Caleb looks up, not at the boy or his father, but past them, to where the open window sits, the curtain opening and closing, now and then giving him a glimpse of the afternoon sun.

He steps onto the Indian, still in the Tin Man costume, hits the kick-start with his boot. He rides west for a couple of miles then stops at a give-way sign, sits with his hand resting on the throttle. He takes off fast, cutting across the path of the car behind him to turn left. Turn south.

Traffic on the motorway slows to stare at him. A police car pulls close and the officers turn, then shake their heads and carry on. At the turnoff to Mount Iris, a child points at him, then waves. He waves back. When Isaac walks in to the visiting room and stops and stares, Caleb sets his whole face and body in tune with the Tin Man's metal grin.

'Be careful,' says Isaac, 'the wind might change and you'll stay like that.'

Caleb reaches into a pocket, squeezes an air horn. He sets his satchel down on a table.

They sit near the window. Isaac has had his hair cut short, and grey spikes of it stand in the sunlight, like a glimpse of a distant cemetery.

'I didn't expect you back for a couple of weeks,' says Isaac.

Caleb pulls a cigarette from the door in the front of the costume. He goes to light it, then stops and smiles.

'What?' says Isaac.

'I forgot. These ones explode.'

'Perhaps not, then.'

Caleb reaches into the door again, lifts out a crumpled packet. He looks at the orderly and the orderly nods and he lights his cigarette, then Isaac's off his.

'Akiko had the baby,' he says.

Isaac leans back.

'A little girl,' says Caleb.

The edges of Isaac's eyes crinkle.

'We were never going to be together,' says Caleb. 'Though I suppose now, I always wanted us to be.'

'Is that what's troubling you?' says Isaac.

Caleb frowns.

'Then what is?' says Isaac. 'You didn't come all the way down here, dressed like that, to tell me what you're not.'

'No.'

'Then what?'

'Tell me about Antarctica.'

'Caleb, we've been through this.'

'Tell me.'

Isaac looks into the smoke glass of the window.

'The dreams have come back,' he says.

'Have you told the doctors?'

'No.'

'Why?'

'They'll just use it as a reason to keep me here.'

'Tell me about Antarctica.'

Isaac doesn't answer.

'Are the dreams about Antarctica?' says Caleb.

'Sometimes.'

'Tell me,' says Caleb.

Isaac draws on the cigarette and the smoke hovers across his face. He blinks his eyes, raises a hand to flick it away.

'On my first night there I roused in the bright light of three am and walked to the window. Even in summer it was so cold the warmth in my raised palms set condensation free on the glass pane. I stood at the door, then moved out onto the rocky ground, noticing only after a few minutes the absence of trees or even grass. There was nothing green – no trees, no grass – for miles in any direction.

'On my second night I woke again in light, my fingers clawing at my sleeping bag's fabric. My sharp breaths steaming. The dream was so real I sniffed the air for the scent of trees.'

'What was the dream?' says Caleb.

Isaac shifts in his seat. He looks down at the burning cigarette in his fingers. When he looks up there are smoke trails in his eyes.

The traffic light turns green and cars begin to move. A breeze rattles the leaves on the trees above the river. A child's ball rolls from the playground out into the street. The child runs after it, stops at the kerb to watch the cars slowing. The driver stops and waves and the child steps out and picks up the ball and turns back to his friends.

'Who was the child?' says Caleb.

Isaac sits forward, his hands steepled on the table. He speaks with his head lowered, as if he speaks into his hands.

'The next day I stood out on a rock shelf in the Salmon Stream Valley,' he says, 'where there were no salmon, nor streams to hold them. The pilot stood topping up the helicopter's oil. The grey stone and shale valley walls rose up around us, distant mountain peaks rising over their ridges. In the endless twilight I walked out a half mile, the rustle of my parka's hood rubbing against my ears and the crunch of my boots on the stony ground the only sounds anywhere. After a couple of hundred yards it was still easy to imagine there might be a town or a ski camp over the next hill. Music on a radio, a stove, a clink of glasses and bleary-eyed laughter. After another couple of hundred yards that seemed no longer possible. I may as well have been on Mars.

'In the desert-dry air I tired fast, so I sat on a rock, the cold reaching my bones even through the heavy fleece-lined coveralls and my trousers beneath. I lifted the hood away for a half-minute, braving even the sudden growth of new ice on my skin, just to try and hear something. Anything. With the stilling of my movements there was nothing to hear.

'When I got back to the helicopter one of the crew was setting a fire in a little self-contained drum. Burning a shit he'd just had. He made sure none of the ash escaped into the air, where it would sit – an intruder – on the valley floor. In the Dry Valleys even the ash from burned human excrement lasts forever.'

Isaac looks up from his hands.

'Can I see one of those exploding cigarettes?' he asks.

Caleb lifts one from his pocket. Isaac turns it over in his fingers, lets it sit flat in his palm. Somewhere beyond the hospital a dog barks, another dog answers. Isaac takes another draw on his cigarette, blows the smoke out over the table.

On the ice they move out again in their converted farm tractors. The puffs of dark smoke from the exhausts are like holes in the white of the snow beyond. The air is so clear that hills that seem ten minutes' walk away are in reality fifty miles distant. Isaac sits on a strange rock shape, a ventifact, its wind-sculpted form detailed enough to be the fossilised echo of a dinosaur. The wind sends messages from ice wall to ice wall. Isaac helps a team of three biologists set up their instruments then asks them when they're flying out. Not for hours. He puts his rations into a back-pack, pulls his hood up over his head. Though the sun is quite warm and the air at least liveable, the wind spirals the thermometer downwards with each gust. He walks up a bank of scree, leaves the jade haze of Lake Vanda below. What seemed like a walk of a few hundred yards turns out to be miles. Isaac climbing, his feet feeling a strange familiarity. Another hillside comes to mind, dark grey, desolate. He stops and looks down at his boots, the line of his footprints stretching away down to the valley floor. With the weight of his gear he begins to tire, stops and sits on a rock and looks around. Black hills, white hills. Boulders that look like pebbles but which he guesses are the size of a trolley bus. He starts again, the slope steepening, his lungs tightening in air drier than he can imagine. He reaches a crest and looks down over the rim. A glacier, a white highway with an edge a hundred feet high. He walks down the slope towards it, his feet quickening, his steps losing their semblance of order on the slippery ice. He begins to slip. Dust rises around him and keeps rising, the wind blowing it ahead of him. He slips again, this time where the gradient has turned treacherous, and he loses his footing, tumbles down the slope. His pack breaks free. He tries to grab for it but shadows loom. He looks up, raises his hands over his face as he smashes against something huge and white. The glacier wall.

In the dream a cat sits washing in a doorway, glancing up to where a bird flies. A woman looks from where she pushes her pram to a man trimming his rosebushes. They smile. An old man with a walking stick stops, bends to pick up a leaf.

He tries to stand up from the ice, but falls when a knee gives way. He rises again, his head pounding. He looks around, knowing he is too tired, too sore to try to climb the incline. Instead he walks along the defile, the thin passage between the glacier and the hillside. He can't see his pack against the grey and black stone. He shakes his head and moves on, knowing he will be almost invisible in the lee of the glacier, but he is unable to find a way back up the hillside. He keeps moving, once or twice thinking he hears a helicopter engine. Thirst gnaws at him now, and he grabs a sharp-edged rock and scrapes away a few inches of the glacier wall, crushing it with a larger stone. Trying to break it down into something resembling water. He takes off a glove and tests the ice's temperature, rubbing it hard against his palm until his skin stings. Then he puts a fragment into his mouth and sucks on it, his tongue tinder dry. He stops, sits down to rest.

In the dream the postman slows his bicycle, looks up to where a pair of thin trails arc in the morning sky. He listens hard for the sound of an aeroplane engine, but there's only the wind in the leaves.

Isaac rests every half-hour or so, reciting mathematical conundrums in his mind as he walks, keeping his focus. Daylight will last until well after midnight. He walks on. Hours later he senses the glacier's wall vanishing in the distance. He begins to run, knowing that his tiny figure is covering in seconds what the glacier covers in a century. At last the white wall breaks west and a corner appears. An edge. He rounds it, stops in its lee. Allows himself to lie in a ball, conserving body heat while he rests. In a few minutes he is sleeping. In his sleep a line of hills ease beneath him, a bay, the tiny imprints of houses. All far below, like a Lilliput landscape. He clutches his arms to his chest, focusing on the central core of lights, a city.

The B-52 bomber's doors open for me and I slip away. No one below is aware of me. My head and my body, encased in their metal sarcophagus, are two separate nuclear weapons. In my head a ring of high explosives surround a central compressible core of plutonium 239. An implosion bomb, a Fat Man. My heart is a rod of plutonium 239 surrounded with a jacket of lithium 6 deuterate. Around those is a mass of styrofoam. No one below is aware of me. The antenna in my nose-cone sends out a stream of signals, bouncing them off the earth, sensing the distance, waiting for my barometric pressure switch to find its preordained point. When each altitude signal bounces back from the ground, the pressure switch readies. At 1,500 feet a tiny electrical pulse, perhaps just enough to burn a corner of a postage stamp, initiates the firing sequence. I have begun.

Another signal detonates the high explosive and a compressional shock wave begins to move inward. faster than the speed of sound, moving in at all points on the plutonium sphere at the same instant. The pressure on my core builds, its density increases, the mass becomes critical, then supercritical, and the fission chain-reactions multiply. Now the initiator is released, producing a host of neutrons, and the chain reaction continues until the energy generated in my head becomes so great that the internal pressure generated by the energy of the fission fragments exceeds the implosion pressure generated by the shock wave. My plutonium bomb's casing cracks, then flies apart, and the energy moves out in the form of X-rays, down the inside wall of the casing.

The X-rays work their way past the uranium 238 tamper, past the shield, heating the styrofoam beneath my skin to a plasma. The tamper burns away, and so the X-rays and the molten styrofoam squeeze inwards, crushing the molecules of the lithium deuterate. Shock waves smash against my plutonium heart and new fission begins. I am near. The fissioning rod sprays radiation, thousands of degrees of heat, free neutrons to bind with other atoms. The lithium deuterate evolves into another isotope of hydrogen – tritium. My heat and pressure is more a child of the sun than the earth. Fusion runs wild; tritium–deuterium and deuterium–deuterium. More heat, more radiation. By now someone shadowing my flight might glimpse my skin buckling, cracking, the first rip sending searing light into the last picoseconds of blue sky.

From first trip of the altimeter switch to explosion has taken me 600 billionths of a second. Beneath me, skin peels, eyeballs melt, bones become liquid.

Isaac wakes in deep Antarctic twilight, shivering, hands fighting off insects whose existence here is impossible. He stands and moves on up the valley, knowing the sea lies a few miles distant. Red and gold and bronze and green nacreous clouds hang like burning banners in the sky. The ground is ash-grey. He covers perhaps a couple of miles before the first of the figures appears. Withered flesh over pale bones, the skull open to the wind. He stands looking down at it, a Weddell seal, miles from the safety of water. He walks on, then slows and stops. Another mummified seal, then another. Perhaps a dozen. He moves among them, among their death caravan. All following the one he'd first come across. A decision in the wrong direction. Heading inland where there was nothing to feed them. Their desiccated bodies could be dozens or hundreds or even thousands of years old.

He sits, a terrible weight in his own bones, in his eyes, his fingertips. He blinks to a Nagasaki morning. A child's toy train, a woman's sandal. He keeps walking, as he had that Nagasaki day, searching each inch for some sign of life. But now, as then, there is none. His knee gives way crossing a small crevasse and he lies back, his focus ebbing. He looks up at the midnight light and screams, watching the woman walk out through the sparse grasses and stand, just as she always has, looking into the setting sun.

When the helicopter crewman leans over him, he peels back the rim of his fur hood.

'What woman?' says the crewman.

Isaac stares, listening to the helicopter's blades send shock waves into the air.

'You mentioned a woman,' says the crewman. 'What woman?'

'I don't know her,' says Isaac.

The crewman's question is the last he will answer for a decade.

New Zealand Herald.
Auckland. February 10, 1959.
Isaac Simeon, English-born nuclear physicist and latterly anti-nuclear weapons campaigner, was committed today to a mental institution for an indeterminate time …

Caleb stands and walks to the window.

'They're never going to let you out,' he says. 'Are they.'

'Never's not a word I use,' says Isaac.

Isaac takes the crumpled cigarette packet from the table, lifts the tin foil out and stubs his cigarette out against its shiny silver skin. He still holds the exploding cigarette in his other hand.

'You came just for that?' he says.

'I came to tell you that I don't blame you,' says Caleb.

Isaac stands, walks to the window, looks at his hundred tiny faces in the scales of the smoke glass.

'I don't know if I could've stopped your mother from going,' he says. 'Even if nothing, none of this, had happened. If I'd never gone to Antarctica and everything had stayed. Your mother is the one you shouldn't blame. She among us was the only one who struck a blow. I like to think that every photo she has had published has scrubbed one day off the war. Off all wars.'

Caleb swallows.

'I know,' he says. 'But that doesn't make the gap any harder to cross.'

Isaac nods.

'Antarctica,' he says. 'I'd spent a decade there without even knowing it. Every empty mile, every breath of graveyard wind had my name on it. A name like mine, arrogance like mine. I just never realised it until I stood on it, set foot with my flesh instead of my mind, my imagination. You know what hurts the most, Caleb. That I gave it all up when I was satiated. But I'd already spoonfed the monster, fed and clothed it and pushed it out in a little red wagon, out into the world.'

'You were too late,' says Caleb.

'I'd decided ahead of time, without even knowing, that I'd be too late.'

'I'm not sure I understand.'

Isaac sits in an empty chair beneath the window. He puts his head in his hands.

'We make our own Antarcticas,' he says.

Caleb goes to him, reaches down and cradles Isaac's head, his Tin Man's silver hair across Isaac's grey bristles. He holds him for a long moment, then reaches into his satchel and takes out the straw hat. He bends down, kisses his father on the forehead, then puts the hat over his grey hair.

'Mum had it with her,' he says.

Isaac looks up, puzzlement in his eyes. Caleb steps back, his mouth twitching. He flicks a couple of fingers in the air.

'So long, kid,' he says, in his best, twitching, Bogart voice.

Isaac looks up, reaches for him, but Caleb has already stepped away. He walks to the door, nods his head at the guard and goes through.

'Caleb,' says the voice from behind him.

But he doesn't look back.

XII

Armistice Day

November 10, 1970

In the evening when Troy walks down Akiko's hall there is music coming from her workroom. He touches the door open a sliver, seeing her record player's needle on the vinyl disc. Crimson fabric spreads on the table as she runs edges of it through her sewing machine. Her foot works the pedal in time with the music. He taps on the door and she turns.

'Is that a new costume?' says Troy.

'Yes. For the peace rally. I'm going to do something there.'

'Are you sure you're up to it?'

'Yes.'

'About the rally. One of the new guys had a beam fall on him, so I'm pulling extra duty for a couple of days.'

'Oh. How is he?'

'Not too bad. But it means I can't take you to the rally now.'

She touches her hand against the fabric, nods her head.

In the night he slips from the sheets. He sits for a moment then gets his T-shirt and boots and jeans and walks down the hall. He is driving for ten minutes before he makes his first conscious decision as to which street to take, more than mere reaction. He gets on the motorway and heads north, the harbour water falling away beneath the rising span of the bridge.

He takes the road across the top of the harbour, out west, all the way out to Rangimoana, easing down the slope in the dark of three am. Around the estuary and on. He swings the Chev about at the road's ramshackle end, sits with his headlights illuminating hints of the swingbridge. A faint light comes through the trees above him on the slope. He crosses the bridge, walks up the path and up onto the deck. A single candle burns on a table, the wax on its tip melted like icing, pooling in the cracked china cup. Caleb half-sits, half-lies on the couch, one leg stretched forward of the other. Eyes closed. Beyond him the shadows consume the edges of the room. Troy raises his hand to knock but stops, looks at his hand in the faint glow, then past it to Caleb's sleeping figure. He tries the handle and it turns. He slips off his boots and steps in, the rimu floorboards giving with a creak beneath his bare feet. Caleb still lies prone, eyes closed. Troy sits on the floor, against the wall opposite, his hands resting on his knees. When Caleb stirs he glances at Troy and sits up.

'Li'l brother,' says Troy.

'Not so little,' says Caleb.

'You look a bit worse for wear.'

Caleb seems to try to turn around, but gives up with a hiss.

'Ma's sleeping in the other room,' he says. 'If that's what you came for.'

'It isn't.'

'Should I feel touched?'

'When did you become such a smart-arse?'

'I was always a smart-arse.'

Troy smiles.

'Yeah,' he says. 'Yeah. You and your old man.'

'He was your old man too, you know.'

Troy looks into the shadows.

'Is it too girly to say I've missed you?' says Caleb.

'No.'

'I'm glad, about Kiki. She thinks somehow you'd be my last choice.'

'As what?'

'The baby's father.'

'Not sure I'm following you.'

'You won, man. And you didn't even have to throw a rock to fool me.'

'Eh?'

Caleb smiles.

'Remember when Ma used to say you were an island unto yourself?'

Troy nods.

'But sometimes stuff changes,' he says.

'Yeah.'

'Yeah.'

'You could wake up Ma,' says Caleb. 'She'd be jazzed.'

'Nah.'

'Then why did you come out?'

'To say hello, I guess.'

'In the middle of the night?'

'In the middle of the night.'

Caleb now looks away into the shadows. Somewhere a dog barks. There's a rustle of leaves coming from beyond the open window and a rasping sound, sandpaper on gnarled timber.

'You be good to Kiki,' says Caleb.

'I'm gonna try.'

Caleb tries to move again, seems to struggle to swing his feet around onto the floor. It is then Troy realises that the rasping sound is Caleb's breathing. Caleb stares, beyond Troy to some point on the wall, though Troy knows the wall is bare.

'Remember Dad's story about the twins paradox?' says Caleb.

'The two kids on the spaceship.'

'One kid on the spaceship, one left on earth.'

'Okay. Yeah.'

'You ever wonder which one was you and which one was me?'

'No. We ain't twins.'

'Beyond that.'

'I always struggled with that shit about time not being the same for everyone.'

'Even if it is the same, what we do is different.'

'That's not news.'

'What are you going to do from here?'

Troy closes his eyes, opens them again. Caleb's face has darkened with the burning down of the candle. His cheekbones are skeletal now. His eyes are caves.

'Funny,' says Troy, 'for the first time, I reckon, I know where here is. I know where there is.'

Caleb nods.

'That makes sense?' says Troy.

Caleb's rasping breaths silence for a moment, then begin again.

'Remember when all the kids used to rampage through the dunes with those crappy old guns?' he says.

'Old broom and mop handles with a bent nail for a trigger?'

'Yeah. And no one used to want to play with you cause you couldn't stop shooting people. Even when you'd shot everyone.'

'Yeah. Went through mates awful fast.'

'We used to just stop, watch you go searching the next dune for someone else.'

Troy swallows, runs his palms across the knees of his jeans. He picks at a loose denim thread.

'You still looking for that next dune?' says Caleb.

Troy looks at his brother. His clothes baggy, a scare-crow's garb. For a moment Akiko's shadow appears in the space between them.

'Has she ever told you what she sees when she dances?' says Troy.

'In a roundabout way, yes. Though I kinda wish she hadn't.'

Troy looks up at the open window, the night's chill a sudden visitor at the edge of the waning candlelight.

'Do you want me to tell you?' says Caleb.

'I thought I did,' says Troy. He shakes his head.

Caleb smiles.

'What?' says Troy.

'I'm glad you came,' says Caleb.

'Yeah, me too.'

Troy stands.

'You get some sleep,' he says, 'you look like you could use it. Catch ya around.'

'Yeah.'

Caleb passes a hand across his face, a slow withdrawing of a tide.

Troy walks towards the door, but stops. He looks into the shadows of the hall. The floorboards creak again a couple of times as he walks to the end, but not enough to wake the figure on the big bed. He looks beyond her to where the window glass inside the open curtains catches a faint glimmer from the moon. He crouches next to the bed, looking at Etta's sleeping face, the first face he knew. She rolls over in her slumber, faces away from him. He crouches there for a long time, listening to her breathe. He bends, kisses her on the cheek.

When he gets to the front door he looks down at his boots on the darkened boards. He crouches, reaches for them but stops and stands again, then walks, barefoot, on down the steps to the path. He is a couple of paces past the edge of the deck's awning when the candlelight vanishes. He stops for a moment, then walks on, the moon his echo through the trees.

In the whirr of the tyres on the road he hears it, in the motor's hum he hears it. The lullaby Isaac used to sing to Caleb, leaning over his cot. Troy stood in the doorway, leaning against the jamb with his height markings scratched into them. Listening.

Laila, Laila, itsmi et enayich
Night, Night, close your eyes
Laila, Laila, bederech elayich
Night, night, on the way to you
Laila, Laila, rachvu chamushim
Night, Night, they rode in full armour
Numi, Numi, sh'losha parashim
Sleep, Sleep, three horsemen
Numi, Numi, sh'losha parashim
Sleep, Sleep, three horsemen

In the morning Etta sits up in the bed, the dawn light coming through the French doors. She yawns, opens the doors and walks onto the deck and looks out over the road, to the dunes. She goes through the house to the shed and looks in the window. The Indian sits on its stand. There is no sign of Caleb so she drapes her black duffel coat on and walks down the drive and across the road to the sand.

He is sitting on a driftwood log, wearing a pair of beach baggies and a torn T-shirt. His hair flicks in the wind. He doesn't turn to look at her when she sits next to him.

'I was standing about here when I first saw your dad,' says Etta.

He nods.

'He apologised for disturbing us,' says Etta.

'Us?'

'Troy and I.'

'Okay.'

Caleb's thin arms are shivering, so Etta lifts off her coat, sets it over his shoulders.

'He's tired of apologising,' says Caleb.

'I know.'

'Do you?'

He turns to face her, a slight stubble on his unshaven chin. Something she has never seen.

'There's no need to tell me,' he says, 'that one day I'll understand.'

Etta stares into the distant waves.

'I've followed your photos,' says Caleb. 'Magazines, books. I used to sit looking at them, running my fingers over the paper. Trying to get some sense of you.'

She thinks of putting a hand on his shoulder, but doesn't.

'I saved some of the pictures,' says Caleb, 'cut them out to take them to Dad, as some kind of proof of ... I don't know what. That you were still there? The doctors wouldn't let me show them to him. Said it would be regressive for his therapy to show him such violent images. I hadn't really noticed they were violent – strange as that might seem – just your name on the credit.'

He turns back to the sea.

'I lost both parents,' he says, 'very careless of me. But then I got lucky and one came back.'

'Caleb –'

'And now you've come back too.'

He stands.

'But I've lost nothing I won't lose again,' he says.

'He didn't recognise me, Caleb.'

'I know. But it's not about what he knew or didn't know. It's about what you promised.'

'To stay with him? The only promise I ever made to Isaac was to one day ride to the cape with him.'

'I don't understand.'

'No. I suppose I don't either. Not all of it. All I know for sure is that I'm here now, we're here now.'

'You have lousy timing.'

'How do you mean?'

He smiles, though without warmth. His eyes reflect the sand hazing in the wind.

In the patients' communal room Isaac looks up when the orderly approaches. Next to him at the table two other men sit, one playing solitaire and taking five minutes to place each card. The other watches him, laughing at each move, so that the first man changes his mind, attempts to start again. Over and over. Few of the men, including Isaac, have touched their lunch.

'Visitor,' says the orderly. 'A woman.'

Isaac sits looking at him.

'Let's not wait all day,' says the orderly.

He is shown into one of the visiting rooms. No one else is about. He sits, looks out of the barred windows at the cloudy day.

Etta comes in carrying a leather bag. He finds himself looking at the bag – he's not interested in what is in it, but he just wants to avoid her eyes. She wears a black beret, her hair tied in a pony tail. Her boots clunk on the floor. He fidgets with the collar of his gown. She glances down at the chair, then at Isaac.

'Go ahead,' he says.

She sits, looking around at the bare walls. Then back to him.

'You don't look so bad,' she says.

'Can I use that as my epitaph?'

'No daggers, Isaac. Would it help if I said please?'

'I suppose I should say it's good to see you. Something of a surprise.'

'I wasn't going to.'

'What changed your mind?'

Etta frowns the question away.

'Caleb says I shouldn't ask you how you've been,' she says.

'Caleb would be right.'

'All right.'

For a moment, neither speaks, nor even moves.

'I need to ask you,' says Etta.

They sit looking at the walls, at the window, at their shadows on the tiled floor.

'Every year or so they reassess me,' says Isaac. 'Like an old house no one has the heart to pull down. See if they need to nail up a few more planks, another set of shutters. I sit across from a couple of tables where people in suits sit jotting down notes with stainless-steel fountain pens.'

He draws the lapel of his robe across, tugging the material over his chest.

'I thought I was the one that was missing,' says Etta. 'But everyone is. Everyone I ever cared about.'

She leans back in her chair.

'The first night I came back,' she says, 'Caleb was writing a series of equations on your old blackboards. Or one long equation, I could never tell the difference. It was like time had just stopped, changed into reverse. You were writing on that blackboard.'

'Caleb isn't me.'

'I'm not sure whether that is a good or a bad thing.'

'Neither. It just is.'

Isaac looks towards the window, then back at her.

'How did we get to this?' says Etta.

'I came here by train,' says Isaac.

Etta opens and closes the clasp of her bag.

'That's not what I meant,' she says.

'Einstein had a thought experiment,' says Isaac. 'Two men, one on a train, one on a railway-station platform. The train passes the station, travelling at the speed of light. Two lightning bolts strike the train, one at each end. The man on the platform sees the two lightning bolts strike at the same time. Simultaneous. The man on the train, because the train is moving towards one lightning bolt and away from the other, sees the lightning bolt strike the front of the train first, the rear second.'

'Riddles?' says Etta, 'that's your answer?'

He stands and walks to the window. Some of the patients are walking on the grass. A nurse once again throws a rubber ball to a small gathered circle. They all catch it except for the one man who raises his arms to catch, but never does.

'Who is right?' says Isaac.

She looks up, takes her beret off and sits it on the table. Her dark hair has scratch-marks of grey through it.

'Isaac, when I left, you couldn't talk. You wouldn't talk. It was impossible to know whether you even saw or felt. They said they'd saved you from freezing, but you had frozen. You froze minute by minute, inch by inch. Long before you went to Antarctica. I wasn't going to be one of those dogs that lay by their loved one's corpse, not out of loyalty. Not even out of love.'

'Love was the one thing we couldn't mention, Etta. Remember?'

'And we didn't.'

'Didn't we? Not as a word, perhaps.'

Etta takes an edge of the beret's cloth, crunches it in her fingers. She nods her head.

'I didn't abandon you, Isaac. You weren't there to be abandoned. Before you went to Antarctica your guilt was consuming me. When you came back, your guilt had been handcuffed by silence, but that silence was still going to imprison me.'

'You've come all this way to tell me what I already know?'

'Well, maybe it's for my sake.'

'And how have you forgiven yourself for leaving your son?'

'I haven't.'

She takes the beret in both hands, closes them over it.

'I haven't,' she says.

She lifts a pack of cigarettes from her coat's inside pocket, fumbles with a lighter. Isaac's shadow from the window darkens her hand so the flame flares brighter than in daylight.

'You know,' she says, smoking now, 'I told myself for years that I never loved you. That ours was a marriage of convenience. That I only ever loved Joaquin.'

'Told yourself?'

'Yes. It was easier, you see. Easier to give up something that had only so much value, easier than watching someone I loved turn to stone.'

She stands, walks towards him.

'Do you know how many dead people I've seen, Isaac? Hundreds. Day after day of them. Have you ever actually seen anyone dead?'

'No, as it happens.'

'Not one?'

'No.'

Caleb rides the Indian through the gap in the dunes, then along the beach. Sea spray on his hands and face. He is an hour riding in from the coast, slower than the hundreds of other times he has ridden this road. Savouring each turn, each glade he almost feels he has to duck to go through. The Auckland motorway traffic clangs against the memory of soft sand.

He meets Weston on a street corner in Ponsonby, talks to him for only a moment. Weston gives him the address and he rides on uptown then across Grafton Bridge and pulls into the domain, in the gate beside the hospital, glancing up at its white walls, its chimney. He parks the Indian and walks back out of the park and along a couple of streets until he finds a car with its doors unlocked. He slides into the driver's seat, reaches beneath the instrument panel and hotwires the ignition. The address Weston gave is an old house, abandoned, rubbish blowing across the cracked and broken driveway. He walks around the back to where the drum sits in the musty half-light of a crumbling shed. He takes a deep breath, takes the smaller drum next to it and opens both lids.

Akiko draws her crimson costume down over her, straightens the few crumples. She puts on her yukata and lifts Rai out of her cot. She dresses her and puts her in the pram. She looks skyward where a weak sun struggles overhead with a spider's web of cloud. She puts a hat on Rai's head, pulls the collar of her pink jumpsuit up around her neck and pushes the pram out to where her Mini is parked in her driveway. A crêpe-and-silk crane face-mask in one hand, her bag in the other.

A few people are already gathered on the domain's grassy slopes when she arrives. She glances up at the pale hulk of the museum, huge like a sleeping elephant against the sky. She parks and walks past the old gun where it stands pointing out to sea.

She sets up her props on the grass, in front of the makeshift wooden stage. She glances up, scanning the growing crowd for faces she knows, pausing when she sees in the distance, propped on its stand, the Indian.

Four protesters bluster and threaten through a megaphone, their voices metallic, crackling. A row of hooded figures stand holding grim reaper scythes made of wood with cardboard blades. A police car sits beyond the crowd, a handful of uniformed officers drift at the gathering's edge. A banner the length of a school bus drapes across the back of the stage.

Leave Vietnam to the Vietnamese

She has a friend sit next to Rai's pram, kisses her daughter's tiny face, then puts on her paper crane mask and walks out onto the stage.

'Look what the cat's dragged in,' says Monty, as Troy drops his leather jacket on the fire station's kitchen table.

'Oh, you missed me?'

'Reckon I was worried.'

Troy raises his eyebrows.

'You're not gonna give me that bullshit about guys with stuff to lose, are you?' he says.

'No.'

'You could just make me a cuppa.'

'Just cause I'm not that pissed off to see you, doesn't mean I'm gonna be your slave.'

Troy laughs, walks out of the room.

Akiko slips out of her coat and yukata and climbs up the ladder leading to the platform. The music begins. She steps mid-stage, the trailings of her crimson costume billowing behind her. She begins to dance, a dance she has practised behind closed doors in her flat, the home she now shares with Troy. With this man who came to her trying to save her. From what, he didn't know, any more than she did. She has searched herself for something in her gestures, in her eyes, that says she needs saving. Trying hard to dismiss what could be his own selfishness in imprinting his sadness, or perhaps his road out of sadness, on her. She who has never sought anyone's help to move out of her own sadness. Who has viewed each opening of her eyes in the morning as a victory.

She has not allowed the organisers to announce her as hibakusha, though that knowledge may add poignancy. It is her knowledge alone, captured, contained, burned into each step of her dance. And as she dances she lets long silk ribbons fly behind her, her feathers, her tail. The paper crane's tail.

Beyond the point of the mask's beak she can see her mother's face, her father's face, neither of which she has a memory of beyond photographs. They're with her now. The pigeons from the peace park in Nagasaki swirl around her also, are part of her dance. As is that kiwi soft toy with the broken eye at Auckland Airport. She swoops and rises on the wind currents, currents she wishes could flow against history, wear it down like the sea wears away stone cliffs.

She centres in her eye a carved figure, half-naked, his eyes closed. The ground zero monument in Nagasaki. Its stone finger rising to point to the sky. She dances until she runs out of music, then she stops, stands still, as she had that first moment when Troy came up onto her stage, touched her with a single finger. Behind the mask, where no one can see, a tear touches against her cheek.

Caleb sits in the stolen car, the petrol can full of napalm in the back seat. In the distance music plays – Japanese – and he sits listening. He raises the bottle of liquid morphine to his lips, drinks again.

Armistice Day.

Yesterday was his father's birthday and for the first time in years he didn't celebrate it with him. With a small cupcake and a single candle. He hopes Isaac will forgive him this small indiscretion.

He fumbles with the keys for a moment, then starts the engine.

Akiko hears the car before she sees it. The engine grows louder again, a small rip lengthening. She walks to the edge of the stage, puts her yukata back on.

Isaac turns from the hospital window. He looks at Etta for a moment, then through her, at a lone seal sitting upright in death, ice beneath its brittle bones. Desiccated, ageless. Leading hundreds, thousands, millions away from the water.

'Did Caleb ever tell you why he never replied to your letters?' says Isaac.

'No.'

'I've always wondered, but never had the guts, I suppose, to ask him. A father afraid of his child's answer. Letters, hell, we're always giving each other pieces of paper. Books to read for those who seek answers. Forms to commit people to an asylum. Bills of sale and trade. At the site of the Trinity test I watched as a scientist signed a delivery docket handed to him by an engineers' corpsman, to confirm taking possession of the bomb's plutonium core. The army had to account, after all, for all the millions of public dollars that went into it. I'd like to think that I wondered then, if those millions would equal the number of children who would never be born because of what we were doing. But I didn't. I brushed a table clean with the edge of my hand, so we could get on with our work.

He grasps the metal mesh over the windows.

'The bomb project was a playpen for me,' he says. 'It's where I grew up, if I grew up at all. Sure, I was busting to do my bit to end the war, but I was playing with building blocks that transcended all politics. All argument and positioning, all right and wrong. I saw myself – my public self – fighting for the allies against the Nazis, then against the Japanese hordes, but would I have turned down my role had I been in the German machine?

'I didn't feel guilt for helping to build the bomb that destroyed a city. We were at war. A terrible trade in a terrible moment, thousands of their lives for thousands of ours. No. My tears were for me. For the realisation that a part of me would've worked on the bomb no matter what, no matter where. Beyond even ego I was guilty of one of the most precious of human gifts. Curiosity.

'They say that nuclear weapons kept the peace,' says Isaac. 'In a bizarre way that's almost true. They keep us suspended at any given moment, an inch from world war, but what we're left with isn't peace.'

Etta stands at the window next to him.

'Do you think I don't know that?' she says.

Caleb eases his way into the gathering. People step aside, some banging on the car's bonnet and roof. He taps the horn a couple of times, leaning away from reaching hands. The smell and taste of kerosene metallic against his tongue. He drains the last of the morphine and drops the bottle over the seat. It clangs against the petrol can. In the clearing he stops, turns the car side on to the stage, steps out and lifts the petrol can from the seat.

'Everyone move back,' he says.

Some do, but most just stare. He lifts a Zippo cigarette lighter from his pocket, raises it.

'For your own safety,' he shouts, 'move back.'

The first murmur of tension in the crowd. He raises the can, then the lighter. The closest people shout, push backwards, a circle of twenty yards of empty space appears around him in seconds.

He climbs up on car's bonnet and onto the roof and sits, his legs dangling over the edge.

'My father has been put away for years because they think he's crazy,' he says. 'Because they need him to be crazy.'

His voice is hoarse, his weakened lungs stripping its power.

He looks into the crowd where two policemen have pushed forward to the edge.

'I wouldn't,' he says.

They stop for a moment, then begin to walk towards him. Caleb tips the spout of the jerry can, pouring petrol down the car's windowglass and panels. He holds the cigarette lighter in his other hand. The policemen stop. One lifts a radio device from his breast pocket, talks into it.

'Back!' says Caleb.

The policemen don't move. He splashes some more petrol onto the car. The rear policeman steps back, calling to the first. The first policeman stares at Caleb, his arms raised.

'Son,' he says, 'it isn't worth it.'

'Worth?' says Caleb. 'You want to talk about worth? About value?'

'Son —'

Caleb holds the lighter over the petrol, the lighter's cap still on. Both policemen step back. He sits watching them, watching the crowd. The fear in their eyes. Those who had come here today with picnic baskets and prams.

'Caleb.'

A voice from behind him. A voice he knows. He closes his eyes, wishes the voice away.

'Caleb, don't do it.'

He opens his eyes, turns to where Akiko stands on the edge of the stage, looking down at him. Crimson stockings beneath a black yukata. She has one hand raised in front of her.

'Caleb, put down the lighter.'

'I'm already gone, Kiki,' says Caleb.

'I know. But don't do this.'

A siren in the distance, growing louder.

'I have to,' he says.

'No, you don't. You can die with arms around you. People who love you.'

A police car, then another, moves up through the trees. Then a white van with blue police markings on it.

'Kiki –'

'I'm coming down there, Caleb.'

'No.'

He raises the lighter again but she ignores it, steps down the stairs.

Troy holds on to the edge of the seat as the fire engine accelerates.

'Some nut threatening to set fire to himself,' says Monty, the radio receiver in his hand.

'Eh?' says Troy.

'At that hippies' rally in the domain.'

Troy fastens his boots, looks up at the trees flying by, the wail of the sirens turning heads as they head across Grafton Bridge.

Caleb looks down at his hands, a petrol can in one, a lighter in the other. A US Army issue Zippo, purloined by the boy Caleb from his father's possessions. The first time he had visited Isaac in the hospital, Isaac just sat staring into nothing. Etta reached out and took Caleb's hand in hers.

'He's ill,' she said. 'That's all. He's not ignoring you.'

The boy sat, watching his silent father. He raised his own hands, began to form the shadow puppets they'd once projected by torchlight onto the walls of Caleb's bedroom. But Isaac just sat. Caleb leaned forward, looked close into his eyes. He saw only his own figure, twinned, a boy in each eye. Etta tapped him on the shoulder, then leaned him against her, his hand still crossing Isaac's empty stare.

'Caleb,' she said, 'we have to go.'

He watches the police cars pull up, the white van. Uniformed men step out of the van. Two of them reach into the van's rear and reappear, the thin vipers' bodies of rifles stark against the sunlit grass. The other siren howls louder. There's a flash of red through the trees.

The policemen with the rifles move closer, the others ushering the crowd away.

'Caleb,' says Akiko. 'You don't have to go this way. Come home with me.'

'I wish I could, Kiki. More than anything else I've ever wished, I wish I could.'

He stands. The policemen pause.

'My father was accused of a crime of which he was innocent,' he shouts. He feels his voice fade, senses the crowd is too far away to hear. He swallows, trying to give his throat strength. 'The only crime of which he was guilty was realising we all went mad. For that he was called mad. They called him a trouble-maker, a communist, even a traitor. But he was none of those. He was just a man who had found himself out. Found all of us out.'

Akiko's footsteps turn his head. She stands on the grass now, moving clockwise to his vision. Around in front of him.

'Don't come any closer, Kiki.'

'You won't hurt me, Caleb. I know you.'

There is a ripple of movement over her head and he looks up to where the fire engine parks on the grass. Figures step out.

Troy walks away from Monty, from the others. He knows not so much the figure of the guy standing on the car's roof, but the woman moving between them.

'Whoa, boy,' says Monty, grabbing at him. Troy pushes

him away, glancing at the two armed offender's squad officers moving beside him, rifles raised. One of them hisses at Troy.

'Get back.'

'Piss off,' says Troy.

The other officer sticks the butt of his rifle in Troy's ribs, halts him. Troy looks down at it.

Akiko keeps advancing, each step silent. She is aware of other footsteps behind her. Boot steps. She reaches inside herself, pushes all other sound out of her mind.

'I'm not leaving you here, Caleb,' she says.

A voice from behind her, familiar.

'Kiki, step away. Caleb, drop the lighter.'

Familiar to her now as her own outline in a mirror.

'Kiki, step away.'

'Troy?'

'Yes.'

'I can't.'

Troy holds the two of them in his eyeline. Akiko takes another few steps forward and he knows she won't stop. Not in this moment, when he knows, finally, what she sees when she dances. Not what she dances towards but dances away from. A man holding the means to make fire in both hands, weighing her life in his scales.

She is only a couple of feet from the point of no return, poised to cross. Caleb raises the lighter again, flicks open the cap. Then the flint's switch. The flame tip waves in the wind. A heartbeat of fire.

Akiko steps forward.

Troy glances beside him to the armed officer, snaps his elbow against his jaw. A punch to the ribs then a kick to the stomach downs him, Troy pulling the rifle from his hands.

Akiko half-turns as Troy steps one pace to his right, cocks and raises the rifle and shoots, past her frozen stare. Past her to where the bullet pierces the centre of his little brother's head and jolts him backwards, toppling onto the car's roof. One leg twitches against the glass, then stills. Petrol bleeds down the pillar, down the shuddering glass. Akiko sinks to her knees, her scream rising with the petrol fumes, rising against the path of the lighter as it bounces against the roof, against the pillar and door handle and falls spinning into the pool of kerosene.

Akiko kneels with her head bowed.

The officer lies stunned.

The kerosene ignites, flames unwinding like venomous streamers. Monty sprints past Troy, drags Akiko away kicking. Troy walks towards the fire, the heat searing his face, only Caleb's feet visible among the flames. Suddenly he is on the ground, his ears screaming, as the jerry can ignites. His throat choking. He gags, spits into the grass, reloads a cartridge into the rifle's chamber. Napalm smoke in his eyes now. He narrows his stare, stalking the fire's perimeter. Knowing also, for the first time, what he sees when he dances. A scared young man sits on a landing craft, palm trees bending with the wind. Another island, another war. Flak smoke, mortar smoke. American and Japanese bodies washed high and dry above a coral reef. Troy shoots into the fire. Reloads. Shoots. Reloads. Caleb with him now, his ghost on his brother's shoulder as Troy carries him out of here, back along the railway tracks.

'Do you reckon it's true,' says Caleb boy's voice into his ear, 'that when you put your ear against the railway tracks, that you can hear a train coming.'

'I don't know,' says Troy.

Caleb giggles, pulls out his penis and aims a stream of urine down, into the fire creeping up the length of the tracks towards him. He giggles again as the flames reach his toes.

Troy turns, to where the figures are all drawing away from him, from the burning. He raises the rifle, shoots at the police van, reloads, shoots at the fire engine. They are obscene to him now in their voyeurism, this moment with just he and his brother.

'I don't know,' says Troy.

'I do,' says Caleb.

Troy shoots again and one of the upper windows in the museum shatters. All around him, up the grassy slope, figures are lying prone in the grass. He can't tell if they're cowering or sleeping or dead.

'How do you know?' he says.

'Because I've heard them,' says Caleb. 'I've heard the trains.'

Troy looks back, to where his brother lies once again in the fire, alone now. He lowers the rifle. A voice. He turns. The old Vietnamese man stands in his sodden peasant's suit. And if men with three heads and wings of fire drop out of the sky, I'll fight them too, he says. Troy nods. But this time the old man has a gun. He raises it. Troy touches his finger against his own trigger.

'Put the gun down, old man,' he says. 'I don't want to kill you anymore.'

But the old man doesn't respond. He just smiles, shrugs in resignation, the rain falling from his wet hair, down over his bony cheeks. Troy shakes his head, raises his rifle.

'Why don't you just die,' says Troy, 'just fucking die. How many times do I have to kill you?'

He hears the rifle crack, looks down at his finger. It hasn't moved. He is still looking at his motionless finger when he falls to his knees, then crumples down onto his side. The grass is warm against his cheek, warmer, he suspects, than the old man's rain. Warmer even than the blood that now drips into his hands, onto his trigger finger. Warmer even than the fire that fades, pulse by pulse, into the horizon.

May, 1989

Akiko walks to the window of the bedroom she once shared with Troy. She puts a cushion on the wide sill and sits against the corner of the wooden frame, one foot up on the sill. Her bare toes touching a small, dried piece of a cracked leaf.

Once, when Rai was small, Akiko made a bird house in her back yard. She assembled some wooden boards for the sides and base and roof and fixed them together. Rai asked her if she could paint it. Do some part of it. Akiko showed her how to mix the paint, how many coats to put on. When it was finished they made a picnic lunch of egg sandwiches and herb tea and sat out by the birdhouse. Akiko went to take one of the sandwiches but her hands had a tincture of solvent from the paint, so she went in and washed them but couldn't get all the smell off. It seemed to stay for days. Days she and Rai would check at odd times to see if there were any birds in the house. But there never were. After a while they stopped looking. The house was there.

There.

Here.

That was all they needed to know.

She used to watch Caleb polishing the Tin Man costume until his hands were red, raw like the inside of a flower. He never told her why it was so important. He never told her a lot of things. He had some other costumes; clowns, tramps. Akiko made him a kind of psychedelic scientist costume; a white lab coat with crazy equations painted or sewn onto it. She drew some make-believe calculus with pen then cut the material out around them, so the numbers were just slashes. She hung small, broken pieces of blackboard from pieces of electrical cord. She made a bright gold, mop-haired wig. He wore it once and laughed but then looked in a mirror. He stopped laughing and took it off.

Today I found another flat stone, a New Zealand kind of stone. A toheroa shell. I didn't draw anything on it.

Today I learned there are some pains we can never talk to.

I am forty-four years old and I'm still here. That's a long reprieve.

Isaac contacts a couple of acquaintances at the Royal Society of Physics in London. He asks for a copy of the press conference notes, and material relevant to the University of Utah's announcement of their lab tests producing cold fusion. He asks for the information to be faxed through to the number of the local stationery shop. He rides there each day for four days, waiting for an answer. On the fourth day a woman points to him as he goes in the door, then ducks behind some shelves. She comes back with a manila folder, hands it to him.

He eases the motorbike to a stop in front of the train carriage. He stills the engine, opens the folder. A quick glance at the headline, then chapter summaries. Cathodes and diodes immersed in heavy water. A claim of 4.5 watts of heat out for every one watt of power in. He flicks to the last page where a line catches his eyes.

Fusion products produced as the result of the test – Nil.

No radiation.

Whatever they had produced in their lab, it was unlikely to be nuclear fusion. He closes the folder, looks away into the marshes.

'A riddle unsolved,' he says to the wind.

Inside, he takes the old pint milk bottle from the windowsill and runs it beneath the tap. He walks from flowerpot to flowerpot, tipping a thin stream of water. He goes back several times to refill, finishing out on the carriage's rear deck, looking past a sand-coloured ceramic pot in a hanging basket when Rai's Volkswagen comes rolling across the grass. He leans on the rail, waiting to greet Rai, but it's Etta that steps out, stands on the grass looking at him.

Neither say anything for a good while, then;

'I'm still not much of a drinking man,' says Isaac, 'but I do have some tea.'

'Sold,' says Etta.

Rai walks out into the back yard with the hose. She goes to the garden she has dug over and wets the soil, pausing a couple of times to drink from the nozzle. Water drips down her chin, splashes against her T-shirt. She takes another swig, then bends a section of the hose into a hairpin knot. The water stops, except for a faint trickle running down over her wrist. There is movement down the slope and she turns to where Akiko comes walking through the wild grass towards her.

'Hey,' says Rai.

'Hiya,' says Akiko. 'Gardening? You?'

Rai laughs.

'Yes, me!' she says.

Rai goes back into the shed and comes out with the wooden seed tray in her hands. She walks along the edges of the slight troughs she has dug, pauses at one end and turns back to Akiko.

'Want to give me a hand?' she says.

Akiko puts her bag down on the grass, takes a couple of handfuls of seeds from the trays. The women walk down the rows, sifting seeds through their fingers.

Rangimoana
November, 1970

The days before the funerals the wind blows hard against the terraces of grass and flax and toetoe on Koroheke's back. Leaves split, flax flowers fall into the sea. By the time the cemetery workers ease the two coffins into the ground the wind has stilled. Even the surf sweeps to shore in gentle arcs. Akiko stands watching them bury Troy and Caleb next to each other, Rai's carry-cot against her legs. When the vicar closes the bible and looks up at the small gathering she lifts Rai, holds her against her chest. People step forward and lift white flowers from a glass bowl. Students and a couple of tutors from the university, faces she has seen around the village, a group of men in fire-service dress uniforms. The uniformed men brought Troy here from the church in an antique fire engine with a small boy ringing an ornate bell instead of a siren. Caleb came in a hearse. Separated again, though they are side by side now.

Monty walks up to her, hands her a folded New Zealand flag, as the woman had handed her a cloth kiwi all those years ago. Akiko nods. Monty and the firemen walk away. She glances across the graves at the woman in the flak jacket and beret. Others had glanced at the woman during the funeral, canvas pants and black boots out of place among the suits. She hadn't returned anyone's stare. Akiko is about to step forward, after everyone else, and take a flower from the bowl, but the other woman does so instead, her face lowered. She takes a flower for each, drops it in the grave then turns towards the sea. Akiko doesn't drop any flowers, just a crimson paper crane.

She closes her eyes for a moment. And in that moment she sees the crane's wings rise up out of the ground, over the two piles of dirt; and over the people's faces and over the fence bordering the hilltop and out over the waves.

'Were you born in the autumn?' says Troy and Caleb together as they ride between the crane's wings.

'Yes,' says the hibakusha girl, 'but my daughter was born in the spring.'

'Hello,' she says when she goes to Etta standing by the cliff. 'My name is Akiko.'

Etta turns. Akiko looks down at Rai's sleeping face.

'And this is your granddaughter,' she says.

May, 1989

Etta follows Isaac into the train carriage, looking around at the strange collection of paraphernalia. A Hebrew candle on a small table. A vase of red begonias sitting on the edge of the sink, a couple of flowers fallen into the tub. Isaac holds a hanging curtain aside and she walks into another section with an old settee against a wall. He motions for her to sit. When she looks up she grimaces.

Woman in the Setting Sun, hanging on the wall opposite.

He brings her a cup of tea and some biscuits and they sit sipping.

'Where are your blackboards, Isaac.'

He comes back, puts his fingers into a gap in the wall panels behind the painting and swings the wood outwards – painting and all – to reveal a blackboard. Etta looks up to where he stands.

'You've carried everything with you,' she says.

'Everything that could be carried, yes.'

'I have my gear bag and three cameras.'

'Did you ever need more than that?'

She shapes to answer but doesn't.

'What ever happened to that old Beau Brownie?' says Isaac.

'It's at the house.'

'It'll outlive us both.'

'Everything will.'

'Not everything.'

Isaac looks up at the painting.

'I almost threw that away,' he says, 'after you first pooh-poohed it. In a fit of pique. But I didn't. I was glad later, as I've stood with that woman in the setting sun for thirty years. Whispered to her to come in. Put a shawl over her shoulders, against the evening chill.'

'Did she ever come in?'

He looks at Etta, full in the face for the first time.

'Maybe it's time she did,' says Etta. 'At last.'

'Perhaps it's time we both did.'

At the Rangimoana house the next day Etta takes one of the sheets of first prints from her bag and holds it against the glass of the window, uses the little viewer to look at each frame. She marks a few with felt pen, then picks up another sheet and runs the viewer's end over each photo. She glances up, the sound getting louder, closer. She looks past the ladders of pictures to where a shape flickers beyond the lower branches of the trees, the sound almost upon her. She stands back from the glass, her eyes widening, as the Indian comes up the drive.

'I wondered if I'd forget the way,' says Isaac.

'Once you're on this road, there's nowhere else to go.'

He looks down at the Indian.

'Remember when we had that plan,' he says, 'to take a ride north on it? All the way to the cape.'

'Te Rerenga Wairua. Yeah.'

'Do the spirits still leave from there?'

'As much as they ever did, I guess.'

'If we need them to.'

'If we need them to.'

'Why did we never make that trip?'

He follows her up the steps and through the door, glancing down at the man, the young physicist, screwing the hinges into the wall a half-century before. The young man looks up at him and Isaac nods hello to himself. He nods also to the Isaac who stands painting the hallway wall, the Isaac screwing the light fixture into the living room ceiling. A paint-spattered T-shirt above his faded military issue trousers. Each of them stands above floorboards Isaac has not set his tread on since the day before he climbed up the steps onto an aeroplane that took him to Christchurch to meet another plane, in Air Force livery this time, to take him to Antarctica.

Etta motions for him to sit on the couch, and he does, his body stiff. Hands clasped in his lap.

They speak of moments, not years or grand decisions, but seconds. Gestures of eye or hand or snippets of conversation that passed in a blink. Isaac's shadow puppets on the walls, Caleb's magic acts – rabbits that never came out of hats, cards guessed that never matched the cards his audience held.

Then Isaac walks from room to room, taking in the dozens of photographs, most of which he has never seen. A fluffy cat in a village of ruined brick and stone buildings. An oriental woman in a bikini holding an automatic rifle while a soldier sleeps in a tumbledown cot behind her. Three young Asian men, posing in cool nonchalance on their motorcycles outside a nightclub, a rat snaking in the shadowed gutter beneath them. A water buffalo standing in regal repose in the grass at the edge of a runway where a huge military jet takes off.

Etta appears from the small bedroom, the Beau Brownie in her hands.

'Well I'll be,' says Isaac.

He takes the camera from her, its brown skin faded, stained. He turns it around, looks into its eye where another Isaac, an old man this time, looks out at him. He hands it back to her.

They walk down the steps from the deck. She is a few paces past the Indian when Isaac smiles, gets on and starts it. She turns, staring. He turns the bike around and rolls towards her, stopping a few inches from her toes. He shifts forward on the seat and she wraps the camera's cord around her neck and steps on behind him, cursing at the effort in raising her legs to clear the seat. He turns and chuckles, and she pokes her tongue out and settles behind him.

They ride through the gap between the dunes, through the high tide line and onto the harder packed sand stretching towards the surf. He gets off and she follows. He puts the motorbike on its stand.

She gestures him, on foot now, down the sand to the waterline and on into the smallest of the waves and he turns, looking over his shoulder at her. Surf breaks against him and he teeters then regains his footing, breathing hard against its power. She walks into the water with him, reaches to undo the buttons of his shirt. He peers down at his bony chest, skin crinkling like paper left in the rain.

'Isaac.'

He looks up. A man of waves and troughs, a sea-spray smile.

When Rai arrives home in the early afternoon she drops her bag on the bench, walks from room to room, stilling when the piece of paper on the coffee table catches a hint from the breeze from the open door, drifts down onto the rimu boards.

Kid, be back in a couple of days.
Nan.

The motorcycle heads north through Hellensville. Isaac glances at the hardware store windows. Weekly specials, timber offcuts for bargain prices. A sudden flash of sun on a motorbike's tank. Two figures. He changes down a gear and works the throttle, feeling his pillion passenger draw closer against him, against the acceleration.

They take the two-lane highway skirting the southern rim of the Kaipara Harbour, the road rising now and then to edge across hillsides, drop into troughs. They meet the main highway in Wellsford and carry on past where a roadside sign welcomes them to Northland. They stop to rest and eat at the crest of the Brynderwyn Hills, then Isaac powers across the long straights past the refinery and on up through Ohaewai and on to where the Mangamuka River cuts the bush-laden hillsides in half, the asphalt of the highway through the gorge strobing from baking sunlight to night dark and back again in seconds.

At Pukenui they stop again, for the evening this time. Isaac walks stiff-legged from where he leaves the Indian on its stand and over to where Etta has their motel cabin's kettle boiling. Two beds, a couple of tables. A toilet and shower, the wooden frame of a skylight through which the moon rises lit and elegant like a silent movie star. They eat fish and chips from the local takeaway off newsprint, the heat moistening the scratched surface of the table beneath. Etta looks up through the skylight. Isaac follows her stare. The glass hasn't been cleaned in a while, the stars hazing. When she looks back down she blinks a couple of times. Then again. She closes her eyes.

'Thinking about the boys,' she says.

'I know.'

Isaac looks back out the window. Beyond the trees Mount Camel rises, singular, blocking out a hundred stars behind it. Though even the smallest of them is a million times its size.

When they lie silent in the empty dark Etta's voice comes soft, rough at the edges.

'You never filed for divorce,' she says.

'Neither did you.'

He looks over towards her but there's nothing but shadows.

'By the time I was aware again what divorce was,' he says, 'you were so far away it seemed not to matter.'

'Was that the real reason?'

'Maybe.'

'A lot of things that used to matter, don't any more.'

Isaac closes his eyes.

'You know what I never bargained on?' he says.

'What?'

'The older I get, the closer things become. Memories. It's as if each footstep isn't overlaying other footsteps, but walking among them. I'm never alone now.'

'I think I am. Except for ghosts.'

'I wouldn't wish your ghosts on anyone.'

'Nor yours.'

'But we're still here.'

'Yes.'

'Maybe there is no reason. Just a stake in the ground.'

'One stake for each, your name and mine.'

'Two stakes?'

'Or one?'

They lie for a while longer, then their eyelids yield to tiredness.

Rai puts her programme down when the house lights go off, leaving only the stage lit. The music begins. Pachelbel, Canon in D. Dry ice begins to drift across the stage, enough to cloud the floor, the rear and side walls. A single dancer emerges from the mist, wearing aqua. She moves, spinning, across the stage's front, a yellow ribbon trailing from around her shoulders. Another woman emerges from the other side, clothed in yellow, this time with an aqua ribbon. Then another, a man this time. One by one the dancers appear out of the mist, then vanish back into it.

Rai had gone backstage before the show, to wish Akiko and her troupe luck, and Akiko had stood almost without acknowledging her, just staring towards the stage door. So still while the dancers fidgeted around her, applying make-up, doing last minute costume alterations, going through their stage roles in their minds. Akiko provided the only tranquillity amid the nervous laughter and chat. She greeted Rai only with a clasp of both hands and a nod. No words. Then Rai left to go and find her seat.

There are six dancers. Three women, three men. The last dancer to emerge is awash in crimson. This dancer at first circles the stage in a frantic rush, stepping, leaping, falling and landing, but then she eases into the centre and the other dancers circle her. No matter how many times the other dancers swap partners, man woman, woman woman, man man, she always finishes each sequence in the stage's centre.

Its core.

Rai sits back in her seat, closing her eyes for a moment, not to block the dance out but to take it inside her.

When she opens her eyes again the dancers form a tighter circle and move like a single being. A sea anemone.

In the morning Etta stands with one foot up on a stock fence, turning to cross the deserted highway again when Isaac puts the petrol pump nozzle back on its bracket. The attendant stands smirking, perhaps at their grey hair sprouting beneath their helmets. She buys a couple of chocolate nut bars from the station shop and they ride chewing, Etta stuffing both the wrappers in her jacket pocket. The war photographer's code.

Leave no trace but your pictures.

When the few buildings of Te Kao appear Etta taps Isaac on the shoulder, gestures for him to take the smaller road west. Toetoe sprouts from roadside culverts, cabbage palms stand like road signs. They pass a tractor, a four-wheeled farmbike. A lone woman walking, carrying a flax kete. The woman waves. Isaac slows as the man-made road gives way to sandy soil, then beach, as the vast strip of Ninety-mile Beach stretches away to the north and south.

Into the sea wind they ride, this old man, this old woman

on a forty-year-old motorcycle. Their physical bond is no more than the grip of two aged hands around an aged waist. Taut but tenuous. Yet their bond is also as strong and as frail as the love of two young men for one woman. But through it all, through the breezes of decades, carrying sand grains and dust and seed spores of memory, two small figures ride an ancient motorbike, north, further north, knowing they will stop only when they run out of land. Needing to run out of land.

Akiko sits among the costumes of her workroom. Silks and satins and Indian cotton. Ballet, vaudeville, tap. She stands and goes to her CD player and lifts the cover, looks at her shelves of music. She flips down the cover again and goes to her wardrobe and lifts out her old gramophone. The blue vinyl covering is ripped, stained. She plugs it in and opens the lid and sets the speed to thirty-three rpm. She puts a record onto the turntable, chuckling when it goes into a drunken dance, the album warped. She sits watching the stylus struggle to stay on, then closes her eyes when the music – scratched, warped, dusty but still alive – begins.

In her mind her mother's face appears. A face built cell by cell every day Akiko has woken to the dawn.

> *Today I had another pain, this time in my heart. Maybe that's where they were all along. I asked it what it wanted to be, but it didn't answer.*
>
> *Today I realised you never left me. That you were the pains I felt. My reminder.*

Etta taps Isaac with the forehead of her helmet, then again, but he doesn't turn, doesn't even slow. Perhaps he senses that she doesn't want him to, that it is just her voice reduced to its essence. She glances sideways at the pages of the immense book of ocean waves leafing down onto the sand. She taps her helmet against Isaac's one last time.

Click.

Akiko stands from her work table, watching the vinyl disc circle. She waits a few bars then begins to dance. Here, with only her costumes and sketches and books as her audience. The leaves on the trees surrounding the yard. A birdhouse. She stops and takes off her clothes until she is naked. Lets her scars feel the air, the scars she has carried since the day she was born. Scars she has hidden from almost everyone. Baring them to the music.

Acknowledgements

As always, I am indebted to many people for their help in this book. John Huria, for his editing. Robyn and Brian Bargh, Katrina and Renee and everyone at Huia Publishers for their support and wairua. Also Susan Sayer, of Sayer Literary Agency. Thanks also to Andy, Elaine, Helen, Nina, Sheila, Stephen and Trisha for their feedback during the long writing process.

Special thanks to Te Waka Toi (Creative New Zealand) for their grant in the initial writing stages and their continuing support since.

There were many books that were important in my research. *Too Hot to Handle*, by Frank Close, for its information about cold fusion. *Dark Sun*, by Richard Rhodes, about the building of the hydrogen bomb, *Children of the Paper Crane*, by Masamoto Nasu, about A-bomb survivors. *Heroes*, by John Pilger and *Tears before the Rain*, by Larry Engelmann for their narratives on the fall of Saigon. Also *The Untamed Coast*, by Bob Harvey, for the information and marvellous photographs, by Ted Scott, of Auckland's west coast. In addition, the Vietnam War photographs of Larry Burrows and the documentary film about photographer Jim Nachtwey, *War Photographer*, for its searing images and insightful and moving narrative.